Kerebos

Kerebos

Nicholas C. Prata

Arx Publishing
Merchantville NJ

First Edition

ISBN 978-1-889758-79-4

.

Manufactured in the United States of America

Library of Congress Cataloging-in-Publication Data

Prata, Nicholas C.
  Kerebos / Nicholas C. Prata. -- 1st ed.
      p. cm.
  Prequel to: Dream of fire.
  ISBN 978-1-889758-79-4
  I. Title.

PS3566.R267K47 2007
813'.54--dc22

2007007393

"Is any man as evil or great as rumor makes him?"
Lasctakos Ikar

BOY

erebos *Ikar* was born Livios Rapax in the rural southwestern corner of the *Chaconni* province, Ios. His parents, Daedilos and Neva, had despaired of having children when Neva finally got pregnant. It was a difficult nine months for the woman, who was confined to bed and never fully recovered from delivering the thirteen pound baby. A season after giving birth Neva removed to Ios' capitol, of the same name, to be tended properly; her father, an affluent merchant named Zathis, brought her home under the pretense of supplying medical care, but it was no secret he disliked Daedilos and felt Neva had married down with the landed but poor farmer.

Daedilos remained home to mind the crops but visited daily his wife and infant son. On the occasion that Zathis barred him from the house, Daedilos forced the door and made off with Livios, recently weaned. Daedilos tried to reconcile through a messenger, but Zathis would only demand the child's return.

Daedilos eventually arranged to visit his wife, though Zathis insisted on being present. Daedilos was brought to Neva's bedchamber, which was larger than his house, and knelt beside her bed. Neva was wan and gaunt and scarcely to be heard.

"Please bring him," she implored softly.

"I won't lose both of you to your father," Daedilos said.

"It's best for our son."

"Having a mother *and* father is best for him. Why not return?"

Neva wept. "I would, husband, but haven't the strength. I suffered the farm only because I loved you, but returning would surely kill me. Look at me! How could I tend you two?"

Daedilos took her cold hand in his. "It's I that'll tend you, wife. Just come home."

Neva shook her head. "Can't. Come back when you may." She looked to her father. "Promise that he can."

Zathis didn't answer.

1

As time passed Daedilos grew to regret separating mother and child and sought to reconcile with Zathis. One day he presented himself at the manor and, to his surprise, was granted an audience.

"Give your word that I can see them when I choose, and I'll bring Livios back," Daedilos began. "Your money would buy him a better life than I could provide," he ended bitterly.

"So, you want money?" Zathis sneered and flung his purse at the farmer. "There! Now leave and don't return!"

Angered, Daedilos threw the coins at Zathis and ran out before retainers could grab him. He never returned.

The next seven years were hard on Daedilos, who did his best to provide for Livios. When the yield on his two hundred acres was insufficient, Daedilos labored for the rich in Ios. He earned enough to stave off the governor's tax collectors but the brutally long days whittled his sturdy constitution. His cropped black hair went swiftly gray and toil lines etched his angular face. By the time Livios was old enough for chores, little of the vibrant, handsome man Neva had fallen for remained of Daedilos.

One season Livios fell ill with a pestilence that swept the province, and Daedilos sold his horse to buy medicine. When Livios did not improve, Daedilos tried to unload a parcel of land, but the new shire magistrate, Aedilos Zathis, blocked the transaction. Luckily, Livios rebounded from the sickness, proving as rugged as he was large. He topped one hundred pounds before his seventh birthday.

Daedilos also suspected that Zathis barred Livios' enrollment into the king's school, because a week after receiving the written declination (Daedilos was a lettered man) he was presented an offer from Zathis.

It read:

"Sirrah, as you may have heard, my daughter has died—you have played no small part in her death—and I wish to honor my promise that I shall provide for my grandson. Though I have not seen him in years, I extend an offer of housing and schooling. In addition, he shall be allowed to visit you if he desires.

I shall expect the lad at the end of the season. Aedilos Zathis."

Daedilos tried to conceal his grief, but to no avail. "My Neva," he sobbed, remembering her as he had first seen her, the sun in her bronze hair.

"What's wrong?" Livios asked excitedly. "Is that from mother? Is she coming back?"

Daedilos rubbed his dark eyes, the shape and color he had passed to his son. He bent to look Livios full in the face. "You know your father loves you?" he asked gently.

Livios' lip quivered. "Mother?"

Daedilos hugged the boy to his chest.

At ten, Livios was as tall as his father. Though he had yet to grow into enormous hands and feet, he had lost most of his baby fat and was more than equal to the chores of the two-room house. He had become an adequate cook, which lifted much drudgery from his father, but was especially fond of woodworking and showed promise as a horseman.

"If only you'd slow long enough to fill those sleds of yours," Daedilos laughed, tapping Livios' foot as it slid into the stirrup. "You'd make a fine officer in the Royal Guards."

The lad beamed from the saddle. "Can I ride to the river?"

"Aren't you and Felix hunting today?"

"He broke his bow."

Daedilos rubbed the roan's nose; the horse had already put in a full day. "I don't know, baby giant. Old Herakles sounds a bit winded. It was a hot afternoon."

"I'll wash and scrub him afterwards. *Please.*"

Daedilos chewed his lip, causing his leathery, tanned cheek to dimple. He managed a weary smile. "Okay, but no jumping."

"Thanks, dad!" Livios kneed the horse, which bolted off with surprising enthusiasm.

"Be back before sunset to practice your reading!" Daedilos yelled after them but could tell the boy had not heard. He watched with pride as his son thundered over the softly sloping plain. *I should've taught him letters before now*, he thought.

Livios and Herakles maintained a swift pace. They soon left the Rapax holdings and tore across undulating green hills toward the distant creek Livios knew only as "the river". It was a fine summer evening. The air was warm, but held little moisture, and the sky was clear and blue.

"Faster!" Livios urged the horse as they reached the ancient ruins of Fort Vesta, whose broken walls stuck from the earth like rotten teeth.

Herakles rolled on at speed, his hooves thudding like a muffled drum. Livios extended his right arm, pretending he held a sword. He brought the invisible weapon forward in a fluid motion, slicing an unseen foe.

"Kings Guard!" he cried, then laughed. "Faster, Herakles!"

The green slopes became increasingly rocky as they approached the river. Livios eased the horse to a trot and descended to the wide sandy beach. The gurgling stream covered less than half its bed this time of year but was unusually clear. Some willows lined the closest beach, and a large bog of cattails sat across the water. The buzz of insects and stench from the fen was in the air. Herakles crunched over the white sand, reached the water and began to drink. Livios patted the steed and slid off its back.

"Not too much, boy," he warned.

Livios picked up some small, smooth stones and tried skipping them. He was not very skilled, though, and couldn't cross the narrow span. He bent for more rocks, then another handful, then another, grimly determined to master the trick.

"Got one, Herakles!" he chirped and pointed across the creek. "See that?"

Herakles appeared unimpressed.

Livios pulled off his shirt and breeches and waded out into the tepid water, his feet sticking to the muddy bottom. He tried floating on his back, but soon wearied and went to lay beside Herakles. The sun had begun its descent, but the air was still balmy. Livios looked into the blue heavens.

Is mother up there? he wondered. *What was that?*

Voices!

Livios bolted upright, heart racing. He glanced down the stream and his stomach jumped into his mouth. A sizable detachment of warriors was watering themselves not fifty yards away! The swordsmen, all in black, were filling waterskins and lounging on the opposite beach. A few wore bandages, but even these men seemed in high spirits. Not until some slaves were herded onto the scene did Livios realize how enormous were the soldiers; they towered over even the tallest captive. Each looked capable of throwing Herakles over a shoulder.

Landesknectos! Livios thought. He had never seen the dreaded legionaries—they rarely bothered with Ios—but had heard many tales. He could only stare, too terrified to move.

"Hey, boy!" a warrior cried, not unkindly.

"Come over here!" called another. "There's one for you, Vex!"

Livios was on the horse so fast he forgot his clothes. The *landesknectos* howled as Herakles labored up the sandy incline.

"No need to be afraid!" one shouted, almost in Livios' ear—or so he thought. "Don't like the Legion, eh?"

Livios reached home in record time. He reined Herakles to a stop at the thatched cabin's door and leaped from the saddle, shouting, "Dad! Dad!"

Daedilos burst from the house, knife in hand, the light of battle in his eyes. He looked about and demanded, "What is it?"

4

"*Landesknectos!* Hundreds of 'em!"

Daedilos' muttered under his breath. "Where?"

"By the river!"

"Did they see you?"

Livios nodded wildly.

Daedilos stuck the knife in his belt and grabbed his son by the shoulders. "Calm down, baby giant," he said. "The Legion's not interested in the likes of us, and even if they were, it would take an hour to march here, as they have no horses."

Livios mastered himself.

"But just in case, we'll spend the night in town," Daedilos resumed. "Sack enough food for us and come right back. Understand?"

"Yes."

"And grab yourself some clothes. Get to it."

Livios set off as ordered and Daedilos took mental note of his valuables. There weren't many, but Herakles could not carry both humans and baubles.

"Going to have to hitch up the cart," he sighed; the wagon had a bad axle and squeaked loud enough to wake the dead. "God help us."

Livios at age fourteen was an imposing specimen, a head taller than Daedilos and much broader across the shoulders—he had to turn sideways to enter the cabin. His muscles were wonderfully developed, sculpted by backbreaking farmwork, and he had earned a reputation for strength at festival contests the previous two years. He had already caught the eye of the local marshal but Daedilos wanted a more prestigious position for his son and had petitioned the provincial recruiter in Ios regarding enlistment in the Royal Guards. The recruiter had heard of Livios and expressed interest, but suggested he wait until his sixteenth birthday before trying for one of the coveted posts in the distant capitol, Korenthis.

Nor was interest in Livios limited to the military. A baroness twice offered to hire the lad as a "bodyguard" but Daedilos declined; the woman had a notorious reputation. Also, he was deeply attached to his son and planned to keep him as long as possible.

Livios resembled his father, which spared him ribbing over paternity. He had his sire's hawklike nose, sharp chin and flat cheekbones. His eyes were very brown, almost black, and he had a straight set of strong teeth. Also his raven hair recalled Daedilos', before it had gone gray, though he wore its curls shoulder length.

Livios was quiet but had a generous nature, and never bullied other children. He frequently joked with those he knew best: Daedilos, his friend Felix, and the neighbor's daughter, Vara. He had inherited Neva's sense of humor, or so Daedilos said.

Livios and Felix had crouched by the deer path for hours with no luck; they hadn't even seen a bird. By now they were getting restless, and since nighttime was fast approaching, contemplated calling it a day.

I hate being the first to quit, Livios thought. He smiled at Felix, who smiled back.

The grin came naturally to Felix's swarthy, round face, as fleshy as Livios' was chiseled. Nearly as tall as Livios, but paunchy, he was nevertheless quite an athlete. He could ride, too.

"Thinking about knocking off, eh?" Felix whispered. "I can tell."

"Not yet."

"Liar." Felix drew the bow. "Maybe we should shoot and dress you?"

"Maybe I should break that bow over your head?"

Felix laid the weapon aside. "Did I tell you Vara kissed me?"

Livios pointed. "Stay away from my girl."

"Yours? You're too young, Rapax. She has five years on you. Vara needs a real man."

"A real *fat* man?"

Felix jabbed his friend with the bow. "Why don't you—"

Both turned at once. A buck had emerged from a copse and was headed straight for them. The deer, a ten pointer, stopped suddenly and lifted its head, twenty yards out.

Can't smell us, Livios thought, heart aflutter. *We're still downwind.* He motioned for the bow and Felix surrendered it at once. Livios picked an arrow off the ground and rose to his knees, careful to not rustle leaves. His head and shoulders stood above the brush. His heart was pounding as he slowly drew the string to his ear. The long yew bow creaked slightly. The deer looked right at him.

"Eye," Livios breathed as he loosed.

The arrow flew true and sliced into the orb with a brief "ffft". The deer dropped onto the narrow path. The boys jumped from their hiding place, whooping as they ran to the fallen prey. The buck lay with head on splayed hooves, looking very much asleep. The arrow had failed to penetrate the back of the skull, but had snapped inside the head, judging from the fletch. A single tear of blood wound down the animal's face.

Felix grunted admiration. "Nice shot, Livi."

"Thanks! Did you hear me call the eye?"

"Yes. He's a big one. Hundred and fifty, I'd wager."

"My dad will be pleased," Livios said, already basking in Daedilos' praise.

Felix drew a long knife from his boot. "We'd better be quick about. It's almost dark." As though on cue, a wolf howled in the distance. Livios drew his own blade to help.

The boys arrived at the Rapax house after nightfall, the buck hanging from a branch slung over their shoulders. Livios saw gray chimney smoke against the sky but could smell that Daedilos had not cooked dinner. A welcome red glow shone through the window slats.

"Hello there!" Livios called. "The butcher has arrived with a special delivery."

Daedilos came outside, shaving lather on his face. He gave a low whistle. "Nice one! Who got him?"

"I did," Livios replied proudly. "Ten points."

"I see that. Guess we'll have to make room for them over the fireplace."

Livios could only smile.

"Hang him in the barn, sir?" Felix asked.

"No, bleed him from the tree. Nice and high, too. Don't want any bears to get at him. I'll finish dinner. You are staying, Felix?"

"Yes, sir."

As they settled around the small table, Daedilos said, "Felix, take old Herakles tonight. Come back in the morning with your father's cart and we'll divvy up the meat."

"Yes, sir."

"Did you two wash your hands?" Daedilos asked.

The boys looked at each other.

"Be quick then, I'm hungry."

Livios and Felix found a bucket of water and did a fast job. Daedilos lifted the iron lid and a toothsome smell filled the room. Livios reached for his plate.

"Prayers," Daedilos said.

Livios put his hands together. "God bless and keep us. Forgive us our sins. Thank you for the meal we're about to eat, and may we never go hungry. And may next harvest be a good one." He looked at his father.

"Good enough," Daedilos said.

Next day Livios rose early and quartered the deer. Felix soon arrived with his own mule and wagon, Herakles in tow.

"Morning," he said and climbed down.

"Hello. I did the dirty work. Bring any sacks?"

"Yes," Felix replied and reached into the wagon. "You done cutting?"

"I am."

Felix stood over the venison. "You pick first."

7

Livios chose the cleaner ham, Felix the other. They traded turns until the beast had been split evenly, but Livios appropriated the antlers and heart as trophies.

"You know, I haven't had breakfast yet, but I'm not the slightest bit hungry," he admitted.

"Know what you mean." Felix eyed the sky. "Thunderheads rolling in. I'd better be on my way."

Livios helped load the wagon, and Felix pulled the smoker from the barn.

"That should do it, Livi. See you."

They clasped hands.

Felix climbed into the driver's seat, which gave voice beneath him. He smiled as he snapped the reins. "I wasn't joking about Vara," he said as the cart lurched forward.

"What?" Livios replied, momentarily puzzled. "Oh, get out of here before I give you a beating!"

Felix made a semicircle and headed back the way he had come. Before he had gone far down the dirt drive he passed a young woman bearing two buckets over her shoulders. They waved at each other.

Livios' ears burned. "Good morning, Vara."

Vara eased the yoke onto the grass. She smiled as she straightened, exposing a small space between her two front teeth. Her honey-colored hair was lighter than most *Chaconni*'s, and so were her blue eyes. Livios loved her eyes. Her nose was small, slightly upturned, and her lips the same color as her rosy cheeks.

"Why's Felix leaving?" she asked.

"Can I have the milk, please?"

Vara laughed, a sound both intoxicating and infuriating. "Didn't I just set it down?"

Livios tossed her a packet of venison brisket.

She dropped it, stepped forward and grabbed his belt. "Why such a sour face? You'll spoil the milk."

Livios looked into her eyes, then away.

"Felix told you?" Vara laughed. "I hoped he would."

Livios swallowed on a dry mouth. "I thought you liked me."

Vara leaned into him, standing on her toes. "I do, baby giant," she replied in a low tone that chilled his spine. "How long you going to make me wait?"

Livios swallowed again, too terrified to speak.

Vara pursed her lips. "Kiss me."

Livios was incapable of motion.

"Morning, Vara," Daedilos growled as he arrived, hoe in hand.

8

"Thanks for the milk. Tell your mother I'll send the wheat directly."

Vara's expression became passive. She turned to Daedilos. "Hello. I'll tell her." She grabbed the yoke, unhitched the buckets and set the wood over her shoulders. With a last backward smile, she began walking. Father and son watched her swaying hips for a long moment.

"Put your tongue back in your mouth, son," Daedilos said.

"I'm not sure I can."

"I think she likes you...a little too well."

Livios nodded.

"How old is she now, anyway?" Daedilos asked.

"Nineteen."

"Too old for you. And I don't like the rumors I've heard about her in town. I'm going to talk to her parents."

Livios felt a maelstrom of emotions in his breast. He couldn't quite sort them. "Uh, can you not, dad?"

Daedilos looked thoughtfully at his son. "Very well. But keep her at arm's length, you hear? *You hear?*"

"Yes, sir."

Daedilos tossed Livios the dusty hoe. "Hang that for me."

That night Livios had an evil dream.

He was trapped in some subterranean maze, feeling his way along the cold and muddy walls. He sensed something awful sneaking up on him, but the faster he blundered along, the more twists and turns confronted him. Even worse, he suspected he was working toward that which stalked him. His breaths come in gasps.

"Dad!" he cried.

Livios awoke. Daedilos was leaning over the cot. "You're dreaming, son!" he said, his face craggy in the candlelight. "You okay?"

Livios sat upright.

"What was it about?" his father asked.

Livios waded through the dream, but as is often the case with night-mares viewed afterwards, there seemed little to justify the dread that had possessed him. "Sorry to wake you," he grumbled at last.

Daedilos straightened. "No worry, I wasn't sleeping. There's still some night left. Get some rest." He went back to the table and hunched over a parchment.

Livios eased back onto the cot, but kept his father in view. Daedilos' sharp profile was dark since the candle sat on the table's far side. Livios snuggled into the straw mattress, savoring a sense of security.

Daedilos reread the parchment, silently lamenting his sloppy cursive.

Daedilos Rapax to His Honor, Lord Praxis—

Greetings. I gratefully accept your offer to trade one quarter of my acres for the 3-year-old stallion and saddle in question. It is very important, though, that my son test the mount. He must be comfortable with any animal with which he will be linking his professional future.

Daedilos sighed and leaned onto his elbows. He could ill afford to lose the land, but Herakles was getting old. Besides, Praxis's stables were famous for warhorses and Livios would need that advantage when he signed with the Royal Guards.

Daedilos shook his head, thinking, *Maybe Praxis will let me share-crop?*

Livios woke to an empty cabin. He washed, ate the food his father had put aside for him and pulled on soiled work clothes. After tidying the place, he went outside.

It was a bright, beautiful day. The sky was a deep azure and the breeze carried the scent of pine from a distant copse. A buzz of insects was in the air. Livios crossed the yard and followed the cart path to the barn. The large double doors were closed, but not bolted, which puzzled him until he remembered Daedilos had taken Herakles; his father would be gone all day. He opened the valves and stepped out of their way; sunlight filled the barn. Claiming an axe and wedge from the wall, he went back outside. He began splitting the logs on the barn's north side, muscling them around with an ease unimaginable to most men. Before long he worked up a sweat and removed his shirt.

Livios sang as he banged away, marking time to an old soldier's chant. His booming voice carried across the fields of wheat.

> "Knew a man, 'twas a farmer's son,
> The days were long, he worked for free,
> He spent his life tied to the plow,
> Til' he signed with the infantry.
>
> Knew a man in the infantry,
> The pay was poor, the marches hard.
> Fell in love with a rich man's girl,
> Then he rode with the Scarlet Guards.
>
> Knew a man in the Scarlet Guards,
> Who led a life of luxury.
> Put his hands on a noble's wife,
> So now he works the farm for free."

There was a squeaking sound as he drew for another stroke and the axe blade stayed in the wood. "Damn," he said and inspected the naked handle; the tensing nail had somehow worked loose. He went into the barn, opened his father's cavernous tool chest and rummaged for the perfect nail. The chest's musky odor brought back childhood memories.

A woman laughed. "Just look at you all lathered up."

Livios whirled toward Vara, who was leaning against the jamb. Not dressed for farmwork, she wore a skirt and gossamer blouse.

"Scare you?" she asked.

"Maybe. Don't sneak up like that."

Vara sauntered over, a curious gleam in her eyes. "Lots more hair on your chest than last time I saw it, baby giant."

Livios stood his ground. "So. Jealous?"

Vara laughed again. "Oh, I don't think so. Guess what I'm doing here."

Livios felt at once uneasy and excited. He swallowed hard and glanced past Vara as though expecting, or hoping, to see Daedilos striding into view.

"Who you looking for?" Vara laughed. "I'm right here." She slid her hand under his arm and placed it on the goosebumped flesh of his naked back. "Your daddy wouldn't approve, is that it?" she asked, her tone still playful but now tinged with disdain. "Can't you look at me?"

Livios steeled himself as he gazed down at her. "I'm not afraid of you, if that's what you mean," he lied. "But I've work to do." He tried to twist away but found that she had somehow manipulated him nearer; they stood so close he could feel her shirt buttons on his stomach. Again he looked toward the barn door.

"No one to save you, baby giant," Vara purred.

"I have work," he said, struggling feebly. Or had he struggled at all? Again, against his will, he found himself trapped in her blue eyes. *Keep her at arm's length*, Daedilos had said.

"It can wait," Vara rasped. She placed her hands behind his head and whispered: "Kiss me."

Livios suddenly closed his eyes and thrust her from him. For his life he couldn't remember having decided to push her. He lifted a hand, intent on trying to explain his feelings, but found no words forthcoming.

Vara, a few paces away, wiped golden locks from her face and gave an impish smile. "Do I have to get Felix to do it?"

Daedilos turned off the King's road, an overgrown stone highway with a history that stretched back a millenium, and coaxed Herakles

11

over a hedgerow. His farm sprawled before him, and he was happy to see it; it had been an irritating day. The wait at Lord Praxis' had been shorter than he had anticipated, but no less galling; he had stood outside Praxis' walls all morning before being granted the briefest of audiences.

"Rapax," the nobleman had greeted as Daedilos was led in. Praxis lifted a parchment, saying, "These terms are acceptable." He signed the contract, blew on the ink, and handed the scroll to his factor, an elderly Northman named Kall. "Send your son tomorrow to try the horse. Good day."

And that was it.

Nobles! Daedilos thought with disgust. *They should try my life for a month or two.* But the rancor ebbed as he mulled the future he'd bought Livios and looked forward to telling him about the new charger. *The lad's expression alone will be worth the price.*

No smoke rose from the cabin, which meant Livios had found the oats and ham he'd prepared for him. *He should be done splitting those rails by now. Throws them around like toothpicks*, he thought proudly.

The logs came into view but Livios was nowhere to be seen. The barn was wide open. Daedilos swung from the saddle and briefly massaged his hamstring. He walked Herakles up the scant incline. *What's that noise?* he wondered, tensing.

Vara suddenly strode from the barn, her hair disheveled and her blouse buttoned out of sequence. "Hello!" she said and stepped briskly past.

What's this? Daedilos thought as he watched her go, then cold realization washed him. Furious, he entered the barn. A barechested Livios stood near the tool chest, looking quite guilty.

Livios saw his father stomp inside and prepared for a sharp dressing down.

"Have an interesting morning?" Daedilos growled as he stopped a few feet away. "Working hard while I was gone?"

Livios' shrug might have seemed to lack contrition but he was simply at a loss for words. He was sickened at having disobeyed Daedilos—and that was only the beginning of his shame; he could hardly believe what had passed. He feared to speak lest he surrender the whole story.

"Answer me, boy!"

Livios looked away. He felt small; at least it seemed that his father towered over him. "I thought you'd be all day."

"Is that right?" Daedilos asked hotly. "If only I'd come home sooner! Didn't I tell you to stay away from that tart? You want to ruin your life before it even gets started? Let's pray you haven't done anything that can't be undone! What happened?"

Livios felt sodden and wretched and wished Daedilos would stop yelling. He wanted badly to run from the building but knew that would only make matters worse. He felt tight in the chest and cold in the stomach but, most of all, disgraced. How could he have so failed his father? His eyes started to sting.

"Answer me!" Daedilos shouted.

Livios stood mute.

"I sold much of our land today to get you a good mount, and this is your reply?" Daedilos railed. "I should just take it back because if you can't follow simple orders, you'll never make a soldier!"

Livios felt the tears coming; he was worthless and dirty. Did Daedilos hate him now? Why had Vara done this to him? He felt a rising fury with the girl. Hadn't he told her, many times, to leave him be? Without fully comprehending it he turned to slink off.

"Don't turn from me, boy!" Daedilos cried and grabbed Livios' elbow.

Livios yanked his arm free and threw Daedilos into a stumble. Daedilos righted himself and jumped after his son. He took Livios roughly by the shoulders and forced him back around. "Can't you hear me?" he shouted.

In truth, Livios hadn't, struggling as he was to overcome the unwarranted, disconnected rage that he was experiencing for the first time, but would become a mainstay of his life. His vision took on a red cast.

"Answer me!" Daedilos demanded.

Vaguely aware that he must escape the situation, Livios again turned away; Daedilos again grabbed him.

Something snapped in Livios and before he knew it he wheeled and launched a mighty blow at his father's head. There was a sharp "crack" and Daedilos fell in a heap. It was moments before Livios realized what had happened but when it hit he knew he'd never be the same. Nausea swept him and his knees buckled. He dropped to the dirt beside Daedilos. "Daddy! Daddy!" he wailed, gathering his father into his arms.

Daedilos' neck was obviously broken; bone had pierced skin in two places. His dark eyes held a look of infinite sadness.

Livios squeezed his father close, kissing him, slobbering on him. "*Goddddd!*" he cried, snorting and coughing. He shook Daedilos as though to wake him. "Daddy!"

"You killed him!" Vara shrieked from the door. "You killed him!" She had sneaked back to eavesdrop and had gotten much more than she bargained for.

But Livios did not hear, nor did he mark when she finally ran off. He was out cold.

13

OUTLAW

Livios opened his eyes; the webbed recesses of the peaked barn loomed above. *What am I doing in here?* he wondered. He rolled onto his side, saw Daedilos, and memory swept him like a cold, sickening wave.

"Oh, dad," he groaned. He snuggled up to his father and placed his head on his chest.

The tears came again, without their prior urgency, but rather like the steady ebb of a mortal wound. He cried until his eyes ran dry, then sobbed until hoarse, and all the while prayed for death.

Time passed.

The sun sank and the barn cooled. Livios crawled to his breeches, pulled them on, then went back to his father. Daedilos was staring at him, and it was more than he could bear. He curled into a ball and wept more, rocking slowly back and forth. He longed for Daedilos to wake him, but the realization that this was no dream only sharpened the pain.

Daedilos was dead. Forever. *And I killed him,* he thought. *Killed my own father.*

It was nearly dark before the news reached Felix. A shaken Vara had given her parents a fairly accurate account of the proceedings and they immediately summoned the shire constable, Felix's uncle Achillis. As chance had it, Achillis was passing through the district with a captured horse thief and safeguarded the criminal at Felix's before seeking Livios. Felix took his father's horse and reached the Rapax farm even as starry night fell.

"Livi!" he cried, swinging off the colt's back and running to the barn. It was very dark inside. "Livi!" he repeated and groped for the lamp just inside the door. Working by feel he sparked the lamp; white flame bloomed and shadows crawled across the floor.

Livios was slumped beside Daedilos. Felix choked up as he approached them.

14

"You okay?" he asked quietly.

Livios' head shot up, madness in his eyes. He sprang to his feet with a growl. "Get out of here, damn you!" he screamed and grabbed the lamp. He choked Felix with his free hand.

Felix knew fear of Livios for the first time. It was as though some devil had possessed his friend, and his malice was tangible as a punch in the gut. Livios bared his teeth and squeezed.

"I killed him!" he shrieked and burst into tears. He blubbered a moment then released Felix and sank to his knees.

Felix staggered off to catch his breath. When he looked again Livios lay in a heap, sobbing. Fear left Felix and he was overcome with grief and pity. He peered at Daedilos, who lay in his son's shadow, and sighed. "I know, Livi. Come, let's look to him."

"No," Livios croaked miserably, shaking his head. "I don't want him to leave."

Felix laid a trembling hand on Livios' curly head. "I know." He eventually coaxed Livios from the barn and they headed for the cabin. The stars lent cold light to the world. "Let's get you something to eat," he said as cheerfully as possible. "Will do you good."

"Give me the lamp."

Felix obeyed, then pushed open the front door. "Come, you'll feel better after a bite," he said with a forced smile.

Livios stared at Felix, who had the distinct impression that some-one other than his friend was looking at him. "No I won't," Livios said tonelessly. "Wait here," he commanded and trudged back to the barn.

"Livi!" Felix called after him.

Livios entered the barn and clanged shut the heavy door; the yard was again dark.

Felix heard the shatter of glass. "Hey!" he cried. Another moment. Rays of light stabbed through the slatted woodwork. Thin puffs of smoke issued from the triangular roof. "My God!" he yelled and sprang into action. The smoke grew thicker even as he ran to the structure. He wrestled with the doors, but they were secured from inside. For the first time he heard the crackle of flames and smelled burning hay.

Felix thought fast. He knew there were no locks on the inside and concluded that Livios had jammed the doorhandles. He ran to the woodpile and grabbed the heaviest log he could manage. He puffed up the grade and was at a trot when he rammed the latch. The recoil from the blow knocked the wind from his chest, but he was rewarded with the sound of snapping metal. Wheezing, he wiggled the pig iron handle from the door and burst into the building. And stopped at once. There was already a hellish blaze and the heat stole the air from his lungs. The entire west wall was afire above the shards of broken lamp; the flames

15

tickled the ceiling.

Livios lay with his head on his father's chest. Felix crouched under the thickest smoke and stumbled to his friend. The heat and noise left him disoriented. He fumbled for Livios' belt and inched the young giant across the dirt. Felix could hold his breath no longer, inhaled, and began to cough. He couldn't see through his tears but pulled on the belt with his remaining strength.

Felix felt afire but maintained his sweaty grip. He muscled Livios slowly backward, and just when he could endure no more, felt the welcome cool of night. He crashed onto his back and gasped for air, his eyes too full of smoke to make out the stars. Sweat poured from him in torrents.

"Livios!" Felix called. Forcing his body into motion, he dragged the unconscious youth onto some damp grass and rested again. The flames were a roar now and the acrid, creamy smoke curled into the sky.

*   *   *

Night was falling before Constable Achillis turned south for the Rapax farm. Having learned of Felix's disappearance, he surmised his nephew had ridden ahead but that didn't bother him. He knew Livios well enough, and suspected the lad wouldn't run. Other than his colossal stature, there was little to say of him (certainly nothing bad), though Achillis felt a tad envious of the interest the King's Guards had shown in Livios. Achillis had tried to enlist with that elite force, but his horsemanship was at best average. The recruiting officer had dismissed him after only the briefest consideration. *Some folks are just born to ride*, he thought grudgingly.

The stallion which bore him down the inky, overgrown highway was in many ways like himself: lean, dark, unkempt and perhaps a bit old for his job. The horse even had a long braid, as did his master. Achillis had already squeezed a full day's work from the animal and was beginning to wonder if he should pull into the knot of cedars yonder for some sleep, and put the Rapax matter off till morning. If Livios *had* bolted, it certainly made more sense to track by light of day. Anyway, Achillis was bone tired and would like time to consider the issue. If young Rapax held up under interrogation and corroborated that tramp Vara's story, he might just give him some lashes and remand him to Felix's father.

Without even realizing it, Achillis had turned into the trees and dismounted. He liked bedding beneath coniferous trees; they gave year-round cover and the ground beneath was usually dry. Besides, they smelled nice. Achillis tended the horse, then struck a small fire. He ate a meager meal and stretched out for the night, dagger beside him.

Achillis was nearly asleep when the earth brought the report of hooves. "Damn," he cursed and smothered the blaze. He had rarely been accosted on the highway—people usually tried to *evade*, not *find* him—but his was a suspicious nature. *More than one rider, by the sound of it*, he thought. *They're really moving, too.*

Soon he made out half a dozen riders. Even at night he identified the gaudy striped livery of Lord Praxis' henchmen and wondered what they were doing so far from town.

The lead horseman slowed to a stop not far from Achillis and gazed toward the campsite. "Can see the smoke, constable," he called. "Can I come over for a chat?"

Achillis recognized Praxis' elderly seneschal, Kall, and sheathed his dagger. Though he and Kall had been friendly once upon a time, he had no intention of making it easy on the retainer. "Just you," he replied. "And leave your weapons."

The request was unnecessary as Kall, an aged *Boru*, had twenty years on Achillis, but the constable was cranky about being wakened. Besides, there was always a chance Praxis' stooges were up to no good. How frequently did they ride in the dark, anyway?

Kall gave instructions to his soldiers and swung from the saddle. He left his sword behind and leaped the roadside drainage ditch.

"What is this?" Achillis demanded. "Can't a working man get some sleep?"

"Sorry. If you haven't guessed already, I was looking for you." Kall sat beside the smoldering embers. He pulled a pipe from under his brigantine jacket and lit the bowl with one of the coals. He puffed until tobacco scented the air. "Please, constable, have a seat," he laughed. "Do I really look that dangerous?"

Achillis sat. In truth, Kall did look harmless; he was long and thin with advanced gout in his fingers. What remained of his gray hair scarcely rimmed a pate discolored by splotches dark enough to stand out at nighttime. He had aged much since Achillis had last seen him. The constable hoped Kall wasn't thinking the same of him.

"What brings you out?" Achillis asked.

"A matter my lord can't trust to them," Kall replied with a nod at his skulking comrades. He took a puff on the pipe and a red glow lit his face. "And, yes, it has to do with money."

Achillis shrugged. "We all know Praxis."

Another draw on the pipe. "I assume you're making your way to apprehend the murderer, Livios Rapax."

Achillis perked up. "'Apprehend' and 'murder' are words I haven't settled on. What's it to you?"

Kall chuckled and glanced furtively about. "Please, not so loud. Do

17

you know my lord had recently signed a contract with Daedilos? Bought his land?"

"Bought Rapax's farm?" Achillis snorted. "I don't think so. I would've heard about it. Estate transactions go through the aedile's office. You know that."

"Well, maybe not *all* the acres," Kall conceded. "But I brought the deed with me."

Achillis waited.

"Lord Praxis would like to keep his claim to the land, that's all," Kall continued with an oily smile. "And you might help him with that."

Achillis guessed where this was going. "And if Livios were killed, that 'not all, initially' might flower into something more? Might help you slide the title past the aedile?"

Kall smiled again. "Exactly, constable. But who's talking of killing? Enslaving the boy would do the trick. Anything to eliminate his claim."

Achillis had nothing against Livios and saw no reason to destroy his future. Yet. "You're living dangerously," he said. As Kall opened his mouth, Achillis interrupted: "Trying to bribe me is a capital crime, mind you."

Kall leaned closer and whispered: "But what if it's a *really good* bribe?"

*   *   *

A drab dawn was at hand when Achillis reached the Rapax farm. Clouds had moved in during the night and a summer dousing was not far off. The remains of the barn were still smoking and a halo of scorched grass ringed the site. Achillis saw two horses tethered to a post but the boys were nowhere to be seen. A white chicken darted across the yard.

"Hello the house!" Achillis called before the door.

There were some scuffling sounds before Felix poked his head out. His hair was mussed and his chubby face grimy. "Uncle," he replied, blinking.

"Is he here?"

The barest hesitation. "Yes, sir. It was an accident. Livi tried to kill himself last night."

Achillis felt a twinge of guilt. "He'll have to tell it to the aedile. Send him out."

Felix's jaw dropped. "The aedile? Why you taking him there?"

Achillis glared. "Did you hear what I told you, boy? Get moving!"

Felix disappeared and Achillis heard muffled conversation. Achillis'

18

intuition said Livios would come along quietly, and that was a considerable comfort. The pup would have been a handful otherwise. *Never heard of a man being killed with a single punch,* he reflected. He heard Felix's quick, hushed tones an instant before Livios filled the doorway. *Good God, he's grown even since harvest!*

Livios' soot-covered torso resembled those of the gladiators Achillis had seen in Korenthis; he had to bend to exit. He trod heavily toward the constable, showing the hollow gaze of a condemned man. Tear tracks lined his dirty face. Achillis again felt remorse.

"Hello, Livios," he said gentler than he wanted. "I must take you in."

Livios merely raised his hands.

"Uncle!" Felix called from the steps.

"Get his shirt," Achillis said tonelessly and pulled rope from his saddle.

"What about his other things?" Felix demanded.

Achillis studied Livios, who stared at the ground. "Won't need them where he's going. Now shut up and obey me before I give you a thrashing."

In the end Achillis did have to rough up his nephew, which proved harder than he thought. Felix fought with surprising skill, or maybe it only seemed so since Achillis' heart wasn't in the matter. In any event, he only managed to knock out Felix after the lad had split his lip.

Livios stood by the entire time, utterly forlorn and completely disinterested in the proceedings.

Before long Achillis and his captive reached the King's highway. Herakles' reins were bound to the constable's saddle; Livios slumped upon the horse, looking very much asleep.

It was more than ten leagues to Ios City and the grumbling clouds promised a wet trip. Achillis was anxious to finish the road and get his money, if not happy about selling Livios to slavers. *But I need the money,* he told his conscience. *Fifty in gold will go far to getting me out of this business.* Achillis glanced at Livios. *He's no farmer, anyway. And he did kill his father, accident or not.*

Achillis frowned. He was just making rationalizations and knew it. It began to drizzle. He stared ahead, concentrating on the sound of hoof on stone. They passed an ancient granite roadmarker.

Twenty-eight miles to go.

Felix awoke and tasted blood in his mouth. He groaned as he labored to a sitting position and rubbed his head. There were lumps on his scalp and the entire left side of his face felt puffy; the eye was nearly

19

swollen shut. *Damn Achillis!* he thought and tried stand.

Felix had never been especially fond of his mother's brother but now felt downright murderous toward the man. He gained his feet and started for the cabin. The first few steps were shaky but desire saw him through. He staggered into the cabin but soon reemerged with bow and quiver. It began to rain softly as he bent and strung the weapon. He looked for his horse. *Uncle must've run him off*, he thought. Felix tried whistling for the animal, but his lips were too swollen. He tucked the bow under his armpit and loped toward the nearest grazing field.

It took an hour to find the steed. The saddle was gone, but that didn't matter; he rode just as well without one. Felix cut westward across the Rapax lands, pressing the horse. If he pushed it, he might intercept his uncle just outside Ios. He was not sure what he would do if he found Achillis, but knew he would die before seeing Livios enslaved.

The walled city of Ios was located on the undulating plains of southwestern Ios province and boasted dozens of buildings. The governor's keep stood squarely in the middle of town, its spired donjon rose above the surroundings. The sparse woodlands had been cut back a mile to deny an enemy cover.

Achillis was relieved to see Ios. He was drenched to the skin, hungry, and anxious to unload Livios, who had said nothing all journey. The silence was a different kind than Achillis was used to from prisoners, and it disturbed him.

It rained harder.

Achillis felt a savage pain in his left leg and shrieked. He looked and was astonished to see an arrow in his knee! He yanked the horse to a halt and frantically fingered around the wound, unsure how to proceed. Felix rose from a drainage ditch, arrow at the ready. He was covered in mud and had a very serious look on his bruised, pudgy face.

"Afternoon, uncle," he slurred. "The next one hits your face."

Achillis wavered between fear and rage. He settled on both. "You'll hang for this," he hissed. "I'll make sure of it."

Felix stepped closer. "Swing down real slowly."

Achillis contemplated spurring his horse but didn't; Felix was an excellent shot. "I can't stand, fool," he snapped. "You crippled me."

"Then lay in the muck."

Rage started to conquer Achillis. Not only because he was used to being in control, but also because it was Felix who waylaid him. The same nephew he had bounced on his knee. *Or beat bloody*, he reminded himself. He snorted with pain when he tried to put weight on the leg. He eased to the ground. "I should've cut your throat, fat boy."

"I might cut yours if you don't shut up," Felix replied as he took

Achillis' horse. The constable glowered while bleeding onto the wet cobblestones.

Felix approached his friend. "You all right?" he asked softly. No reply. "Livi!" Livios slowly looked up, his expression morose beyond words. "Rouse yourself. We're leaving."

Livios shook his head.

"Don't be stupid!" Felix said. "Do you think your father would want to see you hanged?"

Livios stiffened in the saddle.

"I'm not planning to kill him," Achillis said.

"Quiet!" Felix roared, then turned to his friend. "Well?"

"Whatever you want. I don't care."

Felix called his mount, which emerged from behind a distant aqueduct. Very soon he, Livios and all the horses were ready to depart.

Only now did he fully comprehend what assaulting a constable, even his uncle, meant. He felt himself softening a bit and tossed Achillis a balled scarf for a bandage.

Achillis smiled grimly but snatched the cloth. "I'll see you hang," he promised. "You and your mate, there. Unless you get me into the city."

Felix steeled himself and notched an arrow. "You may be right, uncle. Guess I'd better kill you."

Achillis didn't think Felix had it in him. "But you won't. So help me into the saddle."

Felix shot the other knee.

*   *   *

The outlaws reached the Rapax farm. It took longer than Felix anticipated, as he had to hold his friend in the saddle near the end. Livios had perked up during the initial mad dash, but soon fell back into lassitude; he sat on Herakles with all the life of a sack of potatoes. No amount of prodding roused him, either. Felix was concerned and annoyed.

"Come on, gather supplies," he said and dismounted.

Livios seemed not to hear.

Felix collected food, weapons, bedding and clothes as quickly as possible, but it took so long he expected an army of constables at any moment. He looked at the bundled sacks. *What am I forgetting?* he wondered while lugging the sacks into the yard. The rain was coming in torrents. *Good. Make it tougher to track us.*

Livios sat motionless on Herakles; wet hair snaked over his forehead. "Tinder," he said softly.

21

Felix turned on a coin. "Eh?"

"And flint."

Felix smiled, so happy was he to hear Livios' voice. "Knew I was forgetting something." He finished lading the horses and grabbed Herakles' reins. "Let's go."

Felix knew good hiding spots in the district but Achillis knew them, too. Thinking of his uncle caused a sinking sensation in his stomach. *I should've killed him,* he thought. *Would've been the smart thing. Maybe he bled to death?* he considered with little hope. *No. Things like that have a way of not happening when you need them. Kind of like starting a fire: you freeze to death while attempting a blaze with embers, oil, and seasoned wood, then some fool drops a spark in a wet field and your whole crop goes up.*

At last Felix settled on a place. There were some salt licks near Cemetery River that had hollowed nicely into good, deep caves. Even better, it fell outside Achillis' jurisdiction. True, the caves were technically in Ios, but they were so close to the Legion's territory that no one dared go there.

"Livi, we have to ride hard," Felix said above the stinging rain. "Can you please try to stay on this time? *Please?*"

"Right."

Livios exerted enough effort that Felix soon stopped worrying. They made off south and covered the thirty miles as swiftly as they might across the muddy, roadless land. There were no forests to slow them but they infrequently passed the remains of a manor or farm; the province had been far more populated once upon a time. The closer they drew to the river the less common this became. Felix pondered glumly that the Rapax house was now deserted, too. He thought of his uncle and imagined a posse on his trail; the image of he and Livios swinging by the neck caused a shudder. Suddenly the salt licks didn't seem so remote and secure.

Should they flee *Chaconni* lands altogether? *I don't speak any other languages,* he thought.

The skies had cleared during the last hour, but the sun had begun its descent. The boys eased the lathered horses down a rocky slope that spilled onto a floodplain. Felix saw that vibrantly green sward stretch into the distance where it terminated against a ribbon of white sand. Dusk was enough at hand that he couldn't see Cemetery River's broad brown water, but he heard the distant roars of the sharks that had ventured onto land.

Somehow Felix had forgotten the sharks. The mottled orange, purple and gray monsters that flourished in Cemetery River were much to be feared. Not only were they huge and incredibly ill tempered, but they had legs. They did not venture far from the water, so he felt safe in the licks, but God help the fool who found himself near the river at nightfall. The "legionary sharks" could outrun a man and, after centuries of feeding by the *landesknectos*, had developed a voracious tooth for humans.

It was almost dark when Felix found the desired cave. A quick inspection proved it all he remembered; it stretched many paces into the incline, forking off just as it seemed to be petering out. Livios was staring into space when he returned.

Felix was near the end of patience by the time he dragged Livios off Herakles, and of course his listless friend was no help caring for the horses. After a long while, Felix staggered into the cool cave and dropped onto its smooth floor. He was asleep before closing his eyes.

Felix was lost in a dream when something hot stung his nose. He opened his eyes and slowly focused. Livios was squatting before him in the gloom, a sizzling piece of pork an inch from his face.

"Breakfast," Livios said swinging the ham.

Felix rubbed his eyes then took the offered spit. "Thanks. Good to hear you talking."

Livios nodded as he stood.

Felix took a bite of the smoked ham. Rarely had he tasted something so good. A thought struck him. "You started a fire?"

"Uh, huh."

"What of the legionaries?"

Livios looked worried. "I forgot. I'll put it out."

Felix took another, larger bite, burning his tongue. "We should only make fires at night."

The next few weeks passed without event and the boys settled into a routine. Besides his very intense nightmares, Livios was feeling better each day—unless Daedilos' name came up. Truth be told, the boys rather liked their new life, which seemed an extended camping trip once they got over the shock of being outlaws. For one thing, they didn't have to work. One would have to be a farmer to fully realize the drudgery involved in their previous lives. The sweat required in raising crops and stock was only part of it; there was always another task on a farm and it was usually backbreaking. Now they slept until dawn!

Even necessary chores became fun, as they were only accountable to each other. For example, when Livios lost a bet and had to ride to a nearby brook for water, there was nothing to prevent him from taking a dip before napping in the sun. When he returned to camp hours later no explanation was required, though the absence had given Felix time to fill his bed with snakes. Livios soon retaliated and sabotaged Felix's boots with secretions from a female *cheruba's* scent gland. Felix never determined why male *cherubae* (dog-sized weasels) stalked him, with the clear intention of mating, until Livios sickened of weasel meat and revealed the secret.

Other tasks were downright exhilarating. God help those in Ios who had ever mistreated the youths. After it became apparent that no one was on their trail, and with an eye toward winter, they began their nocturnal raids and quickly filled a nearby cave with food. They almost got caught stealing some shirts from a clothesline, but Livios was on friendly terms with the guard dogs, which settled down after a few barks. They never rode near the Rapax home, though. The matter went undiscussed, but Felix knew when his friend thought of Daedilos. Livios would fall silent and that faraway, empty gaze would return.

Life was not all good, however. Both of them contracted dysentery near the end of the season and Felix almost died. It was then that Livios repaid him when, despite his own illness, he nursed Felix back to health. Neither realized how sick they had been until they saw vultures circling the camp.

Then there was the time that a bear attacked Felix. He put two arrows into the beast as it lumbered towards him but it had life enough to maul his arm while dislocating his shoulder. He never again shot with his former proficiency.

A fishing trip at the river very nearly ended in disaster. One overcast day, the boys were having such good luck they failed to mark approaching dusk. At last Livios said: "It's getting dark. We'd better get."

Felix looked at the sky. "Naw, we have time."

There was a sudden roar and a giant shark lunged from the water and sank its teeth into Herakles. The shark, easily twenty feet long, had no problem lifting the screaming horse and slapping him into the murky river under a rainbow of blood. A tangled mass of fins cut the surface where Herakles hit.

The companions dropped their poles and bolted. Felix even forgot his own horse, which eventually found his way home. Later, over a quiet dinner, Livios burst into tears. Felix was a little surprised, though he had thought Herakles a fine horse.

"Was thinking about dad," Livios later explained.

A few months passed. The autumn rains had come and the land was dreary and blanketed with mist. The trees surrendered their leaves with the first frost and the days grew short. The boys rarely ventured into the weather and spent long, tedious hours inside the cave. For the first time they spoke of home life and the simple comforts they had taken for granted.

Efforts to procure a new horse proved unsuccessful. Neither of them had any desire to steal such an important item from a farmer, and forays into Ios city had nearly ended in disaster. On one such trip, though, they heard that Achillis had survived his wounds, but had lost a leg. They had also learned that a bounty of one hundred gold pieces lay upon their heads for "attempted murder of a King's man."

"They'll be coming after us in the spring," Livios said one night as he tended the small fire just inside the cave.

"Likely," Felix agreed as he fingered his throat. His tonsils had already swelled and would remain so until spring. He would probably lose his voice before year's end.

They sat in silence. Livios was tired of playing cards and considered going to sleep. Thunder rolled in the distance. "God, I wish it would stop," he sighed at length. The cave, damp under the best of conditions, had grown downright wet with the rains. The walls seeped constantly.

"Yes."

The heavens redoubled their efforts. Torrents spilled onto the plain and angled into the cave. The fire sputtered.

"Kick it out, Livi," Felix muttered. "Let's sleep."

Disgusted, Livios literally kicked the brands from the cave but didn't follow his friend's lead. He shuddered; every night he burned alive in his dreams. It seemed so real he almost smelled the roasting flesh.

"Why, God?" he asked the falling water.

The rain continued.

RECRUIT

The next day brought more rain. The boys, drenched and miserable, huddled far back in the cave. Both had colds. Felix's voice was little more than a whisper. Livios shivered inside his wet cloak.

"Don't think it's let up a bit," he muttered.

Felix nodded.

"Maybe we should build a cabin come spring," Livios suggested.

"Good idea."

Livios rose and sloshed toward the cave mouth. An ugly morning was at hand. He strained to see the distant river. *How I'd like a nice soup. Perhaps one of the chickens should go?* he thought, recalling the first he had butchered.

It had always looked so easy when Daedilos did it; he gave the chickens' heads a quick turn and they simply snapped off. One day Livios decided to surprise him with dinner but the plans went quickly awry. The feisty bird drew blood in a dozen places before Livios secured a hold and, try as he might, he had no luck "snapping" the neck. It was a mess. He finally ended the squawking nightmare with an axe.

Daedilos was initially angry but Livios looked so pitiful, covered with oozing scratches and feathers that he soon forgave him. "Next time don't choose our best egg-layer, son," he advised.

Things were never as easy as he made them look, Livios thought, relishing the memory. *Dad could do anything…*

"Livi?" Felix said.

Livios resented the intrusion. "What?"

"Off one of the birds and I'll make soup."

Livios wakened with a snort and a cough; he was freezing. He sat upright in the dark cave and tried to get his bearings. It took a moment to realize he was sitting in a half foot of water, and it was rising fast.

"Felix!"

"Huh?" Felix replied sluggishly. "The fire's out."

"We're flooding!"

A few seconds passed. "Damn! Let's get out of here!"

They frantically searched the darkness for his boots. The water was already twice as deep as it had been.

"Come on!" Felix called.

Livios grabbed his knife from under the bedroll, tucked it into his belt, and stumbled after his friend. The cave's mouth was a gray semi-circle above swirling black water. Dawn had arrived and it was still raining hard.

"Hope the horse is okay!" Felix shouted.

They were halted in their tracks by a deep, belching roar. It was very close. The water grew even colder around their knees.

"That was a shark," Livios said.

"I know."

The water kept rising. Livios had a terrifying mental picture of one of the larger bulls squirming into the cave, its dead eyes wide above snapping jaws. He envisioned the floodplain. It was a good mile from the cave to the river, but the slope was gradual. There was probably less than a five foot drop altogether. He inched to the mouth and scanned the murky morning. The river obscured everything but the bare branches of trees—and the swirling congress of fins that cut the water where Felix had hitched the horse.

Livios' blood froze.

"Got to move fast!" Felix said.

Not fifty feet away, a massive shark emerged from the water. It slid up the bole of an oak and stood with stumpy forelegs against the trunk, like a dog for a treat.

"Mmmrrraaahhh!" it bellowed, flashing a mouthful of dagger-like teeth.

That put the boys in motion. They waded into the water, away from the sharks, and headed for the natural steps on the cave's hillside. Livios' heart was in his throat as he flapped toward the distant steps. He fully expected to feel very large teeth before reaching the goal.

The shark roared again and others joined in; Livios knew he had been seen. "Hurry, hurry!" he shouted at his friend's back.

Felix redoubled his efforts, splashing Livios' face. Livios stumbled forward, nearly blind. He tripped over an unseen stone and slipped beneath the surface. As water filled his ears he heard the sound of claws scratching rock. He shot from the water in time to see Felix scuttling up the slick shale incline. Felix reached the top and looked down at, then beyond, Livios. His brown eyes grew wide.

"Swim!" he cried above the gale.

Livios was sick with dread. He felt he was wading through syrup. The world slowed and he clearly saw the individual rain drops. The sharks were close enough for him to hear them scrambling through the water. *They're going to rip me to pieces!* he thought.

Somehow he reached and began to crawl up the mudslickened rock. He barely felt the jagged shale chew into his flesh.

Felix peered down from the plateau, looking even more scared than before. "For God's sake, hurry!"

Livios found himself wondering when Felix had regained his voice. Then he felt a slight warmth on his back followed by a loud click. Felix picked up a rock and heaved it, missing Livios' head by an inch; it slapped something meaty and a shark grunted.

Livios cleared the top and sprawled into a puddle. Felix was screaming at him to get up and run. The grassy puddle before Livios looked as though it were boiling under the torrential rain.

The boys were on their feet and running hard. Now the world moved in real time, Livios thought. He followed Felix until the path widened and he could pass. They sprinted to the nearest woods without looking back.

The rain tapered off and stopped before dark. The exhausted boys slept beneath piles of leaves. When they woke next morning, weary and hungry, it took a few moments for the previous day's disaster to fully sink in. Certainly all the food, as well as their horse, had been lost. With winter only weeks away, the realization was as a great weight.

Livios sat dejectedly on his leaves, still warm from his body heat. He tried rubbing the soreness from his neck, but was little helped by the cold breeze. "We'd better go take a look," he suggested.

Felix stirred from his nest; thin steam curled from his hair into the brisk morning. "Damn, Livi," he groaned. "I don't have shoes."

"Me, either. Let's go."

It was a slow walk through mud, but they reached the decline without event. The river had returned to normal. The floodplain looked quite the same as ever, but for long brown divots the shark claws had swathed in its green skin. Livios noted the swath's peculiar pattern, as though the animals had hugged the plain's perimeter.

"Come on," he said wearily and started down the steps.

The caves were a depressing mess. Everything was gone except for a knife, two blankets and one of Felix's boots. Livios wondered if the sharks had eaten his cookware. "How the hell are we going to make it till spring?"

Winter came early and announced itself with a dusting of snow.

Luckily, Livios had contrived some moccasins from a section of blanket but even the modest weather showed how sadly prepared they were for the season. It was not long until they broke their ban on daytime fires, but they burned only seasoned hardwoods to minimize the smoke.

Foraging went on daily in an attempt to replenish stockpiles, but their success was greatly hampered by the lack of a bow. Livios did bring down a small doe with a spear, jumping on the deer from a branch, but he ruined the meat while salting it. Nor could they range far without a horse. When they managed to steal some grain from the closest—but by no means close farm—it took two days to lug the bags to the cave.

Firewood was proving a problem, too. Without axe, hatchet or saw, the outlaws were reduced to gathering sticks and fallen branches. The area was soon picked clean of ideal fuels, and pitch-filled softwoods fed the fire. The black smoke that twisted heavenwards was seen by many.

*   *   *

Boros *Sestar* sat legs crossed in his tent, poring over documents. He shook his dark head in disgust. *Damn,* he thought. *I hope the others did better.* As chief recruiter for the Black Legion's Second *Elhar,* he was expected to deliver at least two hundred bodies to his commander, but pickings had been very slim; he had rounded up only six score that met the size requirements. The trail was at an end and he would soon be crossing Cemetery River into *landesknecta* territory. He could already hear Lasctakos *Cohar* grousing him in his polite yet biting manner; it made his stomach hurt.

And those I have are a sorry looking lot, he admitted silently. *Gonna need a lot of whipping into shape. Most won't survive training, not to mention the branding.*

Legionary Enyo shoved his scarred, bald head into the tent. "Sir, can you take a look at this?" he asked, his deep voice giving away nothing.

Boros turned piglike black eyes on his ugly subordinate. "Hope it's good news," he replied. He grabbed his swordbelt and exited into the blustery evening.

The small camp consisted of four black tents circling the recruits, who huddled together in the windswept grass. Boros cared nothing for their discomfort and wouldn't have provided tents had he the means. If they couldn't take a little cold they would never make legionaries, anyway. Had he taken time to view the lot, he would have seen a collection of huge young men in paupers' clothing, each wearing expressions of mingled fear and defiance. It had been the same in his day, though training had quickly pruned the defiance.

29

The recruits marked Boros *Sestar*, though. They saw a towering figure in plain but expensive black armor. A rugged, square-jawed man who wore arrogance with his kit, who, even when he looked at them, didn't see them; they might as well have been rocks.

Enyo joined his mates, Laertos and Argos, as they gazed south. Boros stopped beside his men, giants armed just like him.

"What am I looking for?" he asked, squinting.

"See the smoke, *Sestar*?" Laertos asked.

"Hmm. Can't be any of the other arms," he thought aloud. "We're the only ones still north of the river."

"King's soldiers, sir?" Enyo suggested without fear. Any *landesknecta* would fight an entire army, if ordered—an attitude not lost on the recruits.

Boros shook his head. "Not likely. We'll investigate before hitting the bridge."

*   *   *

Felix wakened Livios with a shove.

"Wuh?" Livios said.

"I was getting wood and saw some horsemen on the high plain. Three of them."

Livios shook off the remnants of his nightmare. "King's men?"

Felix kicked out the fire. He shook his head. "Don't know. They were looking at our tracks, though. And one of them sure seemed shy a leg."

Livios was suddenly very much awake. "Achillis?"

"It's snowing again. Let's lie low and let it cover us."

They followed Felix's plan for three days and only left the cave to relieve themselves. The days were long, cold and boring. Their diet consisted of water and dry grain. At night they maintained a fire, which became the centerpiece of their meager existence.

Felix looked at his friend's troubled face and broke a long silence. "God, Livi, something has to give."

Later that night, something did.

Livios sat upright on his bedroll. Someone had kicked his foot.

Two very large armored men stood above him; one held a torch. Felix, looking scared and rather small, was already captive between them.

"On your feet, boy," an ugly man with a hideously scarred face growled. "Hurry!"

Livios scrambled to his feet. Scarface bound his wrists with coarse rope and pulled the bonds very tight. "You talk, or try to get out of that,

30

and I'll cut off your stones," the man said. "Out of the cave!"

Livios was scared. Their bulk, bearing and arms identified these men as *landesknectos*. Both were roughly his size but exuded an air of lethality that cowed thoughts of resistance. The legionaries moved so lightly, despite their armor and greatshields, he had to jog to keep pace. It was still dark as the boys were herded onto the snowy floodplain. A shark belched in the distance but the warriors showed no concern.

"Hurry," Scarface repeated.

They made a brisk pace for a while, the water growing ever closer. Livios saw large shapes hulking about in the distance. He thought: *Are we just going to march down their gullets?*

Scarface stopped suddenly, bent and grabbed a short rope and peeled the plain's white carpet peeled back, exposing a trapdoor. "Swing it open," he commanded Livios. The small door opened upward, revealing a chamber of utter blackness. A sour smell wafted into the night. "In you go!" Scarface snarled and kicked the captive into the hole.

Livios landed hard in shallow, frigid water. He saw nothing, but heard his own rapid breaths against nearby walls. The crawlspace wasn't much larger than six feet square.

"Ahh!" Felix shouted before crashing onto his friend.

"Move out of the way, idiots!" a legionary berated them.

The boys huddled against a wall and the *landesknectos* dropped into the cell with a splash; the door slammed shut. Complete darkness. Something wriggled from beneath Livios.

Scarface's deep voice boomed: "Sit next to each other for heat. Sleep."

"No talking," the other man said.

Just then they heard scratching overhead. "Shark," Scarface told his comrade. "That was quick."

"Good thing Lasctakos armored this box."

More claws tore the earth, followed by the screech of talon on metal. The water suddenly grew warmer around Livios. *Felix wet himself*, he thought. *Feel like doing it, too.*

The predators roundly assaulted the cell before giving up. When the pawing stopped, Livios heard Scarface's snores. *Ice in his veins*, he thought. The idea of attacking the sleeping man popped into his mind, but was immediately discarded.

The boys shivered in the pool for a long time and tried to cope with the situation. In the unlikely event that someone had an interest in rescuing them, it was probably not possible. Even the *Chaconni* kings avoided the Legion, and with reason. The last time Korenthis had challenged the *ikar*, the *landesknectos* had destroyed two divisions and depopulated most of Ios. *What do they want with us*, Livios wondered?

31

The trapdoor opened with a creak and sunlight blinded them. An upside-down helmet poked into view.

"Comfy, Enyo?" the head asked Scarface.

"Shut up. Find any more?"

"No." The head turned toward the prisoners, shook a few times, then withdrew. Blue sky filled the door.

"Out!" Enyo boomed.

Livios stood, hit his head on a beam, then sloshed to the trapdoor. It took a few jumps to free his cramped feet from the mud. He got a grip on the doorjamb and pulled himself upward. Squinting, he emerged into the bright morning and sprawled onto the slushy grass; the snow had begun to melt. Five legionaries surrounded him. Dozens of recruits sat nearby. A bedraggled Felix scratched out next, followed by Enyo and the other legionary.

"Morning, sir," Enyo greeted the *sestar*.

"Morning," Boros replied and drew a small leather pouch from his cloak. "Chew some *kraal*."

Enyo dumped two small leaves into his palm, offered one to his comrade, and then stuck the leaf into his mouth. He drew the pouch string and returned the drugs. "Thanks."

"Go clean up," Boros ordered. He turned to Livios. "What were you doing in our caves?"

Livios looked into the *sestar's* dark, lifeless eyes, then at the recruits. He thought fast. "We want to join, my lord," he replied, then sneezed.

"Stand."

Livios rose; he was slightly taller than the *sestar* and broader. Boros squeezed the farm boy's shoulder and grunted. He gave a quick, shrill whistle and someone threw something at Livios' head. Livios plucked the stone from the air without thinking.

Boros' brows went up a quarter inch. He nodded at Felix: "Up, fat boy."

"Sir, riders approaching!" a *landesknecta* said in disbelief.

All gazed northward. Three horsemen were crossing the soggy plain.

"Enyo," Boros said calmly.

The warrior looked up from a wash pan. "Sir?"

"You and Halesas secure the new meat. Put these two with them."

"Sir!"

Enyo and Halesas, an older man who was Livios' other captor, sprang into action. They barked orders and the recruits were soon kneeling, legs crossed behind them, hands on heads.

"If any of you move, I'll kill you all!" Enyo thundered.

"*Sestar* into a tortoise!" Boros ordered.

Enyo, Halesas and another man grouped together in a tight triangular formation, their shields overlapping. They pulled short throwing pila from sheaths on their backs and lifted them overhead. The other three legionaries did likewise, forming two paces to the left. Boros drew his sword and waited between the triangles.

The riders stopped just beyond pilum range. Two bore crossbows.

Livios swallowed on his raw throat and looked at Felix. Achillis was one of the horsemen; his left leg was gone above the knee; the stirrup had been modified. He glared at the boys then hailed the *sestar*.

"Greetings, legionary," he said without enthusiasm. "I am the governor's constable. May I approach."

"Why are you on our land?" Boros demanded.

"We're north of the river."

Boros stewed a moment. "Unbolt those crossbows," he demanded.

Achillis said something to his companions, men in Praxis' livery, and the crossbows were cleared. Achillis rode to within a dozen paces.

"What do you want?" the *sestar* asked.

Achillis pointed at Felix. "Them," he said through clenched teeth.

Boros looked bewildered. "So? They're mine now."

Achillis shook his head. "The big one killed his own father, and the other shot me."

"Good."

Achillis shifted in his saddle. "They have to hang, *sestar*. Give them to me."

Boros looked even more surprised. "What? **What?** Are you insane? Get out of our lands!"

Achillis raised his hand and his companions reloaded. "I'll kill you all and still get them. This is your last chance."

Boros snorted. "No, little man. You'll get the bolts off, but won't pierce our armor. When your missiles are exhausted, you'll ride off like cowards. By midday I'll report your stupidity to my superiors and by tomorrow we will have razed Ios to the ground. All because of you."

Achillis grimaced at the irony.

Boros continued matter-of-factly: "After my men have ravished your family, we'll kick open the children's' heads and eat their brains. If you're still alive, I'll feed some to you."

Livios couldn't believe his ears and glanced at the other recruits. Some were obviously disturbed. Felix was bug-eyed, his chunky face pale.

Achillis started to speak, but stopped.

"Enyo!" Boros cried.

A pilum soared through the air and struck the horse. Achillis' crossbowmen fired but the bolts stuck in the legionaries' greatshields. They reloaded and fired again. Achillis, a poor rider even before losing his leg, could not control his mount. The horse snorted and bucked until it had thrown him, then tore across the plain.

"Forward!" Boros howled. The *landesknectos* immediately repositioned themselves between Achillis and Praxis' men. The crossbowmen shot again. At the recruits. A bolt slammed into the head of the man before Livios. The recruit toppled backward and lay convulsing across Livios' knees.

Boros placed his sword to Achillis' throat. "Lose the bows."

"They'll shoot you," Achillis choked.

Boros pricked the constable's Adam's apple. "The bows!"

"Drop your weapons!"

Livios couldn't see Achillis' face, but the terror in his voice was evident. He almost felt sorry for him.

Boros tapped Achillis' stump with his blade. "Did the boy do this? That why he has to die?"

Achillis nodded wildly.

Boros laughed. "Enyo, Hals, step on his elbows. Laertos, the foot."

The legionaries jumped to comply. Achillis groaned beneath their weight. Boros sauntered around the scene, then exploded into action. Moving faster than sight, he chopped Achillis' leg just above the knee. The blade slurped into wet earth. Achillis gave a chilling shriek, which rang over the field. He lay moaning in a growing red puddle. Boros grabbed the leg by the ankle and swung it over his shoulder; blood dripped down his back. He grinned at Achillis, saying, "Guess I have to die now, too."

Achillis sobbed.

"Quiet!" Boros snapped and began beating the constable with his own leg. Blood splattered with every blow until Achillis lay still.

Boros stood panting over his victim, his face dripping. Even at a distance, Livios saw the change that had overcome the *sestar*, whose listless expression had been replaced by one of intense glee. His eyes shone with a savagery that was painful to behold.

Livios sank onto his hams. *What have I gotten myself into?* he wondered.

Boros had them soon underway and made a pace that left the recruits reeling. The sun was unseasonably warm and the snow continued melting, which made for tough slogging. Livios grit his teeth and kept in step, but not all were so lucky. One man swooned and fell and, without a word, Boros ran him through.

The detachment shadowed the broad river for some miles; a black wall rose slowly from the plain. Livios couldn't take his eyes from the wall. He guessed it thrice the size of the governor's in Ios. He had heard that the parapet extended as far under ground as above. Armies had broken themselves against the "black rock".

They reached a low wooden bridge, which had a thick vertical pole on either end.

"Halt," Boros said and approached the nearest, which boasted many hundreds of black nails in its wood. Boros drew similar nails from his purse and tacked them in with his dagger pommel, one for each recruit.

The *sestar* turned and proclaimed, "Most of you will never again cross this river. When you die, you'll be fed to the sharks. Those of you who survive will be men." He nodded toward the other side. "Proceed."

The walkway was wide enough for six but had no railings. Livios wondered how many had accidentally stumbled into the water over the years and, weighed by armor, sank to the muddy floor. He imagined sharks lurking beneath the gently swirling current and shuddered.

The plain on the other side was flat as a table with many claw marks in its green scalp. The grass was very short, suggesting there were livestock about. *Must move them down in the morning and back at dusk,* he surmised. Something bumped his elbow; Livios turned toward Felix, who looked horrified.

They walked another mile before coming to a cavernous dry moat. The ditch was thirty feet across and at least as deep. Livios later learned it encircled the fort and had six retractable bridges, one for each side. Each black wall boasted a crenellated tower half again taller than the forty-foot curtain. Helmeted warriors peered from between the crenels. A number of huge tents were grouped at regular intervals around the walls. Many recruits were milling about.

"Hullo, Boros!" a sentry called from a tower. "Only you and Cilix are still out." Boros gave a halfhearted wave.

The recruits were ordered across the bridge and herded to some tents. Boros was approached by a Negro *sestar*, and they clasped hands. Livios stared; he had never seen a black man.

"Kill any of 'em yet?" the black asked and offered a water skin.

"Thanks, Melas. One. Couldn't keep up."

Melas chuckled. "You sound disappointed. Lasctakos wants you so you'd better get inside.

Boros nodded. "I'll be back."

"Sit!" Melas bawled at the recruits. "No talking, no walking, no thinking!"

Livios parked himself in the wet grass. It seemed ages since he had been warm and dry. He thought of the happy days back on the farm. He looked at Felix, who managed an uncomfortable smile.

Boros approached the main portcullis as twelve legionaries exited. These newcomers caught Livios' eye. He was astonished that *any* men could appear nastier than the *landesknectos* he had met, but this group looked absolutely demonic; their eyes bore a terrifying malignancy. They fanned out around the wall, two to each recruit camp.

Boros soon returned. He placed himself before the seated recruits, hands on hips.

"I am Boros, Second *Sestar* of Lasctakos *Cohar*," he said loudly. "I am your master, and you will call me 'master' until you are dead, or graduate. You have come here of your own free will, but shall not leave of it. None of you are permitted to speak unless so ordered by a Brother," here he waved at the six men who Livios knew from the day's march. "None of you are permitted to eat, sleep, stand, sit, walk, or scratch unless ordered. You are not permitted possessions or opinions. Any infraction of any of our rules is immediately punishable by death. Is that understood?"

"Yes, master!" they cried.

Boros pulled his sword, stepped forward, and clove a man's head to the throat. He ripped free his blade with a splash of blood.

"Not loud enough! Do you understand?"

"YES, MASTER!!!" they screamed.

"You and you," he pointed out two recruits. "Drag this crap over the moat."

"Yes, master!" The men jumped into action, colliding with the effort.

Livios saw Enyo laughing. The legionary whispered something to Boros, who shook his head, saying: "Nah. More will be joining him before long. Recruits, on your feet!"

Livios was up before he knew it. Boros ran to a man and sheared his head clean off his shoulders; the body stood at attention for a moment before crumbling. "Don't be last, either," he counseled.

Livios risked a glance at Felix, who looked faint.

The men on corpse detail returned. "Take this one, too." Boros ordered.

"Master!"

The legionaries arranged the recruits into rows of three and four. Boros pulled a recruit out from the others; the man stood trembling. "Be still," Boros said. He lifted a charcoal pencil into the air. "I will assign you each a number. It will be written on your forehead so I can see it. Learn it." He reached out and scrawled "2111" across the recruit's damp brow.

"The Legion's tactical order of command runs: *Ikar, elhar, cohar, sestar*, legionary, you. This turd is now '2111,'" he said. "That is his name until he dies or is awarded a *chiampuglia*. 2111 means Second *Elhar*, First *Cohar*, First *Sestar*, recruit 1. Get back in line."

"Yes, master!"

They were numbered without event until Felix. Boros studied him with a hard eye. "How tall are you?"

"Six feet, three inches, master!"

Boros drew his dagger and slammed it into Felix's stomach so hard black steel sprang from his back. Felix coughed and fell onto the *sestar*, then to the ground. He lay twitching.

"Too short," Boros said. "Any others under six-four?"

One man broke rank and jumped into the moat. Ugly Enyo leaped forth and ran to the ditch. He yanked a knife from his belt and threw in a smooth motion. The man screamed. Enyo walked back through the recruits and slapped one's head, saying, "Fetch my sticker."

Livios stood in silent shock. Tears spilled down his face and his legs threatened to buckle. He turned toward Boros with murder in his eyes, thinking, *I'll kill him when he approaches!* Still, he barely kept from charging the *sestar*.

"Boros, Lasctakos wants you!" a sentry called from the wall.

"Enyo, take over," the *sestar* said and sheathed his dagger.

TRAINING

uckily for Livios, the next segment consisted of Enyo rattling off a list of rules. He didn't even try to listen, but stood at attention while his heart slowly chilled to stone. He thought of Felix and their lifelong friendship, which dredged up painful memories of Daedilos. Images of lost loved ones flashed through his mind, but none brought warmth. He felt stranded and alone, unable to recall any good in his life; he found it easy to blame himself for Daedilos' and Felix's deaths. Self-loathing choked him like a strangling snake. Breathing grew difficult.

I should've hung, he concluded.

Enyo droned on.

Boros returned with two of the legionaries Livios had noted previously. "Have 'em sit!" the *sestar* said.

"On your asses!" Enyo shouted.

Boros muttered something to Enyo, who looked disgusted, then turned to the recruits. "About now some of you are feeling you've made a mistake joining up," he began. "Perhaps you have. Nothing you can do about it, though. All things must run their course." He waved the two legionaries forth. "These are the *elhar's* Judges. You try to escape, and they'll judge you. If you assault one of your masters, they'll judge. Let me demonstrate." He turned to Enyo. "Anyone try to rabbit?"

"No, sir."

"Very well." Boros stepped forward and grabbed a blond recruit by the throat. He shoved the rawboned teenager at the Judges, who stood with vacant stares. "Here's a volunteer. Begin!"

The Judges moved with stunning speed. They grabbed the "volunteer", stripped his meager clothes and slammed him to the ground so hard wind whistled between his teeth. The recruit started screaming as he was bound with leather strips. One Judge plopped onto the recruit's chest, the other across his knees. The Judges stared at each other, evil sparks in their eyes.

38

Livios couldn't help but watch, having even forgotten Felix.

"Get to it, boys!" Boros ordered.

Out came the knives. The Judges passed sentence in Ancient *Chaconni*, then began to cut flesh from the recruit as he bucked and shrieked. The screams were unlike any Livios had ever heard and he would long remember them.

"For God's sake!" someone cried.

Boros took no notice.

The Judges ate at a deliberate pace, oblivious to the thrashing "volunteer." It went on far longer than Livios thought it could. Somehow the Judges avoided killing the victim until his chest, stomach and thighs were virtually denuded. Only when they started on his organs did the recruit cease struggling.

Blood was everywhere. The Judges were painted entirely red. The grass was black and slick. Boros gazed proudly over the proceedings. "That'll be all, I think," he said.

A Judge looked up; his white smile contrasted vividly with his bloodsmeared face. "I need a drink, sir," he said in a hollow tone.

"Both of you get one. Go clean up."

The Judges staggered off like drunks, leaving behind a corpse gleaned even cleaner than Livios had suspected. Numerous bones were visible. As Livios came to himself he saw, and smelled, that nearly every recruit had vomited. Rivers of viscous liquid glistened in the winter sun.

A group of dispirited slaves emerged from the gates. Every race of Pangaea was represented, though all wore dun breeches and shirts. Each man bore cavernous baskets of bread. A last slave waddled from the fort beneath a mound of water skins.

Boros made the recruits sit in their own vomit. "Lunch time," he said.

The next few days were brutal. The recruits got less than two hours of sleep a night. They huddled into a massive, communal tent but were given neither blankets nor bedrolls. The ground was cold and hard but so overcrowded (at first) they managed not to freeze. Nevertheless, there was not a dry nose in the camp by week's end.

The recruits logged endless laps around the fort. Boros spurred them on by killing the slowest man at the end of each marathon. Livios always finished near the front. They did push-ups beyond the pain, and then sandbags were laid across their shoulders before doing more. At the end of a particularly grueling session, the recruits were led onto the open plain and made to lie in a gigantic circle, head to heel. There were less than one hundred of them at this point.

Enyo started clapping slowly. The sound snapped in the crisp air.

"More push-ups, you scabs!" Boros shouted. "Keep pace with Enyo!"

At first Livios could barely start. It felt his pectoral tendons had torn. *Have to move!* he thought. *If you don't, he'll kill you and you'll never get him!*

Boros stomped around the circle, hands on hips. "By the *ikar*, the first man who stops gets slit from nut to neck!" A little later he kept the promise.

The recruits were given a short rest after that one. Livios crashed onto his chest with a groan, his arms quivering. He was asleep within moments. A light snow started.

"On your feet!" Boros screamed. "Wake up and on your feet!"

A recruit kicked Livios, who rose slowly. The recruits stood at attention.

"We have a special visitor," Boros said, then wheeled toward the nearest bridge, which two armored men had crossed. Boros and his squad saluted, fist over heart.

"Lasctakos *Cohar!*" they cried enthusiastically.

Livios was close enough to get a good look at the visitors. Neither wore helmets, both had dark, cropped hair. The taller man was strikingly handsome, very lean and walked with smooth grace. His amber eyes regarded them benignly. Livios instantly sensed that someone important had arrived. The man possessed a gravitas even weightier than Boros' terror. He looked familiar, Livios thought.

"Is all well, *sestar?*" Lasctakos asked. His polished voice was resonant and unmistakably stamped with the accent of Korenthis, the *Chaconni* capitol.

Money, Livios thought, tensing. *Definitely a noble. How'd he wind up here?*

"Yes, sir!" Boros replied, still at attention.

"At ease, gentlemen." To Boros: "Walk with me."

The three officers marched around the ring, stopping near Livios.

"Twenty-one dead in two days?" Lasctakos asked Boros.

Boros counted on his fingers. "Right. Sorry, sir. A damn poor crop. Not done yet, either."

Lasctakos shook his head. "Have many succumbed to the weather?"

"Six, *cohar*."

Lasctakos approached the nearest recruit, a *Boru* bruiser with tattoos down both arms. Lasctakos said something in the guttural *Boru* tongue and the recruit responded. The *cohar* changed languages.

"Yes, Master!" the recruit replied.

"Very well," Lasctakos said quietly, then moved on. He turned to his companion, who was staring at Livios. "Vexaras?"

"Yes, sir?" the First *Sestar* replied.

"These men are in rags. Provide them clothing."

Livios almost thanked Lasctakos; rarely had he felt so grateful. *How do I know him?* he wondered.

The officers continued around the ring. Lasctakos shared a brief laugh with Enyo and the others before heading for the bridge. Livios admired the way the *cohar* glided over the grass.

Boros looked thoughtful. "Well, some of you will die warmer. The *cohar* has seen fit to clothe you. Be *very* grateful. As you aren't Brothers, he's paying out of his own pocket." He gazed after Lasctakos with undisguised awe. "He'll be *ikar* one day. Deadliest blade in the legion."

It suddenly dawned on Livios why Lasctakos seemed familiar—he looked remarkably like a young Daedilos!

"Back on your faces!" Boros snarled. "Let's try them with one hand."

The recruits slept very well that night. For about an hour. Boros' squad roused and chased them from the tent into the torch-lit yard, where two large squares had been cordoned off in the grass. Shovels lay all around. Enyo broke the shivering recruits into two teams. Legionaries laughed from the castle wall.

Boros walked purposefully around the squares. The torchlight made his visage more sinister than usual. "These boxes must be emptied to a depth of ten feet," he told them. "This one for team A, the other for B. Don't be on the losing team."

The recruits were still blinking at each other when Enyo cried, "What are you idiots waiting for?"

The exhausted, arm-sore youths blundered forward like old cripples. Many toppled and had trouble regaining their feet. Others were so sore they had to crawl.

"Hurry!" Boros yelled.

Livios was on Team A and a glance suggested that was the wrong one to be on. Many of those he had been lumped with bore gruesome injuries and some had that empty, faraway stare so common among the failures Boros had found worthy of dispatching.

"By the *ikar*, don't you want to live?" Enyo scolded.

Livios grabbed a shovel and stumbled to the proper square. He and some others commenced digging but the ground was very hard. The going was extremely slow, further hampered by the fact that they were not allowed to talk. Despite the cold, they were soon sweating.

The recruits dug throughout the night. Neither team achieved the required depth by daybreak, so both were punished. Boros picked the sickest looking fellow from each team, threw him into the hole, and had his comrades bury him alive. The condemned were too exhausted to scream.

Slaves brought breakfast, which the recruits ate standing, then Boros directed them onto the open plain. The sharks had only recently departed; Livios saw large depressions in the grass where they had lain.

"Let's start with push-ups!" Boros said as the sun peeked over the horizon.

Livios was so woozy he didn't realize he had already begun the exercises. He no longer felt the pain in his chest or his bleeding hands. *No way I'll make it through the day*, he thought groggily.

Enyo started clapping the cadence.

Second *Elhar*'s recruit class was down to eighty by the end of the week; most of the casualties were from exhaustion. The communal tent was getting roomy, and colder, but Lasctakos' clothes kept them warm enough. By the end of the third week the class had been pruned to seventy two. Most of the recently killed had fallen to their deaths during "string drills." String drills consisted of knotting ropes to the wall towers and having the recruits climb to the top—after the knots had been set on fire. Luckily for Livios he had lost weight or he never would have managed it; he barely reached the tower before the rope burnt through.

Six other men were not so lucky. Each hit earth with a sickening crunch. Two others were even less fortunate; they were fed to the Judges after a failed escape attempt. Livios was forced to watch the execution, but it made little impression. He had grown used to ugly sights.

But I'm still going to get you, Boros, he thought, staring at the *sestar* as he lorded over the execution. The pain over Felix had dimmed. The edge was gone, salved by torture and deprivation. Livios had to prod the anger to the fore. *How had that happened?* he wondered. Wasn't Felix his best friend? When did it come to pass that he had to stoke the embers of vengeance?

That he had changed so much hurt worst of all.

On day sixty the recruits were called onto the plain and ordered to sit in the snow. The cold didn't matter at this point. The fifty-three survivors were inured to pain and weather; their muscles had hardened along with their wills and hearts.

Boros stood before them. "I see promise," he said flatly. "Some of you will make *landesknectos*, that is to say, men. You've passed your first hurdle and have crossed into a broader world, a world of discipline and weapons." He pulled his bastard sword and held it aloft in the watery sun, staring lovingly at the black blade. "Nine years I've known this cold bride. Without her I'm naked, and naked with her, I'm clothed. It'll be the same with some of you." He sheathed the sword with a hiss and a ping. "But not yet."

Livios hated Boros as much as ever, but couldn't help but feel proud that he had survived this far. Indeed, he had thrived. His thews had stopped shrinking and, fueled by massive meals of bread and beef, had bloomed to sizes he had never dreamed. He could do push-ups for hours and run from dusk till dawn. Clambering up the rope was no longer difficult, he could even do it with someone on his back, and sleeping in snow caused only the slightest discomfort. True, he could not see the pits beneath his eyes, or the ugly light that burned inside them, but he wouldn't have cared.

Boros had them pair off and Enyo supplied wooden swords.

"You'll learn these first," Boros said. "But will eventually know all blades. Stabbing, slicing, chopping—makes no difference. They're all the same after the metal becomes part of you. Watch Enyo, now."

Enyo demonstrated the proper method of drawing and presenting a sword. They practiced this simple maneuver for hours, and though he frequently beat them for their mistakes, he seemed sincerely pleased when they got it right.

Boros walked between the rows of recruits, hands on hips. "Learning the sword is like learning to walk," he told them. "It takes a lot of practice. From this day you may now ask questions without being ordered, as long as you "master" your trainers. Is that understood?"

"Yes, master!" they screamed.

"Enyo, balance drills," Boros said.

"Yes, sir! You boys get in single file! Move it!"

The following days were a revelation to Livios. The wooden sword was like an extension of his arm and he had little trouble disarming most recruits.

Enyo told Boros: "By the *ikar* that lad's fast. He hit four stones I pitched into the air. Balanced, too. *Very* strong. Got it all."

"Who? 2122?"

"Yes, sir."

Boros grunted. "Yeah? How about that *Boru* with the tattoos?"

"Real solid. Not as good as the boy, though. That redhead and the assassin have something, also."

"Guess this lot wasn't a total waste. We'll see how they react to blood."

"Yes, *sestar*. How are the other *elhari?*"

"We've lost the most recruits."

43

Enyo nodded. "We usually do."

Boros scowled. "Let's make sure we don't take casualties against First *Elhar* next week. And pencil their numbers again. Lasctakos might come out today.

"Understood, sir."

*   *   *

"Balance drills" scared Livios half to death. They scared most of the recruits. As soon as they saw the thin tree stretching across the dry moat, the legionaries-in-training knew they would have to walk it. The first few times across were bad enough. The bark was slick with frost and the thirty-foot drop killed two men. This incensed Boros, who berated the entire class, then ran across the span. And *backwards*.

"I guess you sons of bitches need an incentive to stay balanced," he muttered then stomped off to the castle. He returned within moments, which suggested he had planned the "incentive" all along. He led a throng of slaves, who pulled a mammoth, wheeled pen, its contents obscured by leather flaps. "Faster!" he barked, though the men's faces twisted with effort. The cage slowed as it eased off the path into deeper snow.

Livios stood at attention as the slaves passed. The big coop smelled like rotten fish. Enyo lurked nearby, an insidious grin on his ruined face.

"Master, what reeks?" a recruit asked.

"You'll find out, boy," Enyo answered.

The cage was muscled to the moat. Boros glanced into the ravine then turned to the slaves. "Remove the cover."

The leather went and a medium-sized shark was revealed. The orange and purple creature lay despondently against the bars, its stubby feet in the air. Livios' heart sank.

Boros chuckled softly. "Don't worry, he'll wake." To the slaves: "Dump him in!"

Two thralls worked a winch and the cage started to tilt. The shark pepped up and rolled onto his bulging stomach. A slave grasped the lock dowels and looked at Boros, who said, "Spill him." The dowels were pulled and the gate fell away. The shark roared as it tumbled into the moat. It thrashed a few times then waited beneath the tree like an expectant dog.

He knows what's going to happen, Livios thought. He looked over at #2112, a narrow-eyed *Hsia*, who cursed in disbelief.

"That's right," Boros called out. "Line up. Single file. Any of you don't want to go, tell it to the Judges."

They lined up by number, which put Livios near the front. His heart pounded. *Same as last time,* he told himself. *Don't look down.*

"Stand at attention!" Boros cried.

"At ease," Lasctakos said as he arrived.

Livios thought of his father and felt a sharp pang. He wished for the thousandth time that Daedilos was alive and they were together back home. *Wonder if anyone's living there now,* he mulled.

"A word with you, *sestar*," Lasctakos said; his even tone somehow indicated annoyance.

"Yes, sir!"

The two officers walked out of earshot.

"A little soon for the shark, no?" Lasctakos asked.

"Sir?"

"Every year you bring him out earlier. Why teach these lads to run before they can walk? We are already burning through them at a stiff clip."

Boros looked rebuked and a little afraid. "My apologies, *cohar*. I won't do it again."

Lasctakos smiled. "I know you won't. Remember what I've told you and the others—'tough' and 'sadistic' aren't the same thing. Be tough."

"Yes, *cohar*. Should I scratch the drill?"

Lasctakos shook his head. "Too late for that. We can't have you appearing soft. Go through with it, but don't lose too many. Clear?"

"Absolutely, sir."

"Go to work."

"Yes, *cohar*!"

Boros turned on his heel.

"And *sestar*?" Lasctakos called loud enough for all to hear.

"Sir?"

Lasctakos smiled again. "Congratulations on tying the *ikar*'s record for training classes. Drop by my quarters tonight for a bottle. That's not an order, but an invitation."

Boros beamed. "Thank you, sir!" He marched back to the others with renewed purpose. "Let's get on with it!"

The recruits gasped suddenly. Lasctakos had marched onto the tree and on his way back they could see that his eyes were closed! He stopped directly over the shark, opened his eyes, drew two knives and juggled them with one hand. He strolled back to the group and sheathed the weapons.

"Balance is here, gentlemen," he said, tapping his brow. "Along with everything else of importance. Show me a poor soldier and I'll show you a stupid man. See you after mess, Boros."

"Yes, *cohar*."

The recruits were now anxious to try the tree, and said as much. They didn't lose another man that day.

BLOODED

The weeks passed and the class dwindled, but now when a man was grievously hurt he was sent to the hospital instead of being run to death or buried alive. It had been some time since Boros had killed a recruit. Indeed, he and his minions spent long hours on personalized instruction and even doled out occasional praise.

One day Enyo matched Livios against two recruits and when Livios "killed" both opponents with his wooden sword Enyo grunted, "That's the way, boy. We'll make a swordsman of you yet." Livios didn't like Enyo, but it struck a chord that the legionary appreciated his skills—some of them, anyway.

"When do we move on to the bow, Master?" Livios asked.

Enyo's eyes bulged. "*What!* We don't learn the goddamn bow! That's a coward's weapon! Didn't you learn anything about us while shagging sheep on your farm?"

"Not much, master."

Enyo rubbed his blonde stubble. "Any woman can draw a string, boy," he said at length. "There's no honor in killing a man like that. You can't see his eyes."

"Yes, master."

In time Boros' recruits were stacked against those from other *elhari*. Boros took these tests *very* seriously. After losing a marathon relay to Sixth *Elhar*—Livios had the distinct impression that Boros disliked his counterpart in the Sixth, a disfigured fellow named Daphonos—the *sestar* killed his two slowest men, beating them to death with his dagger. Boros' recruits usually won, however; they were better conditioned.

Usually, but not always. Once Livios and his comrades were unable to maintain a shield wall against an overwhelming force of pikemen. It was the first time that they had handled the tall, hourglass-shaped shields, but that didn't matter to Boros, who cut the drill and marched

47

them onto the snowy plain. They were lined in single file before the fuming *sestar*, who bent a wooden sword in his hairy hands.

"You bastards won't fight, then you'll get a beating," he said. They were then made to attack him one at a time and he left them all bruised, bloody and/or unconscious. He broke the sword over the last man's head and stalked through his victims on the way back to the bridge. "You fight like a bunch of women!" he declared. "You lads better get hard or I'm going to kill every last one of you!"

Livios sat in the snow, massaging a bruised jaw. He had attacked Boros with murderous intent, but had been quickly leveled. He couldn't even recall what had happened. Thoughts of vengeance, which had grown along with his confidence, flickered and almost died. *I'm a long way from being able to handle him,* he thought glumly.

Enyo laughed at the forty-six recruits sprawled about the bloody snow. "You idiots. He bet two pouches of *kraal* on you, and you couldn't even hold a simple wall. Maybe you're not strong enough?"

"But we were outmatched three to one, master!" someone complained.

"So? Think you'll get such kindly odds in real combat?"

They did push-ups and leg squats until dark.

Another month trimmed the class to thirty, but thirty even Boros approved of. He reviewed the recruits at attention; all were dressed in brown, black shields before them, wooden swords on their hips. They looked "controlled furious" he thought, just as he liked them. The fat had definitely been trimmed.

Boros called a recruit: "2311, present arms!"

That man did as ordered, and crisply.

Boros swat the sword with his palm. "How many movements in that execution?"

"Four, master!"

"Who's in your trident?"

"2323 and 2316, master!"

"Name the six *elhari*, in order."

"Phaetonis, Endios, Menestheos, Anios, Naiphios and Polyphemos, master!"

"Good. Sheath your wand." Boros continued down the line.

"Not bad, not bad at all," he allowed, though he frowned.

Can't imagine why he looks so glum, Livios thought. *He hasn't lost a bet in weeks.*

Boros stood before a small wagon, hands on hips. "Think of how far you've come since staggering across the river," he said. "You've that far again to yet travel. But that you *have* learned, and faster than the other

48

classes, is what's important. Geraestos *Ikar* is pleased to recognize you for that and is entrusting you with new toys. Enyo, break 'em out."

Enyo pulled a black sword from the wagon. "2111, step forth and surrender your wand."

The recruit fell out and handed over his notched wooden sword.

Enyo hoisted the new weapon. "This blade isn't yours. You can't name or sharpen it, and death will swiftly find you if you use it against another except by command. Do you understand?"

"Yes, master!"

Enyo handed over the weapon, pommel first. "Sheath it and return to ranks. 2122, step forth."

Livios obeyed. Later he would recall little of the brief ceremony except the charge the cold hilt gave his body. He was soon back in ranks and unsure how he felt. Though he hated Boros and the Legion, he was, nevertheless, exquisitely proud of his new "toy". So proud he wished Daedilos could see him, until he remembered why he had joined the *landesknectos* in the first place. His pride swiftly turned to remorse. *I wish that at least Felix had made it this far*, he thought, feeling dismal and alone. But he knew his friend would never have survived to this day.

When Enyo was done, Boros gave a lecture about the proper maintenance of swords, then dismissed them. Suddenly finding themselves with a brief leave, the recruits looked at each other then slowly broke ranks.

Livios wandered down to the river, deep in reflection. He stared at the churning brown water. "I'm sorry, dad," he sighed at last, sounding very much like the boy who had fled Ios. *A lifetime ago*, he pondered. Then he thought of Felix. *Hope you're in heaven, brother—where I'll never be.* It was a short road from there to Boros. *That demon*, he thought coldly, remembering how quickly the *sestar* had defeated him. He shook his head. *Take years to get that good, unless I outthink him.* He ran through some plans in his mind.

Another recruit joined him. "2122," the man greeted. It was the tattooed *Boru* Livios knew only as 2142.

"Hello."

"You're pretty good with a sword."

Not a bad accent for a barbarian, Livios thought. "You, too."

"I'm older than you and have had lots of practice."

The remark put Livios on guard. Was the *Boru* poking fun at him? "How old do you think I am?"

"Don't know. Young." 2142 snickered, but with good humor.

Livios was surprised to find he was amused, too. "I'm Livios," he said and offered his hand.

The *Boru* stared a moment, then shook hands, saying, "Krynn of

Kobald. Not that it matters. They'll change our names before long. Who'd you kill to end up here?"

Livios stiffened. "It was an accident."

Krynn shrugged. "Usually is. I'm a pirate and a thief. Ever heard of me?" he asked hopefully.

"Sorry, no."

"I lifted the governor of Ios' payroll. You sound like you're from there. Never heard of that?"

"No."

"Oh, well," Krynn sighed. "I got caught."

"Tell me."

Krynn embarked on a short but colorful description of his adventures since leaving Kobald, a *Boru* island, some ten years earlier. He ended with the failed payroll heist. "So there I am, half in, half out of that ratty thatched roof screaming 'It wasn't me! It wasn't me!' as coins spilled from my pockets. I had bags over both shoulders, too. Lokks, they were heavy!" He laughed. "The guards didn't believe me."

Livios smiled, which felt strange. It had been so long. "I know that guardhouse. Why didn't they shoot you?"

"They did." Krynn lifted his shirt and displayed two scars. "Anyway, the roof caved in and I fell, crushing one of the governor's painted lads. How he squealed! By the time the guards had broken the door, I was gone."

Livios felt homesick. "What happened to the gold?"

"The bags split when I hit the ground. Ended up with a handful, that's it. Hel's teats!"

"And now you'll be a legionary?"

Krynn yawned. "Why not? I was a soldier before. Wish we could get more sleep. The food's not bad, though."

Livios noticed the sun had nearly set. "We'd better go."

By muddy spring Livios had earned the reputation as a most promising swordsman. Enyo called him a "natural" and proclaimed him "the fastest pup I've seen in years. Dangerous with either hand." He also reminded Livios that there were a few "kinks" to work out of his style.

Livios promised to work harder, but the kinks remained. He wanted them there and visible. More importantly, he wanted Boros to see them.

The *sestar* did. "Watch that backslash, 2122!" he berated Livios. "It's too slow and you always deliver it upstairs! Mix it up or it'll get you killed someday."

"Yes, master!" Livios replied and sped up.

"Not that high, damn it! Footwork's very good, though. The rest of you watch his feet. He's always on balance. Staying level makes him very dangerous."

Livios also excelled in other areas. He was lead prong of his "trident", a three-man shock formation, and displayed a knack for tactics. Sometimes when his team was on the verge of breaking, he simply took over and led them to victory. Boros didn't mind initiative and particularly liked it when Livios' trident broke up the Sixth's shield wall; he rewarded the recruits with *kraal*. Livios disliked the drug, it made him nauseous and irate, but appreciated how it soothed his aching limbs.

Livios proved handy with a pilum, too, throwing the spears with distance and accuracy. He privately attributed the talent to having learned archery but kept the revelation to himself.

Enyo watched with satisfaction as a stream of pila arced over a palisade into straw horses. "Born to kill, lad, born to kill," he raved. "Excellent! Being able to break up cavalry's about the most important thing there is."

"Yes, master!"

"I want you to teach the rest of your trident to throw like that."

"Yes, master!"

Spring was ending when they entered their last week of training. They had lost only one man in the preceding month, and that was to pneumonia.

Boros addressed the twenty-eight recruits. "I thought you were a waste of flesh the first time I clapped eyes on you, but don't feel that way now. Only the branding and naming remains, and then you'll no longer be recruits." He looked unusually pensive. "I'm surprised to say you're one of the best classes I've had. Who would have thought it? Get some sleep because you'll need it."

Enyo screamed, "Fall out!"

Boros looked at Livios. "Come here."

Livios ran over. He hoped hatred wasn't showing in his eyes. "Yes, master?"

Boros chewed his lip before saying, "Come."

Livios was suddenly very worried.

They went through the gates and into the keep. Livios had never been inside and was impressed. The black castle was bigger than he had imagined and cleverly constructed. Six wings spoked from the enormous, hexagonal, main hall. There were hundreds of legionaries milling about the parade ground, laughing, drilling and fencing. There were slaves working, too, most of them female. A white flag hung above each wing; each bore the Legion's clenched, black gauntlet and a number. They entered number two.

The barrack was nearly as austere as the recruit tent. Cots lined the walls, and large, standing crosses lined the cots. Some of the crosses held armor, but most were bare. Livios was led into Boros' small room. The *sestar* lived as simply as his men, though there was a bottle of wine beside his bed and he owned an extra suit of armor.

"Stay here," Boros grunted and rummaged through his footlocker. He found and hefted a sheathed dagger. "Know what this is?"

"No, master."

"I award this sticker to the outstanding recruit from each class. Wear it until you die or are blooded, whichever comes first."

Livios felt taller. "Yes, master!"

Boros clasped the dagger to Livios' belt. The boy was so confused he could only stare ahead.

"I carried that same blade many years ago," Boros said. "So did two *ikari*. Bear it with honor. Dismissed."

Livios snapped his best salute. "Thank you, master!"

He walked back to the recruit tent, though he would later swear his feet never touched the ground.

*   *   *

The recruits were roused at first light and fell into formation. By the sound of it, the other classes were up as well. A pillar of smoke rose from the other side of the fort. Boros looked more anxious than usual. "The screaming is going to start with First *Elhar* but will visit you before long," he said solemnly. "I think I can tell you, in all truth, that you'll soon be in the greatest agony of your lives. If you survive, you'll be legionaries. Undress."

The recruits obeyed after the slightest hesitation and stood naked in the morning sun. The *Boru* shot Livios a quick wink.

Piercing screams shattered the morning from the direction of First *Elhar*. The cries multiplied and intensified. A smell like burning pork filled the air. Livios glanced at Enyo, whose face revealed nothing. Boros licked his lips in pained anticipation. Eventually the screams trailed off.

Livios thought he heard sobs. Sweat dripped down his cheek.

What's going to happen? he wondered frantically. He didn't have to wait long to find out.

A slave-drawn, black wagon squeaked into sight. The wain carried a large cast iron stove that issued a ceaseless breath of gray smoke. A slave fed and stoked the red-hot oven. A train of *landesknectos* marched behind the cart, including Endios *Elhar*.

Livios had only seen Endios once, at a distance, and that quick glance had not prepared him for the man's ugliness. The skinny, bald

52

elhar was preposterously tall with a nose so long and shapeless it wagged like an elephant's trunk. His uneven, discolored teeth were enormous and poked from his mouth like dirty fingers—Livios wondered how he ate—giving an overall appearance that was at once idiotic and frightening. That said, Endios allegedly possessed a fine mind and was the Legion's expert on "Desian Orthodoxy".

Boros saluted.

"Ready?" Endios asked in a high-pitched voice.

"Yes, sir!"

"Begin."

Boros turned to the class. "I'll call you by number. When I do, lay beside the wagon. When I'm done, stagger back to the tent or pass out here, it doesn't really matter. 2121, you're first."

A recruit walked bravely toward Boros, who indicated the ground.

2121 plopped down and legionaries bound him hand and foot, then spiked the bindings into the earth. Enyo reached onto the wagon and pulled a sponge from a bucket and smeared shiny grease onto 2121's chest and stomach.

A slave tonged a large iron rolling pin from the whistling oven and gave it to Endios. The *elhar*, who was wearing special gauntlets, accepted the glowing Brand, which bore many lines script on its gleaming surface. He straddled the frightened recruit, saying, "You've come of your own free will for this." He chanted a few words in Ancient *Chaconni* then lowered the Brand onto 2121's chest.

"AAAAHHHHHH!!!!" the recruit screamed, thrashing.

Endios slowly rolled the Brand from collarbone to pelvis, searing the Legion's laws into flesh, which sizzled and spat like bacon. He smiled through the thin smoke as he stepped back; Enyo slopped more grease onto the victim, who had fainted.

Livios almost retched at the sight and smell. *God, I can't take that!* he thought.

Endios scraped toasted flesh from the Scriptus then gave it to the slave, who placed it back into the oven. "Boros, move him."

The *sestar* unbound the unconscious recruit and dragged him a short distance.

Endios grinned, his teeth sticking out in all directions. "Next."

"2122!" Boros snapped.

Livios felt dizzy. "Here, Master!" he called weakly and lumbered forward. His feet felt heavier than iron.

"Ah, lad!" Boros chuckled. "Let's see if you're worthy of that dagger. You saw the drill."

Livios was in a state of delirium as he lay down and offered Boros the dagger.

"It's yours," the *sestar* said. "Use it. Chew on it."

Livios complied, though it seemed he moved at a fraction his normal speed. He bit down hard on the scabbard.

"It's best to go early," Enyo intimated as he tightened the bonds.

A smiling Endios hovered above as lard was slopped onto Livios. The smoking Brand was pulled and Endios held it aloft.

"You'll like this," he said and lowered the Brand.

Livios had never felt such pain. His mind filled with blinding light and his teeth sank into the metal scabbard as the Brand sputtered down his torso. He heard a tooth crack. Blood filled his mouth, then he knew no more. He was dragged to 2121's side.

"Next," Endios said.

The recruits sprawled throughout the tent in agony. The smell of burnt flesh lingered, mingling with the stench of gangrene. Fortunately for Livios, his burns had bubbled, scabbed and begun to heal. Half of the men hadn't been so lucky. Enyo and other legionaries came through the tent twice a day, looking for dead or dying. Bodies were carried out on a regular basis.

"Master," Livios croaked at Enyo.

"What?"

"Why not take us to the hospital?"

"Have to pull through on your own, boy," Enyo replied. He eyed Livios' pitted, discolored flesh. "You'll make it."

Livios wasn't so sure. The pain made him want to die. "I don't think so," he replied. There was a popping sound and fluids oozed down his stomach.

Enyo looked contemptuous. "Argos," he called a legionary, "come here and unstrap me." Enyo removed his breastplate. He pulled up his shirt and revealed his own Scriptus scars. "Toughen up!"

Livios kept quiet until he finally drifted into a restless doze.

It was two weeks before Livios was up and about, but he was unfit for anything but the lightest duty. Most of his peers suffered even worse. Of the twenty-eight men Endios had branded, fifteen never regained their feet. Most had contracted infection and died quickly, though the strongest lingered until abscesses consumed them. Enyo eventually dispatched a few hard cases who refused to die.

Graduation day finally dawned. The communal tent was struck and the recruits were issued new clothing; each received two simple black tunics, a belt and good leather boots. Livios was allowed to retain his dagger until he was absorbed into a *sestar*.

After breakfast, Boros reviewed them for the last time. He was in full dress and was even wearing a cloak. He looked at the class with a peculiar expression of mixed condescension and pride. "Today is graduation day, men," he said. "I call you men, for that you are. Five months ago I herded one hundred and twenty slaves across the bridge, but you thirteen legionaries have replaced them."

Livios was appalled that Boros' words touched him. *He killed Felix*, he reminded himself.

"Your training was hard," Boros admitted. "It had to be, for what's required of you will be even harder. Be proud, always, of what you've suffered to become *landesknectos*. Wear your scars with conceit. You *must not* confuse yourselves with common men or with what you were before I got my hands on you. You have been distilled into something better. Don't think on those who died in training, either. They were weaklings you would've had to kill someday, anyway."

Livios hated Boros talking that way about Felix but he knew his friend wouldn't have survived to this point.

Boros eyed each man. "When you got here we numbered you. We did that to show that it didn't matter who you were before you crossed Cemetery River. Now I'm going to give you names—names you've earned. Be proud of them as well, for though many thousands have held your numbers over the centuries, your *chiampuglia*, your 'battle name', is yours alone until you die. It also comes a lot closer to describing you than the handle your mother spewed out because she thought it sounded pretty. Enyo, bring me the book."

"Sir." Enyo produced a large, ironbound ledger.

Boros took the tome. "2121, step forth!"

"Yes, master!"

"Don't call me that anymore, any of you. 'Sir' is fine. From this day on you are 'Neleos', which means 'the ruthless' in the ancient tongue. I like the way you trample the slow and ailing," Boros explained. "Single-mindedness is a great gift."

"Thank you, sir!"

Boros penciled something into the ledger. "You would've come to Second *Sestar* but are going to Vexaras' instead since all his recruits died. Get back in formation."

Neleos saluted and stepped back.

"2122, step forth!"

Livios obeyed. "Sir!"

Boros chuckled. "I've given your name a lot of thought. It had to be something special for the 'outstanding recruit'. From this day you're known as 'Patricides', which means 'father killer'. You're coming to my *sestar*, which is good. Get back in line."

Livios felt punched. His eyes watered.

"Get back in formation, Patricides," Boros growled. "You gone deaf?"

So, today's the day I die, Livios thought. The realization calmed him. *God, just let me take him with me.*

Boros glared. "What's wrong with you?"

Livios took a deep breath. "I want another name."

"You what? And put a 'Sir' on that!"

"I don't like that name. Give me another," Livios replied louder.

Boros appeared ready for a fit but suddenly burst into laughter. He tossed the book to Enyo. "Looks like the class is down to twelve. You don't like your name? Too bad! Shouldn't have killed your old man."

Livios half reached for his dagger.

Boros' look of astonishment faded into understanding. He nodded. "A brooder. I had you pegged wrong," he leaned close enough for Livios to smell his breath. "Pull that blade, idiot, and it'll end up like the one I used on your friend."

Livios cursed and shoved Boros hard.

The *sestar* had his sword out before he stopped backpedaling. "Yes, you're a sensitive one. That's a bad trait for a soldier. Don't worry, though, you won't have it long." He nodded at the dagger. "Draw it."

"Knife against sword?" Livios' voice sounded alien in his own ears.

"I didn't tell you to turn traitor, recruit."

Livios shook his head. "Legionary. I've been branded."

"By the *ikar*, you're right! Enyo, give him a sword."

Livios' heart raced. *I'm going to die today!* he thought. A sword dropped onto the grass before him.

"Pick it up," Boros ordered.

Livios tried but couldn't move.

"Pick it up!" Boros screamed. He stepped forward and slapped Livios. "And when you see your father in hell, tell him he raised a coward."

Livios took a half step. Somehow his body wasn't quite working.

"Kill me and pick your own name," Boros prodded.

Livios scooped the blade off the ground. He could hear the crowd for the first time.

"Stand down, fool!" Krynn cried from the end of the line.

Livios steadied himself and moved forward at a crouch.

Boros laughed but kept his thoughts to himself. "Come on, Pa-tri-ci-des," he beckoned. "My sword's itching to taste you." They circled each other at about five paces. "Been killing men for years and years," Boros said. "Killed my first before you were born. Never grow tired of it, though." Livios concentrated on the *sestar's* sword. "That's right," Boros

56

said, "eyes on the blade. My words can't hurt you, only this sword will."
He lunged and Livios stumbled backward.

"It's easy to look sharp in training," Boros laughed. "Combat's another thing, as I'm sure you're realizing. Gets your heart all drumming but your hands go at half speed. The worst is how your fuzzies creep into your throat. Don't worry, Patricides, it'll all be over soon."

Livios leaped forward and took a mighty, hissing swipe at Boros' head. The *sestar* ducked in plenty of time and smiled as he lifted his sword to catch the inevitably high backhand stroke.

But it came low and very fast, catching him in the naked spot just above the boot with a "click". Boros crashed onto his back, too shocked to scream. He stared up in wonder as Livios stepped over the squirting, severed limb and onto his swordarm.

"Hold!" Enyo shouted.

Livios froze. He didn't know what to feel.

"Step away!"

Boros was still shaking his head but his eyes had gone glassy. He gave a rasping laugh. "Fooled me."

Livios moved from the pool of blood and dropped the sword.

He tossed his dagger onto Boros' heaving chest. The *sestar* cursed as his skin went white. After a short while his eyes fluttered and he lay still.

Enyo looked from the dead *sestar* to Livios, eyes wide. "Damn it! Damn it, damn it!" he said. "Laertos, get Vexaras! Damn it!"

Laertos took off at a sprint. Enyo pushed a dagger to Livios' throat. "I never heard of such a thing!" he complained. "Really now! Unblooded boy killing a *sestar*?"

For the first time since enlisting, Livios had no purpose. He had survived training to avenge Felix. Now what? *They're going to kill me*, he thought. *So? You deserve to die*. Tears crawled down his face.

"Why'd you do it?" Enyo demanded.

"I didn't like the name," Livios whispered.

TRIAL

n *elhar*'s barrack was precisely laid out. Each two-story structure stuck like a black spoke from the *ikar*'s castle and came to a peak forty feet above the ground. The "spokes" were two hundred feet long and eighty feet wide, distinguishable only by the unit flags above their iron-plated doors. An inner chamber ran the length of the spoke. Legionary cots, grouped by unit, stood adjacent to *sestari* quarters—nine of the junior officers lined each wall. Three *cohari* were also housed on the left of each floor, and the *elhar*'s spacious quarters were located just inside the entrance. Senior officers had external, as well as internal, access to their rooms.

The mess hall was situated against the castle, on the first floor, with an armorer's den above. A flight of stairs stood at both ends of the spoke and two majestic fireplaces graced each floor. The walls were bare stone, the floor polished wood. All areas were immaculate. A legionary convicted of something as trivial as an "unkempt bed" might find himself incarcerated. Graver violations, such as improperly maintained arms, were punishable by a scourging or even death, though an *elhar* might commute such a sentence.

Each spoke had a jail in the crawlspace beneath the mess hall where conditions were made as uncomfortable as possible. A man unlucky enough to get locked up swiftly decided to not revisit the jail, no matter what. Beatings by the guards, who were borrowed from other *elhari* to curtail soft treatment, were common. Food was limited to water and the vermin a prisoner could catch in his cramped, dripping cell. Starvation took a heavy toll.

Livios found himself in just such a place for two days. After the obligatory roughing up, which seemed mild after his training, he was stripped and shoved into a tiny cell. The ceiling was low and the dirt floor cold. The jail was so dark he could not tell how many inmates it held but heard their coughing and hacking.

And the rats! Livios had never liked rodents, and had killed them whenever possible on the farm, but these were like something from a bad dream. He only actually saw one once, when a guard shoved a torch into the cell, but it looked two feet long; he was often wakened by sharp teeth in his flesh. By the time guards dragged him from the cell he had so many rat and spider bites on his body his fevered skin felt like leather.

Livios was forced up the ladder into the mess hall where Enyo and the obviously insane Argos bound him. Enyo seemed incredulous. "Stupid, stupid, stupid. Survive training so Lasctakos can kill you?"

Livios was marched into the spoke. It must've been nighttime because the house was full. *Landesknectos* were talking, sleeping or gambling; dice seemed popular. Oiled armor hung on crossbars beside beds. Most of the men paid Livios no mind as he passed, though one laughed and another drew a finger across his throat. *Guess the story is out,* he thought. He didn't mind the idea of dying so long as Boros was dead. *Surprised I've lived this long.*

As First *Cohar*, Lasctakos' room was beside the sentry post and directly across from the *elhar*'s. The door was closed, but Livios heard noises within.

"Keep your mouth shut, that's my advice," Enyo said, then rapped on the door.

"Yes?" came the muffled response.

"We've brought him, sir," Enyo replied.

"Enter."

*   *   *

Lasctakos was in poor temper. Though skilled at cards he had already lost his favorite dagger and some *kraal* to his *sestari*. He looked across the table at First *Sestar* Vexaras, who swept some coins into a woolen purse.

"Fortune hasn't smiled on you this evening, sir," Vexaras said with a grin. His was an unremarkable face though his eyes held a little madness.

"No," the *cohar* agreed. He looked at frowning Melas; who was still upset over Boros' death.

"Don't fret, sir," jowly, gray-haired Pielos said. "Vex'll give it back. Always does."

The bearded Fifth *Sestar*, Oenos, motioned to a slave girl, saying, "More wine."

"Come, come!" Daphonos croaked from beneath a grotesquely protruding brow. "Whose deal?"

"Mine," Lasctakos said. He collected the cards and began to shuffle. His hands moved quicker than sight. *Damn Boros,* he thought. *Getting himself killed. Now these men expect to get bumped.* It was true. Melas had already hinted that he wanted Second *Sestar*. Lasctakos didn't have to promote him, but it was expected and to not do so might cause problems. To do so always encouraged legionaries to challenge their new *sestari* come Winnowing Day, though, which meant more deaths.

Lasctakos began to deal. "Nothing wild, gentlemen." A knock on the door. "Yes?"

"We've brought him, sir," came the muffled response.

"Enter."

The door opened and Enyo stepped inside, followed by a bound youth and Argos. The curly-headed youngster was big, even for a *landesknecta*. The skin on his chest and stomach was discolored and cracked from the recent branding. Lasctakos recognized him. *Doubt he's eighteen*, he thought. "So here is our murderer?" he asked. "You two are dismissed."

Enyo and Argos saluted and left.

Vexaras began to fidget. "He sure has pretty curls. Maybe I should give him a proper haircut?"

Lasctakos shook his head. "He has been branded and named. You may not touch him."

"Pity."

"Hard to believe he killed Boros," Melas growled.

Lasctakos studied the prisoner. He saw animosity and, more importantly, intelligence. "Actually, it's not at all hard to believe. Boros allowed his nature to cloud his judgement. Have I not told you he would meet such an end? Vexaras, unbind him."

All the *sestari* looked surprised.

Vexaras cut Livios' bonds and remained standing.

Lasctakos rose, walked around the table and sat before Livios, who remained outwardly undaunted. "Death is the penalty for killing your commander before the Winnowing. Did you know that?"

Livios shook his head and recalled how the *cohar* had walked across the fallen tree. *While juggling daggers.*

Vexaras slapped the boy's posterior. "Answer!"

"I didn't know," Livios said.

"Then you are foolish as well as rash," Lasctakos replied. He pointed at the Scriptus scars. "You wear the law over your bowels."

"I can't read, sir," Livios replied.

Vexaras made an obscene noise. "Another farmer. Lovely."

Lasctakos' head tilted. "Why did you kill Boros?"

Livios was astounded by how the simple action made Lasctakos even more closely resembles his father. "He asked me to. Sir."

"Oh?"

60

Livios nodded. "Said I should kill him if I didn't like the name he gave. Told me he'd let me name myself. He slapped me in the face and drew a weapon, too."

Lasctakos raised an eyebrow at Vexaras.

"Boros did corner him, sir," the *sestar* reluctantly confirmed. "I'm told it was one of those 'fight or be killed' situations."

Lasctakos eyed Livios with growing interest. "Fight **and** be killed, I suspect. And an unblooded boy slays my best swordsman. Remarkable. So you didn't like your *chiampuglia*? What did he dub you?"

Livios' shoulders sagged.

"Stand at attention!" Vexaras snarled and backhanded him.

"That one will leave a bruise," Melas praised. "Hit 'em again, Vex!"

"Patricides," Livios ground out. He glared at Vexaras, who blew a kiss.

Lasctakos looked thoughtful. "You murdered your sire?"

"I didn't mean to, sir."

There was understanding in Lasctakos' eyes. "I see. So you joined the Black Brotherhood to conceal your sins? How old are you?"

Livios lowered his eyes. "Fifteen, sir."

Lasctakos' jaw dropped. "Fifteen? *Fifteen!* That damn Boros! If he wasn't dead, *I'd* kill him!"

Vexaras looked furious. "It's a sickening thing," he said and others agreed. Only Daphonos, Boros' enemy, remained silent.

Lasctakos stewed for a moment, then laughed. He shook his head. "Fifteen. I guess the *ikar* is raiding cradles. So you don't like your name, Patricides?"

"No, sir."

Lasctakos placed his palms on the table, leaving his swordhilt unprotected. "I suppose you would like to kill me for calling you that?"

Livios stood mute.

Vexaras struck again. "Answer!"

Livios ignored the blow, though his teeth hurt terribly. He stared at Lasctakos. "I suppose I would."

"We must score him highly for honesty, gentlemen," Lasctakos said.

"Vexaras?"

The *sestar* was staring at Livios. "Sir?"

"I think this child stumbled into a trap. I elect trial by ordeal. A night with the sharks will show if he has what I need. Jail him until tomorrow evening."

Vexaras looked dubious. "As you say, sir."

Lasctakos nodded at Livios. "Survive that sentence and you'll be worthy of your scars. Remove him."

Livios tried saluting, but Vexaras grabbed his hands and tied them. Lasctakos went back to his seat and began to shuffle. "Hey, boy?"

"Sir?"

"Choose another name. What grabs you?"

"Shouldn't we wait to see if he survives?" Vexaras asked.

Lasctakos shook his head. "No. I have a feeling about this one. "What will it be?"

Livios thought hard. *What was that three-headed dog from the myths?* "Call me Kerebos."

Vexaras grabbed him by the scruff. "Only if you survive, pretty boy! Enyo!"

It took a moment for the guards to arrive. Vexaras returned to the game. He wiped his brow and looked with surprise at the moisture on his hands.

"This is where he gives the money back," Pielos chuckled.

Vexaras' eyes flashed. "Shut up."

Lasctakos began to deal. "You shouldn't irk that cub," he warned. "One day he might kill you."

Vexaras looked scornful. "Oh, please!"

"After this game, bring me Boros' recruit ledger."

"Yes, sir."

*   *   *

Livios was back in his cell, which seemed damper and cooler than before. He heard the steady drip of water all around. The smell of decomposition was in the air, which brought the sharks to mind. He remembered their snuffling from his first day as a recruit. How might a man survive an entire night with those beasts? *They'll sniff me out.*

The jail's trap door fell open and he covered his eyes as a ladder lowered into sight. A legionary climbed down, then reached up for a torch. Livios recognized Daphonos *Sestar*, whose protruding brow looked even more disfigured by torchlight. Daphonos stumbled to Livios' cell.

"You in there, Sir Kerebos?" he slurred.

"Yes, *sestar*."

Daphonos coughed. "Smells nice down here. Someone must've died." He shoved the sputtering torch between the bars. "Crawl where I can see you."

Livios obeyed. He smelled wine on the *sestar*, whose watery eyes stared down at him for some time. *What does he want?* he wondered.

At last Daphonos spoke. "I wanted to thank you for killing Boros." He swayed where he stood and touched his bumpy forehead. "Hated him. Did this to me."

"Yes, sir."

Daphonos leaned against the bars and smiled. "He was my brother," he whispered.

Livios inched away.

"Where you going? Didn't I say I hated him? I did! Joined up just to get him, you know." Daphonos grabbed a bar to steady himself. "Well, just wanted to say thanks before the sharks chewed you."

"Yes, sir."

Daphonos gave a sloppy salute. "Goodbye, Kerebos. See you in hell." He turned to leave.

"Sir?"

Daphonos turned and belched. "Yeah?"

"Can I have a last request?"

Daphonos looked irritated. "Do I look like the *ikar*?"

"I don't want much, just some spices to flavor my rat meat. Pepper, maybe?"

Daphonos blinked as though he didn't understand, though he must have because later that night a guard tossed a pouch into Livios' cell, saying, "For your rat meat."

Livios hadn't slept when soldiers came for him. They were Argos, Laertos and the new *sestar*, Enyo. Lasctakos had promoted from within Boros' squad rather than going the more traditional route of dropping Enyo to the junior Sixth spot.

"Time," Enyo said smugly.

They unlocked the cell and Livios crawled out. He was pulled to his feet and shoved toward the ladder.

"Let's go!" Enyo spat.

Livios reached the steps and climbed. The rest of the *sestar* waited above, including the newest member, Krynn. The *Boru* had yet to receive armor but wore sword, dagger and helmet.

"Evening, Krynn," Livios said.

"It's Luecos, now, friend."

"Evening, Luecos."

Enyo climbed up. "Be quiet, the both of you. Lead us out, Luecos."

"Sir!"

They marched through the empty spoke and exited into orange dusk, where the entire *elhar* had formed in the yard. Enyo brought the detail to a halt.

"The legionary Kerebos, formerly recruit 2122, step forth!" Vexaras cried in a loud voice. Livios complied. Vexaras unrolled a scroll and read. "This man has violated code two of Desia's law—unsanctioned killing of a superior. The fact that he was judged as provoked, and committed the crime without premeditation, has caused the remanding authority, First *Cohar* Lasctakos, to commute his sentence from summary execution to trial by ordeal." Vexaras rolled up the scroll and looked at Livios. "The prisoner must spend the night beyond the moat and in view of the walls. The prisoner must take no weapons. The prisoner must make no attempt to reenter the walls until first light. Violation of any of these edicts shall void the trial by ordeal and the prisoner will be immediately Judged. Has the prisoner any questions?"

Livios shook his head.

Vexaras nodded at Enyo. "Carry on."

Enyo nudged Livios. "Come."

Livios was brought to the gate. As they waited for it to open, Luecos waved, saying, "Die well."

Livios walked through the gate, which boomed closed behind him. Never had he felt so forlorn as when he gazed over the darkening plain to where large shapes were emerging from the distant river.

"On the other side of the moat!" a sentry cried from the wall.

Livios looked up and saw that a crowd had gathered above. A pilum struck the ground between his feet. "Other side!" the sentry ordered.

Livios thought briefly about taking the spear, but decided against it; it would not have been much help, anyway. It was almost dark now, and he could hear the sharks fighting among themselves. He knew it was only a matter of time before they smelled him and came to investigate. He remembered watching sharks from his flooded cave and how they hugged the periphery. *At least they'll start that way*, he thought. A gentle thud near his foot made him jump. Something struck his head. He bent and picked up a chunk of beef. *Landesknectos* were throwing meat onto the plain!

"Give them that!" someone yelled with a laugh. "Maybe they'll leave you be!"

Livios wished he could get his hands on the man. More food landed around him. A shark bawled in the distance. *I'd better hurry!* he thought and moved out onto the plain. He dropped to the ground and began to dig the soft earth, which was filled with stones. It was rough going and his hands were soon bleeding. He fought through the pain and completed a shallow hole roughly the shape of his body. Lying in it, he found it too small, and climbed out to dig some more. The ground trembled beneath him. *My heart or their feet?* he wondered.

Another shark gave voice, much nearer than had the last.

Livios tried to calm himself, but sweated with fatigue and terror. *They must smell me!* he thought. Another growl. *My god, they're close!* He lay in the widened hole and began to cover himself with mud and grass. It was slow going.

"Mraahhh!" a shark roared. Livios forced himself to look; he made out its shape, a stone's toss away. Was that another one just behind it? No, there were *two*! *Where'd the rest of the dirt go?* He wondered, sick with dread.

When nearly covered, Livios wriggled a hand beneath the cool earth and drew the pepper bag from his loincloth. He prayed the spice was still dry as he pulled the pouch string with his teeth and dusted his body with pepper, saving the last for the mud he patted over his head. A small breathing hole remained for his mouth; he fought to control his breaths. *I've bled so much they have to smell me!* he thought.

Livios remembered his arms and tried to wriggle them beneath his body, but was sure they remained visible. The earth shook as the giant predators approached. He lay as still as possible, though it seemed his heart would burst. The position was made even less comfortable, due to rocks and cold mud; he bit his tongue to keep his teeth from chattering. Time crawled by and the suspense became unbearable. Why didn't they attack?

Livios gave thought to repositioning himself, but couldn't move; his whole body had cramped. Already he heard the sharks' sniffing. For him. *One of my ears must not be covered*, he thought, giving himself up for dead. *Nothing to do about it now.*

Men often talk of "moments like hours" but Livios was confident the phrase was coined under far better circumstances. Every endless second he expected to feel claws and teeth. He pictured his body being torn to pieces, being fought over. Would he still be alive when they began to eat him?

Some sharks got involved in a noisy scuffle mere feet away and his heart nearly stopped. The growling and snarling was so close he was sure he'd be crushed. A very loud roar rang his ear and he almost screamed. *Can't take any more!* he told himself. *Might as well get up and run, rather than wait here!* How far would he get before they dragged him down? *Who am I fooling? They'll chomp me before I make it out of the mud.*

Then came a wonderful sound: a sneeze. Then another. Soon there was a veritable symphony of wheezing. The sharks began to roar again, but this time with pain. The chorus trumpeted around him for a while but at last the beasts began to make noisily for the river. The earth shook beneath their feet.

Livios was alone. He waited until he could take no more of the cold and floundered from the shallow pit. Incredibly, the sharks had gone. He laughed until hoarse.

Dawn found Livios on the bridge before the main gate. He was tired, muddy and had an awful cough but was otherwise unscathed. "You going to let me in?" he shouted at the wall.

A sentry looked down. "By the *ikar*, he's still alive!"

Soon many gazed down at the prisoner. Livios smirked at them.

"How'd you do it?" someone cried.

"I prayed real hard."

The gate cracked open and a guard looked out. "Inside."

Legionaries swarmed Livios, and more were on the way. Enyo arrived in his underclothes. A smiling Luecos was there as well.

Enyo looked crestfallen. "I don't believe it. Nobody's ever beaten the sharks."

Livios saluted smugly. "Sir."

Enyo's ugly, scarred face broke into a reluctant smile. "By the *cohar*'s verdict, I guess you're acquitted. Go wash up and report to mess."

The crowd was large now. Questions and compliments bombarded Livios from all directions. He had never been so popular.

"Good show, lad!" Laertos said with warmth. "Anyone have *kraal* for him?"

Livios spied Vexaras, who blew a kiss.

"You hungry, or what, Kerebos?" Enyo demanded impatiently.

"I don't know anything but the jail, sir. Where's the mess hall?"

"Right. Luecos, show him the way."

"Yes, sir."

Soon Livios had bathed, had dressed and was eating beside the Second's table in the mess hall. As he had not been absorbed into the unit, he had to sit on the floor, but that didn't stop the questions. Not wishing to compromise Daphonos, he fabricated a story of having evaded the sharks by stealth. The astounded legionaries bought it but wanted details. When someone pointed out the sharks' excellent senses of smell, Livios shrugged.

"They can't smell you through a coat of mud," he said.

"I don't know about all that," Enyo interjected.

A legionary arrived. "Kerebos, get over to the *cohar*'s quarters!"

Livios rose to his feet. "On my way. Luecos, watch my food."

"Got it."

Livios remembered the way and quickly found Lasctakos' door. He knocked.

"Come," Lasctakos replied.

Livios entered and saluted. Lasctakos folded his arms on the desk.

"Good morning. I want to confirm what your commander told you, that your sentence has been fulfilled and you are returned to duty."

"Thank you, sir."

Lasctakos lifted Boros' recruit ledger. "On six separate occasions your trainers wrote of your tendency to return strokes high."

"Yes, sir."

"Yet you killed Boros with a cut to the knee?" Lasctakos stared. "I think you planned the whole thing."

Livios felt a sinking feeling. *The Judges, now?* he thought.

Lasctakos gave a paternal smile. "I expect good things from you, Kerebos. Dismissed."

RUNNER

Though he had graduated as Boros' outstanding recruit, Livios soon found he was not as "graduated" as some. Those lucky enough to slide into a vacant slot, like Luecos, were exempt from *feccalas laboris* ('dung work' in Ancient *Chaconni*) and could drill and loaf like regular *landesknectos*. The majority of the recently branded, however, were saddled with perpetual tasks as well as drills.

Livios' first assignment was blacksmith's assistant. Though demanding, he liked the work and discovered a natural talent. His quick mind and hands took to the job as readily as they had to weapons. Unfortunately, it did not last. Vexaras *Sestar*, Enyo's mentor, found a pretext to get Livios back to scrubbing floors. The Master Armorer, a disabled *cohar*, was irked by the loss and approached Lasctakos about the situation but nothing came of it. Livios tucked the sleight in that part of his mind reserved for hating Vexaras.

Livios and the rest were worked nearly to death polishing floors and arms, manning the kitchens and doing anything else an officer could conceive. He and his peers were also used as "runners" and were constantly sent about with messages that ranged from trivial to ridiculous. Enyo once rescued him from *feccalas* only to send him to inform Lasctakos, who was fishing, that mess was ready. When Livios returned from his two-mile sprint Enyo said: "You can run faster than that. Put yourself in for extra fire watch. And shine my boots."

"Fire watch" was unbearable; this worthless guard duty kept Livios awake for hours scouting the barracks for flame, while real *landesknectos* snored fitfully. To his knowledge none of the stone spokes had ever caught fire but that didn't seem to matter to the officers. Even worse, he had to sleep on the hard floor. A few weeks of *feccalas* made him consider desertion.

Livios was on his back, eyes closed. *Why can't I sleep?* he silently lamented. It seemed unfair, considering how tired he was. The floor seemed particularly hard tonight.

68

"Your watch, Kerebos," Neleos whispered.

Livios glared at the lean, dark man, the oldest of Boros' recruits. Was it true he had been an assassin? "Move that lamp from my face."

Neleos scowled. "On your feet, shark boy, before I pour the oil on you."

Livios rose with effort; his eyes refused to focus. He grabbed the lamp and accepted the "fire hat", a ridiculous cap that looked like a cross between a skunk and an ashcan. Neleos slipped away to his own patch of floor, moving with a feline grace entirely consistent with his rumored past.

Livios stared a moment at the stupid hat. He suddenly sensed someone behind him and wheeled to see Luecos. The *Boru* regarded him with pity, asking, "Been a while since you slept, huh?"

"Yes. I'm on edge."

Luecos looked about. "Take my bed for a few hours. I'll stand your watch." He swiped the fire hat from Livios and reached for the lamp.

"Go on. I've only one drill tomorrow. I'll be fine."

Livios sighed. "Thanks, Kobald. I owe you."

"Don't worry 'bout it."

"No, do worry about it," Vexaras' loud voice interrupted. They looked toward his open door and could see him in the gloom. "You can't trade fire watch." the *sestar* spat; men stirred on their pallets. "Do you think this is some holiday?"

"My apologies, sir," Luecos said.

"Apologize to your friend. You just doubled his watch for the month. As for you, barbarian, you'll just have to get by on bread and water during that time. Go to bed."

Luecos, uncommonly fond of food, bit back a comment.

"Go to bed!" Vexaras repeated.

"Sir," Luecos replied.

Dozens of legionaries were grumbling but Vexaras seemed oblivious. He motioned to Livios, saying, "Your hat's crooked. Come here."

Livios was suddenly wide-awake. *How I hate him!* he thought. He stood before Vexaras, who wore only a loincloth.

"Hold out your hand," the *sestar* ordered; he grasped the boy's forefinger and dragged it over the Scriptus scar on his bare stomach. "I know you can't read, so I'll tell you. It says 'death to he who rests on guard duty'." He bit the tip of his tongue and giggled. "I suggest you don't let sleep get the best of you. Lots of nasty things can happen to a lad when he's dead, you know. Dismissed."

The smoky mess hall smelled of fried grains and was filled with boisterous conversation. Livios sat on the floor beside Enyo's squad. He swooned over his plate, eyes half shut.

"Sir, I must start my watch," Luecos told Enyo from the "junior" seat. "May I be excused?"

Enyo belched. "Isn't your bread good?" There was a general laugh.

Luecos stood. "Sir, the water barrel in the guard house is empty. Can I put this runner to work?"

Enyo nodded carelessly.

Luecos kicked Livios' leg. "Wake up. Come on."

They walked through the empty spoke to the guardroom adjacent the entrance. Luecos shut the door then made sure no one was hiding in the chamber, going so far as to look behind a lock box.

Livios grew interested despite his drowsiness. "What?"

Luecos' face twisted with rage. "I'm going to kill him! Thirty days bread and water!"

"Who?"

"You know who. Vexaras."

Livios was suddenly frightened. "You can't, he's too tough," he replied. "You'll never get that good by Winnowing Day."

"*We* can, and I won't need to. We're not waiting till autumn."

Livios shook his head. "Boros was one thing, but this is different. There will be no way for them to ignore this. You'll die and you'll die horribly."

"No we won't," Luecos insisted. "Why do you keep leaving yourself out of this?"

"Because that's where I want to be! This is crazy!"

"Do you think he's just going to forget about you 'pretty boy'? Why do you think he's running you into the ground?"

Livios shuddered. "He can't touch me. I'm a legionary now."

"Maybe not here, but you won't be in the castle forever, *runner*. Vexaras' and our squads are moving out soon."

Livios' heart skipped. "How do you know that?"

Luecos appeared reluctant. "Argos told me. I don't know where we're going, but we'll be away for days. And if you're as stubborn as I suspect you are, and don't give him what he wants, that means you won't be coming back."

Livios felt weighted with bricks. He sat on the lock-box.

"You might have the thews of a man," Luecos resumed, "but you've the eyes of a child. I *know* bad men. I *am* one." He raised an eyebrow. "Vexaras has to go."

Livios sighed. "We'll never get away with it."

Luecos laughed. "We'd better. He's never going to forgive me for being your friend and I can't stand any more of this bread and water nonsense. Soon I'll be too weak to lift my sword."

Livios felt trapped. Killing Boros had seemed the right thing. After all, he had murdered Felix. Snuffing Vexaras, even if possible, was another matter. *I can't just start killing people because I don't like them,* he thought. *That'd be wrong. But I've already murdered,* he reasoned. *What's one more? I'm not even sorry I killed Boros!* His thoughts wandered back to Daedilos and he groaned.

"Well?" Luecos asked.

"I don't think I can."

"Of course you can! You have to. He's not just going to go away."

Livios stood. "I'll think on it."

"You have till the end of the week," Luecos replied. "Fill that water barrel before you go."

*   *   *

The day's drills had been particularly onerous and now Livios stood another fire watch. He limped the spoke at a cripple's pace trying to recall the last time he'd slept. His eyes burned and itched and were so gummy he heard when he blinked. The silly fire cap felt like a rock on his head as he shuffled past the rows of snoring men.

How'd I come to this end? Livios wondered. *Is this typical for the "outstanding recruit?* He doubted it. His fevered thoughts ran over the shark plain to the salt caves and beyond. He saw rolling green fields bathed in golden sunlight, and finally his home. He almost convinced himself that Daedilos was there awaiting him.

"Kerebos," someone whispered.

"Eh?" he answered, looking around.

A bare-chested Vexaras leaned from his room. "Come here."

Livios recoiled but obeyed, stopping just outside the room. "Sir?"

Vexaras smiled hungrily. "Come on in," he said ingratiatingly.

Worn though he was, Livios was instantly suspicious. What price to pay for disobeying such a minor order? "Sir?"

Vexaras' smile faded. "Get in here!"

Livios took one step into the room and Vexaras settled onto the bed. The lamp-lit room smelled of sweat. The very walls seemed to perspire.

"Why so nervous?" Vexaras asked. "Think I don't know how to take care of you?"

Livios was speechless.

Vexaras pat the bed. "Rest beside me."

"I'm, I'm on fire watch, *sestar*," Livios stammered.

Vexaras frowned. "Not so loud. So now you hide behind regulations? I could have you flayed for even coming in here. Did you know that?"

71

Livios was repulsed to his core and weary beyond caution. Perhaps Vexaras had authority to beat him for anything or nothing, but he suspected Lasctakos wouldn't like it. "Perhaps I should ask the *cohar* for permission?"

"Don't ever threaten me, boy!" Vexaras snarled but his face quickly softened. "Wouldn't it be nice to sit? To sleep? I could arrange it. I could make it so you'd never have to stand watch again. All sorts of things I can do for my favorites."

"I'm very tired, sir."

Vexaras smiled. "I understand. Mull my words, though. And think of me as a friend. A boy can't have too many friends, you know. Plenty of favors I'd do for a friend."

Livios felt sick. "Yes, sir. Can I go?"

"We'll talk again soon," Vexaras said with a wink. "Very soon."

The next day Luecos recruited Livios to polish armor. "You'll need oil," Luecos said. "Follow me to the armory." The smiths were busy at their loud work and paid the visitors no heed. Luecos looked concerned. "What happened? You look like hell."

"Let's do it. Let's kill him."

Luecos didn't seem surprised. "Excellent. I have a plan."

Livios recalled Vexaras' lecherous expression. "Let's do it tonight."

Luecos chuckled. "Calm down, now. This is going to take some thought. Not so squeamish anymore, huh? Did he grab you? The pig."

"I can't stand watch tonight," Livios insisted.

A small pouch appeared in Luecos' hand. "Don't worry, you're going to the hospital for a rest. Eat this *kraal*. All of it."

"That's enough for six men. I'll be sick for days."

"That's right. Until we move out at week's end."

*   *   *

It wasn't quite summer, but Livios couldn't remember such heat. Sweat poured from his body as he ran over the plain. The sun burned in a cloudless sky. *Still have a headache from that kraal,* he thought, *but damned if Luecos wasn't right.* The legion's surgeon took one look at Livios in the throes of a puking fit, and quarantined him. Livios got three days' bed rest, and rest he did. *Must've slept seventy hours. Good old Luecos!*

Enyo came to the hospital on Friday morning and talked to the doctor. Livios overheard the conversation.

"How is he?" Enyo asked.

72

"Fine, fine," the surgeon replied. "Has done nothing but sleep and eat."

"Good. I need his speed."

"What have you been doing to him?"

"None of your business, slave. Kerebos, get up!" Enyo shouted. "Prepare for a march. Wear runner's gear."

Livios stirred as though waking. "Yes, sir. I never got my running moccasins."

"Wear boots, then. Hurry!"

They struck a southbound course as the sun baked off the morning haze. Vexaras was in command and Enyo his deputy. Both *sestari* brought their full units plus one runner. The legionaries were armed to the teeth and marched in single file. The runners, wearing only footwear and loincloths, scouted a few hundred yards before and behind the detachment. Livios would run forward a quarter mile, then make his way back so Vexaras could see him. He had no idea how many revolutions he completed before he was reeled in for a brief rest; he'd lost count around fifty.

The legionaries gulped water where they stood. Luecos handed the panting Livios a canteen. Vexaras, covered in dust and pollen, removed his horsehair-crested helmet and glared at Livios, saying, "Don't come in so close before. If I can see you, that's good enough." His voice was all business.

"Yes, sir."

"You're getting sunburned," Enyo pointed out. "Rub some dirt on your shoulders."

"Yes, *sestar.*"

Livios took a moment to pour sweat from his boots and wring his socks. His feet had chafed raw and were bleeding.

"Gonna have to sleep with 'em on tonight," the usually quiet Halesas said. "If you don't, you'll swell. Start soaking your feet in salt water. Toughen 'em up."

Livios looked at Halesas' weathered face in surprise. *First time he's talked to me.* "I'll try that."

Vexaras splashed water on his cropped head then pulled on his helmet. He adjusted the eye slits. "Move out!" he cried.

Livios and the other runner swapped sides and sprinted off. Livios found being rear flanker more demanding than his previous job. He had to run faster on his return to catch up with the *sestari*, as they marched away from him. He deeply regretted not having moccasins and blamed Enyo for the oversight. Not only did the knee-high boots hurt, they slowed him—a decidedly bad thing. Fortunately they were only travelling twenty miles today, through docile country, or Enyo's mistake might have proved costly.

A thought struck Livios. *Enyo's a new officer and he's not in command now. Vexaras should've sorted our kit.* He felt a rising anger. Either Vexaras had forgotten to check the unit's materiel or had deliberately and sadistically allowed him to run scout in boots. Neither explanation made him feel better. *I hope Luecos' idea works,* he thought. Luecos had yet to share the plan, but Livios was confident the plot would finish Vexaras. The notion lightened his feet.

They stopped near a small river before dark. The runners stood lookout as the others dug in. A small, semicircular trench was swiftly finished around the campsite, complete with sharpened stakes. Four tents were erected, one for each trident, and two smaller ones for the officers; runners slept under the stars. There was even a latrine.

Livios watched from a sandy escarpment and pondered Vexaras' bivouac. *Water behind for bathing, cooking and defense. Soft earth for easy digging...the man's no fool.* Enyo gave a long whistle and waved him into camp. *Dinner!*

The meal was plain but decent, and Livios lay down immediately afterwards. The greatest virtue of being a runner was that he was not required to stand guard. This made sense for two reasons. First, the scouts worked to exhaustion and tended to fall asleep while on post, which both weakened the camp and required their execution. Second, they had no armor and were easy pickings for an archer. Either way, Livios liked the arrangement. He was drifting into sleep when Luecos sat beside him.

"Hi," the *Boru* said. "Bet you're beat."

"You're right."

"It's not going to happen till we're on our way back," Luecos intimated as he loosened his armor. "First night on our way back. Maybe in this very spot."

"Where we going?"

"Taking some *Tantorri* hostages for the *ikar*. One of the southern clans has had a change in chiefs or something, and we have to maintain leverage."

The *Tantorri*, a loose association of plain dwellers, had been under the legion's "protection" for centuries and provided food and slaves.

Livios yawned. "All right."

Luecos smiled. "Never been this far south, have you?"

"No. I have to sleep."

"Go ahead, then. And throw a blanket over yourself."

"It's too hot."

"If you don't, the mosquitoes will eat you alive. G'night!"

Livios woke with first light. He was very sore and itched all over. Luecos and two others were frying breakfast.

"Hurry and eat," Enyo cried. "We're moving out."

Livios had a hard time standing. Sharp pain shot through his feet and calves. He staggered over to the fire in boots that felt many sizes too small. "Hey there, pincushion face," Luecos said with a laugh. "Didn't I warn you about the mosquitoes?"

"Uhh."

"Broth?" Halesas asked.

Livios nodded and the legionary handed him a cup of steaming brown liquid. "Broth" was a morning drink particularly favored by veterans. Livios didn't know what was in it but smelled *kraal*. He took a small sip and covered his mouth.

"Good God!" he gasped. "Did somebody piss in this?"

"No god here," blonde Clios growled.

"Just a little bit," Luecos said. "Keeps you on your toes, runner."

Surprisingly, Livios began to feel more energetic and the pain in his legs eased. He finished the broth.

Halesas snorted. "Be drinking it in your sleep before long."

"Bastard!" a legionary growled from the other fire where a runner had accidentally stepped on him. "Luecos, throw me that shovel!"

The *Boru* pulled the tool from the dirt and tossed it over his shoulder without looking. The angry soldier plucked it from the air and began to beat the unfortunate runner. The whole camped laughed, except for Vexaras.

"Knock it off!" he said. "Hurt that boy and you're running in his place! We're moving out as soon as I return." He stomped off to the latrine.

The *landesknectos* smothered the fires and struck camp with impressive speed. They were on the trail within moments.

The *Tantorri* camp appalled Livios. The weatherworn teepees were haphazardly arranged and the ground between them littered with refuse. Dogs and children ran about while men lounged and women worked. The stench of tanning skins overpowered even that of the piles of garbage. The entire scene was disorderly, dirty, noisy and chaotic. But the horses were beautiful. Livios had never seen such beasts; a hand smaller than his Herakles, perhaps, but sleek and clean-limbed. The manes and tails were braided with cloth-of-gold.

"They make a living selling them," Luecos said. "I don't think they treat their children as well. Even Korenthis buys these."

"Why do they suffer such filth?" Livios asked, breathing through his mouth.

"It's the open plain. They ruin an area then move on. Some other clans are far cleaner, though, and even have cities."

"Quiet," Enyo said as he weaved through the trident formations, which bristled with spears. He glanced at the largest tent. *"Give me till midday,"* Vexaras had said. *"If I'm not back, kill everyone."*

"It's not midday, sir," Argos said.

"I know, stupid. I'm thinking."

Argos' hyper intense expression shifted to one of anger. *They were best friends before Enyo's promotion,* Livios thought.

"Ah!" Enyo said as Vexaras appeared.

The senior *sestar* looked pleased. "All's well. No problems. The old boy wanted to feed me."

The legionaries relaxed.

"How many we taking?" Enyo asked.

"Two children. His oldest and youngest sons."

At that moment Livios saw the boys in question. The elder of the short, black-haired pair carried a small bundle. He walked with proud steps, but was obviously terrified. The other boy, no older than eight or nine, wept openly. Livios pitied them; he wouldn't want to be separated from his family, either. They stopped before the towering warriors and bowed.

"Could fit them in my pocket," Luecos said.

"And you might have to if they can't keep up," Vexaras threatened. He barked orders at the hostages in *Tantorri* then pointed at Livios, saying, "Take us out the way we came."

"Sir!" Livios darted from the encampment.

The *landesknectos* reached their previous campsite as night fell. Vexaras had them deepen the dry moat and further fortify it with stakes, just in case the *Tantorri* changed their mind.

Livios had eaten but was too keyed up to sleep. Was Luecos avoiding him for a reason? The *Boru* had disappeared into his tent as soon as it had been erected and hadn't shown so much as a nose. *Tonight's not the night,* he concluded. *At least he can come tell me so I can rest.*

Luecos emerged from the walled tent and walked to Livios. "Sorry," he whispered. "Had to get some information."

"Not tonight?"

"Oh, it's going to happen," Luecos replied with a grin. "Couldn't be a better night—no moon and clouds moving in. And guess who's taken a shine to our little prisoner."

Livios felt queasy. "Did he now?"

"Yes. Vexaras told Hals to bring the kid over after we fell asleep."

Livios shook his head. "What's the plan?"

Luecos leaned closer. "I have third watch, and by then everyone will be out. Halfway through my duty, Vexaras is going to have an accident." He produced a small lamp. "I'll toss this into his tent as you pull the stakes."

Livios remembered his burning barn. "Is there no other way?"

Luecos scowled. "What do you want? This is as easy as it gets. I'll wake you when I come on watch. Keep your eyes peeled for my signal."

Livios was losing confidence. "What if someone sees us?"

"They won't. It'll be darker than the inside of a mule's ass tonight, trust me. A spark and a scream, then no more Vex."

"All right. Wait! What about the boy?"

Luecos mulled the question. "I'll cut a slit in the side so he can scurry out. You just worry about those stakes. You have to get them all."

Livios felt a rising thrill in his breast, not unlike that which had accompanied his showdown with Boros. He wished there was another way but savored the thought of a world without Vexaras. "I'll be there."

Somehow Livios managed to sleep. The next thing he knew Luecos kicked him on the way to his post. The camp was silent, but for snores.

Livios was so nervous he doubted he could uphold his end; he was having a hard time rationalizing the assassination of a sleeping man. At least Boros had had a fighting chance. *It's not murder*, he told himself. *I'm just getting him before he gets me.* Time passed. *What's he doing? Has he scrapped the whole thing?*

Luecos struck a noisy match, lit the lamp and closed the shutters. "Psst!" he signaled, and then made for Vexaras' tent, at the end of the row.

Livios gained his feet and stumbled after his friend. The first stake was very stubbornly buried, so he pulled his bootknife and cut its rope. He swiftly sliced the others. Before Livios severed the last support, Luecos opened the flap, dashed the lamp onto the ground at Vexaras' feet and toppled the pole. The conspirators bolted back to their respective positions as Vexaras began to scream. The tent burst into flame and was soon fully involved. Vexaras tried to stand but the burning fabric clung to him. He turned around and around and got further tangled. His shrieks were terrible. The smell of burning hair filled the heavy air.

"Awake! Awake! Fire!" Luecos cried and ran back to the scene. "Awake!"

"AAAAHHHHH!" Vexaras wailed. One of his arms shot into sight. It was crawling with flame.

Landesknectos poured from their tents.

"Get water from the river!" Enyo commanded. "Hurry! Use the pots and pans!"

There was no thwarting the fire, though. Vexaras soon fell and his

77

cries stopped. The flames had quite burned down by the time legionaries returned with water, though the reek of burnt flesh was worse than ever. Vexaras lay smoking and sizzling in the night.

Enyo was punching his hand and cursing. "Kerebos, feel for a pulse!" he cried.

Livios approached the charcoaled Vexaras and pinched the steaming black throat. He released the crispy skin, which stuck to his fingers, and turned to Enyo. He shook his head.

"Damn!" Enyo said. He turned to Luecos, who was doing a first class acting job and looked genuinely shocked and sad. "What happened?"

"I heard some thrashing, *sestar,* and that's it."

All the legionaries gathered around the dying flames. Livios could see that the boy had been bound and gagged by ropes that had not burned off entirely. He felt very depressed as he gazed at the innocent.

"I'm sorry, sir," Luecos told Enyo.

"Nothing you could've done. I told him to lay off the hostages, at least till we got home." Luecos looked at the men. "Go back to sleep. We'll bury him in the morning."

"His weapons, sir?" Argos asked.

"Take them."

As the legionaries sought their tents Luecos sided up to his friend.

Livios shook his head at his own gullibility. "Nice slit you cut for the boy."

Luecos shrugged. "Rather it was you in there? Nothing to be done about it now. How would've he gotten out, anyway, tied up like that?"

"Then I shouldn't have allowed it," Livios said softly. "We're going to hell."

"Well, Vex will be waiting for us."

Livios glared at the *Boru* then walked away.

Enyo brought the squads back home without further adventure and immediately reported to Lasctakos. To their very great surprise, Livios and Luecos were promptly summoned by the *cohar.*

"You sent for us, sir?" Luecos asked.

Lasctakos looked up from his desk. "The 'terrible two'," he replied lightly. "One moment." He finished writing then let the scroll close. "Quite a journey, gentlemen. Don't you agree?"

"Yes, sir," they answered.

"You've lost weight, Kerebos," Lasctakos observed. "Nervous stomach?"

"I don't think so, sir. I've been running for days."

"'The guilty flee when no man pursueth.'" Lasctakos quoted the *Aharoni* scripture.

78

Lasctakos obviously suspected something but was looking and acting so like Daedilos that Livios felt no fear. Lasctakos reached into a drawer and produced another scroll. "Take this, Luecos."

The *Boru* obeyed.

"Open it and read," the *cohar* said.

Luecos broke the wax seal and leaned forward into the lamplight. He read: "Orders—Legionary Luecos. Recruit 2142 of Geraestos *Ikar's* fourth year. Effective immediately, Luecos is promoted to First *Sestar* and shall assume responsibilities accordingly, except for direct control of his team in combat, reserved by Lasctakos *Cohar* until further notice.' Signed by you, sir," Luecos finished quietly.

"Correct. Do you understand the trust I've placed in you by promoting you above far more experienced men?"

"I think so, sir."

"I doubt it. Men shall want your blood, and will try to spill it come Winnowing Day."

"I don't blame them, sir. I'm not complaining, but why me? I have confidence in me, but don't see why you do."

Lasctakos' amber eyes narrowed. "I have my reasons. Let me simply say that I am trying to eradicate certain elements from my command. I need able, smart men. Strong leaders. Soldiers with vision. I see that in you, to a degree."

"Thank you, sir."

Lasctakos smiled. "More importantly, I need to separate you two."

Livios tensed, and saw Luecos do likewise.

"I don't understand, sir," Luecos replied slowly.

"I suspect you do, *sestar*. Anyway, I've done you a favor. Now Kerebos won't have to kill you to get promoted," Lasctakos concluded with a chuckle.

Comprehension swept Luecos' pale face. He waved the scroll. "You wrote this before we got back?"

"Before you departed, actually."

There was silence while Lasctakos' words settled. Luecos regarded the *cohar* with new respect.

Lasctakos stood, placed his fists on the desk and leaned toward them.

"Gentlemen, I've turned a blind eye to the slayings of Boros and Vexaras because we are at peace and they were bad leaders. To a large part, you did what I hoped others would have done. You displayed ingenuity and bravery, which are qualities I need and admire. I have rewarded you, Luecos, with an officership and shall reward Kerebos with a bed of his own."

I'm a real legionary now, Livios thought with a smile.

"But for every action, there is an opposite, gentlemen," Lasctakos continued. "That part you must concern yourselves with is this: I demand complete, utter and unquestioning loyalty. I endeavor to build this legion into something great and you shall have a part in that, but only if we understand each other."

Lasctakos stared at them in turn. Livios felt the force of the man's personality like a physical thing; it seemed the room was suddenly crowded.

"I'm your man, sir," Luecos said.

"More than you know," Lasctakos replied menacingly. "I see through you, soldier. I have known your kind my whole life—talented men who believe in nothing, leeches that take the good but shirk the bad. I need more than that. I *demand* more than that, and you *will* deliver."

Luecos gazed straight ahead.

"Perhaps a season or so from now you might see opportunity outside the Legion," Lasctakos continued. "I wouldn't pursue it, Krynn Ollafson of Kobald. Such ingratitude would arise in me a most severe reaction. I might just have to Judge your entire family, thief."

Luecos' brow glistened. He licked his lips. "Your knowledge is impressive, sir. You have your way of me."

Lasctakos smiled broadly and the ugly moment dissipated. "Excellent! Report to your men and make known your orders. If you're shown disrespect, handle it as you see fit. If you cannot handle it, I have chosen the wrong man."

Luecos snapped a salute. "Sir!"

"One more thing. Report here an hour before mess every evening. I'll instruct you on tactics and put some finishing touches on your swordsmanship."

"Sir!" Luecos departed.

Lasctakos came around and sat on the desk. He studied Livios with concern. "What's wrong? You looked so satisfied a moment ago. Aren't you pleased with your promotion?"

"I am, sir. Thank you."

"Well? Scared by my speech to Luecos?"

Livios averted his eyes; he didn't want to see Daedilos at the moment.

"Speak your mind," Lasctakos said. "Always do so. To me at least."

"I don't think I'm right for the Brotherhood."

"Go on."

"Killing people is much harder on me than it is on the other fellows. I don't think I'll get used to it."

Lasctakos laughed kindly. "You have it wrong, son."

Son! "I do?"

"Yes. I don't require it become routine. Tell me, did you get less satisfaction from killing Vexaras in his sleep than Boros in fair combat?"

Livios nodded.

"Could you envision enjoying a situation where you might slice a man who really deserved it, someone who killed a loved one, for example?"

Livios considered the argument. "Probably, sir."

"Of course you could! That would be right and proper. When we extinguish the guilty, we perform a just, moral act. The reason you would feel good about it is because it's in accordance with providence. The fact that you are scarred because of that situation with your father is the converse."

Livios sagged. "Converse?"

"My apologies. Let us say, rather, 'the opposite.'"

"I understand."

Lasctakos pulled his dagger and asked: "Can this be other than a blade?"

"I don't think so, sir."

"I agree. If I try it as a fork, for example, it would do a poor job. Using it as a candle would prove a miserable failure. The same is true with men. The closer we act in accordance with our design, the happier we are. I like commanding soldiers, hence my good humor. You have acted contrary to your perception of structure, and have suffered. I ask you, aren't you happier about the Vexaras business now that you know my support?"

Livios nodded once. In truth, it did make him feel better.

"Of course you are, Kerebos. You would feel even better had I commanded you to kill him. My orders would have eliminated your uncertainty, and you could have taken consolation, or even pride, in the fact that you had obeyed your *cohar*." Lasctakos raised an eyebrow. "Agreed?"

"But it would still be wrong," Livios insisted.

Lasctakos shook his head. "Absolutely not. From top to bottom we live in a world of rules. If there was any culpability, blame that is, it would be mine for giving the order. The only immoral act you could have committed would have been to ignore my authority."

Livios saw Lasctakos' point but didn't agree, as much as he would have liked to. *It would make things so much easier*, he thought.

Lasctakos was still smiling, but there was a curious gleam in his eyes.

"Did you attend divine services with your family?"

"No, sir, but my father often read the *Aharoni* books to me."

"Do you recall the story where God ordered Yajiz to sacrifice his own son?"

Livios nodded. That chapter had always troubled him.

"Would Yajiz have been wrong to sacrifice his son?" Lasctakos asked.

"He didn't do it."

"But had he, would he have done ill?"

Livios pondered the question. "The blame, if any, would be in the command."

Lasctakos stood and lay a hand on Livios' shoulder. "My point exactly, son."

Livios felt tired and confused. He wanted badly to be able to go along with the officer's arguments.

"We'll talk another time," Lasctakos said. "Go rest."

"Yes, sir." Livios saluted.

"Kerebos?"

"Sir?"

"If Endios *Elhar* asks, how should I explain the cut ropes on Vexaras' tent?"

Livios stood mute.

Lasctakos shook his head. "We're lucky the point escaped Enyo; sloppy work on both your parts. Go."

ARMOR

Livios found Enyo in the mess hall, which was empty but for a few officers. The *sestar* had cornered a runner and was delivering a severe dressing down. Enyo's grating voice was even louder than usual.

"You call these plates clean, idiot?" he asked the scared youngster while poking his chest. "I wouldn't let a dog eat off them! Did you polish them with your tongue?"

"No, sir!"

"No you don't call them clean? Then why'd you stack them? Trying to make us all sick? How does permanent fire watch grab you? Maybe I'll just sew the fire hat to your head? Sound good?" Enyo had barked the questions so fast the stammering runner couldn't respond. "Speak up, boy!"

"Yes, sir! Anything you say, sir!"

Livios stopped a dozen feet behind his commander. He knew better than to interfere.

Enyo whirled about. "What?"

Livios saluted. "Sorry to interrupt, *sestar*. I just came from Lasctakos. He promoted me into the unit."

Enyo looked disgusted. "You think I don't know? What, are you bragging about it?"

"No, sir. Just wondering where I sleep tonight."

Enyo rolled his eyes. "Take a guess."

"Luecos' old bed?"

"*Very good!* Hope you fight better than you think. Get lost."

"Yes, sir!"

Enyo was screaming again before Livios entered the spoke. *Can't wait to sleep in my own bed*, he thought. The rest of the unit had gathered around his pallet. *What are they up to?*

"There he is," Argos said.

Almost all of us have that crazy gaze, Livios thought. *Do I?* He

83

approached cautiously. "What?" he asked the five men.

"Congratulations," Clios said and offered a bottle of wine.

"Drink," Halesas grunted. "It's good."

Livios popped the cork and sniffed.

Argos' dark eyes shone. "The whole thing, boy!"

Clios gave a lopsided smile. "That's right."

"What's the catch?" Livios asked.

"If you don't finish it, you make our beds for a week. It's tradition."

Livios looked at Halesas, whom he felt wouldn't lie.

"It's true," Halesas said.

"What if I finish?"

Argos laughed. "Nothing! Bottoms up!"

Livios took a deep breath and started on the wine; it tasted very bad. He only got half way through before he retched onto the wooden floor. The red liquid splashed on the other legionaries but they didn't seem to mind. A general applause rose as Livios coughed and hacked until wine seeped from his nose.

Enyo arrived on the scene. For once he was not yelling.

"How'd he do? Oh. Farm boy!"

Livios collapsed onto his bed. He spied a runner sneaking past. "Hey, you," he called. "Get a mop."

The runner soon returned with a bucket and began to clean.

"Sorry," Livios said.

"Don't apologize to them," Clios scoffed. "He'll be dishing it to another before long, believe me."

They hardly knew my face this morning, now I'm a brother, Livios thought. It was a good feeling. He liked to belong.

Halesas' rugged face wrinkled into a smile. "G'night, Kerebos. Tomorrow you're in my trident."

Livios slowly reclined. "Good night." He closed his eyes and saw spots. *I wonder how Luecos is handling his team?*

It took Livios a long while to make the beds and by the time he got to the mess hall, food was no longer being served. He stood salivating over the empty serving pots.

"How you going to make it through the day on an empty stomach?" Enyo called from the table.

Livios looked at the scarred face, but said nothing.

"Since you're not going to eat, get upstairs for measuring," Enyo said.

"Sir?"

"Your armor."

Livios slowly broke into a grin. It was a struggle not to run up the armory steps.

A single blacksmith was at work but the chamber was smoky. Livios liked the acrid smell and found himself wishing Vexaras had not pulled him from the smithies. Lasctakos *Cohar* and the Master Armorer, his bad leg propped onto a barrel, were engaged in a friendly disagreement. Livios waited at a respectful distance.

Lasctakos balanced a dagger on the tip of his finger as he cordially berated his peer. "You are most definitely wrong. I suspect this smoke has addled your brain. Perhaps you require a visit to the hospital?"

"Always been done that way, Lasc," the armorer said. "I can't change tradition. You know that."

"Of course you can. I am telling you to."

The armorer chewed his lip. "Something like that'll have to come from the top. Sorry. Don't want to lose my head over your idea."

Lasctakos laughed. "Attikos, do you know how many will die before I become *ikar?*"

"Ohhh, so you've already asked him. Then the answer is doubly no. Now let me work."

Livios had never seen anyone resist Lasctakos, but the *cohar* took it well. "I hope you can sleep tonight," he said.

Attikos picked up a tape measure. "Don't you worry about that. I'll see you." He motioned to Livios. "Get over here."

"Good bye." Lasctakos replied. He turned, saw Livios and smiled. "Good morning."

"Sir."

Lasctakos walked over. "So you're here for fitting? I suppose the Master looks forward to crafting another breastplate that traps shot," he said loudly. "So how'd you sleep, son?"

"Very well, sir."

"I remember my first night in a bed, after I was promoted. I couldn't drop off. I slept on the floor until my commander caught me."

Livios was smiling, though he knew not why. Maybe it was because Lasctakos seemed so genuine. He hoped to one day so inspire his own subordinates.

Lasctakos' face grew serious. "Have you considered our last conversation? I prefer my men happy in their work."

Livios fashioned a response. "I've thought about it, sir."

"And?"

"I'm sure I agree, sir."

Lasctakos chuckled. "Don't lie, Kerebos, it doesn't become you."

Livios swallowed. "I don't agree with you, sir, but can't find the weakness in your words."

"Good, good! Always search for the soft point in an argument; be tactical. Let me ask you: are you confident you owe me your allegiance?"

"Yes, sir."

"Then measure that confidence against your uncertainty." Lasctakos shrugged. "At least that is what I would do. A very wise man once said, 'it is more important that heaven exists than that we go there.' Ponder that."

"I will, sir."

Lasctakos left.

"I don't have all day," Attikos said.

Livios hurried over. "Sorry, sir."

The smith smiled as he measured Livios' shoulders and scribbled onto a parchment.

Livios noted the grin and felt self-conscious. "Am I doing something wrong, sir?"

The armorer looked startled. "What? Oh, no. I was just thinking about his last comment. He's always saying things like that."

"You used to be under him?" Livios guessed.

Attikos kept working. "No, it was the other way around. Good thing I was crippled and relegated to this duty or he would've killed me on his way up." After a brief pause Attikos added: "We both grew up in Thebis."

Livios was surprised. "You knew him?"

"Of course. You think just anyone talks to Lasctakos that way?"

"And he would have killed you?"

Attikos nodded. "Absolutely. Nothing stops him from his desires—at least not very often. That's why he wants this legion to take Thebis."

Livios digested the comment. "Why would he attack his own city, sir?"

The armorer's expression hardened. "Maybe one day he'll tell you. I'm done."

Livios saluted and left.

Livios never finished the beds in time to eat, though on the last day Halesas took pity and brought him food. Enyo almost caught Livios polishing off some lukewarm milk.

"Kerebos!" he snapped from behind.

Livios slipped the mug under his pallet and jumped to his feet. "Sir!"

Enyo was glaring, hands on hips. "Get up to the armory, your kit's ready."

Livios darted off and found Attikos, who was resting his leg. "I just sat down, damn it! Did you run up here?"

"I must admit, sir."

"Don't blame you, the *Stalenzka* and I are that good," Attikos replied with a nod at his thralls. He threw Livios a padded gambeson. "Slip into that."

"This looks new!"

"Of course. You're a *landesknecta* not some damn conscript. Do as I say."

Livios wiggled into the snug, protective garment.

"Raise your arms," Attikos said. "How's that fit? The strings in the back let out."

"Little hard to breathe, sir."

Attikos made some adjustments. "How's that?"

"Good, sir."

Attikos whistled and two helpers carried over a T rack. Livios tried, unsuccessfully, to stifle a grin; his armor looked magnificent. Had he known its cost, he might not have dared put it on; it was easily more expensive than his father's farm.

"You've never worn iron before," the armorer stated.

"No, sir."

"It's not light. About a hundred pounds all told." Attikos lifted a very long chainmail shirt. "Arms over your head."

Livios complied and the shirt rasped down his body, reaching his knees. He was surprised by its weight.

Attikos asked: "Heavy?"

"A bit, sir."

"Then you'll love this. Bring the plate." Another man stepped forward with a painted, black breastplate and buckled it over the shirt.

"How's it fit?" Attikos asked.

Livios wiggled the breastplate. "Seems a little loose, sir."

"Yes. You'll grow into it."

"Grow into it?"

"Believe it or not. You'll get bigger after wearing that for a month, especially across the chest."

Attikos' men slid spiked gauntlets onto Livios' arms. The plated leather was snug yet comfortable.

"Now these feel good!" Livios exclaimed.

"Your hands breathe through the special mesh in your palm—my invention," Attikos said, then handed him a helmet. "Keep the eye slits open for a few days. If you've never worn one, you'll find it quite constricting."

Livios slid on the helmet and retracted the slits, finding his peripheral vision greatly reduced.

"Buckle it under your chin," Attikos said.

Livios fumbled with the strap. He started to remove his gauntlets.

"Stop! Keep them on!"

It took a few moments but Livios eventually succeeded.

"Good," Attikos allowed. "You'll soon feel a headache and maybe a touch of nausea, but don't take off anything. The longer you keep it on, the sooner you'll get over it. Bring his shield."

The greatshield was black with the legion's clenched gauntlet etched into the finish. Livios said: "My name's on the back."

"It's etched on each piece. Don't lose anything, or you'll be sorry."

Livios could think of nothing that would make him part with such treasure. "Yes, sir."

Attikos rapped the breastplate. "Come back tomorrow and show me where it's rubbing you. I can make adjustments for your comfort. Don't listen if anyone tells you to tough it through. Doing so might make you injured or might make you dead. Understand?"

Livios was barely listening. "Yes, sir. Thank you, sir."

"Dismissed."

Livios returned to the spoke. A few *landesknectos* were milling about, including Luecos.

"Get yourself over here, recruit," the *Boru* said with a chuckle.

Livios walked over and gave a lazy salute. Luecos scowled, asking, "What are you smiling at?"

"I'm not."

"Well, you damned well should be. You look like a king in that junk."

Livios blushed. "Thanks." He glanced about before saying, "Any trouble with your unit?"

Luecos shrugged. "What do you think? Nothing I couldn't handle; Vex wasn't all that popular, it seems. I'll get it straightened out when they see me in combat. Enyo wants you outside for drills."

Livios snapped a salute. "Thanks."

Enyo's *sestar* was drilling as the integrated left flank of an anti-cavalry formation. Livios sweated just watching the action. *This stuff's hotter than I thought,* he pondered. Lasctakos called a break and Livios reported to Enyo.

"Take my place, sir?"

Enyo wiped sweat off his bumpy face. "Yes. Drink plenty of water today."

"Yes, sir."

The *elhar* broke into single units and Livios fell in behind Halesas; ambidextrous, he took the left side. Enyo snapped a command and the legionaries maneuvered under his critical eye.

Within moments sweat had soaked Livios' gambeson. He was breathless before long and he found it increasingly difficult to keep up with his trident. The armor became unbearably heavy, making him feel spent and queasy.

During a short rest Halesas asked: "What ails you? Too much water? Why you drinking so much?"

Enyo was not so kind and berated him loudly. "You damned simple fool! You move like my grandfather. What's wrong, shark boy?"

Livios was embarrassed and angry. Was it really possible for a man of Enyo's experience to not realize what had happened? "I don't know, sir. Not used to the metal."

"Not easy jumping around in that stuff, is it? I guess you now know what Boros was up against when you got lucky and sliced him."

Livios instantly saw the larger picture; Enyo had never forgiven him for killing Boros and was using this instance to humiliate him. He had sometimes suspected that Enyo had it out for him but had written it off as mere recruit hazing. Now he knew better. "I'll try harder, sir," he said.

Enyo was still frowning. "You will not take that armor off for an entire month, even to bathe. Sleep, eat, march, drill, whatever. That'll toughen you up."

Nearby, Daphonos *Sestar* looked upset but didn't intervene.

"Yes, sir," Livios answered.

Perhaps Enyo had hoped for a disagreement; he looked perturbed by the obedience. "I'm not finished. In addition, you'll serve double drills, alone if need be."

Livios hid his rage. "I understand. Sir."

Enyo stepped closer. "Winnowing Day's at the end of the summer, if you got a problem with me." He straightened and shouted: "Back to work men!"

Livios managed to keep up but wheezed like a bellows. He felt better after throwing up, but the relief was short-lived. Finally the drills ended; he crashed onto his posterior as the others headed for the baths.

"Eat salt," Halesas advised as he walked by.

Luecos got his men squared away then came over. "I should've warned you about the armor," he said. "It didn't really bother me, though, since I've worn it before."

Livios could only nod.

Enyo arrived and glared at Luecos. "Don't have enough work with your own men?"

Luecos smiled. "Perhaps you've advice for me since we got our squads in about the same way?"

Enyo looked at Luecos while saying, "Kerebos, I think you need more exercise. Run down to the river and get me a bucket of water, and I do mean *run*. If you're not back before I clean up, you're going again." He smirked at Luecos then walked away.

Luecos helped Livios to his feet, saying, "I believe he doesn't like you."

"Don't I know it. I'd better get started." Livios spied a new tattoo on the *Boru's* arm. "What's that?"

Luecos looked sheepish. "It's the date of my promotion. I suppose Lasctakos was right; a man has to believe in something."

Livios nodded. "See you later."

"Wait." Luecos produced a shiny green *kraal* leaf. "This will help." Livios would have declined but the *Boru* said: "Take it! This isn't the last chore he'll have you do tonight."

A month passed.

Livios had absorbed Enyo's endless drills and came away none the worse, rather the opposite. His muscles had swelled until his gambeson ripped, and he grew so agile in armor that officers used him as a sparring partner. His name was on many lips and men he barely knew had risked death by sneaking him food. None of the new legionaries were regarded half so highly, it seemed. Besting Boros, surviving the sharks and his frightening weapons talent marked him as special. Even so, he was embittered by Enyo's treatment. All he had sought from the Legion was anonymity but the *sestar* maliciously forced him to the fore at every chance. Why should he be singled out? It seemed so unfair. *Is the entire universe always unjust?* he wondered. *Why didn't Lasctakos commute my sentence?*

As Livios grew sullen, Enyo became increasingly polite. Startled by Livios' development, he would have called off the "punishment" had he not made such a show of the sentence. It was not that Livios could already best him, but even the dullest realized that he would be a superlative swordsman. With some actual combat under his belt, he might easily outmatch Enyo by the Winnowing.

The last day of the month Enyo halted drills early. He looked at Livios and proclaimed: "I knew I'd make a first class fighter of you!"

Livios merely headed for the barrack. He fumbled with his armor until Halesas helped him with the rusted straps. "Attikos will replace these," he told the youth. "If you hadn't been ordered to sleep in it, you'd be executed for the state of your kit." The breastplate eventually came off and a stench filled the room.

"Go outside," Clios muttered from his bed.

"Quiet," Halesas said. He helped Livios with the chainmail and gambeson; skin came off with the protective garment. "I got a grease for those sores."

Argos wandered over, grinning broadly. "Looks like you've gained twenty pounds of beef," he said. The others agreed. "You not talking, Kerebos?"

Livios couldn't chase Enyo from his mind. "What should I say?"

Argos shrugged then sauntered over.

Halesas called a runner and ordered him to polish Livios' armor.

"Thanks," Livios said.

"Rest."

Livios nodded.

Lasctakos stepped into the common room. His handsome face was stern. "I want the *sestari* immediately."

The officers, in various states of undress, jumped at the command.

Lasctakos' quarters reeked of oily smoke. He commanded the *sestari* to sit at the table.

Pielos asked: "Sir, what's this about?"

"We're moving within the hour, gentlemen. The *ikar* has learned that a force of *Kabu* has raided our beloved *Tantorri* subjects. We must expel them."

The *sestari* turned to black Melas, a *Kabu*. "What?" he demanded.

"In what numbers, sir?" Pielos asked.

"That is unclear."

"How many *cohari* are going?"

Lasctakos hesitated. "Just ours."

"Forty-three men? No wonder you're angry, sir."

Lasctakos nodded. "Endios *Elhar* would not even consider that this might be a trap. We must be extremely cautious."

"Go over his head, sir," Luecos suggested.

Lasctakos stared through him. "*Landesknectos* do not go over their superiors' heads, Luecos, unless they wish to lose their own."

"If the *ikar* has dumped it on Endios, he's got to take care of it," Pielos told Luecos. "He'll only be questioned if we fail."

"Bring food and water for a week and extra pila. I've appropriated more runners for improved surveillance. That is all, gentlemen."

The *sestari* sprang to their feet and saluted.

Alone, Lasctakos quickly donned his armor. *Pielos is wrong,* he thought. *I'm not angry, I'm furious. If Endios wants to kill me, he need not waste so many men to do it. This is just the sort of stupidity I'll eradicate when I'm ikar.*

Lasctakos checked his weapons, blew out the lamp and left the room.

The *cohar* marched ten hours before sunrise. Though their destination was south, Lasctakos had struck west to mask his movements. This puzzled the more thoughtful legionaries.

"Sun's rising behind us," Livios told Argos, who marched beside him. "Why we going west?"

"To elude scouts."

"But the *Kabu* don't have horses, so they wouldn't scout this far."

Argos looked confused.

The *cohar* stopped at midday for a meal. Lasctakos limited their intake of food and water. After a short time they hit the trail again, headed south, and marched all day. As the sun sank they dug into a position that commanded a good view of the grassy plain. No fires were allowed.

Inside his tent, Lasctakos briefed the *sestari*.

"We've not seen horsemen today, which may not mean much. Nevertheless, I see no reason to rush to the *Tantorri* aid since any raiders are probably long gone."

"Unless they're sitting on the territory, sir," Daphonos interjected.

Lasctakos smiled. "Then they'll still be there when we arrive. Enyo?"

"Sir?"

"Tell me about that terrain."

"Fairly flat, two rivers nearby. We can make a quick pace."

"Any place for an ambush?"

Enyo rubbed his scarred jaw. "I wasn't in command, sir, so I didn't get the reports. I do remember Boros talking of hills to the west of the village, though."

"Could a force hide there?"

"I never saw them, sir, just heard about them."

"Do you remember what runner scouted those hills?"

"Yes, sir. Kerebos."

"Good. Get him in here."

Livios arrived fully armed, having been on watch.

"At ease," Lasctakos said. "Tell me about the terrain west of our destination."

Livios thought a moment. "Odd, sir. A dried riverbed surrounded by hills. Short grass and no trees."

"Why is it odd?"

"There are mountains in the distance, sir, but these are the only heights for many miles. I remember wondering if the river had created them."

The last comment seemed to amuse Lasctakos. "I suppose a force could hide there?"

"Yes, sir."

Lasctakos looked to his *sestari*. "We'll approach that way. Thank you, Kerebos."

Livios didn't leave. "May I speak, sir?"

"Go ahead."

A few heartbeats passed.

"Speak freely," Lasctakos commanded.

"Might we not aim a few miles west of that target? We can strike the riverbed and follow it, unobserved, to our foes, wherever they may be." Livios thought it a long time until Lasctakos responded.

The *cohar* chuckled. "A fine idea, son. We'll do just that. Dismissed."

BATTLE

The sweating *landesknectos* approached the dried riverbed from the west, moving stealthily across the grass; the sun beat down mercilessly. The terrain had remained flat until within a few miles of the riverbed, but now yielded increasingly graded slopes. Snowcapped mountains lay many miles behind them.

Livios marched beside Lasctakos, proud of the station yet anxious about the approaching battle. *Will I disgrace myself?* he wondered. *How many men look sharp in drills only to die when blades get pulled?* He considered what Daedilos might think of the situation.

Lasctakos stopped at the foot of a hill and signaled a halt. He whispered for the *sestari*. The word was passed and the officers quickly arrived.

"Melas, how many strides since we last saw the forward runner?" Lasctakos asked.

"Eleven hundred thirty nine, sir."

Lasctakos brooded. "Almost a mile. Far too long."

The officers nodded.

"Keep still and quiet," Lasctakos commanded and lay down his greatshield. "Kerebos, follow me."

The two of them ran up the hill and dropped to their bellies on the broad, round peak. They gazed across a shallow valley toward another, taller, bluff. A gentle wind blew across the grass. A short while passed.

"Nothing," Lasctakos muttered. "Not even vermin. Does nothing live around here?"

Now that the *cohar* pointed it out, Livios had seen no animals all day. Even the termite hill he had earlier rested against had been dead.

"Look familiar?" Lasctakos asked.

"Not really, sir. This is not the valley, though. Not nearly steep enough, and the bed was rocky."

"Withdraw."

"Sir!" Livios gasped and pointed east. The runner had returned.

"Quiet," Lasctakos said. "We'll wait for him."

The runner moved at speed and headed straight for them. He had nearly reached the hilltop when Lasctakos said: "Over here. Where have you been?"

The startled runner immediately changed course and collapsed onto the grass beside Lasctakos. It was moments before he could speak. Lanky and dark, he was unfamiliar to Livios. *Must be from First Elhar,* he thought.

"Where have you been?" Lasctakos repeated.

"Sorry, soor, but I was almost founded out!" Livios didn't know the accent, but *Chaconni* was obviously not the man's native tongue.

"Who?"

"*Tantorri* scouts, soor. You tolded us not to let them see us, soor."

The runner's *Chaconni* distressed even uneducated Livios. *Like a not too clever six-year-old's,* he thought.

Lasctakos handed the runner a canteen. "I did indeed. You escaped detection?"

"Yes, soor, but I wuzzed almost atopped of them. They're in the valley just like you thought, three hills over and the *Kabu* are with 'em!"

"Calm down, son, what do you mean?"

Livios felt a spasm of jealousy at "son".

The runner finally caught his breath and spoke slower. "I sneaked up on them, soor, and peeked downed that dried bed. There are *Tantorri* horsemen and a score of *Kabu* war-chiefs, a painted up, eating and drinking. If they fighted each other, I'm a wench!"

"Why do you think they are chieftains?"

The runner snorted. "I *Razkuli* and kilded my first of them before I shaved, soor. They my people's great enemies. Just when I was done counted and ready to run, some cavalry from the north pinned me. I made like grass till they arrived and reported to their bosses." The runner finished off the canteen and frowned. "Sorry, soor, I polished it."

"How many men did you see?"

"I counded one hundred seven *Tantorri*, soor, their horses posted. Then those black fellows too, only twenty, but done up for war." The runner's brown eyes narrowed. "I supposed there could be men in them tents."

"How many teepees?"

"Three, soor."

"Those would be for the commanders," Lasctakos said. "Good work. Rejoin the *cohar*." He turned to Livios and smiled. "Fortunate you brought us from the west, Kerebos."

Livios smiled, too.

"Let's go."

Lasctakos had the runner sketch the enemy position and stared long at the parchment. "This doesn't tell enough," he said at last. "I need to see it myself. Pielos?"

"Sir?"

"You speak their language?"

"I do, sir."

"Come with me. Grab Kerebos, too. Melas, you're in charge while I'm gone. If we have not returned by nightfall head home the way we came in."

"Yes, sir."

The three legionaries crossed the riverbed a mile from the enemy and approached the *Tantorri* from the south, which Livios remembered as the steeper slope. Lasctakos led them to a point that offered an excellent view of the camp. This is what they saw.

The dead river had left a path of gravel behind, but the valley walls were green and steep. A horse might climb the inclines, but with effort. The *Tantorri* were milling about, their horses staked on either side of the camp. Eight ash piles from previous fires suggested the sleeping arrangements. Three teepees, one very large, sat nearest the *landesknectos*. The *Kabu*, resplendent in lion skins and hammered jewelry, rested at the eastern side of the encampment.

"Smells bad," Pielos whispered.

"The horses," Lasctakos replied. "This camp is many days old. I've seen enough. Withdraw."

They returned to the *cohar*. Lasctakos dismissed Livios and summoned the officers. He spread the parchment on the ground and they knelt over it. "This sketch is good," he began. "That runner has talent, his butchery of *Chaconni* notwithstanding. We move into position after nightfall. Luecos?"

"Sir?"

"I'll remain with and direct your unit. We'll crawl in from the east to within fifty yards of the *Kabu* and will lie prone until the attack begins. There is no moon tonight, so it won't be tough to remain unobserved."

"Yes, sir."

"Enyo and Melas, you will work down the southern slope into positions to take the men around these three fires," here Lasctakos pointed to spots on the parchment. "I will assign runners to stampede the horses."

"Yes, sir," the *sestari* said.

"Your men, Pielos, shall come up the riverbed from the west. You should be able to hide quite nicely behind the teepees. Have a runner just behind the largest. As soon as the attack commences he must kill their commander. Actually, assign two for the job."

96

"Very well, sir," the gray-haired Pielos replied.

"The Fifth and Sixth will be on the other slope, opposite Enyo and Melas. A runner will be stationed in high points here, here, here and here. If anyone manages to break out, the runners will dispatch him. We could use one or two prisoners, so spare some after the battle is in hand."

"A question, sir," Daphonos said.

"Certainly."

"Why not kill the horses before the attack? If they scatter, some will wander home and the other *Tantorri* will know something happened."

"Killing a hundred horses isn't easy and we'd be vulnerable while doing it. All things considered, it is better to get the men before or just after they wake. Dead men ride no steeds."

"Now do we miss the other *cohar* Endios should've sent with us," Melas grumbled.

"We must make do," Lasctakos answered. "If our positions are compromised at any point, attack immediately, sticking as closely as possible to my orders. Any questions, gentlemen?"

"No, sir," they answered.

"Good luck, then. If I'm killed the most tenured man leads you home. As I do not intend to die, be prepared to move immediately afterwards."

"Where to, sir?" Luecos asked.

"That depends on our casualties. Brief your men."

*   *   *

The night was very dark but enemy fires aided the legionaries' maneuvers. Lasctakos, Luecos and the First *Sestar* crawled to within fifty feet of the *Kabu* fire. The black men had just finished a meal and were passing bottles between them. Laughter filled the air.

Good, Lasctakos thought. *A belly full of food and some alcohol will put them quickly to sleep. We'll be able to dispatch them and cut off the escape route. How fortunate these barbarians don't understand the benefits of a fortified camp!* He looked at Luecos, who nodded. *Nice portions of intellect and will in this one. He'll make cohar, if he survives long enough.*

Luecos' thoughts ran along similar lines. *Got to follow his orders to the letter,* he told himself. *Have to prove I can obey before he'll let me lead.* Somehow, though, Luecos was content to play Lasctakos' lieutenant. *Only a fool wouldn't learn from him and I'm no fool.* Luecos looked toward the enemy, whose skins glistened in the firelight. He knew some of their language, having pirated their coasts, and frequently heard the word for "woman". *Not a bad idea,* he thought. *Can just imagine what it'd be like so*

97

far from home. Got to visit the slaves when we get back.

Enyo's men had belly-slid down into the valley and now waited a dozen yards from a long line of horses. The posted animals had grown restless with their arrival, but no *Tantorri* had investigated. Enyo looked right toward the *Kabu* and wondered if Lasctakos was in place.

Can't see a damned thing over there, he thought. *Hope they weren't held up.* He peered through the horses' legs at the closest campfire. Most of the enemy was already resting. *Be napping permanently soon.* Enyo suddenly realized he hadn't killed anyone this year. *Has it really been since last summer?* he wondered. *Guess I'm still on number forty-two, but not for long.* He glanced left toward Third *Sestar* and saw Melas looking at him.

Melas thought: *He gets one fire, I get two. No matter, I'll see it done. My men and me are far more experienced.* Melas looked through the horse legs at his targets. The sword hilt itched his palm. *We're going to spill lots of brains tonight.* He hoped to capture a *Tantorri* for Lasctakos, too, not least because he wanted to torture the prisoner once the *cohar* was finished interrogating. He thought enviously of Pielos' boast that he had hamstrung a man with his bare teeth and decided to try it himself.

Pielos' group had entered the valley a half-mile to the west and followed the meandering path to within a few yards of the *Tantorri* teepees. He barely made out Melas' men to the right, but Oenos' *sestar* was completely hidden by the tents. Pielos motioned the runners into position behind the largest shelter.

Lay flat, fools! he wanted to yell; their bare skin made them fairly visible. Finally the runners came to the same conclusion and lay down. Pielos settled in for a long wait. As always before a fight, he found himself thinking of the family he had abandoned so long ago and wondered if any were still alive. *Maybe one day I'll come across my sons during battle?*

Oenos had earned his name because his copious perspiration smelled like wine, as it was doing now, though he never drank. *Kraal* was his drug of choice, especially because it didn't dry him out. Could he risk another leaf before the attack?

Oenos couldn't see Pielos' men through the teepees but was confident they were there. Anyway, he'd attack all by himself, if he had to. Killing folks was fun and easy, lots easier than drills and squads and all the other drudgery he had to deal with. *Too bad I can't "Winnow" myself back into the ranks,* he thought. *Wouldn't have to worry about what my men are doing all the time. Wish someone would've told me it'd be like this.*

Daphonos, on the other hand, loved commanding others; he had already repositioned each of his men and was considering doing so again. *Always more that can be done*, he remembered a previous commander's mantra. *And I'm twice the officer he was, so I should be twice as thorough. With Boros gone it won't be long before Lasctakos recognizes my qualities.*

All the scheming made Daphonos' deformed head hurt worse than usual. Laying face-first down a hill didn't help, either. Might he remove his helmet for a nice rub before Lasctakos signaled the attack? *Best not*, he decided. *Never know when the boss will attack. Unpredictable.* He looked left toward the distant *Kabu* and made out the barest gleam of a helmet. *That's Lasctakos*, he realized. *Keep low, commander, we don't need anything to happen to you!* But he couldn't help fondling "Daphonos Cohar" in his mind. *Bless that Kerebos for killing Boros.*

Livios lay with his chin in the dewy grass, Enyo to his right, Halesas left. *Should've pulled my blade beforehand*, he pondered. *Would be too noisy, now.*

He looked for the best path to the enemy. He trembled some but not with fear, exactly. He certainly did not want to die, but his greatest concern was living up to the Lasctakos' tall expectations. He avoided thinking about killing and tried to convince himself that the *Tantorri* had it coming. Had they not lured the Brotherhood south to ambush them? The treachery made him simmer. *Perhaps the cohar's right and I should just focus on my duty*, he thought. But still he held back. *Why can't it be that easy?* he wondered, irritated. *Maybe because we all have our duty, but not all of us can be right...*

Livios' limbs tingled beneath him but he dared not move. Enyo had given strict orders that no one shifted but by his command and he knew that "no one" meant him in particular. Yet he saw something new in the *sestar's* eyes lately; Enyo's attitude towards him had changed these past weeks. *Even he sees my promise*, he thought proudly. His and Enyo's eyes met. *There's that look again. Watch me, sestar, and I'll show you something in this fight!* He squelched the enthusiasm. *If my legs don't fall asleep.*

Night wore on and the *Tantorri* camp dropped off; the legionaries kept quiet vigil, awaiting Lasctakos' signal. Pale stars shed scant light on the little valley that was silent but for the occasional neighing of horses and the crackling of flames.

The Kabu fires reflected in Lasctakos' eyes as he whispered to Luecos: "Crawl forward slowly. Leave shields here. If an alarm is raised, attack immediately. Pass on these instructions."

Luecos nodded then informed his men.

Lasctakos crawled out ahead, hilt in hand, naked blade trailing. Luecos and the others followed quietly as they might but were sometimes betrayed by the chink of mail. The soft grass swiftly ran out, though, and the sand and pebble riverbed confronted them. The Kabu snored fitfully a dozen yards away, assegai in hand.

Lasctakos was continually astonished by the absence of guards. *Do these fools set no watch?* he wondered contemptuously. *They certainly deserve to die.* He turned toward his subordinates and made the signs for "stand" and "run". Luecos and the others nodded. Lasctakos lifted three fingers, lowered one, then another then the third—then jumped to his feet and charged. Luecos' men followed across the noisy pebbles.

The enemy began to stir.

Lasctakos hit the *Kabu* before they rose. He buried his sword into a sleeping man's back, pulled it, and struck another in the chest before an alarm was raised. A skin-clad *Kabu* leaped to his feet, assegai in hand, and called his mates to stand and fight. Lasctakos, sword high, rushed the man and shaved off his face, which slopped onto the ground. The stricken *Kabu* grabbed his head and crumpled to his knees as shiny blood bubbled through his fingers. Luecos' men dispatched the remaining *Kabu* while Lasctakos measured the situation.

The whole camp was astir but most of the *sestari* were well into the enemy. The *Tantorri* tried to resist but Lasctakos could tell that his men had achieved total surprise and had acted with deadly efficiency, except for Oenos' unit, which was just getting into position. Lasctakos wondered at the delay.

Luecos huffed up, saying, "All enemy dead, sir. Shall we help our comrades?"

Lasctakos pointed toward the closest *Tantorri*. "Take three men and aid Enyo, then push toward Melas!" he said. "Be thorough. Inform Enyo of my orders!"

"First trident with me!" Luecos called then headed for the fray.

Lasctakos gave instructions to the remaining trident. "Spread out and deny escape to those who disengage. Stay low and out of sight. Move!"

"Yes, sir!"

"Nearest runner to me!" Lasctakos cried.

From the north slope, Daphonos saw Lasctakos attack and shouted his men into action. "Here we go! Hit them hard and watch each other's back! Remember, this is a skirmish not a shieldwall!" With that he broke through the agitated horses and headed toward where about twenty *Tantorri* scrambled for arms. "Fan out and pinch them!" he cried. "I have the flank!"

Daphonos was gratified by how smoothly his men complied. The *Tantorri* squinted into the gloom and yelled their word for "legionaries".

They're dinky, Daphonos thought as he ran. His eyes stung from campfire smoke but he saw well enough. A spear suddenly screeched off his shield, then he was among the enemy. For some reason the nearest *Tantor* was facing the other way, so he stabbed the man through the spine. The *Tantor* convulsed liked a gigged frog and was still screaming as Daphonos ripped free his blade and scanned the action. The runners were having problems scattering the horses but his men were mauling the enemy. The *Tantorri*, surprised and unorganized, couldn't coordinate a resistance and even when they landed a blow it turned on the legionaries' superb armor.

But the tribesmen did not lack for courage and refused to break. Unarmored and overmatched by talented professionals, they were very quickly slaughtered. The smell of death mingled with smoke and the stench of horses.

Daphonos leaped over a bedroll and bore down on a man half his size. The dusky spearman snarled and thrust at the *sestar*, who chopped the pike in half. Daphonos jammed his shield under the *Tantor's* chin, lifting him into the air, then slashed his throat as he crumpled onto the ground. Daphonos looked for another victim.

"All dead, sir," a legionary reported, matter-of-factly.

"Good!" Daphonos replied, looking toward Fifth *Sestar*, where a melee was still going on. "Oenos has a fight on his hands! Follow me!"

Oenos waited until Daphonos stormed the riverbed before ordering his attack, which proved a little late. Two runners had arrived and were harassing the *Tantorri* horses, which bawled, bucked and further muddled the already chaotic situation. It took valuable moments for Oenos to pick through the mayhem and when he succeeded he found many *Tantorri* awaiting him; a longhaired chieftain, axe in hand, had ordered dozens of warriors into a spear line. Oenos' men were still arriving when the chief unleashed a charge.

The *Tantorri* wailed war cries and darted toward the *sestar*. Oenos quickly ordered a shield wall. *Why'd I leave the pila on the slope?* he wondered. "Steady!" he shouted above the din. "Take what they got, then bend the flanks into a circle!" *Lasctakos didn't plan it this way*, he thought dismally. He could kick himself for having lost the initiative yet knew deep down that this was how he preferred things, himself as just another sword in the line. *Nothing to be done now but give a good account of myself.*

The *Tantorri* tried to crash the shieldwall but to no avail. Not for nothing were the giant *landesknectos* reckoned Pangaea's greatest infantrymen. The legionaries shrugged off the collision and swiftly killed a dozen of the enemy who shrieked louder than their horses.

Seeing the pile of dead appear as though by magic, the chieftain frantically ordered his men to take the *landesknectos* from the rear. Oenos' squad calmly bent into a seamless circle. The *Tantorri* disengaged and began to throw spears.

"Hell fire, sir!" a legionary complained. "We have to put up with this? Let's charge them!"

"Not yet!" Oenos said. "Daphonos is on his way."

Actually, he had arrived; his unit slammed the enemy at a run, hacking and slaying. *Tantorri* limbs flew into the night to the laughter of *landesknectos*.

"Break out!" Oenos cried, and his men charged in all directions.

Many *Tantorri* were caught between the closing *sestari* and quickly hewed down. Just then Pielos arrived from the west and raised a severed head into the air.

"Look familiar?" he bellowed in *Tantorri*.

"Great Chief! Great Chief!" the tribesmen lamented in their guttural tongue. Weapons drooped.

"Finish them!" Daphonos ordered as he sliced off a head.

*   *   *

Pielos was flat on the riverbed when he heard the *Kabu's* first cries. The runners behind the teepee shot glances at him and he nodded; they pulled their daggers and went around the front. There were sounds of a struggle, an abbreviated shout and then the chopping sound of blade on bone. A knife sliced the back of the teepee and a runner's torso emerged.

"The old bastard got Memnon!" he reported angrily. "Here, sir!" he said and tossed a large head at Pielos.

"Go help with the horses!" Pielos replied as he picked up the head by its bloody hair. To his unit: "Follow!"

"Same color as your hair, sir," a legionary pointed out.

Pielos led his men between two teepees and ordered the dwellings investigated while he surveyed the battlefield. *This won't last long*, he thought.

"Empty, sir!"

"Mine too, sir!" legionaries reported.

"Both tridents support Melas." Pielos ordered. "Contain the enemy."

"Sir!" they replied and raced for the fight.

Pielos walked toward the largest fray. He lifted the head for another look; its mouth was open and the eyes had rolled back. Blood dripped from the jagged neck.

Pielos laughed. "Want to pay your men a visit, chief?" He stopped beside the fire and lifted the head. "Look familiar?" he asked the *Tantorri* and watched the fight drain out of them.

Melas' unit had to account for over thirty tribesmen so he attacked the instant Lasctakos stood and was on the enemy before they could move.

"Awake, awake!" he cried and nearly chopped a prone man in half. His men slew many warriors before Pielos lifted his grisly trophy over the field. A lament rose from the *Tantorri*, who began to scatter just as Enyo's *sestar* arrived.

Enyo was fighting off sleep when something caught the corner of his eye. Melas was attacking! Enyo glanced right, saw Lasctakos' charge and yelled: "At them, men!"

Livios pulled his sword and followed Enyo towards the *Tantorri*, who scurried for weapons. Though his first battle, he felt remarkably calm. The eye slits of his helmet, which always irked him, seemed to melt away and left him with an untrammeled, almost preternatural view of the field. He absorbed the developments as though from on high and immediately picked his path and targets. He sensed, like a shadow in his mind, when Daphonos' men collided with the enemy and somehow even knew that Oenos had arrived late. The lofty knowledge thrilled and frightened him. "It was like opening my eyes for the first time," he would one day report.

It seemed everyone else was moving at half speed, so Livios passed Enyo to get at the enemy. A *Tantor* rose, axe in hand, and Livios took him. He ducked as the howling *Tantor* hurled the tomahawk, which hissed harmlessly overhead, then slammed his sword into the man's stomach so hard that spittle sprayed his face. He kicked the body off his blade.

More *Tantorri* attacked. One grappled Livios' legs and he pommel spiked the man's head. Another charged from the side and Livios hugged him with his shield arm while slashing both hamstrings. When the *Tantor* fell, Livios stabbed him through the heart. Three braves prepared to loose spears and Livios launched himself at their bare shins, bowling them over. The warriors cursed as they toppled. Enyo and the others dispatched the fallen as Livios came out of his roll and hacked an oncoming tribesman's groin. The man yelped and fell. Livios jumped to his feet as Luecos' men hit the scene. The remaining *Tantorri* were rapidly killed.

"Over to Melas!" Enyo commanded.

Livios fell in beside Halesas and loped toward the skirmish. "Fancy work," the older man acknowledged.

Livios didn't hear. *Killed my first in battle*, he pondered. He felt proud, guilty and a little awed by how easy it had been.

It was then that Pielos showed the Great Chief's head and the fight devolved into a rout. "Spread out! Don't let them go!" Enyo roared.

The legionaries did their best to contain the *Tantorri*, who darted in every direction. Enyo chased two toward the remaining horses. A runner charged down the hill to help the *sestar* but overran his mark. Presented with a clear path to the peak, the tribesman bolted up the incline.

Enyo dragged his man off a horse and began stomping his head. "Kerebos, get the other one!" he cried, pointing up the slope.

Livios was already in motion.

The unarmored *Tantor* had a wide lead so Livios ran to the incline, drew his dagger and threw it; the knife sizzled into the darkness and the *Tantor* sprawled forward with a cry. Livios shook his head disbelievingly and told the runner: "Fetch my dagger."

Halesas, Argos and Clios were sharing a canteen when Livios returned. Enyo stood nearby and gazed thoughtfully at the youth.

"By the *ikar*!" Clios muttered. "Where in hell did you learn that?"

"What, throwing the blade?" Livios replied. "Don't know. It just came to me."

Clios offered the canteen. "It's Halesas' broth."

Livios suddenly realized he was thirsty and tired. "Thanks."

The rest of the *sestar* gathered round. They talked about the battle in general and Livios in particular. Even gloomy Clios was full of praise. "Five men in your first action," he said. "Very impressive."

"Never saw anyone roll like that in armor," Argos added.

Livios enjoyed the acclaim until the order came to mutilate the enemy dead. "To see if they're faking," Halesas explained.

"Nah, that's not it, Hals," Clios said. "It's to cripple them in their afterlife, or something. Worst thing you can do to a *Tantor*."

Livios was horrified; he imagined someone dishonoring Daedilos' body. "But we can't do that."

Clios laughed. "Why not? They're already dead."

"And if they weren't we'd kill them," Argos added.

"Come, we must obey," Halesas replied and, as though to illustrate the point, drew his sword and started hacking the corpses.

"Get to it, Kerebos!" Enyo shouted from a distance.

Livios took a halfhearted swipe at the nearest body, which lay face up. His sword seemed to bounce off the flesh. The small corpse made him think of Daedilos. *Oh, father,* he thought in despair, no longer the proud warrior.

He jumped when Halesas touched his shoulder.

"You all right?" the veteran asked.

Livios eyed Halesas' concerned, craggy face then his dripping blade. "Sure."

"We'd best finish."

"Okay."

Livios stared at the sky. "What's today's date?"

"Tenth of Aleph."

Livios grunted. "My birthday," he said sadly. "I'm sixteen."

Melas grunted happily when Enyo's group flanked the *Tantorri*; a flurry of *landesknecta* swordplay leveled the enemy. "Save one or two of them!" he shouted as they mopped up. He and Enyo appraised the littered battlefield as Luecos arrived.

"That wasn't so bad," Luecos said and took off his helmet. He wiped muck from his brow. "Except for the smell."

Melas pulled a pouch of *kraal*, took some, and passed it on. "Any casualties?"

Luecos shook his head.

"No," Enyo replied. "Halesas!"

"Sir?"

"Make sure all the dead stay dead. Spread the word."

"Yes, sir."

The legionaries fanned out and hacked the fallen until blood rained over the riverbed.

Lasctakos approached with a runner.

Melas saw him first, saluted and offered the *kraal*. "Congratulations, sir!"

"Sir!" Enyo and Luecos echoed.

Lasctakos waved off the drug. "Good work, gentlemen. Casualties?"

"None, sir," Luecos reported.

"Did any hostiles escape?"

"Not from us, sir. Kerebos brought down the last one with a thrown knife."

Lasctakos grinned. "The lad has a future." He turned to Enyo. "Wouldn't you say?"

Enyo's wooden smile faded. "Yes, sir."

"Gentlemen, I've a mind to capture some horses. Luecos, see to it. Melas?"

"Sir?"

"Set a six point watch so the *Tantorri* can't return the favor. Post them high. Enyo, gather the officers and come to the big tent."

Lasctakos' staff meeting was soon underway. The officers sat inside the Great Chief's teepee. Three lamps illuminated the proceedings.

Two runners had died but only Oenos had lost a full legionary. Lasctakos was furious at Oenos and blamed him for the static defense that made his men easy targets and Oenos' flimsy excuses only made him angrier. Lasctakos finally silenced Oenos with a raised hand; even the lamps dimmed.

"Oenos *Sestar*," he began in a low voice. "If ever again you are last to commit your men, I will personally dispatch you. Were my orders unclear?"

Oenos stared at the ground. "No, sir."

"Look at me!"

"Sir!"

"What were you thinking? Your trepidation would have spelled defeat against a larger force. A shield circle!" Lasctakos raged. "They could've circumvented you and escaped!"

The other *sestari* inched away. They rarely heard Lasctakos like this and were not enjoying the experience. Lasctakos fell into a glowering silence. "Never fail us again, Oenos," he said at length. "This unit is only as effective as its weakest soldier. I do not like, and won't abide, weak soldiers."

Oenos looked miserably contrite. "I know, sir. I'm sorry."

"You will personally bury your fallen man before we leave, and shall yourself bear his armor. Understood?"

"Yes, *cohar*."

Lasctakos fumed a while then said: "We'll speak no more on this matter. Luecos, how many horses did you capture?"

"Only forty, sir."

"Who has the prisoners?"

"I do," Melas replied. "Roped and ready."

"Good. We leave for home after the men eat." Lasctakos read their surprise. "I know, we've defeated the enemy and have a clear shot at his village but I doubt anyone is there. The *Tantorri* would have moved their womenfolk once they decided to ambush us. Also, I suspect there are more hostiles in the vicinity. One hundred braves seem a very small escort for a Great Chief and don't forget the *Kabu*. Perhaps those officers we killed were merely observers but maybe they were an advance party.

We have neither the men nor the supplies to challenge an entire army in a protracted engagement." Lasctakos let the words settle. "We have prisoners and many valuable animals, and shall withdraw under cover of darkness. The *ikar* must know what has passed here."

"Sir?" Luecos said.

"Yes?"

"There are too many braves here for the village I saw."

Lasctakos looked pleased. "Precisely. Since you mention it, let me say that I think we have a rebellion on our hands."

"Then why slow us down with the beasts? Not going to ride them are we?" Luecos asked hopefully. He had owned many horses and was privately opposed to the *landesknecta* injunction against using them.

"They're potential leverage, for allies or enemies. Any other questions?"

No one spoke.

"You have performed well here, gentlemen. Pass my compliments to your men. We will be marching all night, so replenish yourselves."

COUNSEL

The legionaries moved out under cover of darkness, heading west at double time; runners scouted routes of less than a hundred yards. The *Tantorri* prisoners ran to keep pace with their long-legged captors, who suffered stoically their heavy kits.

There was no moon so Lasctakos navigated by the stars. He had ordered silence so every clank of armor seemed a minor explosion, but his *cohar* devoured the grassy miles in relative noiselessness. Possible ambush scenarios flashed through his mind. He wondered how he would pursue the outfit if he were a cavalryman and if his men could handle triple time. *This will be a desperate, close run thing,* he thought.

Sweat stung Livios' eyes as he squinted into the darkness. *How long have we been moving?* he wondered. *Marched all day, fought, then hit the trail. Hope he's not going to keep us going all night. I'm already winded.*

Lasctakos brought them to a halt after an hour. "Rest standing," he said. "Officers up here." He waited for the *sestari*; Oenos arrived last, panting beneath his burden.

"I've changed my mind," Lasctakos said. "We'll head straight home and will press through the night with all possible speed. Heading west won't confound our enemies. They'll easily mark our trail come daybreak, so a meandering path will only strengthen their chance of finding us."

"Sir?" Melas said, the whites of his eyes his only visible feature.
"Yes?"

"What if we stumble across them in the dark?"

"I've considered that. At night the initiative will be ours."

Daphonos sighed. "Irks me to duck and run from these people, sir."

"I feel the same," Lasctakos said. "Yet my mission is accomplished and I won't loiter while supplies dwindle and we are stalked by unknown numbers. Rest assured, gentlemen, the enemy will pay but we must first alert our lord. Take a short rest but don't let the men drink too much water, and save the *kraal* for later. We won't stop again until dawn. We must make at least another forty miles before then. Melas?"

"Sir?"

"Those prisoners will lag, but keep them moving."

"I'll prod and prick 'em, sir."

"Any questions?" No one spoke. "Good."

"Sir?" Oenos said cautiously.

Lasctakos glared. "What?"

"I can't make another forty miles with this extra weight. It'll burst my heart."

"Then die out here," Lasctakos replied.

"Uh, yes, sir."

"Return to your units."

The brief stop only magnified Livios' fatigue but he snapped to attention with the order to move. Halesas had shared the last dregs of broth, grown cold and pulpy, but Livios was still fagged. *March till dawn?* he thought. *No way I'll make it. Won't survive the next leg.* But he did manage that leg, and the next. He concentrated on counting strides. Men huffed and toiled but only Oenos lagged. Livios wondered how Oenos managed as well as he did. *Bet his eyes are popping out,* he thought. *Hell, mine are.*

Time crept by. The pain in Livios' side, knees and feet was terrible and grew with every breath. He gritted his teeth until his gums bled. He finished counting another thousand steps and started over.

Livios was out on his feet when the order came to halt. Some legionaries stumbled on until Lasctakos grabbed them. The column slowly reformed.

Lasctakos reviewed the exhausted men, a weary smile on his face. "Good march, gentlemen," he said. "I'm proud of you. Luecos, post the horses. Melas, drag those captives over here. All ranks get some sleep while I keep watch."

The *landesknectos* sprawled onto the wet grass with many a groan. Livios nearly retched as he lay down, so tight were his stomach muscles. His entire body burned yet his teeth chattered uncontrollably; his feet felt twice their normal size. He looked through tears at the starry sky.

"Don't remove your boots," Lasctakos ordered someone.

Livios knew not to whom the *cohar* spoke, but couldn't believe anyone had the strength to attempt the feat. His mouth suddenly filled with saliva and he had just enough wits left to turn his head to one side before vomiting. Hot, vile acid flooded his mouth and sprayed from his lips. From the sound of it, others were throwing up, too.

The last thing Livios saw before falling asleep was Lasctakos' faint silhouette as he watched over them. The sight filled Livios with a sense of security. *Like a father,* he thought.

A bleak dawn was at hand when Lasctakos roused the officers—no easy task. Oenos was upright only an instant before fainting. Lasctakos waited until the other *sestari* had cajoled, threatened and kicked the unit into formation before emptying a canteen onto the unconscious man's face. Oenos sputtered and convulsed.

Lasctakos identified a few legionaries. "Get him on his feet."

Oenos eventually swayed before his commander.

"You are relieved," Lasctakos said. "I'm breaking you. The only reason I don't leave you to die out here is because I fear your capture by the enemy."

Oenos slurred something.

"Azimos?"

"Yes, sir," a burly, young legionary replied.

"You have Fifth *Sestar* for the balance of the march. Keep your charges in rank and keep them moving."

"Yes, sir!"

"Bind this extra suit of armor to one of the horses, and do so quickly."

"Yes, sir! Indos, give me a hand."

Lasctakos didn't deign to look at Oenos but said: "Fall in, *legionary.*"

Melas came to Lasctakos' side. "Sir, those prisoners aren't walking anywhere. Their legs have gone purple and have swollen like hog bellies."

"Tie them back to back and throw them over one of the beasts," Lasctakos instantly replied. "Have two men hold the reins. Pass the word that we'll dispense with normal scouting. The runners will march normally, but at hundred yard intervals."

"Yes, sir. Relays it is."

When all was ready Lasctakos addressed the *cohar.* "Gentlemen, the worst is yet before us. We shall march until we get home." He studied them with bloodshot, but alert, eyes; Livios had the distinct impression Lasctakos was looking at him. "I've suffered no less than you and know your pain. It is for your welfare that we must accomplish what no other soldiers in Pangaea would dare. I will lead you home or will die in the attempt. Follow me."

The speech pierced Livios' hazy thoughts like a ray of sunlight through the clouds. Tired though he was, the words sparked something deep within him and he found himself sooner prepared to die marching than to fail Lasctakos. Had not Lasctakos foregone sleep, and Oenos lugged two suits of mail? Livios wondered if Lasctakos had planned Oenos' punishment merely to spur the troops. *So smart,* he thought.

Livios cast his mind elsewhere and ignored the pain in his blistered feet. The sun was well into its ascent as he finished counting his first thousand strides. *Going to be another scorcher*, he thought miserably.

Lasctakos allowed a brief rest at midday. Men sat back to back. Livios drained his canteen's last drops of warm water and looked imploringly at Halesas. "Any for me?" he croaked.

The older legionary surrendered his canteen.

Livios took a short pull. "Thanks, friend."

Halesas' haggard face twisted into something like a smile.

A little way off, the officers were in congress. "How are your men, Azimos?" Lasctakos asked the new *sestar*.

"We'll follow you, sir."

"Sir, the horses aren't going to make it," Luecos said. "They're limping like old nags and there's still a half day's march."

"If my men can do it, they can."

"But the critters haven't had water."

"What's your point, Luecos?" the *cohar* demanded. "Do you think I know nothing of horses? Or men, for that matter?"

Luecos fell silent.

"Am I the only one who saw those *Tantorri* scouts earlier?" Lasctakos railed. "Even as we stand here cavalry is tracking us!"

No one spoke.

"Keep sharp eyes on your troops!" Lasctakos ordered. "Count each man every minute. We approach that time when some might wander off." *And counting them will keep your minds working, too*, he thought.

Melas asked: "Who'll keep an eye on me?"

Lasctakos snorted. "That's my task."

Lasctakos kept them moving throughout the day. Men marched through agony and reached, one by one, that narrow sward of gracious oblivion that lies between life and death. Many didn't even realize when their bowels and bladders surrendered. For his part, Livios would later recall nothing of those dreadful final steps; for all he knew he slept on his feet.

The sun was sinking as Lasctakos dragged his fagged unit through the *ikar*'s gate. All were exhausted beyond thought and some near death, but they held formation. A description of the tortuous trail would earn but one sentence in Lasctakos' "after action" report: "Routine forced march after enemy contact, 120 miles, 1 1/2 days, three periods of rest."

Lasctakos ordered his men to bed and immediately sought his commander, Endios *Elhar*.

*　　　　*　　　　*

Lasctakos knocked on Endios' door.

"Who is it?" came the squeaky reply.

"Lasctakos."

Endios grumbled, "Enter." His spacious chamber was remarkably cluttered for a legionary's.

I'd punish any man who lived like this, Lasctakos thought. The *elhar* looked up from his desk, a glint in his steely eyes. *Will I never get used to that horrid face?*

"You stink, *cohar*," Endios growled. "Why are you stinking up my room?"

Lasctakos fought an urge to attack Endios. "My apologies," he replied thickly. "I've been busy."

"Did I see a salute?"

Lasctakos stifled his response and saluted.

"What do you want?" Endios demanded.

"Again my apologies, but I thought you'd like to hear what your men have seen and achieved."

Endios shook his head; his shapeless, hanging nose wagged like a tail.

"Always drama with you, *cohar*—drama and fancy words. What?"

Lasctakos was finally suffering the full effects of the march. Every muscle in his body burned and his nose ran incessantly. He swooned on his feet. "May I sit?"

"Get on with your report."

Lasctakos considered cutting Endios' throat. "We were ambushed by the *Tantorri* we were sent to defend. The *Kabu* fought by their sides. You don't appear surprised, sir," Lasctakos said in a rush.

Endios' protruding yellow teeth made a ghastly smile. "Go on."

"We eliminated a small force and took prisoners. Didn't you hear what I said about the *Kabu?*"

"If you grow any more insolent, I'll have you racked. Finish your tale."

Lasctakos' fever was getting the better of him; he felt his brain was melting, oozing down his throat and nose. "Endios, we need to talk to the *ikar*. Now!"

The *elhar* rose, fists clenched. Veins bulged from his forehead and down his thin arms. "Who do you think you're snapping at? I've half a mind to have you flayed."

"You've certainly half a mind."

A knock on the door.

"What?" Endios shouted, staring at Lasctakos.

"The *ikar* wants you both, sir."

Endios straightened to his full height, his eyes shone with malice.

112

"Guess you get your wish," he said. "Stick to the facts or this will be the longest night of your life."

"Yes, sir," Lasctakos muttered. "I don't think the *ikar* would believe you tried to sacrifice my entire unit, anyway."

Geraestos *Ikar*'s quarters were in the castle proper and much larger than Endios'. Lasctakos particularly liked the vaulted ceilings which reminded him of his familial estate. Endios and Lasctakos saluted then stood at attention.

Geraestos looked ready for bed. Robed and barefoot, he was seated in a great chair, First *Elhar* Phaetonis standing by his side. Armored, sans helmet, Phaetonis was bald but for the topknot that denoted his unit's status as the *ikar*'s bodyguard. A scar ran from his forehead to his chin, directly over the right eye. Lasctakos had never figured out how Phaetonis had kept his sight.

Geraestos' face was ruddy and flabby though he was muscular enough. His short salt-and-pepper hair stood in sharp contrast to his red features; his alcoholism was well known. He might have been handsome if his chin were stronger. Years earlier he had tried, unsuccessfully, to overturn the Scriptus injunction against beards, hoping to mask the flaw.

Such pettiness sums up his rule, Lasctakos thought, shivering at attention. *He's a failure at most everything*. Lasctakos blamed Geraestos for the Legion's current state. It wasn't that the *ikar* was a poor leader (he was) but he was armed with a disastrous philosophy. The Legion that Lasctakos had joined had been dedicated to constant expansion of power. Geraestos' reign was painted with indifference. As long as tribute from vassals arrived on time, he was content. If an issue arose, he dealt with it, but the outfit would have had fewer problems if he were more proactive.

Doesn't see the big picture, Lasctakos considered. *Every commander must learn that his unit is either getting better or worse, never staying the same. Preserving the status quo only hurts you. If he had flexed more muscle the Tantorri and Kabu would never have challenged him.*

"You look salty," Geraestos told Lasctakos. "When have you last slept?"

"Two days, sir."

"Endios, grab some chairs."

Endios soon returned. Lasctakos eased into the seat.

"Pull closer to the *cohar*," Geraestos groused at Endios. "I don't want to have to keep turning my head."

Phaetonis poured wine and Lasctakos noted how quickly the *ikar* finished a goblet. Geraestos suddenly whirled on Endios, saying, "What

113

the hell were you thinking, sending a single *cohar* into enemy territory during a state of war? Are you *trying* to get my men killed?"

Endios' eyes widened. "Sir?"

Tired as he was, Lasctakos was nevertheless delighted by Geraestos' questions.

"Don't 'sir' me, you ugly bastard. Phaetonis told me all about it."

Endios looked at his smirking peer. "You told me to take care of it, so that's what I did."

Geraestos sneered. "I also remember telling you to be cautious. Is sending forty-three men against a force of unknown size cautious? Damn it, man, there might have been ten thousand speartossers down there! Phaetonis, get me a drink!"

Lasctakos was surprised but thrilled by how nasty things had become and took pleasure in seeing Endios squirm. Geraestos must've been absolutely furious to berate him before a subordinate.

Geraestos folded his arms. "Was that cautious?"

Endios rubbed his forehead. "No, sir."

Geraestos' face reddened so it seemed his nose would burst. "Phaetonis, where's that drink?"

"In your hand, sir."

The *ikar* emptied the goblet then tossed it at Endios; he missed and it rattled across the floor. "If I were wearing boots I'd kick your head in," he said. "Lasctakos, run through what happened. Keep it short. No, don't stand."

"Thank you, sir." Lasctakos gave a brief, sanitized account of the operation. He intentionally avoided mentioning Endios, knowing full well that the *ikar* would seize upon the omission.

"Stop there," Geraestos said. "So your orders were to approach that valley?"

"No, sir," Lasctakos replied. "But neither was I told **not** to close from the west. Had we tackled that encampment head on we most certainly would have fallen into a trap."

Geraestos glared so wickedly at Endios even Lasctakos was afraid. "Continue," the *ikar* said.

Lasctakos finished without further interruption, but Geraestos seemed far more interested in watching Endios, who squirmed as though suffering piles. Lasctakos had been silent a few moments when Geraestos said: "Good work, *cohar*. Don't worry about those renegade *Tantorri* or their dusky allies, either. I'm going to paint the plains with their guts, starting with those nearest to us. To think that they didn't warn me!"

Lasctakos was disturbed by the promise.

"What?" Geraestos demanded.

The "nearest" *Tantorri*, tribes *Luw* and *Riiz*, had been faithful servants for centuries and Lasctakos cringed at the thought of punishing them. *We have enough work ahead of us, already,* he thought.

"What is it?" Geraestos repeated, louder.

Lasctakos crafted a response. "My lord," he started softly. "I hold the *Luw,* and especially the *Riiz,* blameless. They hate the southern tribes more than anyone. We'll need cavalry to deal with the plainsmen."

Geraestos pursed his lips but didn't reply. Lasctakos continued.

"I humbly ask you to not eliminate or alienate such large tribes on the eve of war. Take more hostages, certainly, but exercise moderation. We'll need allies to safeguard our lands when we move against the enemy."

Geraestos looked conflicted, and a bit irate.

Lasctakos bowed his head. "My lord, we must not redouble our efforts, yet lose sight of our objective."

"And what is that objective," Phaetonis asked in a booming voice that filled the room.

"To strengthen the Brotherhood, sir."

Geraestos took many deep breaths. "You're right," he said as though it hurt. "The *Riiz* will be left untouched. We'll eliminate the *Luw* and give some of their lands to the *Riiz.* That'll give them much to think about."

Lasctakos found this proposal equally alarming. "Sir, if I may?"

"You may not. I have spoken." Geraestos turned a chilling gaze on Endios, who looked uncertain as to what expression to wear. "Phaetonis, get my whip."

Phaetonis' eyes widened and he bent to whisper in the *ikar's* ear.

Geraestos raised a hand. "Quite right." He nodded at Lasctakos. "A fine job. You're dismissed."

Lasctakos stifled any objections. He knew he'd get no further this day, besides, he was too tired for further debate. He saluted, turned slowly and walked from the room. Closing the door behind him, he slumped against the wall. The stone was refreshingly cool. He gathered strength, thinking, *Doubt I can make it to my bed.* Cold sweat dampened his face.

"You okay, sir?" a legionary asked.

Lasctakos recognized the man. "Yes, Timothos."

"Let me know if you need anything."

Lasctakos nodded and pushed off the wall. A strange, tingling sensation settled on his right arm; the tips of his fingers went numb. *There's that pulled muscle again,* he thought. He repeatedly made and relaxed a fist as he staggered down the hall.

Phaetonis smiled and handed over the *ikar's* heavy whip. Geraestos' eyes lit up as he took some practice strokes. "Take off your shirt, Endios. I'm going to show you how I feel about brainless officers."

"Yes, sir," the *elhar* replied feebly.

"Another drink, Phaetonis," Geraestos said lightly. "We've a long night ahead of us."

*   *   *

Rough shaking wakened Livios. He half opened encrusted eyes to a dark spoke; someone towered over his pallet.

"Up!" a voice said. "Got to get out of that metal."

Livios managed to sit, but was little help doffing the filthy armor. A wet stench joined the air as his breastplate came off. He was made to lie back down.

"And keep your limbs on the bed or they'll swell!" the voice said. "Get up!" the voice told Clios.

Livios slept deeply for the next twelve hours but his dreams were very evil; he dreamed of being thrown into an open grave with Daedilos' corpse and being burned alive. The flames were as a living thing as they spread over his flesh, pried open his mouth and crawled down his throat…

Lasctakos himself roused them next morning. He looked clean, rested and was fully armed. "On your feet, son," he told Livios. "Formation in the yard."

The unit assembled outside. It was a muggy morning and Livios longed for his bed. Lasctakos walked the line of men and personally inspected each, sending three to the hospital. He stopped before Halesas. "Your knee is very swollen," he said, pointing.

Halesas looked afraid. "It don't hurt, sir."

Lasctakos raised an eyebrow.

"I'll make it, sir. I don't need the hospital."

Lasctakos smiled. "Lay flat and keep it elevated."

"Yes, sir."

"And how is young Kerebos?" Lasctakos asked Livios.

"Tired and hungry, sir."

"I don't doubt it. I understand you had an auspicious first action."

"Auspicious?"

"A thrown dagger. Superb."

Livios smiled. "Seemed the right way to go about it, sir."

Lasctakos finished reviewing the troops. "Eat a hearty breakfast and drink plenty of water, gentlemen," he told them. "Then back to bed. Tomorrow's need shall be sterner. Dismissed."

"Dismissed!" The *sestari* shouted.

116

Melas stayed behind and limped to Lasctakos' side.

"Are you injured?" Lasctakos asked.

"Just blisters. I've been greasing them. Sir?"

"Yes?"

"How 'stern' will tomorrow be?"

Lasctakos rubbed his chin. "No, it didn't sound good, did it? I suspect the *ikar* will move against the *Tantorri* very soon. You know how impatient he is."

"Hell."

"Surprise the men with a brief drill and some stretching this evening. That'll keep them limber."

"Yes, sir, prevent them from locking up. I'll keep them watered, too."

"Yes. Hydrate them often."

"I'll see to it, sir."

Lasctakos clapped him on the back. "And see to yourself. I'll get First *Elhar* officers to help."

"I am wound down, sir," Melas admitted.

"And I. Get some rest."

"Thank you, sir."

That night Geraestos summoned the *elhari* to the War Room. A dispirited Endios arrived last, wearing a loose shirt soaked with blood.

"Be seated," the *ikar* commanded. They took their chairs around the lacquered table, which was inlaid with a map of Pangaea. "Phaetonis, brief them."

"Sir. We've communicated with the *Luw* and have demanded more hostages. A full *elhar* will march to their village, under guise of parley, and will destroy them utterly. No outrage will be spared. All must be reminded that the Legion is not to be trifled with."

Geraestos grinned at Endios. "Thanks for volunteering."

Endios nodded vacantly.

"No slaves or booty are coming home with you," Phaetonis told Endios. "Burn the structures and salt what crops they have. You leave in the morning."

OUTRAGE

When Lasctakos learned of the finalized plan against the *Luw* he decided to risk another visit to the *ikar*. Not wanting to buck the chain of command, he sought out and found Endios at a sharpening wheel in the armory. The smell of steel was in the air.

"A word with you, sir?" Lasctakos asked humbly.

Endios looked up from his sword and his features hardened. "Does evil never sleep? What?"

"Have I your permission to speak with the *ikar*?"

Endios' expression grew savage. "Go!"

Phaetonis stopped Lasctakos at the *ikar*'s door. "Only two reasons that'd make you want to see him. Either you want more rest for your men, or you're foolish enough to try to change his policy." He gave a tight-lipped smile. "You're no fool, *cohar*, are you?"

Lasctakos wondered if Phaetonis supported Geraestos' plan. "I'm unsure, sir."

"It's a large 'no' either way," came the strident reply. "The *ikar* wants blood and will have it. Your unit's going along because Endios will behave better with you around. Do you understand?"

Lasctakos nodded.

"You're a good officer," Phaetonis allowed. "Don't meddle in top politics until you know the whole picture. See to your unit."

Lasctakos saluted. "Sir."

Second *Elhar* departed next morning. Two scores of runners, and pullers for the wagons, brought the force to nearly three hundred. Endios had command and Lasctakos was his second, per Geraestos' orders.

It had been years since Lasctakos had observed Endios in the field and was impressed by his imaginative use of runners; at least Endios wasn't taking the enemy too lightly. *Not with his own skin on the line*, he thought.

118

No order for silence had been issued so men talked and swapped grievances.

"Feeling reamed," the ever-irritable Clios complained. "Could do with another week's sleep."

"Don't I know it," Livios said. "Sorer now than when we got home. How's the knee, Hals?"

Halesas grunted.

"Looks like a melon," Clios said. "Want me to drain it?"

"No." Halesas took some broth and handed the canteen to Livios.

Livios drank and smacked his lips. "I must be ready for promotion, because this stuff's starting to taste good." His eyes fell on Oenos. *Looks a bit shagged*, he thought. *Can't even imagine how he feels after lugging two kits!* "Was that your toughest march ever, Hals?"

The veteran shrugged.

"You're chatty as usual."

The corner of Halesas' mouth bent. "Yep." They marched on a bit. "I'll say this. You're a scary swordsman, kid."

"I hate to admit it, Kerebos," Clios added, "but you sure called down the thunder. Five in your first action! Or was it six?"

Livios was too tired to feel shame. Or elation. "Wasn't anything."

Enyo appeared beside them. "Why don't you all bottle it? You're giving me a headache. And if you don't stop patting the pup's back he'll be too bruised to fight."

"Sir, I heard we aren't going to have to fight, just kill," Clios replied.

"Quiet!"

Livios frowned, thinking, *Don't like the sound of that.*

They made the twenty-mile journey in four hours. Livios was astonished how easy the march became once he got moving. They took position just outside town; Endios spaced them against a possible cavalry attack before summoning Lasctakos and Second *Cohar* Rodios.

Enyo stood tall before his unit. "Pull pila."

Livios grabbed a throwing spear from his backpack and gazed toward the village. The *Luw* seemed far more civilized than their southern brethren. Their little town was clean and well ordered and boasted brick buildings. There was even a small aqueduct running toward the distant river. Three large corrals held hundreds of horses. Golden wheat waved in the distance. A *landesknecta* flag, clenched black gauntlet on a white field, flapped above the largest house. *These people have prospered under the Legion. What did they do to bring us here? They're even flying our standard!*

A mounted delegation approached Endios before long. As the ten

Tantorri drew near, Livios was again impressed. These tribesmen were refined—shaved, sheared and dressed in silk. Gilded daggers hung from their belts and their proud horses were perfectly groomed. He briefly thought of old Herakles and riding with Felix.

The riders stopped some distance from the legionaries. One, who wore a silver fillet on his brow, asked in perfect *Chaconni*: "Permission to approach, lord?"

"Come," Endios replied. Livios was amused that the *elhar* had lowered his thin voice several octaves.

The *Tantor* dismounted and walked to within a few paces of Endios; he bowed deeply. This close, Livios noticed wrinkles on the man's dark face. He was older than he had first appeared. "The *Luw* welcome you, *elhar!*" he said sincerely. "I, Tamul Fez, remain your servant and look forward to your pleasure. I hope you and your officers will dine with me."

Must've been schooled in Korenthis, Livios surmised.

"You know why we're here," Endios replied. "I want your entire population out in the open before I pick hostages." He pointed. "Over there."

Fez's smile was forced. "Of course, lord."

"Be quick."

Fez hurried back to his companions, who drew close to listen to him. Enigmatic gazes were leveled at the legionaries before the *Tantorri* rode away. Very soon hundreds of villagers had gathered on the plain. The legionaries, swords drawn, encircled the coal haired men, women and children. Livios eyed the nearest female, who held a child in her brown arms. Her straight black hair depended to her hips and glistened in the sun. The woman and infant at once turned and stared at him.

Endios stepped into the ring, hands on hips. "Fez, front and center!"

The *Tantor* did as ordered. "Yes, lord?"

Endios looked as though trying to work himself into a fury. "I said the entire town! Where are the rest?"

Fez seemed caught off guard. "This is all, lord."

Endios told Enyo: "Cut the truth from him."

"Sir!" came the eager reply.

Enyo dropped his shield and stomped toward Fez, whose people melted away from him. Enyo leaped with a roar, grabbed the small man's throat and flung him to the ground; Fez's feet sailed overhead. Still grasping the throat, Enyo pulled the *Tantor's* gilded dagger, cut his belt and yanked down his trousers. He slid the shiny dagger between Fez's legs and turned toward Endios as women began to scream.

"Where are they?" Endios demanded in his usual, squeaky voice.

Fez's chest heaved. "I speak the truth!"

"Cut him!" Endios yelled.

Enyo obeyed, splashing blood into the air. The *Tantor* thrashed and loosed a tortured wail. Enyo roughly covered Fez's mouth and laughed as the *Tantor* bucked until the grass was slick with fluid.

The *Luw* were really screaming now; even the corralled horses had taken up the cry. The legionaries shifted in place and poked at those villagers who got too close. Livios clenched his mouth tight.

"Finish him!" Endios cried.

Enyo scrambled onto Fez's chest and dispatched him with four blows from his spiked fist.

"Get back into formation," Endios said.

Enyo smiled like a fiend. He shook blood and flesh from his glove then jumped off the twitching body.

Livios felt a growing panic. *What's happening! What's happening!* he thought frantically. *I can't kill these poor people!* He glanced at the other legionaries, who looked both pleased and anxious. *God,* he thought with a sick feeling. *Am I really one of them?*

Endios drew his sword. "Advance!" he cried. "Kill them all!"

The legionaries slowly collapsed the circle, forcing the screaming *Luw* into a shrinking knot; the frenzied *Tantorri* men, knives in hand, got between the *landesknectos* and their shrieking families. Cries rose over the gathering.

Even if Livios had wanted to comply with the order his body wouldn't have listened. He stood aghast as his comrades stepped to their ugly work. The sword trembled in his hand. The legionaries' blades rose and fell. The screaming got even worse. Livios wanted to run but couldn't.

"Kerebos, stay in formation, damn you!" Enyo raged. "Get up here!"

The screams were fewer, now, the grisly task nearly done. Livios was grateful that his comrades' massive bodies obscured the proceedings, though fountains of blood arched into view.

Enyo ran at Livios. "I said keep up!"

Somehow a bleeding *Luw*, his face a mask of horror, squeezed from the pocket and dashed toward the town. After a few steps, though, he whirled on his heel and returned to the slaughter. Yelling incoherently, he jumped onto Halesas' back and began stabbing wildly. The legionary dropped his sword and grappled the unseen assailant.

Livios was moving. Without thinking, he flattened Enyo and sprang on the *Tantor*. He twice chopped the little man's spine, dropping him broken onto the grass. Halesas fought to remain upright but fell. Livios bent over his comrade, whose dark eyes were half closed.

"Battle over?" the veteran asked.

Livios scanned the field. Black clad giants were picking through the

Luw's remains, laughing as they hoisted body parts. "Yes."

"Breastplate."

Livios was at work on the straps when Clios, Argos and finally Enyo arrived. Clios dropped to a knee and helped. The armor was removed and Halesas pushed onto his side.

Livios breathed relief as he surveyed Halesas' corded back. Only two blows had penetrated the plate and undermail. The oozing cuts were deep and ugly, but non-lethal.

"Get some cloth from his pack," Clios said.

The blood flow was soon stemmed. Halesas' tanned features had paled slightly, but he looked sound. He gently slapped Livios' arm, saying, "Thanks."

"You should braid that hair on your back, Hals," Argos suggested.

They all laughed.

"Next time you freeze up, I'll have your head," Enyo wheezed from behind. "Got me?"

I forgot about him, Livios thought, recalling how easily he had tossed aside the *sestar*. He felt *something* larger than himself taking over as he faced Enyo. "Don't threaten me again, sir," he replied with a quiet contempt that amounted to a dismissal.

Enyo's eyes widened. Incredibly, though, he didn't reply but simply stormed off. The "something" departed as swiftly as it had come.

Why'd I do that? Livios wondered, impressed and scared. *Am I going mad?*

Halesas and the others stared up at him.

New orders came almost immediately. One *sestar* was spared to behead the vanquished but the others were ordered into the village.

"Erase every living thing," Endios commanded.

Livios suddenly felt old. He had no regrets about saving Halesas but hated the idea of murdering noncombatants. The thought that Halesas had killed innocents was quickly pushed from his mind; he had only followed orders, after all.

"Help me up," Halesas said.

Livios obliged. "You should rest."

"It's nothing."

"Come, we've work," Clios said.

It turned out Fez had told the truth. Search as they might, the *landesknectos* found no one. Endios, who initially stood aside, cursed as the reports arrived and eventually inspected the houses himself. He stumbled from Fez's manor wearing a face of utter dejection, complaining, "I thought for sure he was lying. You people shouldn't have killed them all so fast."

Livios took full part in torching the village, sleepwalking through the job. Huge sacks of unrefined salt were requisitioned from the wagons and doled to each unit. Crops, plants, flowers and even the grass was poisoned. A section of aqueduct was toppled and a dozen runners were given tools and commanded to break it up all the way to the river.

Endios summoned Lasctakos, who arrived promptly.

"Sir?"

"What about those horses?" Endios demanded.

"I don't recall the *ikar* addressing that. Perhaps we should appropriate them or, better still, give them to the *Riiz*."

"I knew you'd say that. Well, he didn't say anything about not killing them, either. If I don't, he'll find some way to blame me for not obeying him. You'd like that wouldn't you?"

"Not at all, sir. But if sparing them offends him you can always rectify the situation. How would you bring them back from the dead?"

Endios glared. "Just kill them and be done with it."

Lasctakos looked pained. "Yes, sir." He turned to the unit. "Dispatch the beasts! Take out one corral at a time! Move!"

The horses put up a better fight than had their masters and injured a few legionaries, one seriously. It was some time before the equine screams ceased. Desensitized and sickened by the slaughter, Livios sat on an animal corpse and shook sweat from his eyes. The shrieks still echoed in his ears. *What am I doing with these men?* he wondered.

The *elhar* was called to formation before the burning houses. The armor grew unbearably hot. Oily smoke churned into the sky.

For the first time Livios noted that *Luw* heads had been staked around the village. Luckily, the eyes were facing away. Despite his abhorrence, he searched for and found the longhaired woman. *Where's her child?* he thought. The entire scene so thoroughly depressed him he would have happily been dead. He never successfully described his feelings of that moment but years later said: "It was like being all cut up inside. I hated myself, my comrades, and even God, because I knew He was looking down but wasn't stopping us. It wasn't grief exactly, but it was the first time I felt completely alone."

Rodios *Cohar* pulled Endios aside and Lasctakos took the opportunity to review his men. He walked slowly among them and inquired about injuries or thanked them, but without specifically mentioning the battle. Livios read Lasctakos' grave dissatisfaction and marveled that it didn't interfere with his work.

Lasctakos made his way through Enyo's unit. "Show me your back," he told Halesas. "That's not so bad, Hals. Not your worst scar in my service."

Halesas smiled.

123

"We'll get you home in no time."

"Yes, sir."

Lasctakos moved on to Livios and stared long at the youth, as though he didn't recognize him.

"It's Kerebos, sir," Livios said desperately. "Kerebos."

Lasctakos squeezed his arm. "I know, son. It's just that you look so different."

Livios swallowed the lump in his throat. *I believe it*, he thought sadly.

"Sir?" Halesas said.

"Yes?"

"I think it best if the pup heads the Trident."

What! Livios thought.

Lasctakos looked peeved. "If you're that ill, ride the wagon home."

"No, sir, I mean permanent. It's best for the unit. He's a wicked swordsman."

Lasctakos' amber eyes betrayed nothing. "Have you talked with your *sestar*?"

"No, sir. Just came to me."

"Sir, Kerebos froze up today," Enyo interrupted. "He needs lashes, not a new assignment."

"Won't happen again, sir," Halesas said confidently.

Enyo broke rank and stomped over to the injured legionary. "Maybe you need some lashes, too? Did I tell you to remove your plate?"

Lasctakos told Enyo. "You broke parade."

Enyo looked abashed. "I'm sorry, sir."

"Let me ask this," Lasctakos replied. "Which man is better?"

Enyo grew more embarrassed. "The boy, I suppose. When he isn't freezing."

"And giving him a Trident strengthens us?"

"I guess," Enyo muttered.

"No guessing, *sestar*."

Enyo simmered. "Yes, sir, it would."

"Then place your recommendation when we get back and it'll be honored." Lasctakos looked for Endios, who had dragged Rodios out of earshot. The lanky *elhar* was gesturing angrily toward one of the corrals. "Excuse me, gentlemen," Lasctakos said.

Livios' emotions had fractured further. He was pleased by Halesas' faith in him, and by Enyo's humiliation, but doubted his ability to command. "Sir!" he squeaked.

Lasctakos stopped and turned. "Yes?"

Livios didn't know how to respond. He was suddenly very self conscious.

"Come over here," Lasctakos replied gently. "What's wrong?"

Flustered, Livios stood mute. He wished he had kept quiet.

Lasctakos was patient. "You still fear your place in this world? In our legion?"

That seemed to Livios a good place to start. He nodded.

"Understandable. It gets easier though, I promise. Not unlike exercising a muscle, you know. One fights through the pain to realize growth. Even in this mass, here," Lasctakos concluded and tapped Livios' forehead.

Livios admired how Lasctakos always put things into perspective but lamented that the words lost strength after the *cohar* stopped speaking. *Soon I'll be back in ranks and won't know anything again*, he thought. "I see, sir," he mumbled.

"No, you don't. I fear you're more upset than I thought."

"Yes, sir."

"Look at me." Lasctakos' expression was severe. "How do you feel about what has passed in this village?"

Livios felt choked by emotion and clenched his fists in frustration. "I . . . I . . .," he stammered.

"Yes?"

"Why'd we have to kill these people?" he said passionately. "Even the babies? It wasn't right!"

Lasctakos nodded thoughtfully. "You wish you'd missed this assignment?"

"Ha!" Livios barked. "Yes, I do!"

"Then you would have sacrificed your friend, Halesas."

The irony silenced Livios.

"Son, how do you think *I* feel about this mission?"

Livios shrugged.

"I hate it," Lasctakos replied. "It is a waste, a stupid waste of time and resources. And life."

Livios was comforted and looked up hopefully. "Really, sir?"

"Really. I tried through *proper* channels to stop it."

"I didn't know."

"Why would you? It's not your job to know, son. It's your task to obey. Perhaps I could have 'fell ill' and stayed home, but that wouldn't have been right. Tell me, whom would you rather have had in command of my *cohar*?"

"No one, sir," Livios answered truthfully.

"Nor is there any I would have entrusted my men to, son. I might have slid from beneath Endios to please my own senses, but it would have been wrong. Perhaps you might have found some way to buck orders to placate your conscience—though it's not easy for a plain soldier—but that would have been equally corrupt. And Halesas would now be dead."

Livios was stymied; he couldn't find the chink in Lasctakos' defense and at this point didn't know what he'd do if he did. *But Hals is alive, and I'm glad of that*, he thought.

"I remember my first taste of war," Lasctakos went on wistfully. "I disliked it. I even thought of leaving, it disgusted me so. Eventually I saw the larger picture."

"What picture, sir?"

Lasctakos smiled. "That war distills virtue through challenge and self-examination. Since it does that for individuals, why not for states? Or the world? Would you agree that Pangaea needs virtue?"

"Yes, sir. And justice."

Lasctakos chuckled. "Well said. Justice comes later. First we must endure the pain that shapes those robust muscles I talked of earlier. Of course it's not simple and requires a great, collective effort. Mine. Yours. In the final analysis, son, I suppose that is the plainest reason I can offer as to why we should be here when it offends our more tender sensibilities."

Livios saw wisdom in the argument, or thought he did. He felt better. Hope even. "I think I understand, sir."

"I'm sure you do and that will make your path easier, though not easy. Our effort is not welcomed by the weak or sodden, you can well guess, and if we fail those we would've freed shall judge us *without* justice and with our deaths all our trials and heroism, our very communion of spirit, will perish. Even our memory will be spurned. We must not fail."

"I never realized it was such a mighty thing," Livios said.

Lasctakos lifted a finger. "It is, son, and you're part of it now. You can't elect to leave either; other men will no longer accept you. You can, however, improve this vision and bring it to fruition. You feel you've suffered bad commands? Maybe you have. So climb high enough that you give the orders."

Though his head swam, Livios felt completely turned around and longed for some orders to follow. He worshipped Lasctakos more than ever and the thought was oddly comforting. *At least when I ask of him, he answers.*

"Actually, you've taken your first step today," Lasctakos pointed out. "Your promotion to Trident bequeaths authority, given you by a man whose life you saved because you followed orders to come here." Lasctakos chuckled. "Is it chance, Kerebos? I think not."

The last comment brought Livios back to earth somewhat. If it wasn't chance, what could have caused the day's destruction? *God?* he wondered, even while he dismissed the idea. *If that's the case, things are even worse than I thought.*

KASSANDRA

Enyo drilled his *sestar* mercilessly for the next week, keeping them long after other units had knocked off. By the second day it had become clear he was pushing the men solely to trip up Livios, who now headed a Trident, but the boy wouldn't crack. Enyo was loud and brutal in his criticism but Livios absorbed it and was eventually snapping orders to *both* Tridents, and more effectively than Enyo.

Lasctakos saw the youth at work and offered glowing words of praise.

"Is there anything you don't do well, son?" he asked with a laugh.

The comment was the last straw for Enyo, who brought the drills to an abrupt halt after Lasctakos left. "Get out of my face!" he yelled at the unit, disgusted.

Livios was undressing by his bed when Luecos approached.

"How you holding up?" the *Boru* asked. "Enyo still cracking your stones?"

Livios wanted to complain but there were others around. "Fine," he responded. "Why the robe?"

Luecos fingered his finery. "Going to see the women. You should come with me. Actually, you are coming with me, so clean up. Will do you good."

Livios remembered Vara and the day he had killed his father. *So long ago,* he thought. "No thanks."

"Not an offer, but an order. Got your future to look out for and can't have you muck it by looking like you don't care for women. Too much of that in the Legion already."

Livios looked away. "I'm just not interested, Krynn."

Luecos' expression softened. "You got them deep hurts, huh?"

Livios looked at the floor and nodded quickly.

"Come along anyway. Doesn't mean you have to do anything."

Livios cleared his throat. "Let me bathe first."

The female slaves' quarters, otherwise called "the barn", were located across from Sixth spoke. It was a two-storied structure with a thatched roof and tiny windows. Different shades of masonry suggested it had been enlarged a number of times. A small brick well rested near the front door beside a sagging, pathetic excuse for a pine.

The only tree inside the walls and it won't last much longer, Livios thought.

Luecos nearly kicked the door off its hinges. "I'm here!" he shouted.

The door almost hit Fifth *Elhar* Naphios, who was on the way out. "Be careful, idiot," he said. Livios thought he had the look of a man whom had lost a lot of blood.

Luecos saluted crisply. "Sorry, sir. Mother raised a fool."

Naphios' vacant eyes narrowed further. "Luecos? Got that money you owe me?"

"Pardon, sir, but you lost every hand."

Naphios smiled. "Ahh." He headed out the door.

Luecos and Livios stepped into the common room and were immediately assaulted by the stench of smoke, sweat and liquor. The *Tantor* rug appeared the only thing of value in the seedy, ill-lit chamber.

"Nice," Livios muttered.

"Be civil, lad. The Mother has Geraestos' favor."

Five stupefied legionaries, in various states of undress, lounged on low divans. A dormant fireplace, soot trails leading to the ceiling, sat below a mantle that held many bottles of wine. Cobwebs haunted the high corners. A counter barred entrance to a dark hall.

Someone should clean those windows to get more light in here, Livios thought.

Luecos slapped the counter hard. "Let's see the old sow!" he cried jovially.

There were distant rumblings, like the sound of moving furniture, then a huge, ugly woman filled the hall. She waddled toward them, bumping a wall with each step. Her face was deeply lined with scars and age and was caked thick with rouge. Already depressed, Livios wilted further. He had never seen such hideousness and would've run but Luecos grabbed his belt.

"*Ikar!*" Livios whispered. "Her beard's thicker than mine!"

The woman reached the counter a few moments after her perfume and squatted onto a whining stool. Her enormous head leaned towards them. A slight smile shaped her thick lips and her single eyebrow lifted as she studied Livios.

"Bringing new meat, Blondie?" she asked Luecos in a voice at once smooth, sultry and melodious. Livios was astonished the painted cow had managed such an utterance.

"Yes. Nice tent you're wearing, Mother."

Mother hugged her striped dress. "Thanks so much."

Again Livios was amazed. *Guess that's how she earned her keep; men would line up just to hear her talk.*

Mother's thick, bumpy arms disappeared beneath the counter and returned with a leather-bound book. She opened the log. "Sorry, Blondie, but Sazha is with someone. Want to wait?"

Luecos shrugged. "Not really. Anyone will do. More importantly, can you take care of Kerebos, here?"

"What!" Livios cried.

Mother smiled. "Who do you have in mind?"

"Young and pretty. Kassandra, maybe."

Mother shook her head. "I'm sorry, but her regular will be by tonight."

Luecos jerked a finger at Livios. "Look at him. He won't take long."

"He does look nervous," Mother agreed. "Maybe I should do the honors myself?"

Livios' stomach did a flip.

Luecos laughed. "I think he just wet himself. No thanks, Mother, Kassandra will do."

Mother looked undecided. "I hate to irritate the officers, you know. Especially the mean ones."

Luecos dropped a small bag of *kraal* onto the grimy counter. "Give him some of that, old nasty, or keep it for yourself. Now no more griping."

One of Mother's paws covered the bag. "I like you, Blondie," she said. "You're a real man. And you never beat the girls, either. Maybe you'll show pity on an old woman sometime?"

Livios groaned.

"Who knows?" Luecos said without ardor.

Mother summoned a twig of a girl in pigtails. She nodded at Livios. "Take Blackie up to Kassandra."

"Yes, ma'am."

Livios gazed at Luecos then followed the girl down the hall. She led him to a narrow staircase and they ascended to the second floor. Livios was surprised there was another flight; the house had not looked that large from the outside.

"There's a third floor?" he asked.

The girl ushered him past numerous doors; he heard muffled sounds; again that feeling of loneliness. *What am I doing here?* "What's your name, girl?" he asked.

129

"No one can touch me till next year," she responded in a world-weary tone that belied her age.

"That's not what I asked."

She stopped at the last door and stared as though to ascertain if he were dangerous, which amused him because he could have lifted her with two fingers. "I'm Livia," she said.

Like mine, he thought. "A nice name. This is Kassandra's?"

"Yeah, but she doesn't like nobody."

"Thanks."

Alone, Livios contemplated going back downstairs. Was it too late for mess? He looked about, wondering, *Does it have to be so dark in here?* He knocked on the thin door, which rattled with the stroke. No answer. He struck again, harder. Nothing. "Anyone home?" he called.

"Yes," came the unenthusiastic response.

Livios looked inside. The chamber was small and plain but immaculate. There was a thin straw mattress on a low, stout frame. The single window was clear of grime; sunlight streamed in. Kassandra lay on the bed, face down. He couldn't see her face but her short blonde hair curled forward before reaching her chin. She was tiny, not much more than five feet, but very full figured. A thin gold chain encircled each ankle and a tiny, blue tattoo graced the small of her back.

Livios swallowed hard. "Why didn't you answer the door?" he demanded in his "drill voice".

"If you've business here you know what to do, and if you don't know what to do, you've no business here," she monotoned.

Livios now discerned her *Boru* accent. *She really is something*, he thought, and imagined with horror what she must have endured at the hands of his comrades.

"You interested or what?" she asked. "If not, I'll get some sleep."

Livios liked her looks, but there was something else he found even more attractive. *She's not afraid*, he finally determined. He gathered his courage. "I've no interest in you."

"Good. Why not lose yourself?"

Now Livios was angry, and a little hurt. He meant no harm so at least she could be civil. "Don't speak to me like that. Turn over. Now."

Kassandra tensed visibly, but didn't further goad him.

No smart remark, he thought, oddly disappointed. "Turn over!"

She rolled lithely onto her elbows and Livios stopped breathing; she was easily the loveliest creature he had seen or imagined. Her face was exquisite, with high cheekbones, a strong chin and a pinch a nose, pierced by a gold stud. Her naturally red lips wore a sullen pout; her large eyes deep blue beneath dark eyebrows. Locks of pale blonde hair framed her face and curled to her mouth from either side.

130

"Happy?" she asked.

Livios looked at Kassandra's eyes, but certainly not into them. Meeting, their gazes failed even the slightest connection, as though she was blind or wreathed in fog.

She smirked. "You done?"

"How old are you?"

Kassandra's lips parted then closed. "Seventeen."

Only seventeen, Livios pondered. *She looks older.* He gazed a long time at her, unwilling and unable to look away. His battle prowess and even the esteem of Lasctakos seemed a small matter beside her beauty.

Kassandra eased flat and crossed her arms. She looked beyond him.

"You're going to hit me, aren't you?"

A great weariness settled upon Livios. Could she really so mistake him? "You said you're tired."

Kassandra shrugged.

"Sleep then," he said softly.

"I can't sleep with a man in the room."

He laughed without mirth. "Don't worry, I'm only sixteen."

Kassandra raised her head into rays of sunlight.

"You've nothing to fear," Livios assured. He grabbed the dagger Luecos had told him to leave behind and tossed it, still sheathed, onto the bed. "Here, take this."

Kassandra looked hard at the blade.

"You can keep it," Livios said. He sat with his back against the door and admired her.

Kassandra deliberately looked him full in the face and for the first time Livios knew that she *saw* him; the fog had lifted. A spasm of happiness passed through him but then he read the anguish in her eyes. *Like looking into a mirror*, he later realized.

Enyo had had a bad day.

The fiasco with Kerebos was unbearable enough but, even worse, he had kept the unit so long he missed dinner. His favorite meal (pork), too. Nor had it helped that Lasctakos had cornered him for a few moments.

"You're working them hard, aren't you?" the *cohar* had asked.

"Just trying to keep them sharp, sir. Working in the new Trident."

"Good, good. They can never be too sharp."

"Yes, sir."

Lasctakos laughed. "I suppose you've abandoned the being-kind-to-Kerebos tactic?"

Enyo had merely stared in reply.

131

Now, barred from mess hall, he wandered the empty spoke in search of infractions. There were none. How had his men cleaned up so quickly and neatly? Dejected, he returned to his room and found it unbearably hot. This time of year the sun baked his side of the spoke nearly all day. Rest was impossible. *If only Kerebos had cracked I'd be eating right now,* he thought angrily. *Have to find some way to kill him before long.* He envisioned the Winnowing with an inward groan. When had he decided to get tougher on Kerebos and had it been wise to assume he could trip up the boy? It hurt to admit Kerebos might already be able to best him and that the "might" was becoming more of a certainty with each day. The sudden realization that extra drills were speeding Kerebos' development spilled on him like a bucket of ice. *And here I am helping him!* he thought. *But I'm not dead yet.* He would find a solution. He had to.

Rising from the damp bed, Enyo swung the full weight of his foot onto a splinter. Growling, he grabbed his heel and grappled the fat splinter. Blood seeped onto the polished floor. He was beside himself with frustration and longed to work it off; he'd go early to the Barn. *And if anyone's with her, I'll beat them both,* he decided. He grabbed a robe and tightened it around his waist. *Kassandra is going to have a rough night.*

Luecos awaited Livios at Mother's counter, amusing her with sleight-of-hand tricks he had learned in his travels.

"Do that again!" she insisted.

Luecos raised the coin. "Free trials are over. Put up some money."

"Stop! You know I don't have any."

"Like hell," he replied. "You're the only free woman in the house."

Mother wrestled an ingot from her finger. "Even up?"

Luecos smiled. "Fair enough." He dropped the coin into his right palm then showed his empty left. "Ready?"

She nodded.

His hands moved slowly round each other. Now and then the coin peeked through his fingers, first on one hand then the other. At last he extended both fists. "Go ahead, beautiful."

Mother eyed his right. Luecos *had* favored that one, in fact the gold was there, but she should've concluded it was in the left. She started for his right but changed her mind and tapped the left, saying, "Here."

Luecos smiled and opened up. "Sorry." He showed the coin. "Again?"

Mother sighed. "Blondie, I can't believe you'd steal from me."

The *sestar* nodded at the men dozing on the couches. "Can't have them thinking I've gone soft."

"Blondie!"

Enyo burst through the front door, his face a scowl.

132

Luecos tossed Mother the ring. "Remember what you see here," he said.

Enyo stomped up to the counter and demanded Kassandra.

"I'm sorry, *sestar*, but she's with someone," Mother replied. "You're early."

"Don't give me that, cow, or I'll slice out what's left of your womb."

Mother's mouth dropped and she inched away from the counter.

"Mind your manners, brother," Luecos suggested.

Enyo refused to look at him. "Keep your mouth shut," he warned. To Mother: "Who's she with?" The answer was too slow in coming so he grabbed the ledger. "Who's 'Blackie'? Is Melas here?"

Mother looked to Luecos. "What did the boy go by?"

Luecos grinned. "Kerebos."

Mother moved further away. Enyo closed the ledger and turned toward his peer, murder in his eyes. "Kerebos?" he hissed.

Luecos' smile widened. "He'll be down soon. It's been a while."

Enyo's head drooped in defeat. He suddenly twisted at the hip and delivered a right cross that smote Luecos full in the mouth and snapped his head back into the wall. Enyo closed and throttled Luecos, driving him to his knees. Luecos repeatedly punched Enyo in the groin. Enyo threw his head back and howled but refused to loosen his grip; he slowly sank to his knees as Luecos' face turned beet red.

Mother screamed with impressive force. The sleeping legionaries woke and sprang onto the maddened officers.

Phaetonis *Elhar* arrived in full gear. "Stop!" he cried, muscling into the brawl. "Stop!!"

The *sestari* released each other and dropped to the floor. Luecos tried to rise but Enyo curled into a ball.

"By the *ikar*, Yaz and Mitera!" Phaetonis raged. "It'd be bad enough seeing this out of recruits, but officers?! What's this about, you monkeys? And make it good!"

Luecos spat a tooth at Enyo and wheezed: "His fault, sir."

Enyo merely groaned.

Phaetonis looked at Mother. "Well?"

Mother reported what had happened but watered down Luecos' involvement. Phaetonis listened with growing agitation as he stared down at Enyo. "So someone kissed your girly?" he mocked. "You're lucky I don't finish what your playmate there started!" He whirled on Luecos, who had leaned against the wall. "And you! I'm sure you've some hand in this!" Phaetonis rubbed his chin in intense thought. He pointed at Enyo. "Thirty days bread and water. Sixty days cleaning my kit. I'll think of more later. If your performance drops off, I'll have you Judged!" He

133

kicked Enyo in the stomach. "Get out!" He motioned to the skulking legionaries. "Drag him out of here!"

"I'll be back," Enyo warned as the door shut.

Phaetonis stuck a finger in Luecos' face, which had begun to swell. "You're lucky I'm in a hurry, fool. Come by my quarters tomorrow for sentencing."

"Yes, sir," Luecos replied and saluted weakly.

Phaetonis stomped from the house, his topknot swinging from his helmet.

Luecos winked at Mother. "Perfect."

Livios woke with a start to find he was sitting against a door. It took a moment to get his bearings. Light from the window told him hours had passed. He was surprised he had slept so deeply. Kassandra lay beneath a gossamer sheet and he admired her fair face, pained even in slumber. Not wishing to disturb her, he rose quietly, but the floor creaked. Kassandra's eyes flew open.

Livios raised his hands. "I'm just leaving."

The coverlet rose and fell with her breaths.

Livios felt for his dagger then remembered. *Rash of me*, he thought. He would have to procure another as soon as possible. "Goodbye, Kassandra," he said. A thought struck him. "I'm sorry, but I didn't bring money."

Kassandra look fiercely at him."You think I'd do this of my own accord? I'm a slave!"

"Sorry." Livios made his way downstairs. Mother and Luecos were gone, but he hardly noticed. When might he see Kassandra again?

Enyo woke his men early, to much grumbling. They stood at attention beside their beds and exchanged anxious glances, though Livios knew the proceedings somehow concerned him. The rest of the spoke began to stir.

"Eyes front!" Enyo shouted. He, at least, looked fully awake.

Melas arrived in a loincloth and demanded: "What is this?"

"Good, you can help. Surprise inspection."

"At this time?" Melas scoffed. "You out of your mind?"

Enyo approached Halesas. "Produce your sword, dagger and belt," he ordered.

Halesas pulled the requested items off his T rack. The *sestar* didn't even draw them but moved immediately to Clios.

Livios trembled where he stood. How had Enyo found out? His panic grew at Lasctakos and Endios' approach. He tried to recall the penalty for a missing weapon and prayed it wasn't death.

Enyo soon reached Livios. "Let's have them, boy," he said in a satisfied tone.

Livios produced his sword and his belt but made no pretense of searching for the dagger.

"Where's your sticker?" Enyo asked.

Livios read disgust on Lasctakos' face and knew the *cohar* wouldn't intercede. *I'm all alone, this time.* "Lost it, sir. Last night."

Enyo smiled maliciously then turned to his superiors and saluted.

"Sorry to wake you. This man is without full kit, having misplaced a weapon."

Lasctakos shook his head but Endios appeared almost jolly, wringing his bony hands in anticipation. "And what's the Scriptus say about that, *sestar?*" he squeaked.

"The lash, sir. Twenty strokes."

"He'll get them for breakfast." Endios turned to Lasctakos, "Assemble them outside after roll."

"Yes, sir."

Enyo made a point of ordering Halesas to bind and escort Livios into the yard. It was a fine morning, though Livios hardly noticed. He crossed the sward to the whipping post under the eyes of the entire *elhar*. A sense of unreality colored his slow march. Had he really been asleep just moments ago? *I can't believe this!* he thought and envisioned Kassandra. *Why'd I give her my blade?*

Halesas drew Livios' bonds through the hook atop the bloodstained post and pulled him onto his tiptoes. The pole scratched Livios' belly. Halesas reached for his canteen, saying, "Take some broth."

Enyo stalked up. "Stop! Back in ranks!"

Livios looked balefully at his friend.

Enyo marched over to Endios and saluted. "Sir, I consulted Desia's writings regarding this," he said. "As we're in a state of war the sentence should be death, not merely a flogging. I'm ready to exact that punishment."

Endios considered the proposal.

"Sir, Enyo is mistaken," Lasctakos broke in. "He's read but translations of the Lawgiver's work. Desia's exact quote was not 'state of war' but the Old *Chaconni* phrase '*ostilis terminos*'—'imminent battle'. While we may be at war, it is preposterous to say that hostilities are at hand."

Endios frowned. "Why so?"

"Has the guard been increased?" Lasctakos reasoned. "Are we on battle footing, or in enemy territory? When is the last time our castle was besieged?"

Endios massaged his ridiculous trunk of a nose.

"But sir," Enyo began again.

Lasctakos shot him a fiery glance. "If you pursue this course, I'll insist upon a formal inquiry by the *ikar*, as is my right. And if indeed battle was imminent he might wish to know how Kerebos' commander was preparing for that fight. I daresay the *ikar's* justice might well embrace a negligent officer or two."

Endios blanched at 'ikar'. "Tell the whipmaster to double the strokes," he told Enyo.

"Sir, I request the privilege of executing sentence with my own hands."

"A noble but outdated custom," Endios replied. "Have you the skill?"

"I'm good with a whip, sir."

"So be it," Endios decided loudly. "And hurry, I'm getting hungry." He eyed Lasctakos. "Any more objections?"

Lasctakos shook his head.

Enyo approached the post. "Toss me that lash," he commanded the whipmaster and caught it in midair. The whip was a nasty one, twenty feet long. It was two inches thick at the braided handle but tapered to a mere whisker, a tiny bent nail at the tip. Enyo snaked the catgut as he closed with Livios. He ground an iron-shod boot onto Livios' toes and tightened the ropes. Livios focused on the bite marks in the wood. *How'd that blood get there?* he wondered.

"The Brand called for twenty but I got you double," Enyo intimated. "With luck I'll cripple you. Remember Boros before you pass out."

"Commence," Endios said.

Livios had every intention of not reacting, but the thought disappeared with the first stroke. There was a hissing sound then red heat ripped his back. He jerked at the pain, though the sting began to dissipate almost immediately. It was impossible to tell where the whip had landed; it seemed to have covered his entire torso.

"One!" Enyo cried.

Livios placed his forehead against the splintery post and ground his teeth. SSSSSST! The snap rang in his ears.

"Two!"

The pain was worse and lingered longer this time. It had not quite become bearable when the next fell.

"Three!"

Livios bucked but couldn't move much. He savagely bit the wood.

"Four!"

"Ahhh!" he growled, slobbering. Salty tears filled his mouth. He couldn't feel it but blood was seeping into his loincloth.

"Five!"

"Six!"

"Seven!"

By ten Livios felt all the skin had been lifted from his back. Each blow rattled his skeleton; he had the distinct impression that Enyo was flogging bare bones. Incredibly, the pain had grown worse. He tasted blood in his mouth and guessed he had bit his tongue. *God, make it stop!* he thought.

At twenty Livios dangled from the post as would a corpse, his hands purpled with the weight. *Half way there, half way!* his mind screamed. How could he bear any more? It seemed Enyo had been at work for hours. The next lash flecked blood onto the post.

A semi-conscious Livios barely felt number thirty. It was as though Enyo whipped him through a coat.

"Stop concentrating there!" Lasctakos warned. "Don't ruin his shoulder!"

Livios was too far gone to hear. He had the sensation that cold wind was rushing over his body. Enyo moved right and deliberately delivered the last stroke onto the virgin flesh of his face. Livios groaned.

Lasctakos snatched the slick whip from Enyo's hand. "I want you and Luecos in quarters!" he growled. "Halesas, Clios, carry him to the hospital. Gently."

Livios didn't realize when they lifted him but enjoyed the sensation of floating. The last thing he heard was, "What a mess! I think he's dead!"

The thought didn't bother him.

CONSPIRACY

Lasctakos kept Enyo and Luecos at attention for most of the day. The two *Boru* knew better than to complain and fixed their blue gazes over the seated *cohar*. Lasctakos finished reading. He studied his subordinates and slowly shook his head. "At ease."

The *sestari* relaxed with sighs of relief.

Lasctakos crossed his arms. "I finally feel I can speak without smacking your thick heads together," he started. "You have greatly disappointed me. During my tenure I've rarely heard of officers behaving in so juvenile a fashion. Small wonder we find ourselves in our current state if men of example cannot refrain from public displays of stupidity." He shook his head again. "Fighting over a wench."

Lasctakos stared hard at Enyo. "Help me understand how you determined that this girl was your personal property and how you were justified in striking another officer in the presence of subordinates and, very much worse, a civilian?" He had remained calm but the words had a visible effect on Enyo, who grew progressively shamefaced.

"I've no excuse, sir."

"Oh, excellent," Lasctakos sneered. "And for that I am forced to watch you nearly kill the best prospect in the brotherhood? *Over a woman!*"

Enyo swallowed.

"If Kerebos dies, you're next," Lasctakos threatened. "If he is crippled, you shall be too."

"Yes, sir."

"Do you understand!"

"Yes, sir!"

Lasctakos poured water before turning to Luecos, whose bruised jaw had swelled nicely. "I've no doubt of your involvement in this, thief, and hold you also in blame. Some friend of the boy's you are, leading him into such trouble. I won't speculate upon your intentions but will warn you that all such infighting stops here and now. This Legion doesn't exist for your personal amusement. Remember that or you'll find a purple chin and a broken tooth small concern compared to what follows."

"Yes, sir!" Luecos shouted.

Lasctakos looked from face to face. "You men have given me a sour stomach. Don't further irritate me or I'll personally drop you into the river. Out!"

They saluted and turned.

"Wait a moment, Luecos," Lasctakos said as Enyo scurried from the room.

"Sir?"

Lasctakos looked satisfied. "Good enough, so far, but I want him out of the picture. Will Kerebos take him come the Winnowing?"

Luecos gave a lopsided smile. "I guarantee it, sir."

Livios had faded in and out of consciousness during the first two days of convalescence; it had taken him some time to realize he was in the hospital. All he had seen during his initial, fevered state were flames and even now ghostly fire danced on the periphery of sight, but he was slowly feeling better. His back still burned and, despite salve and dressing, blood tickled his sides but at least the inferno had retreated. He had not the strength to scan the common room but stared at the cot beside him. The hospital sounded empty.

Disjointed images of Enyo, Luecos, the whipping post, Daedilos, Felix and especially Kassandra swam before Livios' eyes. He wondered if she knew his plight but suspected that if so, she didn't care. The thought smarted.

The report of boots on stone preceded Luecos' arrival. He sat onto the next bed. "Hello."

Livios grunted and even that hurt.

"You look bad," Luecos said as though surprised. He dragged a finger from beneath his eye to the middle of his cheek. "How'd he hit you there? Gonna be an ugly one."

"Don't know."

Luecos stood and peeled back Livios' crusty dressing. He whistled. "Looks like chewed beef."

"I'm burning," Livios croaked.

Luecos whistled at a slave. "Get some water!" The liquid arrived quickly and he helped Livios drink, though most spilled down his chin. *What a fever*, Luecos thought. *Hope he doesn't get infected.*

"Thanks," Livios sputtered weakly.

"Anything you need?"

"No."

Luecos' expression changed. "Why'd you give that tramp your dagger, fool?"

"Stupid."

"You're right about that. Enyo could've demanded your execution for 'inciting insurrection' had he thought of it, and he would've won. Or maybe he knew that'd finish her, too?"

Livios easily imagined that having held Kassandra, Enyo would not risk losing her. He remembered when she noted him for the first time and his pain eased. "I don't blame him there."

Luecos' brow knit. "Hey. Hey!" he said and smacked Livios' head. "Don't go soft on him. He tried to kill you, remember?"

I do, Livios thought. *I don't blame him for that, either. She's worth killing for.*

"Anyway, she'll heal, so don't worry about her," Luecos added. "Won't be working for a while, though, I'd bet."

Livios' guts constricted. "Why?"

"Why do you think? Enyo beat the hell out of her. Heard it's an ugly sight."

Livios struggled off the mattress but Luecos grabbed his scruff and pushed him flat. "Stay down! What good would you do, anyway?"

Livios pictured the little blonde after a roughing by Enyo and felt sick. "How bad?"

"Bad, I'd guess. I haven't seen her."

"Can you?"

Luecos groaned. "Look, boy, don't go daft like Enyo. You don't own her, he don't either. Get over it."

"Please," Livios asked desperately as fresh blood oozed over his ribs. He sneezed suddenly and the pain was such that he nearly blacked out. "Uhhhh."

"By the *ikar*," Luecos muttered. "All right. I have to cop that dagger from her anyway."

Livios closed his eyes, completely drained.

Luecos gently patted Livios' head. "Have to go, brother. I'll make sure your mates get in to see you," he promised and stood. "Seeing her again won't make her life any easier. Enyo got the word about starting more trouble, but there's lots he might still do and get away with."

Livios nodded. He felt helpless.

"The only way you're going to shield her is by climbing up the ranks," Luecos finished as he walked away.

Livios' eyes opened.

*   *   *

Livios healed quickly.

The warden looked over the wounds and said: "Seen men take ten lashes and not knit so nicely. You're fortunate. Another day or two and you'll be back with your unit."

"How long till I drill?"

"A week at least. You'll be on restricted duty until then."

Livios didn't bother to explain how he longed to practice. He doubted the warden would understand, anyway. He was discharged the following morning and made a dizzy path back to the spoke in time for morning mess.

Halesas smiled when he saw Livios; the rest of the *sestar*, indeed most of the barrack, gathered to welcome him. Men praised how he had suffered the lash and there seemed a general sentiment that Enyo had used regulations to exact a personal vengeance.

Luecos elbowed through the thinning crowd. "You don't look too off," he said loudly and handed Livios a dagger. "Found it out where your commander was running you into the ground. Looks like the hitch snapped."

Men expressed sympathy.

Clios stretched and yawned. "Kill the armorer."

Luecos leaned close and whispered: "She never gave it up, no matter how he beat her. Guess she likes you."

Livios was elated by the news. "Then how'd he find out?"

"Another wench ratted."

Livios grabbed Luecos' hand and shook it vigorously. "Thanks!"

Livios found the mess hall louder than usual. *Because I've been gone so long?* He got a steaming breakfast of eggs and grains then located his table. An inviting sense of community swept him as he scanned the familiar faces. Even Clios looked happy.

Enyo's spot was empty, which disappointed Livios. *I want him to see my full anger*, he thought. *He must know that he's a dead man.* Livios imagined a battered Kassandra and his sight tinged red. For the first time he felt he might actually enjoy killing someone; he couldn't wait till Winnowing. *I'll chop him into pieces.*

A steady flow of well-wishers followed the meal. Lasctakos came over even as Enyo finally appeared. Legionaries made way for the revered *cohar*.

Lasctakos was all smiles. "How do you feel, son?"

"Fine, sir," It was true. Luecos' news regarding Kassandra had assured that.

"No drilling until the surgeon gives the go-ahead."

Livios frowned. "I'm getting out of shape, sir."

"That's an order."

"Yes, sir."

"Let me know if you need anything." Lasctakos strode off without a glance at Enyo.

But Livios looked at the *sestar*. "Hello, sir," he spat, feeling the whip on his skin.

Enyo tried to stare him down. "Hope you got smarter while on your holiday."

Livios smiled grimly. "I did, sir. Made some big decisions."

Enyo fingered a knife, his blue eyes inscrutable. "Don't think too hard."

"I don't need to. My path's clear now. I'm just looking forward to the Winnowing."

Conversation ground to a halt. Enyo's pale face darkened.

He's afraid, Livios thought. "Enjoy your bread, sir." He deposited his empty metal plate into the washbarrel on his way out.

Enyo was soon sitting by himself but he felt eyes from the other tables. He moped in silence. *Winnowing's three months away and they're already writing me off*, he thought, dejected. *And why not, at the rate he's improving? Not a chance in ten that I'll be able to take him come fall. Even if I arrange an 'accident' Lasctakos will kill me.* He eyed the untouched loaf on his plate. *All I ever wanted was to be a soldier. How'd I get into this situation?* For the first time in his life Enyo contemplated running from trouble. The notion was short-lived. *I'd only find myself back here with the Judges, and without honor.*

Melas punched Enyo's shoulder. "Keep sagging and your chin will dent the table."

Enyo was grateful for the attention. "Hello."

"You're not dead yet and you're still a *landesknecta*. Get outside and practice."

Enyo nodded. *He's right. And if I must die, I'll take Kerebos with me.* Vitality crept back into his limbs. *And Kassandra.*

*   *   *

Livios had barely reached his bed when Luecos grabbed him, saying, "Come on." They went out into the yard.

"What's wrong?" Livios asked, confused.

Luecos' eyes blazed. "What you doing, talking to him like that?"

"Who?"

"Don't give me that! Enyo! I thought he was going to fill his pants!"

Livios lifted a palm. "I'm going to kill him, but by the Brand. No one will complain."

Luecos resumed walking. "Let's take a stroll."

Livios caught up. "I don't see how you're upset. Don't you want me to take him?"

"Of course I do. But don't announce it for everyone to hear."

"Why not? He knows."

Luecos sighed. "I keep forgetting your age. Look, *thinking* something and *knowing* something aren't the same. Your public bulletin forces him to admit you're coming for him. Now he has months to prepare and gain allies, or dust you off before the Winnowing. You should've laid low, lulled him to sleep. Smiled to his face and kissed his ass."

Livios felt his friend was overreacting. "I don't see it that way. He had to know I wanted him after that whipping."

"Maybe, but you could've gone the other way with it. Many men become geldings after a good beating. You might have apologized for touching his special girl, or blamed me, or something. There are dozens of paths we could've walked."

No way I'd manage that acting job, Livios mulled. *'Your thoughts are on your face,'* Daedilos used to say. But Luecos was right about learning to scheme. "Too late now."

Luecos nodded thoughtfully. "Keep your eyes open."

"I'll do that." Livios suddenly grabbed the other's arm. "What's really bothering you?"

Luecos looked shocked then pleased. "You'll be a formidable officer."

"Well?"

Luecos waited a long moment. "All right. Look, Lasctakos likes you, everyone knows that, and he wouldn't mind getting rid of Enyo, either. But his liking you will dry up if you make a habit of insulting superiors. The *cohar* requires order or he'd just kill the idiots he doesn't want. You've been valuable but won't stay so if you start doing the very crap he's trying to stop."

Finally he speaks his heart, Livios thought, annoyed. He avoided the obvious next question by answering it. "You were afraid to tell me this because you didn't want my head to swell. Or was it that Lasctakos has chained my future to yours?"

Luecos smiled. "Amazing. Why don't I just hang myself and you take my unit? Did I say officer? I meant *'ikar'*!"

Livios liked that Luecos was orbiting him for once, a scary yet thrilling epiphany. "I won't lose the secret. Next time, though, trust me with your thoughts."

Luecos chewed his lip then slowly offered a hand. "I will," he promised.

143

They shook. By chance or design, their jaunt had brought them near the barn. Livios' gaze was drawn to the ugly structure. *Never knew it was here before, now I can't escape it,* he thought.

"Don't," Luecos warned. "Not yet. Let the dust settle."

Restricted duty left Livios little to do, so Lasctakos used him as an aide. He ran errands, maintained arms and stood countless hours beside the officer observing drills. None of this was very much like work and left him time to think of Kassandra. She even crept into his dreams of fire, which appalled him. *Certainly an evil omen,* he thought glumly. *She doesn't deserve to burn, too.*

Only once did the possibility that she wasn't thinking of him cross Livios' mind but he buried the thought and concentrated on the current "wall and Trident" drill. He found that being unable to participate bred an ache curiously similar to the longing for Kassandra. He had never before been forced to examine his desire for fighting and the conclusions were frightening. *I do like it,* he admitted. After a while he even realized a beauty in the violence, the way the strokes wove together. The defeat of one side suddenly ended the fight, which seemed a shame.

Livios stirred from his trance. *The things I think of sometimes!*

"What's in your mind, son?" Lasctakos asked.

"I'm sorry, sir, I was wandering."

Lasctakos seemed amused. "Where?"

The drill resumed. Livios again studied the combatants but this time saw the rough edges. One man was too slow, another was off balance; nobody looked very good. It was clumsy, sweaty, ugly work, like when they had murdered the *Tantorri.* The image of the slain mother and child passed before his eyes and he was repulsed that he had found the fighting attractive. "I was thinking how good I am at this business, sir," he said quietly. "Better then any of them."

Lasctakos crossed his arms. "Good. You're correct, of course." He viewed the skirmish. "I remember the day I noted that in myself. It was as though a light had illuminated my future. The *Hsia* call it 'the shining path'."

They stood shoulder to shoulder. Livios considered the officer's words, enjoying a contentment unlike one he had ever known.

"There's a light upon you also, son," Lasctakos said with conviction. "Bright enough for all to see. You'll be *ikar* one day."

Livios could not shake the mother and child from his mind. He didn't want to ruin the moment but said: "I don't think so, sir."

"Why on Pangaea not?"

Livios regretted his statement. "Because if I were commanding nothing would've happened to the *Luw,*" he replied bitterly. "I don't have the stomach for such things, chopping children in half."

The *cohar* shook his head. "Open your eyes, son. Even unpleasant actions often support a greater good. Haven't we discussed this?"

"Sir, even *you* didn't like it."

"True, but what should I have done? Argued with Endios in plain view and betrayed my oath? Perhaps I might have found a way to spare the town but that would only have spawned more problems. I ask you: why can the *ikar* lord the Legion undisputed?"

Livios wished he were back in ranks, Enyo notwithstanding. "Because he is *ikar*."

"That is incidental. He holds sway over fifteen hundred souls because *they think he can*. If even one link cracks, the entire chain weakens. Too many compromised links leave it a useless pile. Should I bring down the entire house to satisfy myself?" Lasctakos asked. "What message would that send my men, particularly you?"

"But what if the house is rotten?" Livios answered.

Lasctakos stared at him. "Will I be *elhar* come Winnowing Day?"

Livios pondered the question. "You're too good not to."

"Will my policies then govern one sixth of the brotherhood?"

"Yes, sir."

"And this is preferable to the random silliness we've endured?"

Livios searched in vain for a counterpoint. He nodded.

"Had I disobeyed my commander in the *Luw* incident I would never get a chance at Endios, I assure you. I would've tasted death and rightly so. Many of you men would have suffered by my removal, too. Suffered with your lives. Surely you see that?"

"Yes, sir."

"Then in this case the end has certainly justified the means. I was unwilling to sacrifice you or myself for the sake of strangers—strangers who would gladly see us dead, I might add. This is preferable to the alternative. An unpalatable action eliminated a far worse one."

Livios watched the drill. His ears burned, as they always did when he lost an argument. "But if the house is rotten, why save it?" he persisted.

Lasctakos looked cross. "Don't forget how you got here, outlaw. You can't have the Legion as you would choose, 'this far and no farther.' Obviously it has been of some benefit to you."

Livios shrank inside. "I can't forget," he said weakly.

"Good. Then let's examine the world from your view. Do you really wish to disband the Brotherhood and disperse it throughout the lands? Who would control these men? As long as the nations pay us we leave them be and sometimes we're even beneficent. I suggest you think about that."

Livios had lost the will to argue further. In fact, he grudgingly found himself believing the logic. "All the rotten eggs in one basket," he muttered.

Lasctakos was smiling again. "You are yet a pup, despite your size. You think tactically but not strategically; I must see to your education. Can you read?"

"Not well, sir."

"Magos will teach you letters."

"Who's he?"

"A friend of mine from Sixth *Elhar*, gravely wounded last year. He will never fight again but the *ikar* keeps him on as a chamberlain. He has knowledge of many things."

Livios felt terror at the prospect of an education. "I'll do my best, sir."

"I know you will, son."

A moment passed.

"Sir, what kind of Legion will you make?"

Lasctakos' smile faded. "One day I'll show you."

*   *   *

Dusk.

Livios had meant to avoid the barn, had even promised Luecos, but here he was at its door, the knob slick in his hand. *What if she's not happy to see me?* he anguished but grew instantly angry with himself. *You're a landesknecta! Don't fear a slave!* He went inside. The interior was as remembered but felt altogether different. He slapped the counter hard, as Luecos had done. *What am I going to tell him?*

Mother emerged from a distant chamber and began her heavy shuffle towards him. "Hullo, Blackie," she said and eased onto the stool. "What can I do for you? I don't see you in the book."

Livios noticed a bruise beneath her make up. He simply said: "Kassandra."

The big woman shook her head. "It'll be days until she's up to it. He saw to that."

Livios' jaw clenched. "Enyo?"

Mother fingered her bruise and nodded.

"I have to see her."

Mother snorted. "You and half of your mates. She doesn't want anyone coming up."

Livios touched her thick fingers. "Please."

She shook her head. "Not a good idea, Blackie. The *ikar* won't take any more mischief."

146

"I'm not here for trouble, ma'am."

Mother sat back and regarded him with exhausted eyes. She slowly broke into a smile untouched by avarice or politics. For a fleeting moment she recalled what it was to be young. "Don't give me those brown eyes," she said. "But they are lovely."

Livios laid gold on the counter. "Please," he repeated. "She'll be safer with me here."

Mother pushed the coin back and cut him off before he could complain. "All right. Go up."

Livios grinned but quickly composed himself.

Mother's expression had changed. "You'll kill him in the fall?"

Livios remembered the whipping post. "Yes."

He found Kassandra's room and debated going in. *Why am I so nervous?* he wondered. He didn't want to disturb her but couldn't bring himself to leave, so he quietly opened the door.

A single candle lit the small chamber. Kassandra lay curled in a ball, her face in shadow. Livios leaned to get a look of her but it was too dark. He walked to the candle and picked it up.

Kassandra's entire face was bruised and her left eye horribly swollen. Her lips were bloated and discolored and both nostrils were black with dried blood. Someone had stitched the gash above her cheekbone. Closer inspection revealed bloodstains on the mattress and the wall.

Livios wanted to cry. How could any man have savaged her like this? His thoughts blackened and he again felt he would enjoy killing Enyo. *I won't just kill him, he'll suffer!* he thought. He was planning tortures when Kassandra opened her good eye, which filled with tears.

Livios pounded his thighs in anger. "I'll kill him," he grated. "He's dead. Dead!"

Kassandra blew mucous from her nose. "Go," she croaked, barely to be heard.

"I'll protect you!" Livios shouted.

Kassandra snorted derisively. "Go!"

Livios lowered his head in torment; his breast churned with anger, hatred and disappointment. He suddenly punched the wall and stormed from the room.

SUMMER

A week passed.

Livios tried his best to forget Kassandra but was haunted by the image of her lacerated face. He then attempted to convince himself that he hated her for spurning him but that failed, too. He grew so morose Luecos broached the subject.

Luecos put his foot on Livios' bed and said: "Look, you're even starting to depress me. Pull your head from your ass and concentrate on swordplay. You're fighting Enyo at the end of the summer, you know."

Livios gazed at the ceiling. "Sorry."

"Don't be, just wake up. Desia, even Geraestos' favorite bottle is laughing at you."

"I mean I'm sorry for lying to you about seeing her."

"We'll, forget it. I knew you would, anyway."

"Have you ever been in love?"

Luecos looked terrified. "Striped stinking sharks! What you trying to do, give me a stroke? Damn!" He walked away.

It was Lex Desia's birthday, the Legion's only holiday, and the Brotherhood was at leisure. Livios looked at the dozing Halesas, thinking, *He's been doing a lot of that lately.* "Hals, let's get some practice in."

A grunt.

"Come on," Livios pressed.

"Sleeping."

"Not anymore."

"Urgh. No armor?"

"All right."

Halesas rolled over and sat. "Give me a bit."

They eventually reached the yard, which was empty but for a few slaves. Most of the Legion was resting, eating or beyond the walls.

Halesas yawned. "I'm coming down with something."

Livios pulled his sword and loosened up. "You do look like you lost weight."

Halesas drank some broth, dropped his canteen and charged. Livios caught Halesas' sword arm, kicked his left shin and dropped the seasoned warrior onto the grass.

"You surprised me!" Livios admitted.

"Help me up."

They went at it until Halesas ran out of steam; his blows rapidly lost quickness and weight.

Livios laughed. "Come now! You're not as old as that!"

A grayfaced Halesas bent over and gulped air. "Going back in," he gagged.

Livios decided upon a walk around the castle but knew where the trip would end. He made a slow path to the barn, entered and found scores of legionaries waiting; he hoped Kassandra was still out of commission. Clios beckoned from a corner, so Livios went over.

"Let's get some drill in," Livios said. "You can't want to stand around here."

"Nah, I'm next."

"With all these officers around? Good luck."

Clios avoided eye contact. "There's hardly any for the third floor."

"*What?*" Livios asked in disbelief. The barn's third floor was notorious for unspeakable perversions.

Clios shrugged. "It all feels the same."

Livios pushed through the crowd and out the door. He went back to the spoke and lay down. Halesas was snoring. *I should've put my name in the log*, he thought. *God knows what pig is with her.*

Melas and Enyo passed him on their way out into the yard.

The following month was very hot and dry. The yard turned brown and dusty, making drills unpleasant. Halesas fell out of formation on a number of occasions.

Livios mastered small unit tactics to the point that Enyo stopped criticizing; they even reached a sort of truce. Both men seemed resolved to settle their issues on Winnowing Day, though Livios never stopped watching his step. Enyo grew progressively less interested with the unit's training and more concerned with his own.

Livios spent a lot of time studying with Magos, an urbane, older legionary. Livios displayed a universal aptitude but was particularly talented with languages. One day Lasctakos summoned him to his room.

"Reporting as ordered, sir."

Lasctakos looked up from his work. "Magos has naught but praise for you, son."

"Thank you, sir."

"I'm proud of you, too. I feared your performance on the field would suffer but it hasn't, rather the opposite."

Livios grinned.

"How is your Trident, by the way?"

Livios thought of Halesas and sobered. "Not bad, sir. A few kinks but I'll work them out."

Lasctakos lifted a small, leather-bound book and handed it to Livios. "That is a history of Pangaea. It is very ancient."

Livios examined the book. He had never before held one. "There sure are a lot of words."

"I give it to you."

"Thank you, sir."

"Pay more heed to mathematics," Lasctakos said and returned to his writing. "You'll need it one day. Dismissed."

Livios returned to the barn a few days later. *Just don't think about who visited her,* he warned himself but it was no use.

Mother was surprised to see him, saying, "I figured you'd given up."

Livios shook his head. "Is she up and about?"

"No, Blackie. Hasn't been all this time. Turned out she had three broken ribs. Couldn't support any activity. *Ikar* knows they tried."

Livios was pleased and distressed. "I'm going up."

Mother shrugged. "She'll only ask you to leave."

Kassandra was lying on her back. She wore a short blue gown. The bottoms of her feet stood in stark contrast to the brown mattress.

She looked at him and said: "Please leave."

Livios reached into his pocket and withdrew a bundled cloth. He placed it on the bed. "It's chicken."

"Please go."

"I will," he replied but sat on the bed. "After I get a look at you."

Her eyes glistened as she turned away.

Stomach aflutter, he said: "Kassandra?"

"What?"

"I'm over here."

"Will you go?"

"Afterwards."

She slowly faced him. The yellow remains of bruises remained and there was a pink scar on her cheek. It had been a good stitch job, though. *She's still beautiful,* Livios thought. He wanted badly to tell her that.

"Pity he didn't ruin me for good," she said. "Then maybe you vultures would leave me alone."

Livios nodded unhappily and stood. He touched the whip scar on

150

his face. "They almost match. I suppose we took them for each other."

She looked away.

Livios regretted coming. Seeing her brought no joy. *Why does she hate me? I've done nothing to her.* He cleared his throat. "Of course you did it for yourself, but thanks for not telling Enyo about the dagger."

No reply.

On his way out, Livios resolved to never return.

Drills were over when Clios motioned Livios aside. Livios shook off Clios' hand. "What?"

"Something's wrong with Hals. He looks like a scarecrow over there."

Livios gazed at the veteran, who lay atop his shield. His skin was ashen. "I know. He's been sick for a while."

"He's more than sick. I knocked into him earlier and he rattled like a bag of sticks, and he's been living on broth."

His arms do look skinny, Livios thought.

"If Enyo spent half the time worrying about us that he did about Winnowing he would've cut out Hals by now."

Livios nodded reluctantly. He had successfully covered Halesas' ineffectiveness, telling himself his friend would bounce back, but now something had to be done. "I'll take care of it," he said and walked over to Halesas. "How you feeling, old bull?"

Halesas' eyes shot open. He choked out an apology and tried to rise.

"It's all right," Livios said and knelt. "Rest a moment."

Halesas' expression moved from embarrassment to fear. "I've been trying to keep up."

Livios felt racked with pity. "I know," he replied quietly. He grabbed Halesas and lifted him off the ground, finding him much lighter than expected.

"What you doing?" Halesas asked, struggling feebly.

"You need some rest," Livios said. He had tried to sound chipper but his voice betrayed him.

Halesas coughed. "No hospital. Please."

"It'll be all right," Livios promised.

But it wasn't. The surgeon inspected Halesas and proclaimed: "He should already be dead. Has the wasting sickness."

Livios' heart sank. "Are you sure?"

"Yes."

Legionaries visited Halesas daily but none as often as Livios, who was astonished by his friend's speedy degeneration. There was soon nothing left of the once sturdy soldier but skin and bone. Halesas and

Kassandra's situations dismayed Livios worse than had anything since Daedilos' death.

One day Halesas refused food and the surgeon summoned Livios. "Maybe he'll listen to you," the healer said.

"You must eat, Hals," Livios pleaded. "How you going to make officer?"

Halesas wheezed in reply. Blue veins bulged beneath his loose skin. The death smell lingered over him.

Livios told the surgeon: "Leave us." He sat beside Halesas, face in hand.

"You're filling out," Halesas managed.

"So they say."

Time passed and Halesas' breaths grew labored. "You," he whispered.

Livios leaned close. "Yes?"

"Too good. For." Halesas' mouth stayed open.

"Four? Hals? Wake up!"

"Us."

Livios connected the words and tried to laugh on a tight throat.

"Enyo," was Halesas' last word.

Livios closed his friend's eyes then covered his own. He wanted to find Lasctakos or Kassandra but would they even care? He tried to formulate a prayer for Halesas but stopped because he couldn't find the words. *No matter*, he thought angrily. *He won't listen anyway.* He wiped his face and jumped to his feet as the surgeon ambled into sight. "Take care of him!" he barked and stormed from the hospital.

*   *   *

The weather turned unbearably hot and stayed that way. Every day thunderheads formed over the hazy plains but rain refused to come. The legion's hoofed animals grazed ever farther afield. There were rumors of water rationing and drills were moved to dusk. The stone castle grew so stifling that sleep became difficult.

Livios tossed and turned on his clinging covers, cursing the heat. He flipped the straw pillow. He cursed the night, too. Was it any cooler in the barn? *Damn!* he thought and sat upright, glancing at Halesas' old bed. The unit's newest member, a twenty-year-old redhead named Talos, appeared fast asleep. Livios disliked Talos' servile manner and hated that he had taken Halesas' place in the Trident. *Not a bad fighter*, he thought, *but such a bootlicker.*

152

Talos suddenly stirred. "What's wrong, Kerebos, huh? Need some water?"

Livios could barely remain civil. Talos' anxiousness to please seemed almost a perversion. *Why can't he just be quiet and do his job?* He wondered. "Go to sleep."

"Okay, boss."

Livios snatched his robe and went into the starlit yard, which was as warm as the spoke. Dead grass stabbed his naked feet. Two legionaries approached.

"Who's that? Kerebos?" It was Luecos.

"Right."

"Like an oven in there," Luecos complained. "Nights like this I wish I was back home."

The croak of a shark disturbed the night. "Even they don't like it," Livios said.

"I guess swimming is out."

"Think it's cooler in the wood buildings?"

"The 'wood buildings'?" Luecos laughed. "Don't you mean the doll house?"

"Maybe."

Luecos' teeth showed in the pale light. "At least we wouldn't mind the sweating. Only officers can visit this late, though. Good thing I'm an officer. Let's go."

Mother was closing shop but Luecos charmed her. "I know, it's late," he began. "Say, you're even prettier with your hair messed. I might dance with you first."

Mother cackled. "Oh, Blondie!"

Luecos spun the ledger around. "Hmmm. There's got to be a kitten who wants to play."

"They're sleeping."

"What's this in my pocket? Look, money with your name on it!"

"Blondie, of course it's not too late for you."

Luecos pecked her hairy cheek. "You're a queen. Set up these boys, also." He started down the hall. "I'll be thinking of you up there."

"I want to hear it!" she replied.

"Don't worry, you will."

Mother's eyes were shining. "What a lovely scamp your friend is, Blackie. Doubt he's told a truth in his whole life." Her expression slowly changed. "I know who you want but she's busy."

Livios recalled Luecos' words: *Only officers can visit this late.* "**Him?**" he asked in a low voice.

Mother nodded an apology.

Livios suppressed a curse and ground out: "I'll be back tomorrow."

Kassandra's day began before dawn, when Livia shouted everyone awake. She forced herself from bed to work chores in the morning gloom. She drew water from the fountain out front and carried it to various rooms in the barn. The kitchen alone required ten buckets. Next came laundry duty, which she fumbled through, half-asleep. Cocks were crowing before she stumbled into the common room for breakfast. A dozen girls shared two tables. There was no talking. There rarely was. Kassandra finished her whey and returned to her chamber.

The room reeked but that was to be expected. She had had six visitors last night and the final, Enyo, had stayed for hours. Her skin crawled. *How I hate him,* she thought. Even now she felt his big, filthy hands. *I hate them all, but he's the worst. May they all burn in Lindl.* Enyo had joked about thrashing her and promised to do it again if she ever displeased him. "And I want to know every time Kerebos visits," he said while choking her.

Kassandra sank onto the bed and closed her eyes. She wanted to cry but couldn't; she felt dried up inside. *It doesn't help, anyway,* she thought. Mercifully, she was able to nap. For once she remembered her dreams. She was back north on her family's lands, walking the fields of flowers. It was sunny but cool. Mother and Aunt Hyld were at work in the garden. Kassandra was so happy to see them. . .

Sunlight woke Kassandra. "Mama," she whined and closed her eyes tight in a pathetic attempt to trap the dream.

Before long there were footsteps in the hall and an armored legionary stepped into the room. "Hurry up," he ordered and loosened his belt. "I don't have long."

If only I had the courage to kill myself, Kassandra thought while staring at the ceiling. *Too bad that sestar stole my dagger.*

Kassandra was exhausted by the time Livios arrived. He was robed and washed, his hair still wet. *Tonight's his move,* she thought contemptuously. *Surprised he didn't try after giving me the food.* The chicken had been welcome, though. Mother rarely bought meat—for the girls at least.

Livios looked embarrassed as he closed the door.

What right have they to look like that? she wondered. *They're not defiled. And look at this puppy. Doesn't look too fierce. Why's Enyo worried about him?*

"You all right?" Livios asked quietly.

"Can't you just get it over and disappear?"

Livios sat down with his back to the door. "I'm going to sleep here. Before you complain, remember that if I'm not here someone else will be."

Kassandra showed an icy stare.

"I'd like to help you," Livios said.

"Like hell!" she scoffed then flinched.

"I won't hurt you. Speak your mind."

Kassandra saw weakness and attacked; she so rarely got to. "You look like a lost little puppy to me," she said. "I'm surprised your friends haven't abused you, too."

Livios gazed toward the small window. "One tried."

She laughed spitefully. "Did you like it? Did you weep and bleed?"

Livios scowled. "No, he cried and bled. I killed him."

"Really," Kassandra sniffed. "You must be proud."

Livios stared. "So I took pity on you and gave you a knife? Is that why you hurt me?"

"I didn't ask for it!"

"The lashes felt just the same. Now *they* made me cry, if that makes you feel better."

Kassandra smoldered in silence.

"I'm going to kill him soon," Livios continued. "For that alone you should honor me."

Could he really? Kassandra wondered. *He's big but looks so helpless.*

"How can you do that?" She hadn't meant to sneer this time, but it came out that way.

Livios' laughter was chilling; all vestiges of kindness fled his face. "Because it's what I do best," he said coldly. "It's all God has deemed me fit for." He laughed suddenly, harshly. "You should be thanking me, you little barbarian witch. I could open you from throat to gut and nobody would complain. If I reached down your gullet and yanked out your heart my superiors would applaud me for it. I'm Kerebos. *Kerebos!*" he cried, pounding his chest. "Just ask your next caller what that means."

The transformation that had swept Livios startled Kassandra but she masked her fear. Again she had crossed his 'line' but the reaction was much stronger this time. Scarier. She began to believe he could take Enyo and wondered what other deeds he might be capable of. "What do you want with me?"

Livios' anger ebbed. "Just be nicer to me."

"Why? Because you'll cast him out and take his place?"

"No, because with every breath I regret the evil he does you, and want to stop it."

Kassandra was taken aback. Should she believe him? Could she afford to?

Livios closed his eyes and crossed his arms. "I'm going to rest now. I suggest you do the same."

"I can't with a man in here."

"Then don't."

Kassandra watched him for a long time. His broad shoulders entirely barred the door. *I should stop insulting him, at least until he deserves it*, she decided. *That can't be too long in coming.*

Kassandra did ask about Kerebos and learned enough to satisfy her ambitions. Laconic legionaries described him as "big," "tough," "fast," "mean," "Lasctakos' boy" and "that kid Enyo whipped."

Word got back to Enyo. One night he showed up and threw her into the wall. "What are all these Kerebos questions about? You in love?" Kassandra covered her face. "He just sleeps, I swear!"

Enyo slapped her. "The oath of a bought cow! You'd better cough up new lies."

She was frightened but cried: "Or what, you'll kill me? Do me the favor!"

Enyo laid her out with the flat of his hand and chuckled evilly as she inched across the floor, trailing blood. He watched in satisfaction for a few moments. "I'm not going to kill you, my dear. Not when there are still so many tricks to teach you."

Kassandra's terrible screams eventually summoned a number of her housemates.

*   *   *

Phaetonis *Elhar* bade Livia to fetch Mother, who arrived in a pink-faced huff.

"Hello, *Elhar*," she said as she rested against the counter.

"What's going on here?" he demanded. "I've been waiting forever."

Mother cocked her head. "You didn't hear?"

"No."

"One of your men put down three of my girls. Why, even I'm working now!"

Phaetonis grimaced. "What happened?"

"Enyo *Sestar* beat them."

Phaetonis' face clouded. "Did he now?"

Before long Enyo was on the whipping post. The entire Second *Elhar*, Phaetonis and even Geraestos *Ikar* witnessed. Enyo suffered his twenty strokes and was cast into a subterranean jail.

Geraestos evidently considered the proceedings a major inconvenience, he had to get into full dress after all, and demanded Endios front and center. "Look, I don't care if he dies down there, don't let him out for a week," Geraestos said. "If another of yours pulls a similar trick, you won't live to regret it. Come, Phaetonis!"

156

Discipline rolled downhill and Endios immediately summoned his *cohari*. "The barn is off limits for a month," he told them. "I'll Judge any man that goes within a stone's throw of the place."

Livios, who had relished Enyo's scourging, was appalled by the verdict. *I won't be able to see her until after the Winnowing!* he thought.

WINNOWING

Livios practiced alone in the moonlight, swinging his sword at but never quite hitting the whipping post. The blade continually sliced the air and halted a hair's breadth from the wood. He felt completely in control of the weapon, as though it was an extension of his arm. *How'd I ever live without it?* he wondered, ashamed. *And now it'll rid me of Enyo. Can't believe the Winnowing is here.* He reflected upon the day's drill. *He looks like he's already given up. Never looked at me once.* The *sestar* had virtually slept through the exercises; everyone had remarked upon it.

"He knows he's dead," flushed Talos had whispered during a break. "You going to gig him, boss? Huh?"

"Leave off," Livios growled. "He'll hear you. Hell, I almost feel sorry for him."

"Can't wait to see it! All of us are betting on you!"

Livios glared. "You call me 'boss' but never listen to me. Shut up!"

Talos had lowered his head and skulked off.

Livios took a true cut at the whipping post and his sword bit deep with a "thunk". He released the weapon and sat on the ground. He gazed at the stars that seemed to twinkle more than usual. *I imagine Enyo's somewhere practicing, too,* he thought, picturing the *sestar* at work and doing his best. *But it won't be good enough. I could handle two of him.*

Daedilos' words crept into Livios' mind. *Never pick on those weaker than you, son. It's not right, and it doesn't prove anything except that you're a bully.*

"But he's an evil man and wants to kill me," Livios told the stars. Choking up, he added, "I miss you so much."

The stars twinkled on.

Melas entered Enyo's chamber and shut the door. His face split into a smile.

Enyo jumped from his chair. "You got it?"

Melas nodded.

"Let me see!"

"Shhh!" Melas stuck two fingers under his belt and withdrew a small glass vial, which he held before a lamp; its liquid contents were nearly as dark as his skin. "Told you I'd deliver."

Enyo took the vial.

"It will eat through metal if given time," Melas said.

"We'll put it on his blade," Enyo responded, his eyes glowing.

"No. He'll see that. Under the grip."

"Will it chew the leather?"

"No."

Enyo breathed relief. "I thank you, brother. How can I get it on there, though? His friends will scream if I go within a mile of his kit."

Melas grabbed the vial. "Don't worry, I've seen to that."

Enyo's eyebrow rose. "Who'd you bribe?"

"Not me, you. Give me all your *kraal*."

"What! Who?"

Melas looked around as though the sweltering walls had ears. "Clios," he replied.

Enyo nodded, thinking, *I can see that. He's a sneaky one.* "Again, my thanks."

"What are friends for?"

But Enyo wasn't listening. *Things look good but I can't let Kassandra off the hook after all she's done*, he pondered. *She can wait for her boyfriend in hell. If I live, who cares what happens to her and if I die it'll ease my going knowing she's dead.*

Endios lay in bed, beside himself with fear. Lasctakos would challenge him tomorrow. *Nothing to do about it now*, he thought. *All my schemes have failed.* He ran through the Scriptus, searching for loopholes. There were none. This time the beloved laws worked against him. He couldn't even commit himself to the hospital to get out of the Winnowing. Desia had been *very* specific regarding that. *Even the infirm shall enjoin if challenged*, the law said.

Endios cursed as though the law had been written against him specifically. *But what of the commanders and friends you've winnowed in the past?* he reminded himself. The question gripped him cold. *That was different*, he answered. *They had to go.*

And you don't?

Endios closed his eyes but saw only Lasctakos. He pictured the *cohar* closing in for the kill, wearing that irritating smile of his. *How does a man get so fast and surefooted?* he wondered. *What a nightmare!*

Endios eventually drifted off to sleep but Lasctakos waited for him there, too.

159

Enyo dressed and slid a dagger into his belt then walked to his chamber door to peer into the spoke. Nothing stirred; Livios slept not twenty feet away. *Say goodbye to Kassandra, boy,* he thought. He quietly shut his door and locked it then went back to his bed. Pulling a cloth from beneath his pillow, he drew it over his face and tied it behind him. After gathering his thoughts he slipped out a window and onto the crunchy grass.

Crouching, Enyo silently cursed the full moon. *The one time I could use some darkness.* he thought. Hugging the spoke, he crept toward the barn. *Hope no one's up and about.* He was taking a dreadful chance; Endios had promised a Judging to those who visited the women before Winnowing.

Enyo slowed and stopped. *I'd rather die at Kerebos' hands than be Judged,* he thought, weighing his options for the hundredth time. He wiped a sweaty palm on his leg. Should he just go back to bed? *But she has to die. I want to look into her eyes as I cut her throat. She can scream for her boyfriend all she wants, then.* He imagined Kassandra's hot blood gushing through his fingers and the pleasant thought swayed him. *It's worth the risk,* he concluded and cut across the yard.

Enyo had considered entering through a window but had discarded the idea. Likely as not he would drop in on some cozy couple and a great racket would ensue. *No, I'm going through the front door,* he told himself. *If anyone's there, I'll just turn right around and leave. Nobody would recognize me.* He considered the Judges again as he grabbed the doorknob. He almost hoped the house was packed and he had to withdraw. But if he could get to Kassandra unmarked, he would. He licked his lips in anticipation. *I just have to. I don't have any choice in the matter.*

The legionary sprawled on the couch didn't stir as Enyo slipped past. Nor was Mother around. Enyo moved stealthily up the narrow flight, carefully placing his bare feet to minimize squeaking. The upstairs was dark. He would have been hard pressed to navigate had he not been so familiar with the place. He slipped down the hall and stopped before Kassandra's door. The moist air was heavy with familiar odors.

Enyo spent a moment to calm down and congratulate himself on his stealth. Getting out of the house would be easy. *I need only drop from her window. Nothing can stop me,* he thought. He tugged the mask down around his neck. *She has to know it was me.* He simultaneously drew the dagger and a long breath, then entered. Enough light shone through the window to illuminate the girl's small form curled up on the bed.

Enyo smiled as he stepped toward her. "Wake up!" he said lustily.

"Are you lost?" Lasctakos asked as he uncovered a lamp.

Enyo stopped; Kassandra jumped to her feet and scurried into the corner behind Lasctakos. Enyo stood with mouth open and nearly stabbed himself as his arm fell to his side.

Lasctakos was in battle dress, sans helmet, his face grim. His sword hissed as he pulled it from the sheath. "Need I ask again? Are you lost?"

"S-sir?"

Lasctakos smiled. "Why are you here? Have you forgotten your orders?"

Enyo stood mute.

Lasctakos nodded at the dagger. "Do you wish to die now or tomorrow? The choice is yours. To be perfectly frank, I must admit that I've always wanted to kill you. Perhaps I should just do it?"

Enyo's weapon clanged to the floor.

"I'm disappointed," Lasctakos said. "But I can easily imagine how put off you are at finding me here. Not as put off as you'll be when Kerebos takes your head, though."

Enyo sneaked a glance at Kassandra.

"Look at me!" Lasctakos snapped.

"Yes, sir!"

Lasctakos placed the sword tip on Enyo's chest. "Your days with her are over," he said. "Even if you survive Kerebos, I'll see you Judged." He snorted. "Did you really think I was unaware of your plot? That I'd let you hurt this girl and my plans for her?"

Enyo's head drooped in defeat, then raised again. "But you're here, sir," he pointed out. "Endios' orders were for the entire *elhar*."

"True. Good thing I have a countermanding order from Phaetonis in my pocket. I don't suppose you have one?"

Enyo merely stared.

"Go," Lasctakos said.

Enyo left.

Lasctakos stood long in thought, massaging his hand. He finally turned to Kassandra, who trembled in the corner.

"Thank you, lord," she said. "I've never seen you here before."

"Nor shall you again."

Kassandra drew herself to her full height. "Don't you like girls, lord?"

"I used to," Lasctakos responded quietly. "Get into bed."

Kassandra got under the sheet. Lasctakos sheathed his weapon and walked to the door.

"Lord?"

161

Lasctakos turned. Only her small blond head stuck from beneath the coverlet. "Eh?"

"Will Kerebos make it?"

"Oh, yes. He'll make it all the way to the top."

Morning.

Endios had eaten six *kraal* leaves while he dressed and much of his fear had departed. *I'm as ready as I'll be*, he thought while tightening the breastplate straps. He wiggled on the gauntlets and inspected himself in the mirror. *What's wrong with my eyes*, he wondered, then remembered the *kraal*. He leaned closer to the mirror and plucked his deformed nose. "If I die, at least I'll be rid of this ugly face." He fished the last piece of *kraal* from its purse and sniffed it before placing it under his lip.

Endios sucked the drug in silence, enjoying the heat that flowed from the leaf. His heart beat faster as a sense of euphoria settled over him. *You mustn't be afraid*, he thought. *It's not like you didn't earn your station. You've killed hundreds of men.* "That's right," he told the reflection. "I might just surprise Lasctakos."

Endios' vivid thoughts wandered and he speculated upon the possibility that someone might depose Geraestos. The *ikar* had seen better days and was ripe for the picking. *Hell, I could be rid of both he and Lasctakos!* he thought, smiling. *If someone else doesn't cut the old drunk, I just might.* "Endios Ikar," he said aloud. He checked the *kraal* purse again.

A knock on the door disturbed him. "Enter!" he called bravely.

Lasctakos walked in; he unwound a long string and began to measure the bed, whistling all the while.

"What are you doing?" Endios cried.

Lasctakos looked up from his work, showing that smile the *elhar* hated. "Just making sure my movables will fit in here, sir," he replied.

Endios' drug-induced fantasies began to dissolve. "How dare you," he began.

Lasctakos' smile was now cruel. "Let us recall the times you tried to sabotage me, you trunk-nosed abortion. I am going to carve you like ham."

Endios paled as he gestured toward the door. "Out! OUT!"

Lasctakos saluted. "See you on the field, *elhar*."

The *kraal* seemed to have worn off in an instant and Endios found the old terror had returned twofold. He sank onto a chair and looked around the room, thinking, *I'm going to die today!*

Livios was struggling into his gambeson when Lasctakos strode from Endios' room; he wondered why the *cohar* was smiling. *Wish he'd share the joke*, he thought but Lasctakos went the other way.

Talos watched Livios with an expression of worship.

"You going to get dressed?" Livios asked.

"Yeah, boss."

"Better be about it." *God he's stupid*, Livios thought. He caught Clios staring at him. The blond gave a little smile and turned away.

Endios ordered the unit into the yard for roll call then marched them onto the plain where the other *elhari* waited. Livios felt a heaviness in the air and sensed that something important was afoot. Many ranks would change hands today as men who had saved each other's lives would now take them.

The grass had long been dead, though this morning was cool and overcast. It was a perfect day for fighting. Endios' unit took its place. Fifteen hundred and fifty-five black-clad warriors stood at silent attention. Runners were allowed to observe from the wall, though everybody else was strictly forbidden to watch. Any slave, servant or ally caught spying upon the proceedings would be cruelly put to death.

Geraestos *Ikar* walked proudly before the Legion, his snow-white helmet crest freshly bleached. He stopped beside the Scriptus and studied them with clear eyes; for once he wasn't drunk. "The law says, 'The first week of each autumn shall be dedicated to a winnowing," he cried and pointed at the brand. "Then only shall brothers take arms against each other and in success, shall take their brother's place.'" He let the words settle before nodding at Magos, who limped forward and opened a skin-bound tome before Geraestos.

"Sixth *Elhar* Polyphemos?" the *ikar* called. Dead silence on the plain.

"Sir?"

"Who of your legionaries would challenge their *sestari?*"

Polyphemos got confirmation from his subordinates. "Minos *Sestar* is challenged by Ajax, sir!"

"Have them step forth."

Livios could not see the combatants square off and was pleasantly surprised when Geraestos ordered all ranks to form a circle. The requested formation took shape around Minos and Ajax. Livios vaguely recognized the *sestar* but had never seen Ajax, a Negro. Minos looked furious and bared his teeth as he stared across twenty paces at his rival.

"What particulars has the challenged chosen?" Geraestos asked Polyphemos.

"Shield, sword and dagger, sir."

Geraestos recorded the fact in the book. He said: "Commence!"

The fighters circled each other at a short distance and Livios immediately guessed the source of Minos' anger; he was moving on a sprained knee.

163

"He hurt it practicing with Ajax," Argos explained.

Ajax walked with confidence, sword in his left hand.

"Get 'im, Jax!" someone yelled and the Legion burst into cheers and jeers.

Livios was surprised to find he was screaming, too; such was the electricity over the field.

Ajax suddenly rushed Minos and shields collided with a crash. Minos howled as he was thrown off his feet. Ajax closed, stabbing downward, but Minos brought his shield around in the nick of time. Ajax released his sword, fell upon Minos and pulled his dagger. There was a quick tussle and flurry of hands accompanied by grunts and curses. Minos screamed as Ajax wiggled the foot-long blade into his naked armpit. Ajax rode Minos until he lay still, then withdrew the glistening dagger and rolled off. Dust lingered over the pugilists.

The cheering rose to frenzy as legionaries ran forward to congratulate the new *sestar*. Ajax was hoisted into the air, though he didn't seem to share the elation. He was crying.

Geraestos ordered the corpse removed and commanded them into formation. The Legion pulled itself together with astonishing quickness. Ajax was nearly dropped in the process! Only the stained grass indicated that anything had happened. Again, utter quiet.

Markos opened the book before Geraestos, who quickly scribed the results. "The legionary Ajax, 6444, is breveted to *sestar* pending approval and confirmation. He may not be challenged, nor challenge, again this day. Polyphemos *Elhar?*"

"Yes, sir?"

"Who is next?"

"Legionary Chaereos challenges Second *Sestar* Archastratos, sir!"

"What are the particulars?"

"Pilum and daggers, sir."

"Form a circle," Geraestos commanded.

And so it went. There were thirteen challenges in Sixth *Elhar*, including one of Polyphemos, but only Ajax earned a promotion. A *sestar* and *cohar* did manage to kill each other in spectacular fashion, however. Livios had never seen anything like it. The men had attacked each other with startling ferocity—swords only, no shields or helmets. They banged on each other as their protective gear broke off in pieces and with their last gasps sliced at the other's neck and connected. One head was sheared clean off and the other nearly so. The applause and catcalls were fairly subdued.

Luecos grabbed Livios. "Almost a perfect ending, that one. How you doing?"

"Fine."

"You haven't changed your mind have you? Remember the girl."

"I know."

Geraestos ordered them back into formation and took time wrapping up the legalities. At last he said: "Fifth *Elhar* Naphios, what legionaries shall challenge?"

Naphios must have run a tight unit because there was only one fight. It lasted a long while but the men involved seemed dispassionate after the virile bloodletting of the Sixth. Livios quickly grew bored with the lackluster swordplay and sought Lasctakos for encouragement and support.

Lasctakos was delighted to see him. "Good morning, son!" he shouted above the howls.

"Hello, sir." Livios felt better already. He shouldered next to the *cohar* and pretended to concentrate on the fight. His mind soon wandered. *Has anyone ever challenged Lasctakos?* he wondered as his peers bellowed at the top of their lungs. Suddenly, he understood the Winnowing.

Lasctakos draped an arm over Livios' shoulder, saying, "I know you'll fight well today."

Livios nodded. "I get it, sir."

"What's that?"

"I get it. The Winnowing."

Lasctakos raised an eyebrow. "So tell me."

Livios swept a hand over the proceedings. "It's not for promoting men, is it sir? It's for pressure."

"Come here," Lasctakos replied. They stepped away from the circle. "Continue."

Livios smiled. "The Legion's made up of thieves, highwaymen and monsters who kill their own fathers."

"So it is."

"But there's almost no robbery or murder among us. Why?"

Lasctakos looked impatient. "Tell me."

"We have discipline, which is part of it. The Winnowing's the other. Desia must have planned it; it's a 'lawful' outlet for violence. A man doesn't have to knife his officer in the back if he can cut him down with the *ikar's* sanction, and get a promotion out of it. Understand what I mean, sir?"

Lasctakos nodded.

"It has to be that way, sir. Why else lose so many good men today if not to keep more from dying another time? Right?"

Lasctakos stared in wonder. "More than less," he said. "But keep it to yourself, son."

"Yes, sir." Livios turned back to the fight so Lasctakos didn't see him swelled with pride.

Lasctakos laughed to himself. *I didn't realize all that until I made cohar,* he thought.

The combat came to an abrupt halt and a corpse was dragged away. The Legion was called to formation.

Fourth *Elhar* suffered a dozen casualties, three of them the challenged. Anios *Elhar* was called out but made very short work of his opponent. Livios saw little talent in Anios' victim and wondered why the man bothered to attack a master swordsman.

Third *Elhar* lost three *cohari* and nine of its victors were carted off to the hospital; five of these "winners" would never recover. Livios wasn't familiar enough with the Legion's traditions to know how Geraestos would patch the Third back together, but it had to present quite a problem. He watched Geraestos' stolid expression slowly transform to revulsion then rage as Third *Elhar* slowly dismembered itself. The *ikar* hardly watched the final contest but gazed above the action, frequently licking apparently parched lips.

Bet he needs a quaff, Livios thought. *Even I'm shaken by this mess!*

The Legion was once again called to attention after the Third wrapped up its business; the sun was now directly overhead. Livios felt drained from all the yelling and drama but could only imagine how the *ikar* was doing. *Hope Enyo feels like me, in case I challenge him,* he thought. The notion surprised him. *In case?* He glanced at the surprisingly serene Enyo. *Hate him or not, he's had a hand in molding me. Maybe I should just let things be? He'd have to be grateful if I let him off the hook.*

*And forgive him for **Her**?* Livios' inner voice needled. Kassandra's bruised face came to mind and hardened his heart.

Geraestos finished with the Winnowing diary and nodded at Endios. "What does Second Elhar have?" he asked, exasperated.

Endios showed even less enthusiasm. "Fifth *Sestar* Azimos has been challenged by an entire Trident, sir."

Can they do that? Livios wondered.

"You know they can't do that," Geraestos grumbled.

"Not at the same time, sir," Endios replied. "Nicios has seniority."

"Then Nicios it shall be. Come forward, the two of you." Geraestos half waved, half pointed at Endios. "What are the particulars?"

"Full kit, sir."

Geraestos ordered the circle formed and the cheering started again. Livios watched the combatants maneuver. At least he tried to.

"Boss, you got to get your challenge in!" Talos said.

"Come now," Argos whispered in his ear, "it's time."

"Halesas would want you to do it," Laertos said.

166

Livios felt detached and barely heard them. It was as though they spoke from a distance. He wondered if Nicios had any real animosity towards Azimos. *He can't hate Azimos as much as I do Enyo*, he thought, looking at his commander. Enyo stared back, stonefaced. *Why then don't I want to kill him?*

Livios turned from the *Boru*. When it came to it, he didn't really want to kill anyone. Could he not just take Kassandra and leave? Certainly Lasctakos would understand.

Luecos shoved Talos aside and placed his mouth against Livios' ear. "Damn it, you having thoughts again?" he asked. "Even if you don't want to slice him, he's going to find some way to get you. This isn't some merchant's guild you've joined, you know."

Livios nodded. "I know."

Azimos disarmed Nicios with a nifty swirl of the sword and stabbed him through the heart. Nicios coughed and grabbed Azimos' blade as it slid further into the breastplate.

"Do it!" Luecos shouted above thunderous acclaim.

"I want Enyo," Livios said.

Talos and others took up the cry: "Kerebos challenges Enyo *Sestar!*" The words raced like wildfire through the throng.

Livios may have been biased but the cheers seemed the most enthusiastic of the day; many were anxious to see him at work. He looked over the multitude. "Let's see if this boy's as good as we've heard," the faces said.

"What particulars?" Geraestos asked Endios, who looked to Enyo.

Enyo smiled grimly. "Swords alone, sir. No shield, no helmet."

Endios passed on the information.

"He must be crazy!" Talos screamed (in Livios' ear) as Livios pulled off his helmet.

Livios pushed through the crowd; hands clapped him on the back. Everything slowed as he stepped onto the battle circle, its brown grass shiny with blood. He looked across the span at Enyo who stood with clenched fists, a sneer on his scarred face. Livios wondered that Enyo had forgone shield and helmet, whose weight would have done much to negate Livos' speed.

They faced each other for a long moment and for the first time Livios felt vulnerable. He had frequently known the sluggishness that accompanies danger but it usually wore off quicker than it came. Why did it now linger? He wondered if this was how men felt before they died. Still Enyo glowered, motionless and confident.

A deep, resonant chant started behind Livios, a few voices at first but soon most of Sixth *Elhar* was intoning, "Ke-re-bos! Ke-re-bos!" For an instant he reflected upon his newfound popularity. Men from other units were swept up in the moment and carried the cry as well.

The sun was more or less over Enyo's shoulder, making Livios squint. He must correct the disadvantage as soon as the fighting started. The rusty smell of blood lingered in the still air. Enyo bared his teeth in a hideous snarl.

"Begin!" Geraestos' voice rang out.

All fear departed Livios. He grabbed his sword...and instantly knew something was wrong. Incredibly, the handle's leather twining gave way beneath his grip as though the tang had liquefied. A screaming Enyo, blue eyes wild with hatred, was almost upon Livios before he unsheathed his sword.

"What is it?" Luecos demanded.

"Raaahhh!" Enyo cried as he swung his blade.

Livios parried in time but the compromised hilt snapped in his hands and his blade whirled over the *sestar*'s shoulder. Enyo's snarl became a smile as he planted his feet and sliced horizontally at Livios' waist. The sword caught Livios' sheath with force enough to knock him down. He tumbled to the grass wondering what happened to his sword.

The entire Legion was screaming. Already men accused Enyo of foul play.

Livios made a tuck position, did a full roll and exploded onto his feet. Dexterity served him well; he kept enough balance to run. Even as he took his first step, though, he heard Enyo's swordpoint rake across the chainmail that covered his buttocks. He bolted off as fast as he could, confident in his foot speed. But Enyo's blood was up and he remained close, by the stomp of boots. Livios was nearly panicked as he took the last few steps toward a sea of howling legionaries.

What happened next remained a matter of conjecture for years. Some argued that the suggestion issued from the crowd, but Livios was beyond the point of hearing; it just seemed the thing to do. He grabbed the dangling sheath and unhitched it while diving low into the forest of warriors. He knocked someone over, slid between some legs and scurried from Enyo's sight. A man shrieked as Enyo's sword severed his toes.

Livios was pulled to his feet by dozens of hands and cast bodily back into the arena. He stumbled onto the bare grass not three feet from Enyo, who was frantically scanning the crowd. Livios gained control and whirled on the *sestar*, brandishing the three-foot metal scabbard as a club.

"Here I am, sir!" he yelled and smote Enyo's bare head. A scarlet furrow opened on Enyo's temple and began to gush blood. Livios swung again but Enyo met the blow with the sword sheath; Livios had to retreat for the stinging in his fingers.

Enyo didn't pursue, but placed a palm to the gash. The entire side of his face and neck were red. He glared at Livios and mouthed, "Bastard."

A deep cut to the scalp can be fatal under the best of circumstances, due to the network of veins and lack of soft tissue, but a serious gash can swiftly render a man unconscious—especially if he's fighting.

Livios pressed the action. "What's wrong, sir?" he asked, circling the stationary *sestar*. "Woozy?"

Enyo grasped the hilt with both hands and lunged at Livios, almost connecting. He followed with a swipe at the head and a reverse cut to the knee. Livios was fast enough to parry the latter and kicked Enyo in the breastplate with force enough to topple him. Enyo crashed to earth with a thud. He rolled onto his knees and tried to push off, but Livios sent him sprawling with a punch to the back of the head. Enyo groaned as he dropped face first, making weak movements with his limbs. Blood ran beneath the dead grass, blackening the parched soil.

Livios stared down at Enyo, angered by his treachery. How had he ruined his sword? He again heard the Legion chanting his name.

"Finish him!" someone cried.

Livios approached Enyo and stepped on his sword hand. Kneeling, he grabbed the *Boru* and rolled him onto his back. Enyo's eyes were mere slits, his pasty face coated with blood and dirt. Livios reached for the sword and placed a foot onto Enyo's chest. He leaned forward and roared, "Hey!"

Enyo's eyes widened.

Livios pushed the sword's edge against the *sestar's* throat. Enyo's lips parted as he looked up in wrath. Livios' chest heaved as emotion had its way of him. Finally he said, "I would've followed you, if you'd been fair. I never did anything to deserve how you treated me. Now I have your job *and* Kassandra."

"Louder! Speak louder!" men implored.

Still Livios would have released Enyo, Winnowing or no, had he any faith the officer wouldn't kill him at the earliest opportunity. A single, chilling thought took Livios. *You can kill your own father but not this piece of filth?* He blinked hard. "Say hello to Boros when you see him," he finished and leaned onto the sword. Enyo gargled and frothed as the honed edge severed his windpipe; a dying hoot of air issued from the wound. Livios pushed down until the edge bit bone. Blood spurted from Enyo's jugular, keeping time with his heart.

Livios stared into Enyo's eyes long after their light had departed. Finally he released the sword and absently wiped dripping gauntlets on his chest. He had again forgotten the Legion but not they him. Men swarmed around, shouting their approbation. He was lifted heavenwards to tumultuous, prolonged cheers and paraded around the killing field.

169

Livios lay upon the supporting hands and tried to block out the repetitious chanting of his name. Eyes closed, he silently prayed Daedilos couldn't see him.

Geraestos eventually halted the celebration and ordered the Legion back into formation. Livios gratefully returned to his unit, though Luecos had to remind him to stand at its head. Livios felt naked and wished he was anonymous.

Geraestos himself took a hard look at Livios then motioned to Phaetonis. "Who is this Kerebos?" he asked.

"One of Lasctakos' pups, sir. An up and comer."

"Damnation, you'd think Lex Desia had returned!"

"Yes, sir."

"Endios!"

"Sir?"

"Who's next?"

Wrapped in thought, Livios sat apart from the others as Melas finished off a challenger. He couldn't bring himself to regret killing Enyo, but something about the affair greatly disturbed him. He pictured the departed *sestar* lying in the pile of dead, flies crowding his glassy eyeballs. *And I put him there*, he thought.

Livios would have missed Luecos' fight had not Argos run over and said: "Kerebos, I mean Kerebos sir! Thucydidos and Luecos are going to go at it!"

Sir, Livios thought. *It's going to take some getting used to.* He stared at Argos. "So which of you will test me next Winnowing?"

Argos looked amazed. "Huh? No one, sir! Think we're crazy?"

Livios saw no reason to admit that he did. He allowed Argos to help him rise. "Let's go."

Luecos was without shield and had already pulled his sword. He smiled from ear to ear, as though at some great joke, and hurled insults at his opponent, a dusky brute with sunken eyes and missing most of his nose.

"You know you'll be fed to the sharks afterwards, right dogface?" Luecos asked. "But don't worry, they'll probably find you too ugly to eat. Did your mother slice your sniffer while trying to murder you at birth?"

Thucydidos wouldn't take the bait and quietly awaited the hostilities. Luecos continued. "Or did it get pinched off in Vexaras' backside? I bet he liked that! You did too, right? You really should say *something*, anything really, last words and all that."

Livios racked his brains to recall something about Thucydidos, without success. He nudged Clios. "Is he any good?"

"Yes. Yes, sir," Clios replied without turning. "He's got ten years experience. My money's on him."

170

Livios frowned. "You're betting against Luecos?"

"Gold's gold. Sir."

Livios didn't like the sound of that. He had been so absorbed in his own problems he had neglected to consider that he might lose Luecos, an ally and friend. Now that consideration frightened him more than had the face off with Enyo. He looked anxiously at Luecos.

"Begin!" Geraestos cried.

The men did not move for long moments; Luecos' barbs trailed off and stopped. At last they began to circle each other, a dozen paces apart. Thucydidos displayed an ugly, shuffling gait, as though injured, but Livios suspected treachery. Luecos glided with his usual polish, if a tad too upright.

Get down! Livios thought. *You're too big a target and won't be able to react!* He glanced at Lasctakos, hoping the *cohar* would somehow correct the situation.

Luecos grinned as he resumed his taunts, starting slowly at first but increasing in volume and vehemence. He suddenly laughed. "I'm not buying the limp, you know. I'm your commander, remember? You were just fine yesterday."

Thucydidos smirked as the awkward scuffling gave way to his natural step. He reversed direction and Luecos followed suit. They went round and round in ever smaller orbits. The distance between them slowly shrank.

"Are you going to fight, or what?" Talos demanded. Others felt the same. "Kill! Kill!" they shouted.

Neither Luecos nor his challenger would be hurried, though, which suggested their respect for each other. Thucydidos stopped again. Luecos took two steps toward him then halted. Livios sighed relief as his friend condensed into a compact fighting stance. Nothing happened for a long while; the legionaries' complaints grew louder. This was an unprecedented lull in the day's action. Even the officers grew impatient.

Thucydidos inched away from Luecos' sword arm.

Luecos charged so quickly that Livios started in surprise. The *Boru* chopped at Thucydidos' sword and rode the blade earthwards. They scuffled for an instant, screeching blades locked; dust rose around their boots. Luecos suddenly released his sword, pulled his dagger and skewered Thucydidos' kilted thigh. Thucydidos yowled like a man betrayed and tried to bite Luecos' neck. Luecos slammed his helmeted forehead into the noseless face, and grappled Thucydidos' swordarm, twisting the dagger all the while. Blood spilled from Thucydidos' black kilt and his dark features began to pale. Luecos was laughing heartily as he clasped Thucydidos close and ripped the dagger upward. Thucydidos flailed ineffectively as he weakened but Luecos held him until he went completely slack, then tossed him contemptuously aside to raucous approval. He turned a scowling, sweaty face toward his unit and poked the dagger at them.

"Now I'm warmed up!" he thundered. "Who else wants a go?"

There were no takers.

Livios felt fantastically relieved; he didn't realize he had been holding his breath until it started again. "Luecos!" he cried, laughing. He glanced at Clios, who simmered in silence.

Luecos sheathed his weapons and did a few steps of a *Boru* tribal dance as Thucydidos was hauled from the field. Livios ran forward and caught him in a bear hug. "I thought you looked stiff out there, old pirate, but you did all right!" he shouted as others came forward with congratulations. "You did just fine!"

Luecos laughed, also. "Okay, okay, put me down! I'm fragile."

*   *   *

At last Endios' *cohari* had to declare their intentions and a hush fell over the Legion. It had long been rumored that Lasctakos would challenge the despised *elhar* and everyone, even Geraestos, was keen on seeing one of the Brotherhood's very best in action. Lasctakos didn't disappoint, but stepped forward and saluted crisply. "I am going to kill you, sir," he said nonchalantly.

A great cheer rose, maybe the loudest of the day. Geraestos demanded the particulars of Endios, who wrung his hands in what appeared abject terror.

"Well?" the *ikar* pressed.

Endios muttered something.

"What?" Geraestos snapped, winking at Phaetonis.

"Full kit, sir."

Lasctakos was already on the bloody field. He clasped his helmet in place but raised the eye slits; his tawny eyes blazed with fierce glee. He pulled his sword and balanced the tip on a finger. Endios dragged himself onto the battleground with all the enthusiasm of a man going to a funeral.

Livios was surprised to learn that a man in full armor and facing away from him could look so scared. *Is it the way his shoulders are sagging?* he wondered. *How come I don't feel the least bit sorry for him, but did for Enyo?*

Lasctakos walked quickly towards Endios, smacked his sword out of the way, and then dragged the length of his own blade across the *elhar*'s chin. Lasctakos continued past, leaving Endios pinching shut the wound. Endios staggered forward, apparently fearing that Lasctakos was

172

right behind him, but the *cohar* had walked all the way to the crowd before turning.

"I am sorry, *elhar*," he began with feigned concern. "I fear your face got in the way of my blade."

The laughter was deafening. Geraestos favored Phaetonis with a smug expression, as though he had planned the whole thing.

"We best balance that wound with another," Lasctakos continued. He stomped toward Endios, who alternated between holding his shield and squeezing the oozing cut. "We might as well forego shields, sir," Lasctakos suggested. "They're mighty heavy and it's not like yours will do any good."

Lasctakos cast away his greatshield and paced right up to his commander. He swung at Endios, who lifted his shield, then kicked the scutum hard enough to unbalance the wounded *elhar*. Lasctakos sped up, stuck his sword between Endios' shuffling legs and sent him sprawling. Lasctakos jabbed Endios' cheek with the swordpoint and walked on by. He didn't stop until he again reached the wall of exhilarant warriors.

"Did he rise yet?" Lasctakos asked them.

"Yes!"

Lasctakos looked discouraged. "Oh. Really now!"

Endios had gained his feet and was cursing as he wiped blood from his face. He gestured angrily at Lasctakos, all signs of fear gone. "Try that again!" he screamed and raced towards the *cohar*.

Lasctakos tucked his sword under an arm. "Please, sir, don't be angry," he said. "I'm only keeping my promise to carve you like ham."

"Ahhhh!" Endios bellowed and tried to sweep Lasctakos' feet.

Lasctakos jumped nimbly aside then kicked the bottom of Endios' shield, which crunched into the *elhar*'s teeth. Endios dropped to his knees, face in hand.

Lasctakos chuckled. "And might I say, sir, you're doing an admirable job of holding up your end."

Endios slowly regained his feet and spit blood at Lasctakos. "All right!" he yelled and tossed his shield.

"Here I come," Lasctakos said with a laugh, then closed with the same businesslike march he had used before. They swung at each other's head and the blades clanged loudly together, but as soon as they met Lasctakos poked Endios between the eyes with the point. The *elhar* grunted and went down. Again Lasctakos walked past. "That one will blind him some, men," he said as though lecturing to a recruit class. "Panic will set in and he'll start getting wild."

Endios swore like a madman and charged again. Lasctakos easily deflected a half dozen blows then poked his assailant in the groin, dropping him. The legionaries clapped and hooted, thoroughly enjoying the display but Livios felt strangely disturbed. Lasctakos so clearly outclassed Endios there seemed little contest. *Just finish him off,* Livios thought.

But Lasctakos didn't. A dozen times he attacked and a dozen times Endios screamed and fell; chest, neck, back, stomach, legs and shoulders were pierced but never deep enough to kill. Each time Endios staggered to his feet he was more covered with blood.

Lasctakos faced Endios, who leaned heavily on his sword and wiped blood from his eyes. He paid his tormentor no heed, as though having already conceded defeat.

"Should I let him go?" Lasctakos asked the assembly.

"No!" legionaries cried.

"Maybe I should do this instead," Lasctakos replied and reached behind Endios to cut one of his hamstrings. Endios shrieked and crashed to his knees. He released his sword and pulled the wounded leg to his chest, rolling in the dust.

Lasctakos stood by with dripping sword, wearing a disdainful expression that troubled Livios. This was a side of the revered commander he had never seen and certainly did not like. "End it, sir!" he blurted.

"No!" Legionaries guffawed. "Hit him again!"

To everyone's surprise, Lasctakos wiped his sword on the cursing *elhar*, sheathed it, then kneeled beside him. He grabbed Endios' head and spoke privately into his ear. At length he drew Endios' own dagger and stabbed him slowly through the eye; Endios kicked spasmodically as the blade sank to the hilt.

Talos panted in orgiastic delight beside Livios. He simultaneously whooped and giggled.

Lasctakos walked away from the quivering body; his usual, benevolent gaze had returned by the time adoring men enveloped him. Livios held back until Lasctakos waved him over.

"What ails you?" Lasctakos shouted above the racket.

"Why play with him like that, sir?" Livios asked in an accusatory tone.

Lasctakos shrugged. "He had to die. Why not make him an example?"

"That's what I thought you'd say," Livios grumbled.

When Phaetonis reported no challenges from his First *Elhar* subordinates, typical for that elite unit, Geraestos grunted with satisfaction and said: "That's a steady crew you've got there." He began to call his *elhari*. "Polyphemos, am I going to have to kill you today?"

"Not today, sir!" Polyphemos replied, saluted, and returned to his position.

Geraestos looked pleased. "Naphios, you're not itching for the *ikar's*

174

ring, are you?"

"No, sir!"

"Anios?"

"Geraestos is lord!"

That welcome answer erased the *ikar's* scowl. "Menestheos, I've heard some grumbling from you this year."

"Nothing I couldn't swallow, sir."

Geraestos' relief and confidence had grown visibly with every reply. "Lasctakos, you're not eligible to challenge this year."

"Yes, sir, I know."

Geraestos glanced at Magos. "How many we lose?"

"Thirty-six dead, eleven in hospital, sir."

Geraestos squinted as though in pain. "Guess it could be worse. See to the dead, will you?"

"Of course, sir."

Geraestos gazed at each *elhar*, looking very tired. "The Winnowing is over!" he finally announced. "Magos, close the book." He turned to Phaetonis. "Come on, I need a bottle."

Phaetonis shook his head. "I fear I can't do that, sir."

Geraestos looked baffled. "What? Why?"

"You didn't ask *my* intentions, sir. You best reopen that book."

Geraestos' head snapped. "Are you serious?"

"Afraid so, sir."

A collective gasp issued from those who heard the challenge and the word spread like wildfire. Geraestos stood with lowered head for a moment, muttering to himself. When he looked up his face was red. "Very well, pig!" he growled. "Magos!"

"Sir?"

"I want spears only. Write it down!"

"Yes, sir!"

Phaetonis looked mildly surprised by Geraestos' choice but unhitched his swordbelt and removed his helmet. He walked onto the fighting area as men circled around. The Legion was abuzz with excitement and there were shouts of encouragement for both combatants, though Geraestos maintained a slight majority. Even the *elhari* joined in.

Livios knew neither man well enough to have an opinion or preference, but his heart warned him that a change of *ikar* wasn't a thing to take lightly. He hoped that the winner was the better leader as well as the better man. *We'll need that in the months ahead*, he reflected.

Geraestos' fury at his friend's "treason" seemed only to grow stronger; the swollen veins in his nose threatened to burst. He lay the pilum aside and did some minor stretching, glaring at Phaetonis all the while.

The *elhar* remained impassive and stood with the spear over a shoulder. His bald pate glistened in the sun and the black topknot curled around his throat like a cat's tail.

Geraestos talked loudly to no one. "You raise them up, support them, give 'em friendship and this is how they thank you. So be it! *Phaetonis*," he spat derisively. "Phaetonis, you faithless cur! You ready to die?"

"No, sir."

Geraestos stewed on, never taking his eyes from his opponent. He took a long time to prepare as though to say 'I'm still *ikar* and can do whatever I want'.

Livios saw that three *elhari* had gathered in a tight group. *The jockeying has already started*, he thought, repelled. He suddenly realized that Lasctakos was beside him and was glad of the sight, all previous misgivings having dissipated. "Sir, who'll win this fight?"

Lasctakos mulled the question. "It is long since I've seen either of them in action. Geraestos used to be quite a terror but has been out of shape for some time."

"And Phaetonis *Elhar?*"

"He has talent. No one rises that high without it. I cannot believe he's tasked Geraestos, though. I thought they were joined at the hip."

Livios started to talk but stopped.

"What is it?" Lasctakos queried.

"Sir, what does 'winnow' mean anyway? Farmers just used it for pulling weeds."

Lasctakos smiled. "Magos' books would define it as 'getting rid of something unwanted' but it means much more than that for us. Not entirely unlike pulling weeds, however."

"Oh."

"Go!" Geraestos yelled and the Brotherhood erupted into an ear-splitting, delirious roar. It was not often someone challenged for the top command and the notion they watched history in the making raised the event to a sacramental level. Over half of the soldiers had known no *ikar* but Geraestos.

The combatants charged each other at full speed but Phaetonis halted at twenty feet and hurled his pilum. By luck or skill, the *ikar* dove beneath the spear, crashing loudly to the grass. Phaetonis' weapon struck the hard dirt near Livios' feet to the bloodthirsty whooping of fifteen hundred warriors.

Phaetonis raced to the spear and yanked it from the ground as Geraestos jumped to his feet. They whirled on each other and charged a second time. *The ikar's fast*, Livios thought. *Pot belly and all.*

Phaetonis lunged at Geraestos' stomach but the spear caromed from

176

the breastplate. Geraestos clubbed the *elhar* over the head with the blunt end of his weapon then stabbed him in the left thigh. Phaetonis yelped but didn't retreat; he pivoted and slammed the pilum into Geraestos' chest. Again the spear failed to penetrate the armor but Phaetonis shifted stance and smashed the shaft into the *ikar's* groin. Geraestos' eyes rolled and he slumped forward. Phaetonis let him fall then stabbed him through the back all the way up to the pike's wooden handle. A hush fell over the legionaries.

Geraestos' groans held more disappointment than pain. He pushed himself to his knees and reached behind himself to grasp the spear. His face looked calm but determined.

Can't believe he can move, Livios thought, impressed. *Looks like he got it in the backbone.*

Then Geraestos noticed the spear tip poking from his breastplate. He fingered the metal as though trying to determine its origin.

For some reason, Phaetonis stood by and watched. Geraestos suddenly coughed and bloody saliva flecked his lips; he slowly sat on his calves, supported by the spear. He struggled with his chin clasp and pushed off the helmet, which rattled to the ground. Geraestos' matted gray hair shone dully in the sun. He blinked and called weakly for Phaetonis.

The *elhar* limped closer. "Yes, sir?"

Geraestos' lips curled in a gruesome smile, his teeth covered in a pink film. He gagged with laughter. "You should've killed me last year," he said and slumped to one side.

The Legion was absolutely quiet. Each man considered, in his own way and to the level of his understanding that an era had just closed. Livios had not known the *ikar* but still wrestled feelings of panic. *What'll the Tantorri and Kabu do when they learn this?* he thought.

*   *   *

Kassandra sat on the bed's edge, head on her knees. Thus she had been for a long while, too tired to move. Today there was no "company", as Mother called it, but she had slaved throughout the day, her chores only occasionally interrupted by the howls from beyond the wall. Now, however, the legionaries were quiet and had been for a long time. She wondered what had happened to silence them.

Most of the girls feigned indifference toward the day's events but Kassandra saw through the façade. Hating the legionaries *was* easy but some were definitely preferable to others. *The girls must realize that*, she thought. *Kerebos, for instance, isn't a bad sort. Not yet, anyway. Better than Enyo, surely. How I hope Kerebos wins!*

Kassandra tried, unsuccessfully, to fashion a definite attitude towards Kerebos. True, he was kind and handsome but she didn't ask or need anything from any man. *Their mercies always come at a price,* she decided. *Expecting great gratitude for the smallest consideration, then complaining loudly, or with their fists, if praise isn't immediately heaped on them.* But try as she might, she couldn't lump Kerebos in with other men. *He's never asked anything of you,* she admitted. *Nor would he have to; he could just take if he wanted.*

Kassandra sighed. *If he's anxious to protect me, then I'll let him. What can that hurt?* The meditations wandered into new territory. What else might she get from the boy by applying some skilled attention? *Not that he's ever abused me,* she mused. *Not at all like that pig Enyo.* She cringed as the thought of Enyo, recalling his terrible strength and how he had forced her into such horrible things, as had so many men. All sympathy for Kerebos faded. *May they all kill off each other.*

The room gradually darkened. Kassandra dozed but was suddenly startled by a commotion from downstairs. It sounded as though some of the girls were actually laughing. She considered investigating and looked to the door an instant before it opened.

Enyo! she thought, terrified.

Livia's tiny head poked into view. "Hey, Kassandra!" she called, excited.

Kassandra breathed relief. "What?"

"There's a new *ikar*! That Phaetonis fellow!"

"So what."

"And Enyo's dead! Kerebos killed 'im!"

A flowering of warmth tickled Kassandra's stomach and, against her wishes, changed her pout into the tiniest smile. "Thank you, child," she said softly.

"Are you coming down? The girls are drinking wine!"

"Maybe in a while."

Livia slammed the door and ran down the hall.

Kassandra thought of Enyo lying dead but was afraid to really believe it—at least until she looked into Kerebos' gentle eyes. She sat slowly upright. When had she started thinking of his eyes as "gentle"?

SESTAR

I t became immediately apparent that Phaetonis would run things differently than had his predecessor. He at once attacked Geraestos' traditions and dispensed with the Winnowing Day fête of new, unconfirmed, officers. The day's victors were summoned individually to the *ikar's* chamber where they suffered a barrage of questions. The interrogations went through the night and, quite against tradition, didn't simply serve to confirm the elevations. Four victorious legionaries and a *sestar* failed the test and were returned to their previous unit and rank. The shocking news quickly traveled the spokes.

Still in armor, Livios spent the night pacing the length of his new room. Inheriting Enyo's bed would have proved quite enough to prevent sleep but the report that the *ikar* had downgraded five men made him most uncomfortable. Having obtained the rank, it would be a defeat to lose it. *He'll say I'm too young to be an officer and someone more experience will be elevated,* he thought. *How will I protect Kassandra?*

A First *Elhar* man stepped inside and saluted. It took Livios a moment to remember to return the greeting. "The *ikar* wants you, sir," the man said.

"Thanks." The messenger didn't move. "Dismissed."

Livios grabbed his helmet and swordbelt and hurried from the spoke. The sun was rising behind the *ikar's* castle as he approached. Two topknotted guards saluted. Livios thought: *Never really paid much attention to the ponytails, now I see them everywhere.*

"You're Kerebos *Sestar*?"

"That's what I'm here to find out."

"Go inside, sir."

"One of you want to show me the way?"

"Of course, sir. Come with me."

Livios followed the sentry up three flights of steps before they stopped at a great door, slightly ajar. "Don't forget to knock. Good luck, sir."

Livios didn't need to knock. "Hurry!" called Phaetonis. Livios entered a room half the size of his spoke. It was sparingly decorated but rows of "T" racks lined the basalt walls, which were devoid of ornament. A bleary-eyed Phaetonis sat behind a huge lacquered desk, scrolls before him; Magos sat at a much smaller desk with the Winnowing book. "Sit," Phaetonis ordered.

Livios tried to catch Magos' eye, hoping for support, but his tutor remained dourly unengaged, confirming the suspicion that he faced an uphill battle.

Phaetonis squinted momentarily at Livios. The *ikar* had yet to doff his armor, too. "Scared?" he rasped.

"Yes, sir, I am."

"Why?"

Livios saw no reason to lie. "Because I've heard you didn't confirm some elevations, sir."

"So you fought to advance yourself?"

"Not really, sir," Livios stalled. "But having attained the rank, who'd want to go back down?"

Phaetonis snorted. He stared at some scribblings on a parchment. "First in Boros' recruit class, five confirmed kills in your initial action, learning languages and math from Magos here," he nodded at the chamberlain. "And you don't want to be an officer? Why fight then?"

Livios struggled for an answer. "Sometimes it's better to fight than not, sir."

Phaetonis frowned and crossed his arms. "I'm not hearing anything."

"All right, sir," Livios said. "I fought because Enyo had promised to kill me and this was my only chance of getting him first."

Phaetonis appeared neither surprised nor satisfied. "Why didn't you say that up front?"

Livios lowered his eyes. "I wasn't sure how you'd like it."

"So you lied?"

"No, sir, I hesitated. Nothing I said was a lie." Livios decided to fail in grand fashion. "What would you have done in my position?"

Phaetonis chose not to answer. "Lasctakos *elhar* thinks well of you."

Elhar? Livios thought. *Guess he's made up his mind about that one!* "He's a great leader, sir."

"Because he thinks well of you?" Phaetonis pounced.

Livios shook his head. "No, sir, because he inspires his men and follows orders. He's just and fair."

"Justice has little to do with being a legionary, boy."

Livios felt he was failing the interview so risked a forward answer.

180

"By justice, I mean what exists when our laws are followed, sir. We have codes, sir. If men must be true to themselves, then why not the Legion?"

It was just the thing Phaetonis wanted to hear, apparently, and he smiled. "I agree. Continue."

Livios hadn't expected that.

"Well?" Phaetonis soon demanded.

"Sir, am I right in guessing that you seek honesty?"

"That's a slippery question. What am I, a priest? Explain yourself and make it good."

"You killed Geraestos, sir."

"Yes? Is that news?"

"Wasn't it because you didn't share his vision?" Livios answered.

Phaetonis snorted. "If so, I'm not sure it helps your argument. Actually, at this point I'm not sure what your argument is."

Livios chanced everything on his response. "A man might challenge a superior if he felt the man had led the unit astray, away from its true self."

Phaetonis frowned. "You sure use lots of words. Magos, what've you been teaching him?"

"No rhetoric, sir, I assure you."

Phaetonis' eyes darted back to Livios. "What would you say if I told you I killed Geraestos because I simply wanted to be in charge?"

Livios didn't believe it. "I'd say I'm a poor judge of character, sir, and would probably make a better slave than officer. Also, I'd say it makes no sense for a man interested *only* in personal advancement to spend days questioning his men about their beliefs and phil, phil..." Livios looked imploringly at Magos.

Magos' expression softened. "Philosophies," he supplied.

"Philosophies," Livios repeated. "You have a plan for us, sir, and it was different than Geraestos'. That's why you challenged him."

Phaetonis sat back in his chair. "I'm impressed. And a little angry, I think. You're close to the heart and will learn more when I address the entire outfit. Magos?"

"Sir?"

"How old is he?"

"Sixteen, sir."

"That's mighty young for a *sestar*. Have we ever had one that raw?"

Magos consulted the book. "Yes, sir, two hundred years ago. A man named Hermacratos."

Phaetonis rubbed his eyes. "I had every intention of downgrading you, Lasctakos' recommendation or no," he admitted. "You simply don't have the experience I need. Prove me wrong, Kerebos *Sestar*. Make sure the armory fixes your crest. Magos, write it down."

Livios jumped to his feet and saluted, his fatigue gone. "Yes, *ikar!*"

"I understand you're from Ios."

Livios suffered a sinking feeling as he thought of Daedilos. "That's right, sir," he replied quietly.

"Good. I might need your knowledge of the region." Phaetonis handed a folded piece of paper to Livios. "Take that to Polyphemos *Elhar.*"

"Yes, sir!" Livios whirled on his heel and marched from the room.

They watched him leave. "How many to go?" Phaetonis asked.

"Two, sir."

"Bring them. Have food brought up afterwards."

Livios exited the castle into a bright morning. The *ikar* must have kept him a long time because men were already drilling. He went to the Sixth's spoke and delivered the message then took the long way to his quarters—past the barn. He was disappointed to see no one outside. *Wonder what their mornings are like in there*, he thought. *Probably sleep all day.*

A small woman walked from the house toward the fountain, a bucket on either hip. Livios immediately recognized Kassandra, though her hair was pulled up into a scarf. He slowed to a stop. *She looks tired,* he thought. *But so beautiful. Wonder if she knows about Enyo.*

Kassandra filled the buckets and started back to the house. Livios knew the *ikar* didn't want men pining over slaves but had to call her name. It came out much louder than he had planned.

Kassandra stopped and slowly turned. Livios felt the fool and the hero all at once. He regretted calling her until suddenly she smiled, small at first but it bloomed nicely; he smiled back. Too soon, Kassandra nodded at the barn. "Yes," he mouthed.

She went inside.

Livios viewed the closed door with sinking spirits then turned for his spoke, reliving every moment of the experience. His humor faded as an unbearable thought crossed his mind. At first he had guessed she nodded as though to say, "come see me" but what if she was merely indicating that she had to go back inside, or worse, that she *wanted* to? His mood had blackened by the time he reached his room. *Where's that uplifting love that Magos' poets harp about?* he wondered in irritation. *So far it's been nothing but grief.*

Livios received his modified helmet from the armorers by midday. The tips of the black horsehair crest were now gold. He put on the helmet and admired himself in the mirror. *Now I'm really a sestar,* he thought, smiling. He imagined himself with the all-gold crest of a *cohar,* the red and white of the *elhar,* then finally the snow white of the *ikar.* He snapped a few salutes at the reflection and burst into laughter, which made him look remarkably like an innocent boy. The smile faded as he leaned closer to the mirror and asked: "Where'd you go?"

"It's time, sir!" Talos called from the other side of the door.

"All right," Livios grunted and before he could stop himself punched the mirror, which shattered into hundreds of pieces. As he walked into the spoke he told Talos, "Have a runner clean that mess."

The spoke was largely empty but Livios' unit had gathered near their beds. They saluted as he approached. Talos returned from the kitchen and joined the others.

"Anything about our new member, Clios?" Livios asked.

"No. Sir."

Livios studied their equipment. "Buckle that helmet Talos."

"Strap's broken, sir. Drills."

"Get it fixed immediately afterwards."

"Yes, sir."

"Let's go." Livios marched them out into the yard toward that space between Fifth and Sixth spoke where the *ikar* would be addressing them. Most of the Legion had already massed so he wasted no time sliding his unit into its proper spot. Luecos smirked as though to say, "Nice going, idiot!"

The Legion stood at quiet attention.

Phaetonis *Ikar* arrived; his new helmet crest was blinding white. "At ease," he said as he faced them. "The Winnowing is over but more importantly, we've come to a new beginning. Too long has the Brotherhood accepted mediocrity and weakness, polluted itself with corrupting influences. I don't blame you for these vices but *do* demand your help stopping them. We must all seek, in every word and action, to remember that we are the heirs of Lex Desia. No longer can we emulate those nations who used to fear us as death itself."

Phaetonis walked down the line of warriors. "Time was when no king dared raise his hand against us. When our smallest whim was obeyed by the nations as the unalterable dictate of fate. That time has past. We have grown soft." He stopped walking. "Geraestos was once my friend, but he became a fool. Content to sit back and let the world plot against us, happy to ignore dispatches that could've saved us much effort. He was but a reflection of what the Legion had become: fat, drunken and lazy." A storm brewed in his gaze. "So he got what he deserved—and so will we if we don't heal ourselves."

"The king in Korenthis has many divisions, each bigger than our

Legion. The *Kabu* and *Razkuli* are organizing their hordes even as I speak. Being the best soldiers in Pangaea won't see us through our upcoming battles. We must become *the best soldiers who've ever lived!* Better than Titos *Ikar*'s men who laid low forty thousands before the walls of Thebis, better even than Lex Desia's own immortals. This will not be easy."

Phaetonis sneered. "Some of you have survived the Winnowing and not been promoted. That's just too bad. If you don't like it, sweat out this year and prove me wrong. If you really can't abide it, let me know and I'll have you Judged out of your misery. Either way, I won't suffer any complaints about it; the times are too dire."

"So what do I expect of you all? Just this: help me save the Legion. How shall you succeed? By obeying your superiors, living by the Scriptus and leading by example. And I've some new rules to aid your concentration. First, everyone wears a full kit from dawn till dusk. Second, drills will be lengthened; we've grown far too lax. Third, all wine will be eliminated...look what it did for Geraestos." Phaetonis smiled slyly. "All those things will harden the body but that's not enough. Mental discipline is also necessary, therefore I'm instituting some changes at the barn. From now on you can visit your cows only once a week. Furthermore, I'm removing those little colts some of you have grown fond of. I don't know how this practice started but it's over now."

Phaetonis let the orders sink in. "I see you don't like these changes. You're not supposed to. But ask yourself why you don't. If honest you'll have to admit that it's because we've fallen from our high state to one little better than that of the scum we collect tribute from. Really, which of you joined the Legion to swill wine?" He injected such contempt into the question many of the men were forced to nod agreement. "There's good news, however," Phaetonis resumed. "Our illness isn't fatal and we can yet thrive if willing to reform. I don't ask you to make hard decisions; I've done that for you. All you need do is obey." He tapped his breastplate. "Follow me and I'll lead you to a new and better era. Dismissed."

Livios allowed his men a brief rest between drills. He stood apart, which perfectly reflected the distance he felt between he and his former mates. It wasn't that they didn't obey his orders but they did so without enthusiasm, as though they resented his promotion. *Even though none of them had the nerve to challenge Enyo,* he thought. "On your feet, please," he said. "Let's go again." They rose and stumbled into formation. *They look like hell.* He wished he were a plain soldier again. *Wouldn't have to put up with this nonsense.* Clios' jeering face disturbed him to the point he snapped: "What is it, Clios?"

"Nothing, sir. Just thinking about that wine we had to dump out."

"Well stop thinking, we've work to do."

Clios saluted casually. Livios felt frustration taking over. *Did they forget that I could account for the lot of them?* he wondered. "Just because I'm a *sestar* doesn't mean I can't fight," he said.

Clios nodded. "I know, sir. What do you want from me?"

What DO I want? Livios asked himself. *Something's missing here. I can't put my finger on it.*

They fumbled through a clumsy drill before Livios finally dismissed them and went in search of his commanding officer. Melas had been promoted to fill the vacancy left by Lasctakos but the assignment was probationary. Lasctakos would maintain control of First *Cohar* until Melas proved he was up to the task.

Livios knocked on Melas' door. No answer. He turned to leave and almost bumped into Lasctakos, who had hurried into the spoke; the *elhar*'s armor was dusty.

"He's on an errand," Lasctakos said gruffly. "What is it?"

"Nothing, sir."

Lasctakos scowled. "Come into my room."

Livios reluctantly obeyed. Lasctakos had barely spoken to him since the Winnowing and looked almost hostile today. The *elhar* sat at the desk and indicated a chair for Livios. "Take a seat, son," he said in a milder tone.

Livios was grateful for the words. "Thanks, sir."

Lasctakos chewed a lip. "We haven't spoken in a while, I know. Great things are stirring."

Livios nodded.

"Problems with your unit?" Lasctakos asked.

Livios wanted to open his heart but held back. "I think so, sir. I thought it'd be easier than this."

"What in particular?"

"Everything," Livios moped. "They're fighting me all the time. Sometimes I just want to pull my blade and show them!" He rubbed his temple. "Killing him has only made things worse."

"Kerebos?"

Livios looked up. "Sir?"

"You're trying too hard."

Livios cocked his head. "How can a man try too hard?"

Lasctakos laughed without derision. "You're a man no longer, son, but an officer. Tell me your problems."

"I don't know, sir. No matter how kind I am—"

"Stop! That's your issue up front. You're an officer now and don't need to be 'kind'. Give orders and your men will follow them. You no longer have the time, need, or luxury of coating words in honey, or

185

should you heap praise upon mundane accomplishments. Was Enyo ever pleasant? One day you will learn the arcane tricks of command but until then simply give your orders. That's the drill."

Livios understood the lesson but doubted his skill to enact it. "Maybe I'm not ready," he said glumly.

Lasctakos looked stern. "Do you seek to teach me my job?"

"What? Never, sir!"

"Then why question my judgement? You may be a new officer but I am not. I see greatness in you, son. Your presence here is proof of it; only a bad commander never questions himself. It's your duty to do so, and constantly. That never stops. The trick is to not let your men see."

Livios felt hope. "It's that easy?"

Lasctakos exhaled loudly. "Not really. Sorry. Nothing ever is. I promise it gets smoother, though. All you need do is convince yourself that you belong in your role, the rest follows. And Kerebos?"

"Sir?"

Lasctakos pointed. "You belong. You're a sword that needs honing, that's all. Every good day, every smart command, is as a whetstone to an edge. Am I making myself clear?"

Livios pondered the lecture. "Yes, sir."

"Excellent. You'll be fine, son. Now go keep your men out of trouble."

Livios didn't want to leave, fearing the length of time until Lasctakos would again see him. "Thanks very much, *elhar*."

Lasctakos smiled. "Just because the *ikar* is scalping me does not mean I've no time for my favorite pupil."

Livios felt like a new man. He saluted.

"Send Melas in here when you see him," Lasctakos said.

Livios hardly slept that night, so much he planned for his unit. In the morning he attack the drills with renewed vigor. He started the day by leading them on a fast run to the river then dived right into an intense Trident practice. Nothing escaped his notice and he laid bare sloppy work with a tongue that would have shamed Boros. "Too slow, too damned slow!" he shouted at Clios. "You dizzy on *kraal*?" The exercise ground to a halt and he swiped Clios' sword. "Like this!" he said and executed the proper maneuvers but almost too quickly to follow. He handed the sword back. "See, just like you were doing but fast and like you have a pair. You forget how to fight? You've been doing this longer than me, remember?"

Clios looked humbled. "Sorry, sir. We'll do better."

"You'd better. Now show me." Livios stepped out of their way. "Again!"

They did improve, but not enough. "Stop!" Livios ordered. He faced Clios. "Charge me the way you did him."

"What if I hit you, sir?"

"You won't but if you do, I guess you're boss. Do it!"

Clios attacked and Livios got under the sword stroke; he slapped Clios' cheek. "There, you're dead," he said. "Stop leaving yourself so open. Use your shield, that's what it's for. Again!"

The drill went without a hitch. Clios ventured a glance at Livios, who smiled, saying, "That's better." He saw Melas crossing the yard. "Clios, keep them at it. I need to talk to the *cohar*."

"Yes, sir."

Livios chased Melas, who seemed intent on not realizing he was being followed. "Sir?" he cried before Melas ducked into the spoke.

Melas turned with a grimace. "What?"

Livios stopped at a short distance. "When can I expect my replacement, sir? It's been nearly a week. All the other units got theirs."

"Oh?" Melas replied innocently, which didn't fit his face. "I must've overlooked that."

"I know you're busy, sir. Just want to fill out the complement and get it ready for you."

"Is that right?"

Livios was bewildered by Melas' attitude. "Of course, sir."

"Why not just go over my head and visit the *elhar* again," Melas grated.

Livios was further puzzled. "What? Oh, the other day! I was looking for you and he roped me into his office."

"Where you complained I wasn't giving you enough time or instruction?"

"Not at all, sir," Livios replied. "Did he tell you that?"

Melas regarded him coolly. "No, but he did take a bite out of my ass for not teaching you better. Looks like there's some things you can't do after all."

He doesn't have to talk like that, I'm no recruit, Livios thought angrily. "Look, if I've somehow failed you, I apologize," he said curtly. "I'm just trying to do my job."

"Keep your apologies," Melas spat then continued into the spoke. "See me next week for that recruit."

"Yes, sir. Or maybe Lasctakos can assign one if you haven't the time?"

Melas stopped in the doorway and braced his shoulders. "I'd be careful, boy," he warned in his deep voice. "He won't always be around to protect you."

"I don't need protecting," Livios scoffed. "Ask Enyo."

Melas' nostrils flared as turned. "Don't threaten me, Patricides. I'm a tougher nut to crack than Enyo."

Livios said casually: "Yes, you're better than he was, but it wouldn't make any difference. It really wouldn't."

They stared long at each other, neither flinching. Livios broke the silence. "What do you say, Melas, can we work together? Give me my fair share and I'll make you look good."

Melas considered the offer. "All right, boy, you'll have him today. Anything else?"

"Yes. I want you to include me in the meetings. I could learn a lot from you."

Melas looked as though trying to detect an insult. "My chamber, tonight after mess. Cards and *kraal.*"

That's good enough, Livios thought and saluted. "Yes, sir."

*   *   *

Livios entered the barn and found a packed sitting room. He nodded a few greetings as he slid through the crowd and approached Mother.

"Hello, Blackie," she purred. "Heard what happened with our friend. Congratulations."

Livios had planned to act the *sestar* but Mother's voice made him smile. "Thanks. Is she available?"

"I'll say. She hardly gets any company on the Second's day, anymore; some officers, that's it. I think the plain legionaries are scared to death of you."

"Melas?" Livios asked.

"Not for a long time. You know, I'm supposed to tell the *ikar* if his men get too attached, especially if they start threatening the others. We can't have new *sestari* scaring men off their fun or making extra work for the remaining girls. Know what I mean?"

Livios beckoned Mother nearer. "If there was such a man, don't you think he'd cover his tracks?"

Mother laughed. "Probably. Tell him not to get caught."

"I will. I'll also tell him to remember your kindness," he ended as he walked past.

Kassandra was asleep when Livios entered. He stared at her for a long time before taking his seat near the door. As he drifted off to sleep he wondered which officers from the Second still visited her; he couldn't even think about the other units. Thoughts and dreams began to melt into each other. *I saved her from Enyo and will someday spare her from the rest. Enyo. Laying in the ground now. Shouldn't have beaten her. I'd never do anything like that. Dad didn't, either. I'm sorry, dad…*

188

"Kerebos."

Who's that?

"Kerebos."

Livios' eyes opened. Kassandra was sitting, a wisp of hair caught in the corner of her mouth.

"What?" he asked, disoriented.

"You were making noises."

Livios remembered Daedilos. "Sorry."

Kassandra blew out the lamp and lay down. Livios was distressed that she didn't ask if he was all right. *Why do I even try?* he wondered.

"Thank you for killing him," Kassandra said in a small voice.

Livios felt bathed in light. "I just...well, oh," he faltered, then kicked himself for sounding so stupid. Kassandra didn't reply. Should he resume talking? *That can't be all she has to say,* he thought. The painful silence stretched on and his desire to break it was exceeded only by his inability to do so. His loud sighs earned no response so he crossed his arms and settled back onto the door.

"Kerebos?"

"Yes!"

A long pause. "What's hurting you?"

Livios was touched by the interest. "My heart's broken."

"Why?"

Words stuck in his throat. "I can't," he grunted at last.

Kassandra stirred. "Tell me?"

Livios shed silent tears but refused to wipe them.

"Legionaries don't have hearts, you know," she said as a point of fact.

"I'm not a legionary," he muttered. "I don't belong here."

"Then why are you?"

Livios fortified himself with a deep breath. "Because I killed my father," he said with a sob. "I didn't mean to. God knows I didn't mean to, though God did nothing to stop me."

Kassandra listened quietly, feeling of two minds. *Makes sense,* she decided. *He's two men—the killer and the crier. I need the one but like the other.* She imagined accidentally slaying her mother; the thought was unbearable. "Sometimes the gods speak and we don't hear," she said.

"Right."

"Come sleep on the bed," she invited.

A pregnant silence. "Do me a favor?" Livios said.

Kassandra was instantly suspicious. "What?"

"Don't call me Kerebos."

"Then what'll I call you?"

"By my name: Livios."

189

"Livios," Kassandra repeated. *I like it*, she thought. *Fits better.* "Are you coming or not?" she asked. He must have been moving already because the mattress crunched before she finished talking. She rolled onto her side, away from him. *Why'd I ask him up here?*

Livios tried to get comfortable but it was apparent he'd have trouble; the bed was too small for them to lie next to one another. He finally settled onto his side, taking pains not to touch her. "Good night," he said.

"Good night."

Kassandra had previously reveled in his sorrows but was now shamed by her cruelty. *How these monsters have changed me*, she thought sadly. Would her parents even recognize her? She wondered how Livios had slain his father but, surprisingly, had no problem believing it an accident. *It's not his fault he's with them*, she told herself. *He's not really like the others, and he did rid me of Enyo.* It slowly dawned on her that this was the first time she had thought of Enyo without fear. The comprehension was as a warm blanket. *I've lived in terror for so long.* She was unexpectedly overwhelmed by gratitude and said: "Livios, give me your hand."

"Huh?"

Kassandra reached back, grabbed his big paw and drew his arm around her. She could feel him tremble. *He's frightened!* she thought with strange delight, laying her hand over his. She never would have admitted it, even to herself, but at that moment she fully trusted him. *If he meant harm, he would have done it by now.* "Move closer, please."

Livios snuggled against her.

Kassandra smiled despite herself. She was trembling, too.

*   *   *

Phaetonis commanded the *elhari* to sit. He gazed at them in turn, Lasctakos last. "Lasctakos, how do your men like the new rules?"

"Opinions vary, sir, but they especially resent the exclusion of wine. Some miss their diversions and have turned to each other, I think."

"And you've let them?"

"It doesn't violate the Scriptus, sir, and you did not forbid it."

Phaetonis scowled. "The rest of you have similar reports?"

The others nodded.

"But the units *are* sharper, sir," Lasctakos added. "The extra drilling keeps them crisp. They're a most formidable group."

"They'll have to be," Phaetonis replied. "Magos, bring those scrolls over." The chamberlain brought the requested items. Phaetonis sifted through a dozen parchments, saying, "I hope you all are bright enough

190

to realize that I've instituted those changes for good reason, not because I'm a sadist. Well, not only because I'm a sadist."

"Of course, soor," one-eyed Polyphemos replied in his slow manner. A typical brown, brooding *Razkul*, he had joined the Legion after escaping a *Kabu* slave pen.

"That arse Geraestos didn't do a thing to strengthen our hand last year, even though he got these reports every month from his agents in Korenthis." Phaetonis looked flustered. "For the life of me, I don't know what happened to him, he used to be so capable."

"You did what you had to, sir," Lasctakos said.

Phaetonis slowly nodded. "I suppose. Let me read one of these." He cleared his throat and commenced.

"*Geraestos Ikar, I have confirmed the union between the king and the black kingdoms. The Chacconi have sent Royal Marines to the Kabu capital, if the word may be used, to instruct the barbarians. I have also learned that some Tantorri, though NOT your allies—*" here Phaetonis burst into curses. "So we killed the *Luw* for nothing! Nothing!" He resumed reading. "*—though NOT your allies, are on the crown's payroll. A winter campaign against the Legion is being planned. You still have an opportunity to eliminate the Kabu before they link up with the king's armies. Korenthis' nobles will only support this war if the other races are bearing the bulk; no one wants new taxes.*" Phaetonis allowed the scroll to roll up.

"The others are equally disheartening," he said.

Polyphemos looked smug. "My people would not allow *Kabu* to cross our lands, so they'll have to go the long way around."

"You touch on some good news," Phaetonis replied. "Geraestos did maintain a healthy relationship with your brothers. He spread around an awful lot of coin."

First *Elhar* Tzetzos, who had been elevated to fill Phaetonis' billet, could keep quiet no longer. He slammed a fist onto the table so forcefully his raven topknot jumped. "For Desia's sake!" he cried. "What was Geraestos doing to us, sir? Kissing rumps and bleeding our money? When I first joined the Brotherhood ruled by fear not bribes!" Tzetzos, one of the few almond-eyed *Hsia* in the Legion, had climbed the ranks with Phaetonis and was allowed such outbursts.

"Peace," Phaetonis commanded. "I share your outrage but anger against the dead won't get us anywhere."

Tzetzos eyes sparkled like obsidian. "Sorry, sir."

"Magos?" Phaetonis called.

"Yes, sir?"

"How much money do we have?"

"Three hundred and thirty talents gold, eight thousand silver, sir. We're fortunate it's a tribute year."

191

"Not necessarily," Lasctakos said. "We won't be getting much from our vassal states if Geraestos' man was accurate. Was he, sir?"

Phaetonis frowned. "He's always been before. Distressingly so." He looked lost in thought for a while but finally told them: "Our spreading gold days aren't finished yet, either, but we'll have to be judicious." He made a noise deep in his throat. "Low on funds but stocked with enemies. We're going to be very hard pressed, men."

"We do have some moveable wealth, sir," Lasctakos said. "Those boy slaves for one thing."

"Hm!" Phaetonis snorted. "Good thinking. Ios' governor has always bought from us before. Send a runner."

"Yes, sir."

Phaetonis looked solemn. "Keep your units tight and ready to move. Come back the same time tomorrow."

Livios grew increasingly unhappy as he watched his team flounder through a drill. All the gains they had recently made seemed nullified by the addition of their new recruit. *This is what I pressured Melas for?* he thought as he studied Pachos, a pudgy-faced, big lipped *Chaconni* who was the clumsiest legionary he had seen. As he opened his mouth to scream them to a halt Clios did it for him.

Clios shook Pachos by the breastplate and cried: "Step on my feet again and I'll knock you cold! Hear me? By hell, you've the grace of a pig and are twice as ugly!"

"Sorry, sir!"

Clios looked imploringly at Livios. "Sir, I got to have him in my Trident? He's gonna get me killed. Can't we send him to the kitchens or something?"

"String drills might limber him up," Argos suggested. By the look of his face, Pachos hated 'strings'.

Livios shook his head. "You'll work it out, Clios. Maybe our new friend just isn't used to his armor."

"Good point, sir. Guess he needs some exercise in it. Can I send him to the river?"

"I suppose you'd better."

A screaming Clios chased Pachos all the way to the gate then strolled back to the group, a wicked smile on his face. "If he dallies I'll send him again."

"Whatever you want to do."

A runner wound his way through the drilling units and stopped before Livios. "Sir, Melas wants you."

"Very well. Dismissed." Livios thought about how little he respected Melas. There was simply no connection or comradeship between them,

192

or between Melas and the other *sestari*, apparently. *Some men just aren't cut out for command,* he thought. He left Clios in charge and started for the spoke, wondering if it was too early to label Melas a complete failure as a *cohar*.

Melas looked up from honing his sword. "There you are. At ease." He set the whetstone aside. "The *elhar* has picked your unit for a special mission. He's sending you home, I understand."

"Home, sir?"

"Yes, to Ios. That's where you're from, right?"

Livios nodded.

"You don't seem so eager, Kerebos."

"Anything for the outfit, sir."

Melas looked unconvinced. "All right. You're taking some slaves to the governor up there and are to get two hundred in gold for them. There's not going to be any haggling, the price is set."

Livios felt a rising thrill. *Out on a mission of my own!* he thought.

"This is your first command, so here's some advice. Stay away from points of ambush and use your runners. If you meet bad news, hole up until we come get you. Got that?"

"I do, sir."

Melas went back to work. "The slaves will be waiting for you along with the runners. Take supplies for a week. That's all."

Livios saluted. He walked from the room elated but feeling the weight of command; six legionaries and two runners would be depending on him to bring them home alive. Was he up to the challenge? He had been a runner but had never actually 'used' the scouts. *Melas had to know that and if not, he should've asked,* he thought, respecting the *cohar* even less.

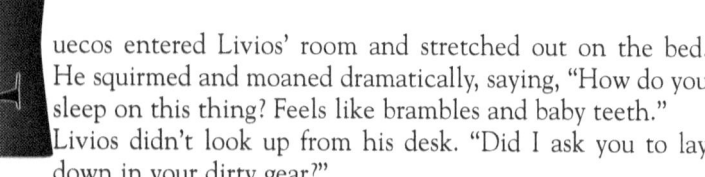uecos entered Livios' room and stretched out on the bed. He squirmed and moaned dramatically, saying, "How do you sleep on this thing? Feels like brambles and baby teeth."

Livios didn't look up from his desk. "Did I ask you to lay down in your dirty gear?"

"I knew you secretly wanted me to. What're you working on?"

"Runners. Actually, come here."

Luecos made a production of standing up then walked over and saw that Livios had drawn two figure-eights, one within the other. "Very pretty," he said. "What is it?"

"Melas made a mistake and assigned me four runners."

"He does that a lot, gives orders and forgets them. What of it?"

"I want to try a different scouting approach," Livios replied. "I remember how boring the job used to get. If I have them do this," he traced the eight with a forefinger, "They'll be looking at new ground all the time."

Luecos sniffed. "I'm sure they'll like that better but we *want* them to see the same ground. That way they'll know if something's changed."

"You're right," Livios agreed. "That's where the second pair of runners comes in. They'll still do it the old way—straight out then back in—but they'll switch off with the 'rounders' every so often."

"'Rounders', huh?"

"Just thought of it. With everyone working like this we won't be doubling the scouted area with the extra runners but tripling it."

Luecos scratched his head. "I don't see how."

"The forward straight runner will get out and back over twice before the 'rounder' completes his revolution, the rearguard straight will make it almost twice," Livios explained patiently.

"Because the unit's moving?"

"Right. One circle's shrinking and one growing."

Luecos seemed confused. "Are you sure?"

194

Livios drew the geometric equation the way Magos had taught him and rechecked his numbers. "Yes."

Luecos pointed at the math. "That's what this says?"

"Uh huh."

"Have you shown Melas?"

Livios sighed. "What'd be the point?"

"He may be a weak *cohar* but he wants what's best for the Legion, not to mention his own hide. Talk to him."

"Sure."

"I'm serious. If he doesn't listen I'll take it up the ladder for you."

"All right. I'd better get going." Livios stood.

Luecos' eyes brightened. "Almost forgot what I came for!" He unhitched his canteen. "I took a stab at copying Halesas' broth for you."

Livios smiled gently. "Old Hals."

"It doesn't taste half bad and it has a kick that would knock the hair off your chest if you had any."

Livios was moved by the gesture. "Made it with your own hands? I don't believe it."

"Well, I didn't wash them. Come back in one piece, will you?"

"I've every intention of it."

"You know the land you're going through. Think of where you'd stage an ambush and stay away from there. Don't look at me like that, I'm serious."

Livios laughed. "Walk out with me."

The *sestar* awaited Livios in the yard and drew into formation as he approached. The runners stood behind the legionaries but before a chain gang of over twenty boys. The slaves were a dismal looking lot, dressed in linens and wearing make up. Some were hanging on each other, weeping.

"Don't whip these ones to keep 'em going," Luecos said. "They might like it."

"No doubt. Clios, shut them up."

The *Boru* soon cowed them into silence.

"Don't make your men carry the extra food, either," Luecos suggested. "Make the slaves do it."

"Right. Do it, Clios."

"Sir!"

After a few moments Luecos said: "I'll see you when you return. Be safe. Don't do anything stupid."

"I'll think of how you'd act and do the opposite."

Luecos muttered something about ingratitude and wandered off. Livios watched him go and took a swig of the broth. Luecos was right; it wasn't bad and packed a wallop.

195

Clios finished his duties. "All secure, sir."
"Move out."

They made good time but stopped frequently for the slaves' sake. The new scouting scheme worked wonderfully after the runners got their timing down; there was always someone approaching the *sestar* with information. As they passed each other runners could now shout directives like "Keep your eyes on that hill" or "Watch that shadowed copse", whereas they would've hardly seen each other under the old rules. By midday the runners were excitedly endorsing the new pattern. Livios smiled, thinking, *I must be on to something. Can't imagine anything that would've pleased me when I was a runner.*

Clios approached Livios and offered his *kraal* pouch. Livios took a big handful, saying, "Thanks. That's some cache you have."

"Yes, sir."

"You've been spreading it around lately. Where'd you get it all?"

Clios stared. "Won a bet with Enyo."

"Hefty bet."

Clios shrugged. "Guess he knew you were going to kill him, sir."

Why's he lying? Livios wondered.

One of the prostrate slaves cried out as Pachos kicked him and writhed on the ground as though dying, making a loud spectacle.

"Quiet down," Livios snapped. "Pachos!"

"Yes, sir, I'll shush him!" Pachos kicked the lad again, harder.

"Pachos!"

The new legionary looked honestly befuddled.

"Brains of a rock," Clios muttered. "I'll take care of it, sir."

Clios quelled the situation while Livios viewed the road ahead and munched the drug in silence. The undulating emerald hills of southern Ios were lovelier than he remembered and he bitterly lamented having left them. He would pass within a few miles of his farm before the day was over. Should he visit? *I want to,* he thought yet knew he couldn't. *I'd go to pieces.* He pondered his life with Daedilos and how different the world then seemed. It pained him that he no longer fit or belonged in that quiet place. *Daedilos, Felix, Herakles, Vara. All gone.*

"Ready when you are, sir," Clios said.

"Give me more leaf."

Clios pulled his pouch and Livios took a generous amount, saying, "Let's move."

Livios pushed them until nightfall. Even his men were tired by the time he stopped and the slaves were barely conscious. The whining boys dropped in their tracks and, refusing food, lay in their own waste. Livios collared Talos, who said: "Yes, sir?"

196

"Make them drink some water. Beat it into them if you have to."

"Sir."

The legionaries squared away the slaves then dug in for the night. "Argos, set my tent before mess. Pachos can help you."

Argos turned to Pachos. "Come on, dummy."

Livios left camp and joined a runner on a distant hill. The scout was tired but had remained vigilant; his footprints were all over the grassy knoll.

"At ease," Livios told him.

"Thanks, sir. I'm beat."

Livios grunted. Time passed and the sun sank.

"What're you looking for, sir?"

"Get back to camp and eat."

Livios couldn't sleep so he roused the men earlier than he had planned. "Hurry," he told them. "I want to be back here before dark."

Breakfast was plain, an affair of grains and water but the legionaries ate heartily. Some of the slaves complained that they were too sore to eat and Livios didn't push the issue. *They'll be mighty sorry before this day's over,* he thought. The fire was smothered, tents rolled and slaves kicked onto their feet. *What am I forgetting?* he asked himself and ran a mental inventory. "Talos, cover the latrine."

They struck out across the dewy grass before sunrise.

Phaetonis ordered the *elhari* seated and got right to the point. "Things are heating up. I got another dispatch from up north. It'll definitely be a winter attack and by a force that dwarfs anything we've seen since the Second Republic."

"Winter's as hard on them as it is on us, soor," Polyphemos said. "Big armies need big food."

Phaetonis ignored the comment. "We can't afford to let the *Chaconni* link up with those black dogs down south. I don't want to tussle the Crown and all the *Kabu.*"

"*All,* lord?" Lasctakos asked.

Phaetonis nodded. "You heard right. King Qetewayo of the 'red feather' clan has been busy, it seems. He's forged an alliance with a dozen weaker nations and they're grouping around his new castle."

Tzetzos laughed. "Them mud huts aren't castles, sir. Our boys will take his place apart and hang him in his own guts."

"They're not mud huts anymore. *Chaconni* engineers have made some improvements. I don't doubt we could take it, but not in the middle of a battle while outnumbered twenty-five, thirty to one. We won't be able to press them if they can retire at will."

"We're legionaries, sir," Tzetzos replied.

"Thirty times is a conservative number, I should think," Lasctakos said. "We must count on them putting at least twenty percent of their population into the field."

Phaetonis frowned. "You may be right. And that's before the *Chaconni* vanguard arrives—another thirteen divisions. And to your point, Tzetzos, yes we're legionaries and we're going to mop the steppe in their blood, but we want to survive the battle *and* return home intact."

"With Scarlet Guard cavalry harrying us along the way," Lasctakos added.

The room was long silent.

"We do have cavalry in the *Rüz*," Lasctakos pointed out.

"Come now," Phaetonis scoffed. "They can scout but they can't take the Guards. They're outnumbered ten to one, anyway." Phaetonis suddenly slapped the table. "Damn it, we're fighting for our lives! Don't any of you have something smart to say? Even without the *Chaconni* we'd be hard pressed to pull this off, not to mention remain combat effective!"

"Gonna have to win convincingly," Polyphemos said. "If we fail that and limp back home all Pangaea will rise against us."

"Then let us keep the *Chaconni* up here, sir," Lasctakos said. "We wouldn't have to do it for an extended period, if timed correctly. These *Kabu* will not long remain allies; they hate each other nearly as much as they hate us. Qetewayo will have his hands full, his castle notwithstanding."

Stress and temper darkened Phaetonis' face and he looked on the verge of saying something truly nasty. When he spoke it was haltingly. "How exactly can that be done, *elhar?*"

"Allow me to elaborate. Magos, bring that map over, please."

Ios city was much as Livios remembered but seemed a disorganized, dirty mess after his structured life among the Brotherhood. The wall was short, thin and inadequately manned. *Could almost push it over with my hands,* he thought. The thatched buildings were haphazardly arranged and the streets a testament to poor planning. He saw few soldiers and those were lightly armed and as slovenly as the population.

Livios made a point of marching through the marketplace. He had bad memories of the place, where Daedilos had tried to sell produce, and enjoyed scattering the merchants before him. Ios' folk had made things difficult for Daedilos and he liked returning the favor.

The legionaries reached the governor's brick-walled palace. Two soldiers stood guard at the gate. Livios glared down at the much shorter men and snarled: "Open it!"

The older of the two sentries swallowed and replied. "Please be patient, *cohar*, I've sent word."

Livios tapped his helmet crest. "*Sestar!* I'm here at his invitation and will not wait!" He realized he was being unreasonable but, for once, enjoyed the fact. He imagined this same cowardly soldier haggling with Daedilos over the price of tomatoes.

An ugly situation was avoided when the governor's own bodyguard opened the gate and stepped forward. This armed man was of typical, unremarkable stock but moved with the assuredness of a career soldier. "Forgive us, *sestar*, you arrived sooner than we anticipated. Please enter with your men and the chattel."

Livios moved before the man finished talking. The interior of the small fortress had been lushly, lovingly adorned. Murals covered the wall and exquisite sculpture decorated the lawn. Tapestries hung in the windows of a gray-stoned, stout donjon. Some stunted, imported palm trees lined the cobbled walkway from the gate to the governor's quarters.

"Would your men need water?" the bodyguard asked.

"Yes. And food."

"I'll see to it. Please follow me to his lordship."

The governor looked the very antithesis of a legionary. Short, fat, bald, bejeweled and draped in silk, he lounged on a divan with serving boys at his bare feet. His pudgy face was drawn into a hilarious, pathetic scowl.

Does he know how ridiculous he looks with that sword? Livios wondered. *God, he didn't even wipe off the dust.*

The bodyguard bowed before the governor. "My lord, the *ikar*'s emissary has arrived." He turned to Livios. "Sir, I present Baron Thracios Kloz Wartos."

The governor looked on with practiced boredom. "You march fast, young *sestar*. You nearly beat my riders home."

And he lisps! Livios thought. *Most unimpressive turd I ever saw.* "We're used to it," he replied then turned to the bodyguard. "Thought you were going to see to my unit?"

The soldier and Wartos exchanged glances.

Livios chuckled. "Don't worry, I'm here for money not fighting. And if it were otherwise, what on Pangaea could you do about it? Go feed my men."

"Do it," Wartos said softly, making a silly pinky gesture at his retainer.

Livios was filled with contempt. "Nice sword, governor. I like the jewels. Does it have an edge?"

Wartos perked up. "Do you like it? Really?"

"Sure. Where's the money?"

Wartos' heavy eyelids drooped. "You brought me twenty new proteges?"

"That's right."

Wartos squeaked with glee and clapped his hands. "I'm so glad! I've grown so tired of these others. I'll probably have to 'put them down', as they say. The spark has quite gone out of them."

Livios eyed the children at Wartos' feet, noting their glazed expressions for the first time. They gave no indication that they heard or cared about the governor's intentions. Livios glared at Wartos, thinking, *I should burn this royal sty with you in it.*

A slave entered with a bag of coins. "Now what did we agree, nine on the head?" Wartos asked.

Livios smiled menacingly. "It was ten, fat boy, and if I hear another word I'll kill you with your own weapon."

Wartos shrank into his cushions and covered his mouth. "Oh my." Terror crossed his face. "Did that count?"

Livios took the bag and told the slave: "Get the rest, now." The man returned quickly.

Wartos directed some noises at the slave who said: "I think his lordship wants to speak."

"Keep it short."

"Thank you," Wartos said. "Are you from my province? You talk like it."

"I am. Hermos Shire."

Wartos' nose wrinkled in disdain. "Oh, Hermos. What holding?"

Livios wanted to slap the man. "Does it matter?"

"I suppose not. Do you like being a slaver more than tilling the field?"

The words stung Livios. Somehow he had avoided thinking of himself as a "slaver". *But that's what I now am,* he realized dismally. He could only guess what his father would think. "No, I don't," he replied. "But I do like killing people who ask too many questions."

Wartos' expression reverted to panic as he sat back and fanned himself furiously.

*   *   *

Livios stomped into his room and threw his helmet onto the bed. He had spent the return journey pondering his interview with the governor and was now beyond irate. Had such degenerates always existed in his homeland? The mere notion jaundiced his childhood memories, which enraged him. He hated the governor for having destroyed his picture of Ios. *And I'm a seller of human beings,* he thought. *I should've killed him for pointing that out. Oh, father, how I've let you down!*

Livios felt betrayed and cheated but the anger proved impossible to vent. He felt filled with poison, as though his spittle might eat a hole in the floor. He hoped to never see Ios again; it had failed him.

A knock on the door. "*Sestar?*"

"Go away."

"Sorry, sir, but Melas wants you. Now."

Livios smacked the helmet to the floor. "I just got back! Can't I have a moment's rest?"

There was no reply.

Livios stewed a moment then leaped to his feet. He made his way to Melas' room, finding Melas and Lasctakos hovered over a map. They finished their conversation and looked at Livios, who saluted.

"What's wrong?" Lasctakos demanded.

"Nothing, sir," Livios lied. He couldn't have explained, anyway.

"How was Ios?" Melas asked.

"Fine."

"That's good, because you're going right on back."

Shortly thereafter Livios found himself at a briefing in the *ikar's* chamber. A score of junior officers were seated on the floor before a hanging map of Pangaea; Luecos was there. Phaetonis, Lasctakos and Magos talked off to the side.

By now Livios' irritation had changed to curiosity. Something unusual was afoot. *Are there any slaves left to sell?* he wondered, then was seized by a sudden terror. *Not the barn's girls! Not Kassandra!*

Phaetonis stood before the map, hands behind his back. "Hold questions till the end. Lasctakos, let's have it."

Phaetonis faded to the side and Lasctakos took his place. Lasctakos said: "Gentlemen, you have been picked for a crucial mission, probably the most important of your lives. Listen with utmost attention." He then delved into an account of the approaching war and the forces being aligned against them.

Livios glanced nervously at Luecos, thinking, *Why is he telling us and not the whole Legion?*

"So why do I inform you of this?" Lasctakos asked them. "Because you shall be instrumental in winning this war. Raise your hands if you speak *Tantorri*."

All but Livios and another raised their hands. *I'm not going to be left out, am I?* he wondered anxiously.

"But you speak *Razkuli*, do you not?" Lasctakos asked him.

"Yes, sir."

"Close enough."

201

Livios relaxed.

"Who can ride?" Lasctakos asked. Everyone responded in the affirmative.

Ride? Livios thought, greatly interested.

"Any bowmen? Don't be ashamed, raise your hand."

Livios and half the others reluctantly obeyed. *I didn't know Luecos could shoot,* he thought.

"Good, very good," Lasctakos said. "Magos, are you writing this?"

"I am, sir."

Lasctakos smiled at them. "Curious?"

"Yes, sir!" And they were. It was not often that they were provided intelligence so long before a battle, certainly nothing confidential. Lasctakos' inquiries only added to the excitement.

"Good. Each of you shall lead a cavalry 'Kommando' of our *Tantorri* allies, the *Riiz*. Your units will be assigned areas of operation within the *Chaconni* provinces. It shall be your duty to harass, destroy, burn and kill as much as possible. And I do mean 'as much as possible', gentlemen. Your Kommandos will be small, thirty to fifty men apiece, but must occupy the enemy as would an army. You will strike trade routes, ungarrisoned towns and other civilian populations until Korenthis is forced to respond." He turned to the map and identified numerous areas. "You must hit where their soldiers are not and not be there when the soldiers arrive. At the very least you must tie down most of the Crown's cavalry and some of its infantry. While you occupy them in the north the rest of us shall move south." He again faced them. "I know it is much to take in and that I am asking you to employ skills you find distasteful. I also know that some of you may feel inadequate to the challenge; you mustn't. Your leaders have weighed your qualifications and are confident in your abilities."

Livios *had* been questioning his readiness to lead a Kommando but was far more concerned about fighting and killing civilians. *He knows I can't do that!* he thought.

"I see questions in your eyes," Lasctakos said and crossed his arms. "Now is the time for answers. Who is first?"

It was Luecos. "Sir, how can we trust these *Tantorri?*"

"A fair inquiry. We can rely on them for three reasons, foremost being that we have hostages. Also, the *Riiz* know that our enemies would covet their lands if we are defeated. In addition, the *ikar* has waived this year's tribute. Yes, Rodios?"

"Sir, I don't like missing the fight against the *Kabu*."

Lasctakos smiled. "Who would? Fear not; most of you will be recalled before the battle. By that time, it is hoped, you will have removed the Crown from the picture. Next?"

202

"Will the *Riiz* be supplying mounts?"

"Yes, Spartos. They'll provide *Tantorri* arms and accoutrements as well. You men will do your best to pass yourselves off as *Riiz*. It is important the *Chaconni* believe the attack independent from us."

"Can't bring my sword, sir?" Spartos asked. Others muttered similar concerns.

Lasctakos looked to Phaetonis who said: "They can take their swords."

Livios raised his hand. "Sir, why are we going in such small units?"

"Concerned about splitting forces, eh? As I said earlier, you'll strike and move. Your Kommandos must not get involved in stand-up battles. The *Chaconni* cannot learn how few you actually are."

Livios felt embarrassed. He should have guessed all this.

Rodios *Cohar* asked: "Slaves or prisoners, sir?"

"No. Cause maximum collateral damage but *do not* get tied down. Fare free and wide. If soldiers try to engage you, withdraw. When they withdraw, return. We are counting on your knowledge of the areas, so you will be assigned to parts familiar."

Livios was so rattled by that statement he didn't hear the remaining questions. *Parts familiar?* How could he be expected to molest and kill his own neighbors! He looked dolefully at Lasctakos who said: "I'll meet with each of you later this afternoon. The *Riiz* fight as kindreds and families and you must get to know those whom shall serve you. What is it, Luecos?"

"Well, sir, I'm sure we'll be moving out today and since I'm not marching with my own men and, uh, there's not too much to plan. . ."

"Out with it, please."

"The barn, sir. Most of us aren't on the slate today."

Lasctakos shook his head in amazement.

Somebody began to laugh; surprisingly, it was Phaetonis. "Anyone who wants to tackle the tarts is allowed, just make it snappy. Markos, write up the orders."

Mother looked bewildered when she saw Livios. "What day is it?"

Livios waved his written dispensation. "From the *ikar*. I want her so clear the book."

"Don't think she's got anyone. Oh, yes, she does but you won't have any trouble chasing this one." She smiled at him. "You know, Blackie, you're getting handsomer every time I see you. Turning into about the best-looking slab of meat in the Legion."

Livios laughed uncomfortably. He made his way to Kassandra's room and heard soft voices from within; he was immediately jealous. "Knock, knock!" he said testily and entered.

Kassandra and Livia were sitting on the floor, a book before them. Livia smiled broadly, she had lost a tooth, and said: "Kassandra's teaching me to read!"

"Is that so?"

"Yes."

Livios looked at Kassandra, who returned his gaze. "I'm sorry, Livia, but you'll have to come back later," he said.

"Oh."

Kassandra closed the book. "Go on, child. Here, take it with you."

Livia frowned but got dutifully to her feet. She slogged past Livios but suddenly tugged his belt.

He looked down at her. "Yes?"

Livia beckoned him closer and whispered: "She isn't mean anymore."

"I'm glad to hear it."

The girl walked from the room, book pressed to her chest.

"What're you doing here?" Kassandra asked when they were alone. "It's not your day."

"Is that some sort of welcome?"

Kassandra's smile was brief. "Of course I'm glad to see you. I just don't want you in trouble."

Livios sat heavily beside her. "I have to go away again."

Her gaze was piercing. "What is it?"

"Just another mission."

"Livios?"

He looked out the window. "I'm ordered back to Ios," he said softly. "My father's own shire."

Kassandra lightly touched his arm. "To fight?"

He nodded a few times. "But I *can't* do it. Lasctakos knows that. Why would he send me there?"

Kassandra moved around in front of him and put her small hands on his shoulders. They stared at each other for a moment then she suddenly embraced him and drew him to her breast.

She smells nice, Livios thought, eyes closed. He chuckled. "You've never hugged me before."

"I know," she replied.

*   *   *

Livios stood before Lasctakos' desk and saluted.

"Sit," the *elhar* said without looking.

Livios obeyed; he could tell that Lasctakos was in no mood for a morality lesson. *How am I going to get out of this one?* he asked himself.

Lasctakos finished working and regarded him intently.

"Son," he began, "I know you're not looking forward to your mission. I also know that the Legion, your true home, needs your help."

"Yes, sir."

"'Yes, sir,' what?"

"To all of it, sir," Livios replied. *Not what he wanted to hear,* he realized, interpreting Lasctakos' expression.

"I am not asking you to enjoy this commission, but am demanding your best, Kerebos."

"But the women and children, sir?"

"That's correct. And the farms, and the beasts. We're not playing games but are struggling for our lives. Let me also point out that you've already abandoned Ios and that we gave you succor. Will you fail us now that we need you? Is that the kind of man you are?"

Livios hated the way he felt, powerless and dishonored. "I won't abandon my mates, sir, but there has to be another way. For me, at least. Please."

Lasctakos leaned onto his forearms. "We've crossed this ground before. Think back to our previous conversations. Did not good come from things that initially reviled you? How much better is the *elhar* now that Endios is gone, or is your unit without Enyo?"

Livios moped in silence.

"I'll offer a deal," Lasctakos said. "Name a man who knows Ios as well as you and he shall take your place."

Livios felt ensnared. "There isn't one."

"So you'll risk our lives to someone less qualified? Not a bright move, *sestar.*"

Livios was as close to angry with Lasctakos as he had ever been. "You know that's not the case, sir."

"What do you think you owe Ios? Are you not an outlaw there?"

"I don't know what I owe them," Livios replied quietly.

"Can we at least agree that you're beholden to us?"

Livios nodded.

"Doesn't a certainty outweigh a doubt?"

"But there are lives at stake, sir!" Livios shot back.

"Correct. Yours, mine and the rest of the Legion. I remind you—*they* will be attacking *us.*"

Livios stared at the *elhar,* unable to argue further.

Lasctakos seemed coldly amused. "One last question. If I don't send you, what monster should go in your place?"

The paradox made Livios flinch. *So it has to be me because I'll kill less people than someone else?* he thought numbly.

Lasctakos walked around the desk and put a hand on Livios' back.

"I'm not unsympathetic, son, but we have so very few cards to play. Do your best for me, that is all I ask." He continued out the door.

Livios sat in tortured contemplation. Interestingly, none of Lasctakos' arguments had borne the authority of his last statement. *I do want to please him*, he thought.

The *elhar* returned and took his seat. "I've sent for your *Tantorri* liaison, so pull yourself together."

Livios sat up. "He's coming in?"

"Yes."

Livios had never heard of such a thing, a stranger in the spoke. "Have you met him, sir?"

"Briefly. He impressed me as a serious and capable man."

A legionary knocked on the jamb. "Got him, *elhar*."

Lasctakos looked past Livios and asked: "Is that his weapon?"

"Yes, sir."

"Give it back. He's here at our invitation."

"Sir?"

Lasctakos smiled. "I think we can protect ourselves."

"Yes, sir."

"Come in, Baso," Lasctakos called.

The *Rüz* was very short with bandy, bowed legs. A studded jerkin enclosed his chest but his long, thick, muscular arms were bare but for an archer's guard. His shiny black hair hung free to his shoulders. He positioned himself before the legionaries and slid a long knife back into his belt.

"Baso, meet Kerebos *Sestar*," Lasctakos said. "My ablest man."

Baso looked at Livios who remained taller, even though seated. The *Tantor's* squinty eyes were the color of flint and just as hard; his grainy skin was weather worn.

Livios could hardly guess Baso's age. *Forty? Fifty? Can never tell with these people.*

Lasctakos broke the silence. "Tell us about yourself, Baso."

"I was ordered here by our council," Baso replied in clean *Chaconni*. "It's my duty to serve you to the best of my ability." His eyes hadn't left Livios.

He's studying me, Livios thought, feeling that some response was in order. "I'm sure you'll do all that's required and more," he said. "Bear with me as I relearn the horse and bow."

Baso bowed slightly.

"You've brought the *sestar* a horse and clothing?" Lasctakos asked.

"Two horses, lord, and my wife's own homespun. I'm not so sure how it will fit."

"Very well. You'll be escorted out now. The *sestar* will join you

206

directly. Guard, take him."

Baso nodded at the officers before being led away. Livios waited until they were alone before saying, "He's a steely looking little fellow."

"Quite the warrior, according to his chief. He's been on their tribal council for decades."

"That's good."

"I wanted you with one of their best."

"Thanks."

"You need not be so gracious to them, son; none would mourn your loss."

"I know. I didn't know what to say."

Lasctakos smiled. "You did fine. Now go prepare yourself. Leave your gear with Attikos so we can bring it down south."

Livios stood and saluted.

"Keep your mind on the task at hand, Kerebos. I'll see you soon."

"Yes, sir."

Livios removed his armor and hung it on the T rack. He shifted uneasily in his undergarments, already missing his kit. He looked at himself in the mirror and flexed his arm muscles, thinking, *Is that really all me?*

A runner entered with some clothing. "Here it is, sir. You have to wear this stuff?"

"Yes. Take my kit to the armorers."

Livios squeezed into the *Tantorri* clothing. The dun-colored, woven shirt fit him across the shoulders (barely) but the sleeves ended halfway up his forearm. The breeches weren't much better. He rolled both articles up to the joints then tried the buckskin moccasins. *These fit pretty well,* he thought, wiggling his toes. He walked around the room, trying to get used to the absence of heels. At last he put on his sword belt and tucked a dagger between his moccasin and calf. He again inspected himself in the mirror and was struck by how closely he resembled Daedilos' son; he pushed the sword out of sight to complete the illusion.

Livios looked at himself for a long while.

AGAIN

Livios kept the band constantly moving during the next week, acclimating himself to the *Riiz* and life in the saddle. He listened much, spoke little, and did his best to learn *Tantorri* ways. His thirty-seven riders proved a dour and doughty lot, longhaired men with hashmarks on their bows for "kills". They took his orders without hesitation and performed efficiently, if not passionately; their demeanor didn't surprise him. No matter how they rationalized it, the proud *Riiz* must have felt pressed into service. True, the *ikar* had given gifts but they couldn't have refused his call for a campaign from which they might not return. For the present, though, they seemed willing to trust his competence. *But what choice do they have?* he asked himself.

Livios eased into command, constantly reminding himself that he was not dealing with legionaries but "allies". He saw nothing to be gained by treating the *Riiz* harshly and hoped the other *landesknectos* had arrived at the same conclusion. He concentrated on mastering their tongue, which proved similar to *Razkuli*. Baso was offended by the suggestion that the *Tantorri* and *Razkuli* were related, however. "They're only pigs that have stolen from us," he said. The matter was dropped.

Livios struggled to get used to so much riding. Believing himself a horseman, he soon found that being able to ride was far removed from being born to do so. The *Riiz*, who could eat and sleep on horseback, seemed entertained by his aches but appreciated his ability to poke fun at himself. "You men look tired," Livios would joke. "All right, we'll stop."

Baso eventually showed pity and offered some riding tips, sitting closer to the horse's neck being one of these. "You won't bounce around so much," he said. Livios thanked him with some *kraal*, which was accepted after a slight hesitation.

By the second week Livios was feeling comfortable enough to proceed to the next stage of his plan. Now he ranged all over Ios, showing the *Riiz* trade routes, hiding spots, and homesteads but avoiding contact with the enemy. A dozen potential campsites were identified and provisioned, including the caves he and Felix had used. He constantly quizzed his men about topography and settlements and even made them sketch the province. His demand for proficiency impressed them and they began bringing concerns directly to him rather than to Baso. Baso himself appreciated Livios' concern for the men and warmed up enough to invite him on a hunting excursion. They didn't bag a deer but Livios learned much about tracking game and got to practice with his bow.

"You can shoot," Baso said after Livios hit his third "soft" target—no need to damage arrows.

"You sound surprised. Didn't Lasctakos tell you?"

"You can *really* shoot."

Livios laughed, but was thinking about the *elhar*. He missed camp life, his friends and his armor. Most of all he missed Kassandra and wondered if she thought of him. He remembered their last meeting and how she smelled. *She didn't want to let me go*, he thought with a smile.

One evening Baso approached Livios as he tangled with a moccasin strap.

"Can I have the *sestar's* ear?"

Livios resented hearing his rank from a non-*landesknecta*; it only reminded him how lonely he was. "What is it?"

The *Riiz's* brown face was unreadable. "I don't understand why you're teaching us all this. Why would a legionary share such thoughts?"

Livios dropped the strap. "I don't know what you mean."

"You're not what we expected," Baso said after a brief silence.

Livios nodded. "I'll bet. How many legionaries have you known?"

"Many."

"It surprises you that I want my men prepared?"

"Why not just order us 'kill' when the time comes? We'll do it. That's why we're here."

"I see."

"And you show us your own land, how to attack it, how to kill your people," Baso went on.

Livios wanted to share his feelings about the mission, how he hated it. *Does he think I'm actually enjoying this?* he thought. "I don't live here anymore," he grumbled. "Would you *prefer* I simply bossed you around?"

Baso stared. "I shouldn't have mentioned it."

Livios suppressed his emotions. "No, this is good. Baso, don't you think I want you to survive this war?"

"Why would you?"

"Why wouldn't I?"

"Because you belong to the Black Legion."

Livios chuckled. "Good point. But even on those terms I'd want to be successful. Instructing you and your kin helps that. Right?"

"I suppose."

"And what if I get killed? How would you get away if I hadn't taught you?"

Baso lifted a crooked finger. "That's what I mean. Why do you even care?"

Livios looked over a rocky outcropping toward the setting sun. "When I was a boy my father told me 'judge a man by his actions because you can't know his thoughts'. You should heed that advice. We all want success and I'm doing my best to see it happens. I'd also like to send you home alive, believe it or not." Thoughts of Daedilos had struck a painful chord and Livios no longer wanted to talk.

Baso looked bewildered. "I believe you."

"Start a fire."

*   *   *

Livios was shaken awake and he labored to sit; it was still dark. "What is it, Harca?" he asked Baso's nephew.

"Have a message for you, *sestar*," Harca replied and placed a scroll on the ground.

"Thank you."

Livios picked his way through the sleeping men and knelt beside the fire. He broke the seal and read: *Greetings, Kerebos. Have any extra arrows? We've been very active already. When are you going to start? Luecos.* Livios crumpled the scroll and dropped it into the fire.

It was a misty, cool morning. *Winter is coming early again*, Livios thought as he crawled from his bedroll. He walked to the edge of the camp and relieved himself near the horses. Baso was nearby doing the same thing.

"Who's our fastest rider?" Livios asked.

"Any of five or six. Why?"

"Last night I got a message from Luecos *Sestar*. Things are pretty active up north and he's short on arrows. I want to send for more."

Baso pulled up his pants. "Good idea. Did he lose anyone?"

Livios recalled that Luecos' men were related to Baso. "He didn't say."

Baso grunted as though to say, "Why would he?"

"Send for the arrows and anything else we need," Livios said.

"Yes, *sestar*."

Livios walked back to his bedroll and grabbed his moccasins. Most of his men were already awake and the previous night's stew was being reheated for breakfast. *Meat again*, he silently lamented, his stomach already hurting. *How I miss my grains.* He again pondered Luecos' communication and was forced to admit that further planning was pointless. *He's right, I've been stalling. It's time.*

The next day Livios' scouts spied a sizable wagon train bound for Ios; he conferred with Baso then moved to intercept. The convoy had probably embarked from Thebis with luxury articles such as textiles, liquor and sugar. Once Livios had watched such a caravan enter Ios, its wagons so swollen they required six horses apiece. He didn't remember it having much of a guard.

Livios and Baso were lying flat atop a hill, watching the approaching wagons. This was one of the most barren sectors of Ios and had long been depopulated. Irrigation ditches had all but filled and some trees dotted the tall grass. It was a raw, rainy day and the *Chaconni* were moving slowly over the ancient road.

"They're still two miles off," Livios said.

"Yes. You haven't eaten."

Livios declined admitting he was too nervous for food. "Nah, I'm fine," he said, scratching his facial scruff.

Baso suddenly laughed, an odd throaty sound. It was the first time Livios had heard such from a *Riiz*. "What?" he asked, baffled.

"Your beard. You'll have to scrape it to pass as one of us."

Livios cursed. "I usually shave every day and was looking forward to stopping. To be honest, I don't need to very often. Unlike my father, who started before he could walk, apparently."

"How old are you *sestar?*"

Livios tensed. "How old do I look?"

"I'm not very good at guessing *Chaconni* ages," Baso admitted.

"Twenty?"

"Almost," Livios lied. "How do you teach your horses to lay down?"

Baso was willing to change the subject and delved into training techniques. Livios listened with one ear while reevaluating his tactics. He had taken Baso's advice about which men worked best together and had broken the *Riiz* into three units. There were twenty riders behind the hill he now lay upon, twelve the next slope over and four hidden on the plain to cut off a retreat. The last group had mounts that would lay prone and silent for extended periods.

The weather grew uglier and hampered visibility. Livios regretted leaving his cloak at the castle, as the poncho Baso had given him was far too small. He longed for the warm dryness of the spoke, and for

Kassandra. He put her out of his mind with only the greatest difficulty.

More time passed.

"I've never used a sword before," Baso said.

He's chatty today, Livios thought. "It's the best weapon. Works for defense and offense."

"May I see yours?"

Livios was startled and checked his initial response; the request would have insulted any legionary. While he was considering a tactful reply Baso turned away.

"Sorry," Livios said at length. He rolled onto his side and unbuckled his swordbelt. "Here."

Baso eyed him but took the weapon. He pulled the blade and the slow hiss sent a shiver down Livios' spine. Baso thumbed the edge.

"Sharp."

Livios nodded, thinking, *I even miss drills.*

"It's lighter than I thought it'd be."

"Most swords aren't more than five pounds or so. We legionaries keep the weight in the handle. Better for stabbing."

Baso nodded. "I've held a Royal Guard's cutlass. The blade was very heavy. For slicing, right?"

Livios was impressed. "Right. Perfect for horseback. I could teach you a thing or two about swordfighting, if you'd like."

"I'm too old to start now. Your leaders probably wouldn't like it, either."

"No, they wouldn't. But I've already earned death by letting you draw my sword."

Baso looked frightened, a remarkable achievement for such a stone-face. "I don't want to get you into trouble, *sestar*." He quickly sheathed the sword and gave it back. "Thank you for so honoring me."

Livios didn't know how to respond. "And thanks for the fine bow."

"No one would kill me for giving it to you."

"Well, I'm not as crazy about my kit as some *landesknectos*. Most of them *name* their swords, if you can believe that."

Baso lifted his bow. "Meet Longclaw."

Livios tried not to laugh but lost the struggle. Baso laughed, too. Livios felt good and didn't want it to end but the wagons were almost in striking distance; he heard their squeaking axles. He fell silent as he gazed at the glum caravan, painfully cognizant that he was, for the first time, going to intentionally kill human beings who had never wished him harm.

"All right, Baso," he growled. "Let's go do this thing."

212

Lieutenant Pylos sagged in the saddle, feeling twice his twenty-five years. The rain was cold, his wet cloak heavy at the clasp, and he hadn't rested all day. The ancient gray road stretched endlessly across the landscape. He turned and whistled for his second in command, Sergeant Ramphios, who rode beside the lead wagon. *Is that scoundrel asleep?* he wondered. "Ramphios!"

The bearded sergeant pushed a drooping hood off his forehead, revealing a steel cap. "Coming, sir." He spurred his steed, whose hooves clapped over the uneven cobbles. Reaching Pylos, he smiled apologetically, displaying yellow teeth. "Sorry. I didn't hear you through the rain."

"Give me your canteen. I'm out of wine and am chilled to the bone."

Ramphios did as ordered and watched sadly as Pylos upended the vessel. The lieutenant could drink heroically, which explained his current, unenviable command.

Pylos lowered the canteen and belched; his haggard face had regained some color. "Have you checked on the men?"

"Yes, sir. First squad's still resting."

"Next time we stop, tell merchant what's-his-name that we're taking over his sleepwagon."

"Naxos?"

"Yes, him. If he doesn't like it tell him to provide us better shelter."

"Got it, sir."

"Here," Pylos said and offered the canteen.

Ramphios reached out and screamed; Pylos screamed, too. A black-feathered arrow had pinned their hands together! They tugged instinctively at the pinion, cursing all the while. Another arrow entered Ramphios' left temple and exploded out the right. Blood splashed Pylos' eyes as the shaft grazed his nose.

"What the hell!" he cried.

Ramphios toppled from the saddle and smacked hard onto the road. Pylos yelled again as Ramphios' weight yanked free the arrow. He tucked his bleeding palm under an armpit and squinted into the rain. Horsemen were nearly upon him! Only now did the figures, fuzzy in the downpour, voice their undulating battle cry. Pylos forgot his injury and pulled his cutlass.

"To arms! To arms!" he cried and charged the raiders who were now close enough for him to get a good look. *Tantorri this far north?* he thought, amazed. The nearest raised his bow. *Can they shoot on the run?*

An arrow slammed Pylos' neck and he crashed facedown into a shallow puddle, wondering what had happened. His head felt hot and he had the distinct impression that his nose had flattened against the road. He tried to move but his limbs would not obey. As he drowned Pylos heard hoofbeats all around.

The driver of the forward wagon saw Pylos fall and steered his horse team off the road. "Get up here!" he yelled to his companion, who was lying in back. Taking the wagon off the road proved a bad idea; its narrow wooden wheels dug deep into the wet earth. Three horsemen gave chase, whooping all the while. "Push out the bags!" the driver ordered as a *Riiz* pulled even with him and drew an arrow, even at a gallop. "No!" he cried and raised his hands. An arrow slammed his side and knocked the wind from his lungs. He grasped the fletch and tried to stand but the wagon struck some stones and he was bounced from the cart. He landed on the arrow and pushed it all the way through his body. Another *Riiz* grabbed the dangling reins and pulled the wagon to a halt.

The remaining *Chaconne* jumped from the wagon and dashed for the horizon. The *Riiz* with the reins whistled to his comrades and nodded toward the fleeing merchant, who was easily ridden down and trampled. The three warriors headed back into the thick of the action.

The rest of the wagon train was faring poorly, too. The second driver tried to execute a turn too fast and flipped his vehicle. The following wagons got jammed behind the wreck and suffered the concentrated wrath of their assailants' terrible recurved bows. The *Riiz* swarmed the now stationary targets and riddled them with arrows. The screams of horses and men rose into the air.

The *Chaconni* were brave and rallied like professionals. Six were in the saddle and charged without hesitation. Voicing their own battle cries, they pulled their weapons but were feathered before they could close. Another half dozen soldiers spilled from a wagon and were shot almost immediately. One man was literally pinned to the cart.

Livios and Baso watched the massacre from a distance. Livios wondered if any of the *Chaconni* had families. "I'm surprised your men shoot horses, as much as they worship them," he said.

"Those nags aren't good for anything but a plow."

The shouts and sounds of violence tapered off. Some of the *Riiz* dismounted and began to search the wagons. Those *Chaconni* who were still alive had their throats cut.

"Come on," Livios said.

They rode to the battle site. It was an ugly scene. Dead men lay sprawled on the grass and road. Crippled horses whinnied and writhed in the mud. Blood ran between the stone cracks. Some *Riiz* were already going through the wagons.

"Anyone wounded, Hamil?" Livios asked a man.

"None of us, *sestar*, but lots of these *Chaconni*."

Livios avoided looking at the corpses' faces. "Start recovering arrows."

The closest wagon's tailgate fell open and a corpse plopped onto the road, an arrow through its head. A *Riiz* pushed the canvas flap aside and looked out at Baso. "Tons of sugar in these bags," he reported.

"Take what we need, burn the rest."

Livios rode behind a wagon and peered in; two dead men lay atop scores of small crates. He smelled wine but the scent repulsed him; he imagined the drink going down warm, like blood. Again he gazed over the carnage he had caused.

Baso rode closer, his hair hanging in wet knots. "Come, we're done here."

Livios felt worse by the moment. Was the murder of these men really that crucial to the Legion? "We can't just leave them lying here," he said. "See if there are any shovels."

Baso shook his head. "We can't bury these men, *sestar*," he said quietly. "They need to be found like this. You know that."

"Like slaughtered sheep?"

"That's how we always leave them. Same as you legionaries do."

Livios shot a dark glance at Baso then pushed past him.

*   *   *

Livios sat on his bedroll, watching his men crowd the fire. They ate and talked casually. He wondered if having destroyed the wagon train at all bothered them.

Baso slipped over and sat on the grass, crossing his long arms. He stared at the sky. "The rain's moved on. Don't think we'll get any more for a while."

"Oh really?" Livios muttered. "How can you tell?"

"By the stars."

Livios didn't notice anything special about them and wondered if the *Riiz* was making sport of him.

"You didn't like killing those men, did you?" Baso asked.

"No."

"Because they're *Chaconni*?"

"I don't like killing innocent people. Any of them. I have orders to follow but I don't have to like them." Livios saw no purpose in pointing out how enthusiastically the *Riiz* had slaughtered the caravan.

Baso looked thoughtful. "I think you're a good man."

Livios smiled ruefully. "For a legionary?"

"Yes. Is obeying your masters worth it?"

Livios glanced away. "That's a good question."

A short while passed. "Many tribes honor the fox," Baso began. "My own is named for him. To my mind, though, the raccoon is the most skilful creature in the forest."

Livios raised an eyebrow.

Baso continued. "He can swim, climb, dig and fish, even has hands. He is brave at need, but crafty and cautious. Even man's settlements don't push him aside; he merely adapts. A raccoon always adapts—"

"At least until the hound's teeth close."

"Yes, but then fights fiercely, turning within his skin, scratching and biting. He has one fatal fault, though; he doesn't know how to cut his losses. Do you know the best way to catch one?"

Livios shook his head. *Can't believe I'm getting caught up in this.*

"Find a small hollow in a rock or tree and drop something he wants into it—a glass bead, a nut—and wait for him to close his fist about it. Once he does, he's trapped. He can't withdraw his hand unless he drops his prize, and that he just won't do. His desire clouds all reason and he'll let you walk right up and brain him."

Livios looked hard at Baso. "What advice would you give him?"

"I wouldn't," Baso replied with a queer grin. "I value his pelt too much. But if he read my thoughts, he'd be cautioned against being short-sighted. He'd be warned not to risk his only skin for some trinket that would profit him little even if he withdrew it, and profits him nothing if he dies." Baso uncrossed his arms and pushed himself to his feet. "At least that's what I think. I'm going to sleep now."

Livios nodded. "Thanks." He watched Baso shuffle off then turned and stared into the night.

Livios woke before the others and stoked the embers into a proper fire. He wished he had some broth; he had long ago polished off Luecos' gift. He wondered how Luecos was faring up north. The *Riiz* began to stir and someone started breakfast.

One of the sentries wandered in, bow over his shoulder. "Morning, *sestar*," he said with a yawn.

"Take some rest."

Baso sidled up to Livios. "How'd you sleep?"

Livios shrugged. At length he said: "Her name's Kassandra."

"Who?"

"My shiny trinket."

Baso grunted. "You can't drop her?"

"No."

Baso's jaw was set in thought. "Then make the hole bigger."

216

Baso was right about the rain; the next few days were warm and sunny. It felt like summer. Livios led his group into a shallow valley and ordered a halt. He slid off the horse and massaged his thighs, thinking, *Will I never get used to this?*

A bedraggled scout rode into the depression and hailed Livios. "*Sestar*, soldiers are coming," he said. "At least a cohort of cavalry."

A few hundred men, Livios thought. "Have they found the caravan?"

"No, but the buzzards mark a path even a *Chaconne* could follow." The scout looked embarrassed. "Sorry."

"How far off?"

"A few miles. They're moving slowly."

Livios smacked the *Riiz's* leg. "Good work, Lari. Switch horses, we're moving out."

"She's still fresh, *sestar*."

"Very well. Baso, leave everything we can!"

They approached the destroyed wagon train to within a mile but were careful to avoid scouts. Livios had sent his own outriders on a long, circular route around the enemy, giving them strict orders to stay out of sight. "Just make sure this wing's alone," he told them.

The unit dismounted and waited in a small wood; they wouldn't attack until dark. Livios and Baso sat apart and talked tactics. Baso etched the dirt with his knife.

"Usually their cavalry beds down like this," he said. "Tents here and here. They don't post many sentries, but they will after finding their dead comrades."

"Night scouts?"

"Depends on the commander. He has much to consider. If he does send them out, we'll kill them. Also, they'll keep their horses together."

Livios tried to put himself in the *Chaconni* officer's place. The man must be livid after finding the slain soldiers. *And here in his own back yard*, he thought. *I know how the ikar would feel!* "We'll wait until midnight before we attack. It'll have to be a brief encounter since we can't expend all our arrows."

"True. We won't be able to get these ones back."

"To be honest, Baso, I'd feel better if you personally appropriated half the men's supply—just in case their enthusiasm gets the best of them."

"I'll do it."

Livios walked to his horse and pulled some of his arrows from the quiver. "Start with mine."

Darkness. Livios and the *Riiz* crawled close to the *Chaconni* encampment, which was laid out as Baso had predicted. The campfires had burned low, but there was still enough light for shooting. The soldiers had cleared away the ruined wagons and, presumably, buried the dead. A number of sentries fringed the camp.

Even now they're not too concerned, Livios thought. *They will be after tonight.* He studied the long lines of posted horses. *At least a cohort.* He waited for his men to form a broad semicircle around the southern part of camp.

Baso slid to Livios' side. "We're ready," he whispered.

"You sure?"

"Yes. Didn't you hear the whistling?"

"Sounded like crickets."

"Some were. They'll join in once your bow sings."

Livios reflected upon his plan, wondering if the enemy would pursue immediately or wait until dawn. He slowly rose onto a knee and notched an arrow. The nearest sentry was only fifty paces away but the poor light made it seem twice as far. He drew the arrow back to his cheek and followed the pacing soldier with the point. The *Chaconne* stopped in front of a dying fire, perfectly outlined.

"Head shot, Felix," Livios said and loosed. The soldier fell forward without a sound but the *Riiz* heard the signal and began to shoot. Strings twanged in the night and the other sentries were dropped. Now shots tore into the tents. Men screamed. Bare-breasted *Chaconni* poured from tents and became immediate casualties.

"Get the horses!" Livios ordered and notched another missile. He shot the nearest animal, which bucked and screamed. Many others were rapidly stricken. One horse rolled through a fire and sent thousands of tiny red embers high into the air, giving the scene an unreal glow.

The enemy camp was in chaos. Horses were pulling their stakes and stampeding as their bawling masters tried to coordinate a response. Livios kept shooting until his arrows were spent. *We got half their horses!* he thought with satisfaction. He jumped to his feet and yelled the *Tantorri* word for "withdraw" before bolting off toward his mount. Breathing heavily with exertion and excitement, he swung up into the saddle and secured his bow as a few *Riiz* reached his position. "Disperse and meet at camp three!" he cried, repeating earlier orders. "Don't approach with men on your tail!" With that he spurred his horse and raced across the inky plain.

MURDER

Kassandra took another sheet from the clothesline which Livia helped fold. It was a blustery day and the cloth almost got away from them.

"Bekkah didn't do a very good job," Livia said. "They're still dirty."

Kassandra nodded as she dropped the sheet into the wicker basket. "Take these inside for me, dear."

"Ok." Livia hefted the wicker and made for the barn's back door.

Kassandra upended an empty bucket and sat down. She was tired and sore; she had had a lot of company last night because the Legion was moving out today. She closed her eyes and listened to the wind rushing past her ears; she imagined the same gust had washed Livios. *I wish I could smell him,* she thought. *He's never rank, like the others.* She remembered the last time they had slept next to each other and missed the feeling of his big arms. *He's still never tried anything,* she reminded herself with a mixture of relief and apprehension.

"What are you thinking?" Livia asked in her little voice.

Kassandra opened her eyes. "Nothing."

They heard voices and the sounds of tramping feet. The legionaries were gathering in the yard.

"Ooh, let's go watch!" Livia said and grabbed Kassandra's hand. "Come!"

Kassandra allowed herself to be led to the front of the house. "We have to stay close," she said as Livia tugged her hand.

"But I can't see!"

"You'll see well enough." And they could. A few hundred legionaries were visible just past the Second spoke; they were in full gear and had extra pila in their back slings.

"That's the Sixth *Elhar*," Livia said.

"I can't tell."

"Is Kerebos up there, you think? He's been away a long while."

"I guess he has."

219

"Where is he?"

"I don't know, child," Kassandra said. A cold thought slowly crept into her mind. What if he was already dead? The notion hurt, which scared her.

"Are you all right?"

"Yes."

"Wouldn't it be nice if me and you and Kerebos could move away?"

Kassandra stared at the little wisp of a girl, thinking, *What made her say that?* "I don't think that will ever happen."

They were both startled to see Mother and other women coming up behind them; Mother's fat face was grim. "You two come along," she ordered. "The *ikar* has summoned us."

Phaetonis gazed down from the flat castle roof. Legionaries, slaves, tanners, armorers and *Tantorri* had crowded onto the grass between First Spoke and the main gate. The Brotherhood's great standard snapped above them.

Have to give them something to remember while I'm gone, Phaetonis thought. "The Legion marches today," he bellowed. "I leave all in Magos' care. He'll have complete control over the premises, people and property. Make no mistake, he *must* be obeyed." He placed his fists on his hips. "Many runners are staying to help enforce his will. I suggest you behave." He nodded at a knot of runners. "Kill twenty slaves."

The runners jumped to action, pulling daggers as they ran. The slaves, packed against the wall, began to shout and some tried to open the gate. The runners butchered the required number before the others could even react and left the quivering corpses on the ground. Phaetonis looked on with satisfaction.

"Don't make it that quick, though, Magos!" he said with a laugh.

"Yes, sir."

Phaetonis gazed over the congregation. "Return to your duties," he said then disappeared, soon to emerge from the spoke. He asked the *Tantorri:* "Your orders are clear?"

"Yes, lord *ikar!*" they replied.

"Good. Lasctakos, let's move out!" he cried.

The gates were opened and the formations passed through in close order. Many wagons waited on the plain. Phaetonis was the last man over the moat. The gate was secured as runners manned the walls.

*　　　　*　　　　*

Livios and the *Rüz* were not pursued and reached camp without incident. There was more good news, too; Baso's man had returned with thousands of arrows. The pack animals were unloaded to the relief of the entire host.

"The *Chacconi* have it hard now," Baso said in his flat tone.

Livios nodded, his face grave.

"We should press them tomorrow," Baso counseled.

"I agree."

"Kill their scouts, shoot into the camp at night. We should put out a party before light to intercept their communications."

"Do it," Livios said. "We're back at it in the morning."

The *Riiz* picked off a number of *Chaconni* messengers the next day and captured valuable dispatches. Another leather-encased scroll was delivered to Livios, who reigned his horse to a stop and read. "I don't believe it," he said and sent for Baso.

Baso was scouting and it was hours until he reported. He found Livios hunched over a stewpot.

Livios looked up and asked: "How'd it go?"

The *Riiz*'s lips tightened into his version of a smile. "A couple more notches on Long Claw."

"The main body hasn't moved?"

"No, *sestar*. Scouts only. They're digging in. We must've gotten more of their horses than we thought." Baso squinted suddenly. "Why?"

Livios smirked. "We killed their commander *and* his executive officer last night. They have two junior lieutenants in charge, and it seems they don't get along so well."

Baso reached into the pot and grabbed a chunk of meat. "How could you know that?"

"The last two dispatches asked for different things and were signed by different men."

Baso looked confused. "What's that mean?"

"That they're divided. They'll break easily without a strong leader. Promise me you nabbed all the riders they sent out."

"We shot all we saw. Maybe these dispatches are a ruse?"

Livios shook his head. "They don't have the time. We'll snipe them throughout the night, ride right up into their camp. If they won't come out we'll bring it to them."

"Good thing they don't have archers," Baso said.

"Isn't it? They won't make the same mistake next time. They'll scrape some bowmen together."

"Mercenaries?"

"Probably *Aharoni*. It'll take two weeks for them to get a force back into this sector, I figure. We won't have such easy pickings going forward."

221

"Those desert rats shoot well," Baso allowed.

"So I've heard."

The *Riiz* killed fourteen riders before dark then tightened the noose around the camp. The *Chaconni* lit no fires but there was sufficient moonlight for shooting. The *Riiz* riddled the enemy incessantly. Baso had been correct about the digging in, but these cavalrymen were no legionaries and their "entrenching" was a sloppy, ineffective, patchwork affair. True, a man could hide behind one of the three-foot mounds, but the horses remained targets. Before long all the mounts were hit. The cavalrymen were incensed; they cursed and oathed at their unseen assailants. A few actually stormed the plain to come to grips with their tormentors but they didn't get far.

Livios looked beyond the riddled soldiers toward the stricken horses. He found the beasts' ceaseless screaming hard to endure. *Why won't they just die?* he thought sadly. He pulled handfuls of grass from the ground in frustration.

"They're big," Baso said. "It takes a while."

"They'll parley in the morning."

"These cavalrymen are no cowards," Baso replied. "I know them. They won't quit so soon."

Livios shook his head. "They've no choice. Their horses are casualties and they're running low on water, not to mention leadership. You'll be talking in my stead, since I can't have them see me."

"As you say."

The *Riiz* continued the assault all night. The *Chaconni* kept their heads down but somehow managed to put the horses out of their misery. Time limped by.

Darkness was waning when Livios told Baso: "We're pulling out. Spread the word."

"Eh?"

"Don't want them to see how few we are."

"What's that matter? They're all going to die anyway." A moment passed. "Aren't they?"

Livios wasn't sure. Could he kill men who tried to surrender? "Let's move," he said.

The *Chaconni* hoisted a white scarf at first light; it was tied to a lance and snapped in the wind. Livios saw it from a quarter of a mile off and sighed. This was the moment he had feared and dawn had brought him no new counsel.

Baso rode up. "You were right, legionary. Now what?"

I've no idea, Livios thought.

"*Sestar*, if I may?"

Livios grunted.

"You predicted they'd fold over divided leadership. We should avoid that ourselves."

He's right, Livios silently conceded but said: "Let's find out what they want first."

Baso looked sympathetic. "All right." He whistled for riders and galloped toward the *Chaconni*.

Livios watched them go with a sinking feeling. He knew what the enemy would request and knew what his answer must be. *God help me*, he thought. *Why'd Lasctakos put this on me?* Baso returned swiftly; his face gave away nothing; Livios resented the *Riiz's* flat demeanor.

"Again you're right," Baso said, his horse stopping nose to nose with Livios'. "They're through."

Livios gazed toward the flag of truce. "What terms?"

"Anything. I even told them they'd have to give up their arms and standard."

"Where'd you leave it?"

"Told them I needed to think. Is that all right?"

Livios closed his eyes briefly. "Yes. Good work."

Baso came a little closer. "*Sestar*, if you let them go we may live to regret it."

"I know."

"If you want, I'll take the men in myself," Baso offered.

"Who gives the orders here?" Livios snapped.

"You. I only wanted—"

"Then why would I let you give this one?" Livios pulled his sword. "I won't ask you to do something I won't do."

Baso's eyes narrowed.

Livios' face clouded. "Dead men tell no tales. Let's go." He ordered his men to ring the camp, telling Baso, "Don't shoot until I say. I'm going in."

"Yes, *sestar*."

Alone, Livios approached the nearest entrenchment; he smelled dead bodies. Heads poked into view as he slid from the saddle, roaring, "Who commands here?"

There was some confusion among the *Chaconni* but an officer in a scarlet-plumed helmet soon crawled atop the mound of dirt. "I do!" he growled. "Lieutenant Samos of Epiros!"

Livios continued across the grass; the death stench grew. "Are you sure? I read your correspondences. Seems you can't really decide."

Samos scowled. He was a young man, but lines of privation creased his face; tawny hair stuck from beneath his helmet. His light eyes were ablaze. "I've offered to place my men in your care. What's your answer?

Wait, you're no *Tantorri!*"

Livios laughed and stopped a short distance from the enemy.

"You've made an offer I don't want and can't accept. Marry yourself to the idea that you're all going to die."

The blood drained from Samos' face. "Barbarian," he spat. "What makes you think we'll go without a fight?"

"There'll be a fight, just not much of one." Livios nodded east and west at the *Riiz.* "They'll drop you all in two sallies. I can't fathom the arrogance that brought you out here so unprepared. Makes me angry, actually." *If their officers weren't so foolhardy I wouldn't be in this situation!* he thought.

Samos' expression was sober but determined.

"I'll give you one last throw," Livios said, bending the black sword in his hands.

"How's that?"

"Engage me in single combat. You best me and your men go free."

"No!" the *Chaconni* cried.

"*Sestar,* don't!" Baso shouted from the other side of the circle.

Samos' face reddened. "*Sestar?*" he growled. "You goddamned renegade! Since when do *landesknectos* command cavalry?"

Livios glared in Baso's direction then back at Samos, who now stood on the tiny hill. "That's right, lieutenant. And that's why I can't let you go."

"I accept!" Samos shouted and drew his cutlass. His men started to rise. "Get back!" he commanded.

Livios waited serenely out on the grass. "Come down, then."

Samos unbuckled his helmet and threw it to the ground, then unhitched his swordbelt. He jumped down, moving away from Livios' sword with quickness that belied his stature. His burnished metal breastplate, gauntlets and shinguards were of obvious quality and provided considerable protection. He moved with caution but not panic; his lantern jaw was set.

He's anxious to tally a legionary, Livios thought. He admired Samos' courage and decided to kill him quickly. He deftly switched hands and charged, blade level. Samos' cutlass angled to intercept but his footwork indicated this was but a feint; when he suddenly leaped to Livios' right he found that the legionary had already countered him! Livios saw the wonder in Samos' eyes as he smacked the cutlass aside and spiked the lieutenant in the throat with the pommel. Samos had yet to react before Livios stepped close and decapitated him with a long, smooth power cut.

Samos crashed forward onto the ground and his head smacked off his back, leaving a smattering of blood. Livios stared down at the corpse, a great anger within him. He glanced at the other *Chaconni*, who were openly terrified.

"At least this one was brave," he berated them. He kicked Samos' head and it bounced off the earthen ramp into the camp. "I was going to give you a chance at me, but you don't deserve it! Baso, finish them!"

He turned from the proceedings and stomped off to the singing of bows and poignant screams.

Afterwards, the outfit withdrew to a region twenty miles southeast of Ios City. Livios was unsure why he chose the spot, except that it was far from the massacred *Chaconni*. He sat apart as the others divvied up the valuables they had stripped from the dead.

Livios saw Baso stand and guessed the old *Tantor* was coming over for a chat. He liked Baso, but was in no mood to talk.

"May I join you?" Baso asked.

"Sure."

They sat in silence for a time, listening to their others squabble.

"We're all impressed," Baso said. "You make good decisions."

"For a *landesknecta?*"

"For anyone. Already you're a better cavalry commander than me, and I'm good."

Livios decided against thanking him. *He's just buttering me up.*

"I'm sorry for what you had to do," Baso continued.

"Had to," Livios muttered.

An uncomfortable silence. "I just wanted to say that." Baso stood.

"It doesn't really bother me," Livios blurted as the *Rüz* turned to leave. "If they're going to ride to war they should come to fight."

"I agree."

Livios eyes stung. He wished desperately that Daedilos was here, or Lasctakos. "They made all the mistakes, not me!"

"Yes."

"Right?" Livios looked imploringly at Baso. "Right?"

"They did, *sestar*," Baso replied evenly.

Livios nodded to himself, rocking back and forth. "Leave, would you?"

Baso woke to cold rain hitting his face and released Long Claw; the clouds were very low in the morning sky. He sat and rubbed his eyes before looking around. The other men were up and about. *I've slept late*, he thought. *Where's the sestar?*

Baso slid from his blankets, drew on his moccasins and took a long pull from his water skin. He stood with effort and attempted to stretch the kinks from his back. *That pain's getting worse every season*, he told himself, rubbing his spine. Thoughts of his first wife crossed his mind and a warmth settled in his breast. *My little Qevva. She could squeeze out the knots!* The welcome feeling ebbed. *Has it really been ten years?*

Baso limped to the fire and held his gnarled hands over the hissing flames. A quick inspection revealed that the hanging breakfast pot was empty.

"Morning, uncle," Harca called as he walked toward the creek. "Don't worry, I saved you some."

"Where's the *sestar?*"

Harca jerked a thumb over his shoulder. "With the horses."

Baso enjoyed the flames a little longer before starting across the broad clearing. The young legionary came into view; he was standing head and shoulders above a gathering of *Riiz*. His face was quite animated, in fact he was smiling.

What on earth did he find to smile about? Baso wondered. Livios waved him over and he squeezed into the tight ring around the legionary. *Who's on guard?*

"So Luecos saw Melas crawling from the tent and slopped the top liquid from the broth," Livios told them. "Slipped in some more *kraal* resin, too. Melas isn't really an early riser, which is why he marches into the night, so it was a good bet he'd appropriate the drink." He chuckled. "No sooner had Luecos scraped out the last then Melas snatched it. 'Thanks, I'll take that!' he says. Luecos didn't try to stop him but did warn that it was 'a tad stiff today'. Melas dirtied his kilt before he got back to his tent. Probably a bunch of other times inside, too; that broth was *strong*. We stayed put that day and Luecos won the bet."

This was just the sort of story that appealed to the taciturn *Riiz* and some of them even laughed. All appeared amused.

"So take care when you swipe a legionary's drink," Livios cautioned. "You men get the camp squared away, now, and pack for a few days. I want a word with Baso."

The knot of *Tantorri* broke up.

Baso was astonished and pleased by the *sestar's* improved attitude and didn't want to ruin it. "Morning."

"Hello!" Livios replied. "Slept in, huh?" They stared at each other for a brief spell. "I'm fine," Livios assured.

"Yes?"

Livios' beatific expression faded. "Yes. If they wanted to live they should have fought better."

Baso wanted out of the conversation. "You called?"

Livios was now facing his horse, roughing the creature's neck. "That's right. I've given thought to our next target."

Baso had wondered at Livios' plans. "Good. Plenty of homesteads to flatten before the king's cavalry return."

226

Livios whirled, all vestiges of amusement gone. "We won't hit any farms, got that! Do you know how hard those poor bastards work just to get by?" He calmed quickly. "No commoners, Baso. That's the way it's going to be."

"As you wish," Baso answered, though he knew the other *landesknectos* weren't so restricted. *Even Riiz like a nice, easy homestead,* he thought. "Where to, then?"

This time Livios' smile reached his eyes. "Something juicy. Ios city."

Livios had no illusions about his ability to capture Ios with his little band but his impression of Governor Wartos made him believe that the *Riiz* could make a royal nuisance of themselves. Ios housed less than a hundred troops and no professional cavalry. It had been ages since an enemy had attacked the town and the 'soldiers' were more police force than fighters. True, they settled disputes and strong-armed the locals, but they were not men of war as far as Livios could tell. Having seen them up close, he was confident they would go to any lengths to preserve their own skins. Add the fact that the citizens were of the sorts who endured a magistrate like Wartos and Livios had few concerns. *Too bad they can't know it's Daedilos' boy doing it to them,* he thought vindictively. His qualms about molesting peasants didn't extend to Ios, not after how they had treated his father. Still, he had no intention of killing noncombatants.

Livios approached Ios from the southwest across broken country. He chose this path to avoid prying eyes (and farms) but if his men knew he had led them twice as far as he needed they didn't seem to mind. The city's walls came into sight as another wet evening settled over the land.

"Dismount but keep your arguments at hand," Livios ordered. He swung from the saddle feeling much sprier for the ride than he would have a few weeks earlier.

"How many live in such a city, *sestar?*" a young *Riiz* asked.

Livios knew that Ios was probably the most impressive town most of the tribesmen had ever seen. It was the biggest he had ever seen, for that matter. "I'm not sure. A few thousand, perhaps." He walked over to Baso, who had plucked Long Claw's string and was listening intently, as would a master musician to an instrument. "Is he okay?"

Baso made a surly face. "Fraying a bit."

"You can still use it?"

"But I'll have to replace it soon." He unstrung the bow and hung it on the saddle. "When do we attack?"

"Middle of the night."

"So late?"

"Yes. That'll be the end of the first watch and the sentries will be far less vigilant. Not that they're eagles, anyway."

Baso scratched his scalp. "You know their leader?"

"I met him once. A little toad of a man. I'd love to get a shot at him."

Baso pulled his bedroll from the horse.

"Send out scouts before you rest," Livios said. "Just to make sure nobody's sneaking up on us."

It continued to drizzle and the temperatures fell enough that the rain began to freeze on the ground. Ios lit up well against the night but Livios' band was too far away to see the guards on the parapet. Scouts returned with surprising information.

"Twenty sentries," Livios repeated. "That seems a lot."

"Do they know we're here?" Baso wondered aloud.

Livios considered this. "Maybe not us specifically, but perhaps they've heard about other trouble. Guess Wartos isn't the fool I thought." Livios clapped his forehead. "The caravan that didn't get through, that's what it is."

"Pricked with our own knives. Twenty. We won't be able to double up on two of them."

"I know. Pick your finest shooters for the solo jobs."

"Then you'll have to take one of them."

"You're joking?"

"I know marksmen," the old *Riiz* continued. "You're one. It hurts to say, *Chaconne*, but you're the best we have."

"I'm flattered," Livios replied sincerely. "I'll do it. We'll time it to one of those owl screeches of yours. One for 'ready', two for 'loose.'"

"Yes, *sestar*."

Livios quietly called the men together and attempted a head count. "We all here?"

"Bol's making a final sweep," someone replied.

"Good. We'll be spread thin around the wall, a mile almost, so I'm giving instructions now. You *must* take out your marks. Dismount and get as close as you can without being seen. Don't go for the head shots, either, but take them at the broadest point. If you get a second shot, take it. Yes? Who is that, Wenni?"

"It is, *sestar*. I'm not much of a shot unless I'm on horseback."

"Stay mounted then. After your kills, regroup off the main gate but stay out of crossbow range. If anyone issues from the town, which I doubt, we'll pick them off. When I give the word, we withdraw together. If you get separated, don't worry; we're meeting here before pulling out. Any questions? No? Then good luck! Baso, make your assignments."

They were soon on their way. Livios was impressed by how silently the *Riiz* melted into the night. There was very little metal in their gear, man or horse, and was therefore none of the jingling that accompanied most cavalry. The horses were not even shod. The unit splintered into twos, leaving Livios to proceed by himself. Before long he heard nothing but rain and the squish of his mount's steps. The drizzle intensified so he recalled a leather cap from his pocket and slid it over his head. *Feels funny with all that hair up there,* he thought, wondering when he last had it cut. *Keeps growing like this and I really will pass for a Tantor.*

The walls grew as he approached and he saw his target pacing back and forth just left of the gate. *Idiots!* he thought. *Why have torches up there? Do they want to be shot?* The sentry wasn't even pretending to watch the plain. *Lazy bastard. Phaetonis would have his head for that.* The guard must have been tall because his chest was clearly visible.

Livios stopped a hundred yards out and eased from the saddle. He pulled his dagger and slipped it into the earth then wound the reins around it; he scratched the horse's nose before claiming the bow and quiver. Noiselessly, he advanced to within easy range and dropped to a knee; cold water soaked his leg. He was breathing hard as he gazed up at the soldier, feeling the excitement he always felt when on the hunt. "Not much of a shot is it, Felix?" he said quietly.

Livios strung the arrow but didn't draw; it might be some time before the others reached position, due to their longer routes. He studied the sentry, marking the way the man walked, noting how he changed direction on every tenth step. *I'm right on top of him,* he thought and decided on a headshot. *Really, if I miss this one I deserve what happens.*

No doubt about that! Felix's voice chimed in.

Livios smiled. "Wish you were here." Just then he heard Baso's unmistakable owl hoot. *That was quick,* he thought and drew the bow, which creaked. He looked the length of the arrow at the soldier's gently illuminated silhouette, placing the point on his head. An endless moment passed; his heart drummed in his ear. The guard reached the end of his path and turned. The second signal came and Livios loosed. The arrow hit the target's ear and splashed from the top of the head. The stricken man staggered and crashed from sight.

Livios exhaled sharply and glanced from side to side. He rose to his feet and listened for screams or signals. Silence. *Good job, boys,* he thought and retreated to his horse. He was well on his way back to camp before an alarm shook the night. There was some shouting at first then a bell. *That'll wake them,* he thought.

Livios sent out scouts before sunrise with orders to keep Ios bottled up and to announce any unwanted visitors. He went over to where Baso was stretched out beneath a tree and found the *Riiz* atop his cover and rubbing his short, crooked legs.

"Lovely day, huh?" Livios asked.

Baso grunted as he pulled Long Claw from beneath the blankets. "I had to keep the strings dry," he explained.

"Get yourself together. You're going in to offer terms."

Harca wandered over. "What about fire, *sestar*?" he asked after a yawn.

"Hold off for now," Livios replied. Then to Baso: "You ready to meet the Governor?"

"What should I say?"

"Demand he surrender the town and be haughty about it. Don't give any conditions. Tell him you've already destroyed the caravan and the cohorts that came after it and you'll do the same to Ios if he doesn't let us in. Let it slip that you want your army to winter there."

Baso frowned. "He'll never agree."

"I don't want him to. I just want to convince him that there's an 'army' out here. We'll keep out of sight and light a bunch of fires to give the illusion of numbers."

"What if he wants to see my army?"

"Ignore the request. You're making the demands, not him."

Baso stood and began to square away his kit.

Livios hoped he wasn't sending the *Riiz* into danger. "Be careful," he said.

"I will."

Baso was gone so long Livios began to worry. He was ready to investigate when the *Riiz* returned, wearing an expression even gloomier than usual.

"What's wrong?" Livios called.

Baso shook his head as he dismounted. "Where is everyone?"

"Who do you think is keeping those fires going around the city? What happened?"

"I rode in like you wanted and demanded the governor. They tried foisting a subordinate upon me but I acted as though I knew Wartos. Good description you gave."

"Continue!"

Baso gave that odd, tight grin and Livios relaxed, thinking, *He's playing with me.*

"The little toad rolled over almost immediately," Baso continued. "Caught me off guard, it was so cowardly."

"Then what have you been doing all this time?" Livios demanded. "I was getting anxious."

"I started making more demands. First I wanted to see all his soldiers—"

"You went into the town!"

"I had them mount the wall." Baso replied. "They were very reluctant to do that. Nineteen of their comrades had been picked off with headshots, you see."

Livios was angry. "I gave other orders."

Baso stroked his chin. "I know. That's why I took my man in the heart. Where'd yours hit?"

Livios scowled. "All right, all right. Go on."

"Then I asked to see his strong room. That took some time. I'm sure his man needed to hide things first."

Livios shook his head in disbelief. "He gave you an inventory?"

"He did." Baso reached under his shirt and withdrew a parchment.

Livios opened it and whistled. "He admitted to all this?"

"He would've yanked out his eyeteeth had I asked," Baso replied in disgust. "I can't decide if he's a gelding or a mare."

Livios was flummoxed. "I just wanted to tweak their noses," he said. "Never thought they'd actually go for it." He looked at Baso. "What do we do? We don't have the men to hold that town. Hell, I don't dare let them know our numbers."

Baso was still smiling. "Don't ask me, legionary, I just follow orders."

Livios thought hard. "We have to demand something he can't deliver," he said at last. "He obviously believes we're here in force and that's all I wanted to accomplish."

"We should at least get the money."

"Oh, yes. Their horses, too. Go grab them while I'm thinking," Livios ordered.

"That works well, his beasts bearing off his treasure. I can't believe such a man lives. I'd rather burn in hell that suffer such dishonor."

Livios remembered Wartos. "Who knows? Maybe he's enjoying this."

Baso eventually returned with twenty-three beautiful horses and six small, ironbound treasure chests. Livios and some of the men admired the booty.

"Those are fine looking mounts," Livios said.

"They are," Baso agreed. "And they're not even *Tantorri*. We should keep these ones."

Aharoni desert breed, Livios thought, noting the horses' lean bodies. *Wartos knows his animals. This had to hurt.*

Baso dismounted and ran his hand over a stallion's shiny coat. "You know he has more treasure in there," he said casually.

"Of course, but we can't carry too much, anyway."

"What're you going to do with it?"

Livios had wondered about that. His orders were to turn over *all* money to Phaetonis—"Whatever falls into your hands" the *ikar* had said. *But these men deserve something,* he thought. "I'd say that at the moment the metal and jewels are in your possession. Why not give half to me as a gift and split the rest among the men?"

Everyone turned toward Livios.

Baso looked surprised. "That's very generous, *sestar*. What'll your masters say?"

"Keep the horses, too. Let's eat."

"Wartos still expects your army to invest the town," Baso said between bites of mutton.

Livios finished his meat and wiped his hands on the ground. The grass was wet, but it had finally stopped raining. "I know. We're going to demand that every citizen leave Ios. He could never agree to that. The king would have his head for abandoning the town with no enemy in sight."

But Wartos did accept the terms! Baso could hardly make his report, he was laughing so hard.

Livios stood in amazed silence.

"I say, *sestar*," Baso managed, wiping tears. "Maybe we should demand he eat his own hands?"

"And his retainers sat still for this?" Livios asked.

"They didn't look very happy."

Livios sat in silent disbelief for a long time but finally his eyes lit up. "I've got it! Tell him we want him to torch the town before we let him leave."

"Torch?"

"Yes, as in burn it."

"What if he agrees?"

Livios shook his head. "How could he?"

A scout rode into camp and cried, "Ios is burning, *sestar*!"

Livios couldn't believe his ears. "What?" He looked in Ios' direction but couldn't see through the trees. "Give me your horse!"

Livios swung into the saddle, wheeled and galloped toward the main gate. As he got round the trees he noted that smoke was indeed curling from the city. He saw Baso parked out on the plain and adjusted direction.

"I don't know how I'm going to put this in my report." Livios said. "The *cohar* will think I'm lying."

Baso sat motionless, a look of contentment upon his face. "They're

232

putting it out, though. Seems the townspeople have finally changed Wartos' mind for him."

Livios turned and saw someone swinging from the wall. It was obvious from the way the man struggled that his limbs were bound. "Is it Wartos?" he asked hopefully.

"It's him. Can tell by that purple robe."

Livios couldn't positively identify the victim but the portly physique fit. Curiosity got the better of him and he rode into bolt range for a closer look. It *was* Wartos. "Now he has a purple face to go with that robe."

Baso rode up. "Look at him kick."

Livios laughed. "The little pimple! Thank God they killed him. It'd be a sin to let him live."

The smoke began to thin. The townsfolk had reached the fire in time.

"I could just watch him swing there all day," Livios said.

*   *   *

Livios led his team southeast. They were short on water but he knew a number of good creeks in the vicinity. The only problem, though, was that the trek brought them within a mile of his old home, the mere thought of which made him tremble. He pressed on.

Livios' excitement peaked with his terror. He wanted badly to visit his farm but knew he couldn't handle the strain. *I'd break down in front of these men,* he thought. *Hell, I'm nearly crying already.* He thought of the people he had killed since Daedilos and felt sick. *Big sestar!* he silently ridiculed himself. *Killed your own father!*

The unit reached the top of a knoll and Livios called a halt. He made a show of getting his bearings but in reality had simply lost the will to proceed. One of the *Riiz* spied a distant covered wagon, headed west toward Ios, and sang out.

"He's speeding up, *sestar!*" another man cried. "Must've marked us!"

"I see," Livios muttered. He didn't want to pursue the wagon, in fact, he didn't feel like doing anything, but he couldn't have the driver report his band's size or movements.

"Take him?" Baso asked.

Livios suddenly kicked his horse. "At 'em!"

The horsemen thundered across the grassland, straight for the wagon. Livios began to feel the thrill of the chase and was able to forget his home as it receded behind him.

Baso began to inch past his commander, the old man tucked over like a jockey from Korenthis' circus. "You're too big to be a rider!" he said, his voice full and vital. The other *Riiz* crept past Livios, too.

"Get it before it reaches sight of the city!" he ordered.

Baso nodded.

Livios tried to emulate the *Riiz's* riding style but couldn't perpetually stand in the stirrups; he was nearly jostled from his horse. *The little bastard's right*, he thought. *I'm too heavy.* He steadily lost ground and was well behind his men by the time they were within bowshot of the cart. The wagon was really moving down the highway, though. The *Chaconni* had completed the road while at the height of their power and this section had been meticulously maintained.

The *Riiz* were now on the wagon's rear and Livios, lagging behind, could hear its wooden wheels over the thudding of hooves. *Must be noisy on that cart*, he thought. Now he heard the wagon master's frantic exhortations and the crack of a whip. The *Riiz* voiced their battle cry to signify the end of the chase and began to shoot. Arrows rained on the wagon and road; brief sparks flashed on the stones.

One of the *Riiz* drew equal with the driver and shot. The team of horses continued at full speed for a short while but slowed as other *Riiz* squeezed the team's leaders.

Livios marveled at his men's skill. The wagon was motionless now and the *Riiz* whooped as they crowded the vehicle. *That's more than the crow of success. They've found something good. Ikar, how much more treasure can we carry?*

The *Riiz* hardly noticed as Livios arrived. "What in hell is it, Baso?" he cried above the din.

Baso rested off to the side. "Woman."

Livios' heart sank. Only then did he hear the struggling female.

Anger flashed within him. "Stop! Get back!" he roared in the loudest voice any of them had ever heard. The *Riiz* halted and turned. Livios called them by name. "Harca, Lua, Cuuar! Get down from there! You're soldiers, not rapists!"

The *Riiz* stared with frozen faces.

Livios pulled his sword. "I said hands off her! Didn't you hear me?" His vision took on that red tint and he knew he was perilously close to losing control. A legionary he may be, but never would he sit back and allow the violation of a defenseless woman. "I'll count to three," he said slowly.

The *Riiz* began to slough off the victim. Many looked shamed and some were asking Livios' forgiveness, but he was not in a conciliatory mood. The last man dropped from the wagon revealing a beautiful, disheveled woman on the wooden seat. Livios pulled his water skin and approached. The woman sobbed quietly, hand over mouth, but managed to thank him.

Livios reached for his bedroll, to cover her, but his heart suddenly froze. "Move your hand," he said.

Blue eyes flashed in his direction and at that moment Livios knew her. It was Vara, his old neighbor, she who had seduced him and had witnessed the killing of Daedilos. At once, his crimes bore down as though God Himself had laid a finger on him. He slumped on the horse.

Vara brushed a lock from her eyes and wiped slobber from her lovely, flushed face. "L-Livi?" she stammered, hugging herself. "Livios!"

The *Rüz* looked ruefully at each other. "Did we attack his kin?" Harca asked Baso.

Vara covered herself with her ripped dress and cried hysterically: "Where have you been? Why are you with these raiders? You killed my husband!"

Livios closed his eyes to shut her out but she only screamed louder.

"Livi, why'd you attack us? Did you kill all those s-s-soldiers?"

Livios remembered the day, so long ago, when she had visited his farm. *And started all my troubles*, he thought. *If she hadn't been there I wouldn't have killed him*, he thought; he felt anger coming on. Vara was still hurling questions but he wasn't listening.

"What're we going to do with her, *sestar?*" someone asked.

"Why not just leave?" Baso suggested.

But Livios didn't hear. He was thinking of Daedilos' corpse on the barn floor and Vara's repeated shouts of "You killed him!" In fact, she was saying that at the moment. He opened his eyes to see her wringing hands over her husband, sobbing, "You killed him, Livi."

"Who was he?" Livios asked.

She turned teary eyes at him. "What?"

"Who—was—he?"

Vara stroked the dead man's hair. "You didn't know him. He's not been around long."

"Really?" he asked dangerously. "Then why are you more upset about him than you were about my father, who you knew all your life?"

Vara had the look of someone caught in a lie. "I cried for him, too."

Livios gave a nasty chuckle. "No doubt; you cry over everything. Doesn't help, does it? So how long did it take you to trick this fool into marrying you? Or did you just ambush him in a barn?"

Vara's lower lip trembled. "Livi, why are you being so cruel? It wasn't like that."

"No? You can't wait to run off and tell everyone I killed someone else, can you? Did you tell them your part in the matter?"

Vara nodded vigorously. "Of course I did! Oh, baby giant, why are you—"

"SHUT UP!!!" Livios erupted. He dropped the sword, leaped from the saddle and yanked her to the ground by her hair. He brandished a giant fist. "Whimpering over that dog like he's someone, with dad and Felix dead!" he raged. "Did you tell everyone how you did them in?"

"Felix?" she whined from a fetal position.

"Apologize!"

"Sorry! I'm so sorry!"

Livios flipped her onto her back and squat on her chest. "Yes, now you are. Where were you when I needed you?" He wrapped his giant hands around her neck and squeezed.

Vara's face darkened as she flailed at his wrists. Her eyes rolled back in her head.

Livios stopped suddenly and sat hunched over her. *What's wrong with me?* he thought in anguish. *How is it that she is here?* When he opened his eyes Vara was again breathing normally. He rolled off her, spent.

Vara lay holding her throat.

Livios gazed up at his men. They all looked spooked except for Baso, whose dark eyes were filled with compassion.

Livios labored to his feet. "Let's go."

"Won't she give us away?" Harca asked.

"No I won't!" Vara coughed, rising to her knees. "I won't! I wouldn't say anything!"

Why doesn't she just be quiet? Livios wondered, empty inside. He bent to reclaim his sword.

Vara misread the action and wailed: "No, Livi, no! I'll never say a word."

He glared at her.

"Don't hurt me," she begged. "I'll do whatever you want!"

Livios took a step towards her. "Then be silent."

"No!" she shrieked. "Please baby giant!"

Somehow, the repeated use of the endearment seemed an unforgivable crime to Livios. He walked forward at a purposeful gait. *Anyway, I can't trust her, not one bit,* he thought. *She'll give us away the moment they ask her.* Even as he lifted his sword he admitted he was lying to himself, that he was killing her for revenge. On who or what, he did not know.

"Close your eyes, Vara," he said in a businesslike tone. She did the opposite, widening them to an impossible degree.

"Please, Please, Livi!" she choked.

Livios had the briefest mental image of Kassandra as he brought the sword down on Vara's head.

236

ASSASSIN

Livios redeployed the unit at once, eager to escape Vara. The adrenal rush and sense of vengeance that had accompanied the murder had waned immediately, leaving only an abysmal depression in its wake. *And it's going to get worse,* he thought with a shudder. *I'm not going to bounce back from this one.* He couldn't force Vara's face from his mind, especially the terror in her dead eyes. He tried to shake the vision but it was useless; he felt worse by the moment. *Oh, why'd I kill her?* he wondered, unwilling to even speculate what Daedilos would have thought. The world dimmed about him and it was all he could do to remain in the saddle. Of course it started to rain again.

"Where we going, *sestar?*" a *Riiz* asked.

Livios remained silent and no one else revived the subject.

They made a meandering path across the district and eventually found one of the campsites. It was dark when Livios dropped to the soggy earth.

"Baso, get things together," he muttered and wandered off into the darkness.

Livios woke suddenly, tasting blood in his mouth. *Bit myself?* he mulled, touching a lip. It was dark and cold, but he made out the images of trees all around. In fact, he was sitting against one. *Where in hell?* he inquired silently. *Why am I holding my sword?* Then memory swept him and he again saw Vara's face. Remorse struck like a blow. He longed for Kassandra, wanting badly her arms around him, but aghast at the thought of relating his deed. *She'd never hold me again.* Some time later he staggered off in what he guessed to be the direction of the campsite. He half feared the men had left. *Wouldn't blame them. God only knows how long I've been gone.*

The men were crowded around a tall blaze. Some marked his approach but he bade them remain seated. Baso rose and came forward with a steaming tin.

Livios took the broth with a shallow nod.

"You've been all night," Baso said.

"That long?"

"Longer. This is breakfast."

Livios sipped the beef stock.

"We looked for you," Baso went on.

Livios frowned. "I wanted to be alone. Is that a problem?"

"No. But you didn't give orders against being disturbed and we got new dispatches."

Livios' glance sharpened. "What dispatches?"

Baso turned and whistled. "Harca, my satchel!" Then to Livios: "A rider found us shortly after you left."

"*Riiz?*"

Baso snorted. "Who else could've tracked us? He was sent from the *ikar*."

Livios was greatly relieved. *Phaetonis is recalling us and I can leave this place!* he thought.

Harca handed a sack to Livios, who removed a leather scroll case and twisted free its contents. The light was poor, so he moved closer to the fire; Baso followed.

"Did you read it?" Livios asked.

"Of course not."

The host fell silent as Livios read. He finished and breathed a grateful sigh. "That's it, Baso," he said. "All legionaries have been recalled."

Livios spent what remained of the night preparing for his journey and giving instructions. He was to rendezvous with the Legion in the land of the *Kabu*, four hundred miles south, where Phaetonis would strike the enemy confederation. *And I'll probably be late, by the date of the dispatch*, he thought; *landesknectos made better speed than most horses. Maybe getting back in ranks will make me feel better.*

Livios checked his kit a final time and mounted up shortly after daybreak. He rode into camp and called the *Riiz* together. *I might just miss them*, he thought. *Why doesn't the ikar use them more?* He thanked them for their service and wished them luck until they joined the effort down south. A few warriors were called out for special praise, which was accepted quietly. "Well, men, make a good end wherever it finds you. Goodbye," he finished.

The men bowed farewell in *Tantorri* style, arms by their sides, and some offered their hands.

Where's Baso? Livios thought as he shook hands. *There he is.*

The old man rode up to the fire, saying, "I'll join you for a bit."

"Good. Harca?"

"Yes, *sestar?*"

"Give Avva and Wenn my farewell when they return."

"I will."

Livios looked over the *Riiz* a final time then kicked his horse. Baso caught up and they rode in silence. At last they halted before a swollen creek, 'the river' as Livios once knew it. They watched the brown water.

A shadow fell over Livios; his old home was less than a mile away. "Thanks for the company," he said at last.

Baso shrugged. "Friendly thing to do."

"Is that what we are, friends?"

"You're all right, for a *Chaconne* and a legionary."

Livios nodded. "Be careful. My friends usually meet bad ends." Again he tried to force Vara from his thoughts.

"Livios?"

It shook the legionary to hear the name. "Yes?"

"Sometimes there are no right choices and even good men can do bad things."

Unconvinced, Livios looked at Baso's weatherworn face. "If you say so." He held out a hand and they shook. "Take care."

"I will. Remember about the raccoons."

Livios nodded, but in truth he had almost forgotten the tale.

Baso whirled the horse about. "When you drop that trinket you'll have a home with us. We can always use another bowman. Farewell!"

"Farewell," Livios replied. He looked after the old warrior and wished for a moment that he were in fact going home with the *Riiz*. Slowly, his gaze was drawn west toward the farm. He was too fatigued to resist the call, *ikar's* orders notwithstanding. He snapped the reins and sat limp in the saddle as the mount followed the creek home.

Livios stared long at the tiny cabin, though the sight hurt terribly. Dejection was far too mild a word to describe his feelings. The little house looked empty and cold, not inviting, as it should; he felt distinctly unwelcome. The door had fallen from its hinges and the small windows Daedilos had purchased at exorbitant price had been shattered. Weeds choked the ruined tomato garden and scaled the wooden walls.

Livios was too numb to do much. Having hoped that the house might revive good memories, he found himself unable to think of anything but Daedilos' death. *I shouldn't have come*, he thought. He gazed at the scorch mark that had been the barn and seriously considered suicide. *Could do it right where I killed dad. No, that wouldn't be right. I'll go over in that row of dead corn. Dead corn, hell! The whole damned farm's ruined.*

The fields he had seen on the approach had been appropriately foreboding. Overgrown and water ravaged, it would take months to whip them into shape; Daedilos would be grieved to know how quickly his life's work had unraveled. Or would he? *He didn't really care for this place, he hated farming,* Livios realized. Only now did he understand his father's subtle complaints about agriculture as a profession. *Just did it to feed me.*

He closed his eyes and prayed that the entire year had been a dream. *I want my life back. Dad and Felix and old Herakles, even Vara.* He dismounted before he realized it and shuffled toward the entrance. Again he closed his eyes. *Please, God, let everything be just as it was. Let dad be in there. I'll do anything you want, forever. Please!*

Livios scanned the room with a broken heart. Leaves littered the dirty floor and a litter of small animals had died in a corner. Most everything had been stolen, too, even Daedilos' old broken chair. Only the shattered bed frames remained. Even empty, the house was much smaller than he remembered. Any junior legionary lived better than had he and his father, with more food and someone else doing the thrall work, with softer beds in a nicely heated spoke. And legionaries had slaves. *Never realized how poor we were,* he thought, ashamed to denigrate the life Daedilos had made for them. *Oh, you're so important now, Livios Rapax!*

Livios retrieved a shard of his father's mirror from the floor. The memory of Daedilos shaving brought a melancholy smile to his face; he had always been impressed by Daedilos' ability to shave, cook and talk at the same time. *What an officer he'd have made, being able to juggle tasks like that.* He glimpsed himself in the shard and flung it away. *Yes, if he hadn't been more interested in rearing his son than killing people.* He felt worse as he realized that Boros would not have even considered his father. *Too short. Not like 'baby giant',* he thought derisively.

Livios drew his dagger as he sank to his knees. He stuck the point against his chest and laid his brow on the rough floor. *Why can't I just go back?* he asked himself, scraping his head against the wood. *Why? Why! I'm not going to live like this any more!* Many times he tried to push the knife into his heart but barely broke the skin. The last time he loosed a battle cry to strengthen himself but his arm wouldn't obey. *Don't do it, stupid!* he berated himself. *Dad would never forgive you.*

Livios groaned as the blade slipped from his nerveless hand. At last he dragged himself onto Daedilos' collapsed bed and curled into a ball. He thought he was going to cry, then he hoped he would, but the sobs never came. They wouldn't have helped, anyway. His despair was deeper than tears.

*   *   *

It took Livios seven days hard riding to reach *Kabu* territory and his lathered horse was spent. He had not made such a pace out of duty but because he wanted to leave Ios. At least the Legion offered combat, and if he died so much the better. *Even his father would understand him dying like a soldier.* But the voice in his head asked: *What about Kassandra?* It was a hard question. He didn't like the thought of abandoning the girl to his merciless comrades.

It was easy to guess Phaetonis' path through the topography. Livios visualized the runners scouting the rocky spine he now crossed. *Would give them a good view of this naked land,* he thought. Naked it was. He had never been so far south and was not impressed. The earth was dry and dusty, its flora sparse. Rivers were few and housed strange animals. The sun was bright now but he knew it was much worse in the summer. *Must be what makes the Kabu black.*

The ridge refused to die so Livios rode it for the rest of the day. Dusk was near when it widened onto a plateau where he finally caught the entrenched Legion, but it was the massive enemy encampments on the eastward flat that stole his attention. *Look at them all,* he thought, awed. *Almost cover the plain.* Closer inspection yielded an even bigger shock—a castle. *I thought these people lived in huts? This isn't good.*

Phaetonis had set up exactly where he should. The meager plateau was only twenty feet higher than the plain, but even that elevation might prove crucial in battle. There was no water nearby, though, suggesting he planned a quick campaign. *Then why such a trench network?* Livios brooded. *Would've taken days to do that. We can't support ourselves for long here so he should fight before water becomes a problem.* The questions begot others. *Why'd the Kabu cede the high ground and why haven't they encircled?*

Livios approached the *landesknecta* camp, which looked pathetically small beside the enemy horde. He could see well-ordered rows of tents but couldn't note details in the fading light. It was just as well; finding his comrades had only made him gloomier. He gazed toward the distant fortress, thinking, *Looks like a fine place to get killed. Good.* He rode into a depression on the northern point of the camp and was hailed long before he reached the first trench.

"Halt and announce yourself!" someone shouted.

Livios noted a black shape beyond the earthwork. "Kerebos *Sestar* from the Second," he said.

Another man ordered: "Dismount and approach, sir."

Livios complied and two runners came forth to greet him, pila at the level. One of the men lowered his weapon, saying, "It's him."

"Am I the last one back?"

"Yes, sir, and we're damned glad to have you. We feared you were lost."

Livios sensed something was wrong. *These men are scared*, he thought. "How are things?"

The men looked at each other before one said: "You'd better ask an officer, sir. We're under orders."

Livios didn't press the issue. "Where's the Second?"

The runner pointed to the far side of the camp.

Livios proceeded forward but was stymied by the trench. It was considerably deeper and wider than was usual. "We got a bridge?" he asked.

"To the right."

Livios rode into camp and was intercepted by men from the Fifth and Sixth. The Officer of the Guard immediately emerged from a tent. "Who's that? Oh, hello, Kerebos," he greeted. "Didn't recognize you with all that hair. Good to see you."

Livios recognized the man from the Winnowing. He wanted to ask questions but knew the officer wouldn't speak frankly with so many men around. "Thanks. Where's Melas *Cohar*?"

"I'll have a man show you. Marios, see to it!"

"Yes, sir."

"You might want to leave that animal with the wagons," the *sestar* told Livios.

"Don't feel like walking. Thanks for the guide. Let's go, Marios."

They soon found Melas' dwelling. Livios chased off the guide and dismounted. "Permission to enter, sir?" he called.

"Who's that? Kerebos? Come in!"

Livios entered. Melas and Rodios *Cohar* were seated on the ground, a lamp between them. They had the derelict look of those sharing a secret. Melas' face registered relief. "Glad you're back," he said. "We need every man."

Livios was surprised by the welcome. "Thank you, sir. Want my report?"

"Not now. What have you heard?"

Livios hadn't relished talking about Ios but was irked to have his labors shrugged off so casually. "Nothing, but I see the men are scared and that we're dug in deep."

"Not deep enough," Rodios muttered.

Livios looked briefly at Rodios then asked Melas: "Are we going to attack or wait until we run out of supplies?"

The lamp spluttered as Melas averted his eyes. "There's a problem."

"Obviously. What in hell has happened here?"

242

Melas spoke as though the words hurt. "The enemy has captured the *ikar*."

Livios almost laughed and glanced from face to face to catch some sign of a joke; the *cohari* remained dead serious. The catastrophic implications of Phaetonis' abduction quickly weighted Livios' shoulders. His personal problems faded as he considered the utter humiliation of an imprisoned *ikar*. *It all fits*, he thought. *The posture of the camp, the jumpiness of the men. Guess that's what happens when our head's cut off.* He barely knew Phaetonis and never would have thought the loss would have any personal effect, but it did. The Brotherhood he had joined was a rigid hierarchy whose rules had, literally, been burned into him. He had never even considered that any external agent could impose *its* rules on a legionary, much less the *ikar*. "Sir," he croaked on a dry mouth. "Mind if I sit?"

"Go ahead."

Livios dropped onto the dirt, suddenly feeling much barer for his missing armor. "How'd it happen?" he asked slowly.

Melas wiped his shiny brow. "We marched here without incident," he started. "The *Riiz* kept us informed of enemy movements, so we knew before we arrived that they weren't interested in the high ground. Phaetonis exploited their mistake and grabbed the ridge, strengthened the position with a weak gully."

Livios nodded to himself, thinking, *That'd be the inner trench. Not severe enough to keep us from sallying.*

Melas continued. "While we were entrenching the enemy emerged from covered holes just behind the command tent. There were scores of them. They snatched Phaetonis right out of his post."

Livios shook his head violently. "No! Where were the bodyguards? How'd any *Kabu* get past the First?"

"There were a few up there, but most were digging."

"Two men killed," Rodios added. "Not counting those who've committed suicide."

"And the enemy?"

"Many," Melas replied. "But they were more interested in running than fighting. Dragged Phaetonis right up the hill and dumped him to a regiment of Scarlet Guardsmen, who rode off with him." Melas rocked in place, eyes closed. "I still hear their taunts."

Guardsmen, Livios thought. "How many *Chaconni* are here?"

"All horse. Two full alaes. Can see their standards in the daytime. The VIIIth and Xth."

Livios was having difficulty comprehending that Phaetonis was snatched from camp. It just did not seem possible. "How'd they know where to dig their holes?"

"The Guards know how we pitch sites," Melas said. "We should've been more suspicious about them leaving us the heights."

The shame Livios felt was turning to wrath. The *Kabu* would have to pay. "So when do we attack?" he asked hotly. "Phaetonis would want that!"

"We're already at a disadvantage—"

"The senior *elhar* takes over and leads us," Livios interrupted. "That's why we have a chain of command."

"There's much to consider," Rodios said.

Livios glared at Melas. "A deal? Is that what we're doing, a deal? Trade Phaetonis for a withdrawal?"

"Enough!" Melas snapped. "When the *elhari* have made a decision you'll know. Until then go clean up and see to your unit."

Livios was disgusted. He didn't know what sickened him more, Phaetonis' capture or bartering for his return. *If we lose face here we're finished*, he decided. *Tomorrow or next year, it makes no difference. No one will respect us.* He stood and gave a brief salute before leaving. Still reeling, he walked to his horse and looked down at the countless enemy fires; passing legionaries greeted him. The *Kabu* were singing what sounded like a mixture of cadence and spiritual. *And why not?* he thought. *They've much to crow about.*

Livios was silently stroking the horse, coveting the seed of an audacious, frightening idea, when Talos and Laertos arrived.

"Kerebos! Kerebos, sir!" Laertos yelled and punched Livios' shoulder. "When did you get back?"

Pale Talos was fairly bursting with delight. "Welcome back, sir! We feared you were lost! I told everyone you'd make it back! 'Can't kill the boss', I said!"

Laertos handed Livios a canteen. "Take some broth, you look tired. Just look at that hair."

Perhaps it was their enthusiasm but Livios was pleased to see the men. "Thanks, you two," he said and took a drink. He smacked his lips. "Staying out of trouble?"

"As much as we can these days," Laertos said gloomily. "Clios has kept us in line."

"I'll bet."

"Have you heard?" Talos asked in a quick whisper.

"Yes."

Talos shook his head. "What're we going to do, sir? We just keep sitting up here, digging in." The veteran, Laertos, seemed equally in need of solace.

Livios had no intention of sharing his thoughts. *Talos would burst into tears*, he thought. "Take this horse up to the wagons and get him fed. Treat him gently. I'm going to see the *elhari*."

"They've been holed up in the command post all day," Laertos said.

The command post was stationed between the First and the baggage wains. The silk standard hung limp overhead. A dozen topknotted legionaries surrounded the tent, swords drawn. Livios saw shadows against the illuminated canvas walls and heard mutterings from within.

Pythen *Sestar* intercepted Livios twenty feet from the post. "Hardly recognized you in that silly get up," he scoffed.

"I need to see Lasctakos."

"No. Orders."

"It's important."

"Not going to happen, Kerebos, so forget it. They almost flogged a man who asked them if they wanted dinner."

"I have orders to report to a senior officer *immediately* upon my return," Livios embellished. "I've crucial information. I suggest you interrupt them."

Pythen's brow knit. "Your ears clogged? How many times I have to say no? Go bother Melas; he's a *cohar*, I hear."

First Elhar! Livios thought angrily. *Acts like he prevented Phaetonis' capture.* "He's not confirmed, and these words aren't for him."

Pythen placed a palm on Livios' chest and shoved him. Other legionaries raced over to support their officer.

"Look!" Livios barked, struggling to maintain his cool. "If it weren't critical do you think I'd risk fighting you just to infuriate the *elhari?*"

A head poked out of the tent. It was one-eyed Polyphemos. "Shut up out here!" he ordered. He assessed the situation. "What's the problem, Kerebos? Didn't he tell you his orders?"

Livios saluted. "Sir. I must speak to you!"

"Devil take you boy, there's no time for that! Now go away."

The bodyguards grabbed Livios roughly. "Sir, if what I have to tell you doesn't warrant my actions, then kill me," he said hurriedly but calmly. "But you'll regret not hearing me out."

The earnestness of the words affected even the bodyguards. Livios felt their grips slacken.

Polyphemos sputtered angrily. "You'd better be right. Get your ass in here!" He let the flap drop and returned to his table of peers, stepping on a large bloodstain; Phaetonis hadn't gone quietly.

First *Elhar* Tzetzos, acting commander-in-chief asked: "What's the noise, Polyphemos?"

"Kerebos *Sestar* is coming in. Says he has news that won't wait."

Tzetzos' slanted eyes widened as he whirled on Lasctakos. "This the way your men obey orders?"

Livios stepped inside and snapped to attention. He scanned the solemn faces and smiled when he saw Lasctakos, so good it was to see him. He almost forgave the *elhar* for sending him to Ios.

Tzetzos leaned forward so quickly his topknot jumped. He seemed anxious to vent frustration. "Did Pythen relay my orders?" he demanded.

"Yes, sir, but—"

"Silence! You will be reduced in rank immediately and incarcerated until hostilities are imminent. After this campaign you'll see formal charges of insubordination. Pythen, come in here!"

Livios' mouth dropped open. "Formal charges" almost certainly meant a death sentence; he never heard of a man being whipped twice. The only reason Tzetzos wasn't executing him tonight, apparently, was because his sword might be needed.

Three men entered the tent and grabbed Livios.

Tzetzos cursed. "I tell you Lasctakos, you'd better teach your team some discipline."

"Perhaps you should hear what he has to say?" Lasctakos replied hotly.

"Perhaps you need to join him in the cage wagon?"

Lasctakos pointed at Pythen. "Wait outside while I confer with the commander."

Tzetzos' eyes stared daggers at Lasctakos but he said: "Go, Pythen. Stay close." The guard obeyed and Tzetzos grabbed Lasctakos' arm. "Explain yourself! Quickly!"

Lasctakos showed anger now that the guards were gone. "Let's assume for a moment that Kerebos has chosen to intrude, at risk to himself, because he has something vital!" he said, shaking off the hand. "Only foolishness would prevent us from hearing him."

"So I'm a fool, am I?"

Lasctakos smiled fiercely. Livios knew that smile and what it meant. Did Tzetzos?

Tzetzos chuckled without amusement. "We'll talk later." He turned to Livios. "What?"

Livios considered staying quiet out of spite, consequences be damned, but Lasctakos had stuck out his neck. "I'm told Phaetonis has been stolen, sir," he replied.

"You think that's news?" Tzetzos railed. "Is this why you've interrupted us?"

"No, sir."

"Out with it!"

Livios smirked. "I can get him back."

The *elhari* almost rose from their seats. Tzetzos asked: "What did you say?"

"I know how to get him back."

Tzetzos appeared ready to say something truly vile but reserved the comment. "You're that smart, eh? What's the plan?"

Livios told them. There was a short silence followed by a barrage of questions, which he handled well. *Anyway, what choice do they have?* he thought. The inquisition wound down.

"It's just a risky plan," Tzetzos said. "You promised success."

"I'm confident, sir," Livios replied. "That's why I bet my life on it."

"You've wasted our time," Tzetzos growled. "You're still in taint of insubordination."

Lasctakos laughed coldly. "Don't you *want* Phaetonis back, First *Elhar?*"

"I've had about enough of you, Lasctakos."

"Then consider this, too. What will Phaetonis say if we buy him back without attempting this plan? If I'm correct, someone will be charged but it won't be Kerebos."

The threat hung in the air until the other *elhari* agreed.

Tzetzos sat back. "All right, Kerebos. Don't fail."

Livios hoped he didn't look smug. "I won't, sir."

"Don't get Phaetonis snuffed with your scheme," he added as an afterthought. "This King Danawayo's no fool and might have planned for some trick. What?"

"I want Melas' command if I'm successful, sir," Livios said evenly.

Tzetzos shook his head, crestfallen. "How dare you hold me for ransom," he said. "You're lucky I'm even letting you try this stunt. Actually, I think I just changed my mind."

"Phaetonis' anger would still hold," Lasctakos pointed out with obvious pleasure. "I was contemplating replacing Melas, anyway."

"If the boy accomplishes this feat, he should get something," Polyphemos added, his one eye bulging. "And if he fails, the situation resolves itself. Let him try, Tzetzos. It's not like the *ikar* won't be grateful."

"Or all of us, for that matter," Lasctakos added.

Tzetzos raised a hand. "Enough. Kerebos, tell Pythen to see to your needs. Leave before I change my mind."

Livios saluted and left. Once outside, he collared Pythen and demanded he locate some items. "I'll be waiting over here," Livios said as he wandered into the darkness. He found a small outcropping of rocks and sat for a breather. The long journey and the face-off had drained him, but he was content. No matter what happened tomorrow, there would be change, and at this point any change seemed good. *Puts distance between Ios and me* he thought gratefully. He briefly reflected upon killing Vara and, of course, his thoughts passed to his old home and Daedilos. *Is it cold out here?* he wondered.

Livios forced the bleak images from his mind and considered the possible outcomes of his plan in decreasing levels of appeal. *I could rescue Phaetonis and die in the escape, get killed in the attempt, or survive and steal Melas' job.* He contemplated the last, his hedge bet against surviving, with a glimmer of enthusiasm. *Would help me protect Kassandra.* He pictured the somber, curvy little blonde, wondering when she had last thought of him, and decided living might not be a disaster. Perhaps Lasctakos was right about life, just make the best of it. *Why be in a hurry for hell?* Struggling to his feet, he sought his horse. The *Kabu* must not suspect he had come from the *landesknecta* camp so he must soon depart. *Too bad I didn't get a chance to talk to Lasctakos or Luecos.* The realization that he probably wouldn't see either man again grieved him. *But they're better off.*

A runner caught up with Livios. "Got your things here, sir."

Livios undid his sword belt and pulled the dagger from his boot. "Deliver those to Lasctakos," he said then took the small bundle from the runner. He opened the buckskin wrap, revealing two flat dinner knives and a scroll.

"That it, sir?"

Livios held a knife against a distant *landesknecta* fire, noting the serrated edge. *Tzetzos was right. Not one chance in a hundred I'll pull this off,* he thought. "That'll be all."

The runner went back down the hill but was stopped near the command post. "Kerebos up there?" someone asked.

Clios and the other, Livios thought, making out figures in black. *Guess I even missed that treacherous albino.*

"Yes, sir, right up there," the runner responded.

"Kerebos, come down before you bolt off!" Clios yelled. "We want to see you!"

Livios hurried up to the wagons and unhitched his mount. He swung into the saddle, thinking, *No, no more farewells for me.* "Let's go, horse," he said and tugged the rein.

*   *   *

Livios rode due north before changing course. Eventually he bedded down a few miles east of the *Kabu* castle. The distant roar of lions woke him before dawn and endured a cheerless cold breakfast beneath an orange sunrise. *Dry down here,* he thought, drinking some tepid water. The horse nuzzled him and he scratched the beast's nose. *What'll happen to this creature? Any way to let him go?*

The bright winter day wore on as Livios played out designs within his head. Convinced he would die, he still wanted to give the best account of himself. *If only I knew the inside of the place*, he thought. After a small dinner he inspected his kit to make sure there was nothing "legionary" about it, then tried to determine if it would pass as a *Puur* brave's. The nomadic *Puur*, the most barbaric of the *Tantorri* tribes and famously neutral, dwelt almost as far from the Legion as the *Kabu*, so he had to rely on Baso's account of them. No sooner had he pronounced the kit "clean" than he recalled that the *Puur* rode bareback. He unstrapped the small saddle, asking himself: *Does that mean they forego reins?* The bridle went in the end, leaving a nagging fear that he'd marked himself for easy detection.

In the gathering dusk Livios darkened his features with mud then quickly removed the braids from his horse's mane. Next he cut holes in the moccasin soles and slid in the flat knives. Walking on the blades proved uncomfortable, but he'd be mounted. Finally he cut some notches in his bow then wedged it over a shoulder; he climbed onto the steed. Luckily he found he could direct the horse by tugging its mane. *But I won't halt him if he's a mind to run*, he thought. He looked west over the tawny scrublands and sighed, fully aware that any half-blind *Tantorri* would instantly mark him as an impostor. *I hope all white men look alike to these Kabu.* "Let's go do this thing, horse," he said.

The squat castle soon came into view; the nearby river shimmered gold in the sunset. There were no soldiers on this side of the water but Livios saw many thousands on the westward plain. The sloppy camps spilled into each other prompting him to wonder if the *Kabu* were incompetent or if such disorder had been forced upon them by the confines of the twisting river. He coaxed the horse into the dark river, finding the balmy water no deeper than six feet. *Do they have sharks around here?* he wondered. Some *Kabu* heard the laboring mount and came to investigate as Livios emerged onto a narrow beach no more than a hundred yards from the torch lit castle door. A cursory inspection revealed the keep to be a windowless, rectangular structure about forty feet high and three times that in length. He couldn't determine if there was a roof but saw that the river wound to within a few yards of the mud brick walls.

A hundred *Kabu* warriors, resplendent in animal skins and uncut, semiprecious stones were nearly upon Livios when he came to a frightening awareness. He quickly removed the scroll case from his belt and tossed it into the water, hoping the enemy missed the action; he wasn't sure the *Puur* could read.

A hulking *Kabu* wearing a golden officer's torque stopped a dozen paces from Livios and began to shout, gesturing with an assegai. Many other black men crowded behind the warrior, echoing his questions and brandishing spears; more approached from the camps.

Livios was distressed to find he barely understood their dialect and struggled to respond. The *Kabu* officer grew swiftly impatient and came closer, the growing throng behind him. Livios was motioned away from the water and obeyed, despite his horse's uneasiness. The crowd pressed in from all sides and he did his best to appear inoffensive, raising his palms as spears prodded him. He could tell by the growing agitation in their voices that he had better reply and quickly.

"I am here to see King Danawayo!" he cried in the *Kabu* Magos had taught. "Take me to him!"

The lead warrior demanded silence of his men and got it. He placed an assegai on Livios' chest and let loose a torrent of words. All Livios understood was "King" "kill" and "who are you". He felt sweat on his temples as he studied the hostile faces.

"I am here with news for King Danawayo," he repeated calmly. "Take me to him."

The warrior smacked Livios' foot with the spade shaped spearhead and continued to berate him. *I'm not taking this from him if I'm going to die anyway,* he thought angrily. He leaned forward and shouted: "You will bring me to your masters or you'll find I'm not the only man getting killed tonight!" He drew a finger across his throat and smiled. "You understand what I mean, you black bastard?"

The warrior understood enough to grow angrier. "Pull him down!" he shouted. "Let's see what color he bleeds!"

Livios heard only "him down" and "he bleeds" but it was enough. He snarled and grabbed for his sword—which wasn't there.

"STOP!" someone cried. The voice was loud and carried unmistakable authority.

The host of warriors parted as a stately, finely knit, gray haired *Kabu* proceeded into view. He walked ramrod straight, chin up, and exuded an air of lethality and importance. A lion's skin served as his cloak, the paws hitched over a bare chest, and a silver filet graced his head. Round, obsidian earrings depended from misshapen lobes but were neither as dark nor as hard looking as his eyes. A brace of short assegai were tucked into his belt.

Livios' interrogator bowed, saying, "General Mbega."

"What passes, captain?" Mbega replied in a toneless voice. His language was subtly different than the others' and Livios followed it easily.

"I don't yet know. We caught this fish belly swimming into camp."

"Why have I not been alerted?"

The captain swallowed hard. "I felt it best to first question him, general."

Mbega looked at Livios, who did his best to copy one of Baso's indifferent expressions. "Who are you, white man?"

Now Livios fathomed the captain's fear. The force of the general's will was disconcerting. "I'm Baso of the *Puur*," he responded, stressing the last word. "I've a message for your king."

Mbega frowned. "There are many kings here."

"For Danawayo."

Mbega's slow laughter was a cruel thing. "Is that so, boy? And you think you can ride in and demand an audience? Are we animals to be so lightly regarded?"

"I ask nothing. I am here at my master's instruction, and he's responding your king."

"How do you know our tongue?"

"Why would I be sent if I didn't?"

Mbega stared. "You did not answer me."

Livios forced a smile. "From my father's slaves."

Mbega grunted. "Tell me of these slaves."

Livios was rapidly exhausting his supply of lies. He hadn't expected these questions and Mbega's deportment gave no indication on how he was faring. Was the general playing with him? *Should I just attack and get it over?* he thought. "He bought some women from the Gazelle Clan."

Mbega nodded. "I knew by your speech that you were taught by a woman."

Livios had no idea where Magos had learned the tongue, so remained silent.

"I have known many *Tantorri*," Mbega said. "You are too large."

"How many *Puur* have you seen?"

"Does it matter?"

"Yes."

Mbega's eyes scanned Livios' kit and came to a rest on the bow. "Give me that."

Livios reluctantly obeyed. "The notches are for kills?" Mbega asked.

"They are."

"Why then are they all fresh?"

"Because they're fresh kills. It's a new bow."

Mbega handled the weapon. "I see," he said. "You feared to bring your favorite with you?"

That's a good excuse, Livios thought. "I left it with my family."

"Then you killed eight men on your trip down here?"

Livios' heart sank. "Two were women."

Mbega plucked the string. "How interesting. Eight dead. You must be quite an archer. You would have to be. Yes, a legionary-sized *Tantorri* with eight new kills."

251

He's toying with me! Livios thought, frightened. *If only I had my sword.* He wondered if he'd be able to throttle Mbega before the other *Kabu* interfered. "You don't believe me?" he said indignantly.

Mbega shook his head. "Our *Tantorri* allies can hit a bird in the dark. Can you?"

"Go find one."

Mbega chuckled. "I have none at present. Captain?"

"Yes, general?"

Mbega pulled one of his short spears and moved behind Livios. "Take twenty paces backward," he said. "The rest of you men move away." The surrounding *Kabu* made room and the captain complied. "Hold up your hand and make a circle of your fingers," Mbega ordered. He smacked Livios' leg with the bow. "Put an arrow through his fingers."

Livios had feared as much. It was a difficult shot under ideal circumstances but now it was nearly dark.

"Come now!" Mbega boomed. "Not a hard task for a *Puur* with eight notches!"

Livios took the bow and checked the string. "As you wish," he replied and started to dismount.

"From the horse," Mbega hissed. "Isn't that how you got your kills, *Tantor?*"

Livios had been mounted long enough to cramp but no true horseman would admit that fact. "Fine. It's easy from any angle," he replied bravely. He drew an arrow from the quiver, notched it, and leaned sideways enough to frame the captain's hand around the castle's torch. *As soon as I miss I'll charge*, he decided, realizing some comfort from the decision. *At least I'll go down fighting.* He loosed and the arrow passed through the warrior's fingers.

Livios suppressed a smile as the blacks howled disbelief. The captain studied his hand, wiggling the fingers. Mbega waved his men to silence.

"The king *has* reached out to the *Puur*," Mbega told Livios. "But that was months ago. You people aren't sure which side to join?"

Livios shrugged. "I don't know what's happened between our nations. I only do what I'm told."

"Very well. Give me your message and I shall relay it to Danawayo."

Livios had anticipated this request but had not figured upon a man like Mbega. He scrambled to fashion a denial that wouldn't give offense. "I can't do that, general," he said humbly. "My words are for the king alone. I'd be killed if I disobeyed my chief in this."

Mbega's gaze was sharper than usual. "I'll kill you if you don't"

252

"Perhaps, but then your king won't get his prize."

Mbega smiled. "You're steely for one so young. Give me the message and go."

Livios shook his head.

"Then I'll draw the information from you."

"My people would think ill of that. Don't you *want* our bows with you?"

That caused Mbega to reflect.

He can't want shooters like me on the other side, Livios thought.

"I'll take that chance," Mbega said. "Captain, go retrieve my questioning knives."

Livios frantically patched together an argument. "So now you'll stall intelligences like your captain did?" he cried above rising cheers. "Danawayo didn't tell you to expect a messenger so you're going to torture his guest to teach him a lesson? Your family will pay the consequences, general, along with your armies!"

Mbega's brow bent and the exhortations trailed off. "Get down," he said.

Livios dropped from the horse and was surprised to learn he towered over Mbega. He was stripped of his visible weapons and his hands were tightly bound with the bowstring.

"Pray to your gods," Mbega warned. "The king is fond of flaying fools and liars." He assigned four burly men to escort Livios. "The rest of you get back to camp. I myself shall see to this matter."

Livios was marched toward the castle. He couldn't see his tingling hands well but felt skin coming off his wrists. *Should've planned on them tying me,* he thought, biting back curses. Being flayed alive was not at all what he had in mind when he proposed the mission. *Not quite the same as catching a spear in the guts,* he thought miserably. It seemed a long walk to the castle. He and his captors crossed the river via a plank bridge and approached the massive double doors. *Cleverly devised,* he silently admitted of the timber valves. *No hinges to be seen.*

The general ordered them to a stop and approached the gates. He slapped the wood. "It is I, Mbega!"

Livios glanced back at the dark water.

"Don't try it, fish belly," a guard warned.

There was the sound of grating metal and one of the doors swung slowly open. "I'll tell the king's minister," an unseen man informed Mbega.

What if he doesn't get in? Livios reflected. *I'll be left to the mercy of his "questioning knives".* Mbega turned and smiled, as though guessing the question.

A considerable time passed and Livios grew concerned. His guards asked Mbega if they might watch the interrogation. *Wish I had my sword,* he thought in despair. *If I somehow make it through this, I'll never again surrender it.* The door opened a few feet. "Mbega," a voice called impatiently. The general disappeared inside. There followed a short con-versation, animated enough to be heard through the gate. "Alright!" someone shouted and Mbega reemerged; he looked most displeased. He nudged the thick door and it swung wide. "The king will see you, white man," he said. "But I doubt you'll come back out."

Livios was shoved from behind but kept his balance. He entered the door and was instantly surround by five swordsmen, hardly smaller than himself, in crude breastplates. *Danawayo's livery?* he speculated. *Didn't know they used swords or armor. Those are Chaconni blades.* He studied the long, well-lit hallway. Torches stuck from the bricks at regular intervals and he saw the sharpened teeth of a raised portcullis halfway down the path. Again he was forced to reevaluate the *Kabu.*

Mbega dismissed Livios' escorts then stepped inside. He shut the gate and used both hands to grind shut the latch. "I will lead," he told the king's men. "Cripple him if he tries anything, but *do not* kill him. He's Danawayo's. Or mine."

The hall was smooth and straight, the dirt floor packed. Even in close quarters Livios could tell these men were marching *Chaconni* style. *Has the Old Kingdom taken to training barbarians?* he wondered. They reached the end of the hall and were greeted by a guarded door on either side. The sentry on the left saluted Mbega and pushed open the gate. Heat, thin smoke and the scents of wine and unwashed bodies issued into the hall.

Mbega drew one of the stunted spears from his belt and poked Livios' stomach before dragging the legionary into the crowded cham-ber.

This is what they saw.

King Danawayo's throne room was forty feet square with a venting hole in its lofty ceiling. A fire pit rested beneath the opening where a glistening slave turned a spitted boar above crackling flames. The walls were sheathed in hammered metal that reflected firelight and torches to dizzying effect. Dozens of generals and witch smellers in feathered capes lounged on animal skins attended by buxom, bare-chested serving girls. Breastplated soldiers stood in each corner.

"Follow," Mbega said.

Livios absorbed the surroundings as he wound through the crowd towards Danawayo's chair. Most of the men wore the glassy-eyed look of intoxication but all were armed. Some sneered at his passing but he knew he was safe until Danawayo pronounced doom; the discipline of the palace guards had disclosed that. He caught the faint outline of a narrow door against the far wall. They rounded the fire pit and the king's ivory throne came into view. Gaudily dressed women in headdresses with two-foot long, curved razors on their hips sat at the bald king's feet.

No concubines, these, Livios thought. *Phaetonis!* The *ikar* had been stripped to a loincloth and was bound hand and foot to a stake before Danawayo's chair. Even in the tricky light it was apparent he had been fiercely beaten. Bruises and blood covered his body and ashes had been smeared over his face. Livios pried away his gaze but not before catching the *ikar's* bloodshot eyes, which bore the wrath of a newly caged animal.

Mbega pulled Livios to within ten feet of the throne. "On your knees," he ordered.

Danawayo took notice of them for the first time and eyed them with a bloodshot gaze. The king was of average height but sported a preposterously protruding potbelly. His black skin glistened with sweat and his cheeks were swollen as though stuffed with food. Close-set eyes beneath a low brow gave him a dim, brutish appearance but Livios knew this was an illusion. Danawayo was smart enough to do what no one had ever done by welding the fractious *Kabu* tribes into a single fighting force. *Not to mention having captured an ikar,* he thought.

Danawayo pointed his skull-topped scepter at Mbega and asked in a surprisingly squeaky voice, "Who have you brought, general?"

Mbega bowed. "He says he's a *Tantor*, Great King. From the *Puur* with a message for your ears only."

Danawayo flexed gouty hands. "And you've brought him here?"

"He wouldn't talk despite my threats, and since we'll soon attack it seemed best not to squander time or an ally's good will." Mbega was now before the kneeling Livios, who prepared for the most desperate action of his life. He slowly slid his left leg forward and reached for the foot with his bound hands.

"This is unlike you, Mbega," Danawayo said. "But perhaps you've a point." His eyebrow went up. "He's mighty big for a *Tantor*. Have you checked his stomach for a Scriptus scar?"

"No, Great Kingayowyowyowaaahhhh!" Mbega shrieked as Livios' knife slammed his pelvic floor with force enough to lift him into the air. Snarling, Livios tore free the blade and sprang at Danawayo.

One of the amazons was already struggling to her feet and bared her teeth while bringing her giant razor into play. Livios launched himself at the throne and kneed her in the face before slamming into Danawayo. The chair went over as screams filled the air. There was a short tussle before Livios wiggled onto the king's chest and got the blade to his throat. Danawayo bucked with great strength until Livios pricked him hard enough to get his attention. "Stop!" he cried. "Tell your harpies to get back!"

The screeching amazons had circled their king. They threatened Livios with their razors, promising dismemberment and death. Livios dug the point under the king's chin. "Back them up!" he ordered breathlessly.

"Away!" Danawayo barked. Then to Livios: "I'll stuff your head with your heart."

"Farther."

"You heard him!" Danawayo scolded. "Over there with the others!"

Livios adjusted his weight for the king was slippery. Was he covered in grease? He inspected the chamber, which looked far different than before. The warriors and priests had crowded the area before the throne; gone was their wine-induced lassitude. Every man had a weapon in hand but none looked as furious as the female bodyguards who were nearly foaming at the mouth.

"Where's Mbega?" Danawayo croaked. He couldn't see where the forgotten general writhed on the floor.

"He's here, Great King," a witch smeller replied.

"Throw him on the fire!" Danawayo shouted.

Livios stabbed until skin gave. "No more!" he warned despite the pleasure of seeing the screaming Mbega tossed into the flame pit. Phaetonis was hidden behind black bodies but Livios heard his raucous laughter. "Tell them to unbind the *ikar*."

"Go stuff yourself!" Danawayo replied.

Livios sliced off one of the king's ears; Danawayo howled while blood squirted the ground. "Your eye's next," he promised.

Danawayo cursed loudly and with pain. "Cut free the legionary!"

"Now listen, king," Livios began. "You'll give him an escort all the way to the our lines. When Phaetonis sounds the Legion horn, I'll release you. Got it?" He pressed hard with the knife. "Do you?"

"All right! Bambuta?"

"Yes, king?"

"Escort that stinking fish belly. No harm comes to him!"

"I'll know the horn, you'd better believe it," Livios said.

"Don't come back until that cursed thing sounds!" Danawayo wheezed.

Livios reduced pressure. "It's less than five hundred paces to our lines. I'll give a count of three hundred."

"Move!" Danawayo yelled.

A warrior in a lion skin and a torque thrust aside the crowd and cut Phaetonis' bonds. The *ikar* had trouble standing. "Good show, boy, good show!" he cackled in Livios' direction. Bambuta pulled him to his feet a number of times before he remained standing. Phaetonis gave Livios a wild grin then shuffled for the door, Bambuta on his heels. Livios glimpsed bloodstains around the binding stake before the *Kabu* pressed in again.

The room fell silent but for Mbega's horrendous screams. Livios was sickened by the sweet smell of burning human flesh. "Make them stop!" he bade Danawayo as the snarling crowd inched forward. Danawayo complied.

They faced off for a long while. Livios felt pride in the fact that he had, unaided, freed the *ikar*. *I'm a legend now*, he thought. "Make them back away and lie down." He jerked his head at the door he had noted. "What's in there?"

"Death for you."

Livios laughed robustly. He didn't fear death at the moment. "Really? Maybe I'll go see."

"You've not heard your horn," Danawayo pointed out.

Livios leaned over and whispered: "There is no horn, fool. Any more than I'm going to let you live."

A spasm of fury crossed Danawayo's face and his eyes narrowed. "So much for your word, white man."

"I'm surprised you believed me."

Danawayo spat on him. "I could carve from a banana an assassin with more sense than you! How can you escape now that you've told me your plan?"

"Simple," Livios replied. "I'm not going to." With that he opened Danawayo's throat from ear to ear, enjoying the feel of crunching sinew; hot blood sprayed his hands. He jumped to his feet and ran toward the camouflaged door. The room erupted in vengeful cries that nearly knocked him from his feet. *Where's the knob?* he thought, eyes dazzled by glittering metal. *Is that a peephole?* Without slowing, he lowered a massive shoulder and plowed the door so hard it crushed the woman behind it; he found her crumpled onto the bottom step of an ascending stairwell but spared her no thought. A glance back into the throne room revealed that the blood-crazed mob was almost upon him!

Fear found Livios. He cursed and slammed the door in a snarling razor woman's face. A search revealed that his blow had snapped the door's lock so he hurriedly tried to wedge the jamb with his knife. The blade was too thin. Bodies smacked the door, which smote his forehead with each blow. He was seeing stars as he tried to muscle the door shut, but it was too late. Arms had squeezed into the opening; some were holding blades. He again lowered his shoulder, placed his feet against a step and pushed with all the strength of his great legs. The advantageous

257

leverage, the door's scant width and his assailants' uncoordinated effort caused a stalemate. Screams of pain mingled with those of rage as he unmercifully crushed the dusky arms. Sweat blinded him as he strained with all his might.

In that moment Livios realized he didn't want to die, at least not here. Why succumb to torment when he might earn glory on the battlefield? An image of Kassandra popped into his mind and he expelled her just as quickly, as though hiding her from the enemy. "You want me, you have to earn it!" he yelled before biting a chunk out of an arm.

A very loud man's voice began to shout orders and Livios felt less pressure against the door. *Someone's taking hold of the situation*, he thought. *Move fast, move fast!* He stood, slid his bound wrists down an amazon's razor, still in her grip, and cast off the bowstring with numb fingers. His hands were free. Using the knife, he sliced the woman's wrist, snatched her weapon and bound up the stairs. The enemy spilled into the stairwell.

Livios took four of the uneven steps at a time, heart in his throat. His arms pumped wildly in the gloom, knife in one hand and the two-foot razor in the other. The amazon's weapon proved remarkably light and well balanced. Sharp, too. He sliced his leg in three places while climbing the dusty flight.

The *Kabu* were close behind, their voices amplified by the narrow path. Something struck Livios' back but fell harmlessly away. He reached the top of the steps, pushed open the door and somehow ducked a murderous sword stroke from one of Danawayo's bullies. The blade barely missed Livios' head before biting into the wall. He slid his razor behind the *Kabu*'s knee and crippled him then stabbed him on the way down. Economizing his motions he dropped his weapons, and looked around as he hefted the body overhead. The dim chamber was full of weapons. Rows of assegai lined the walls and spiked maces hung from the low ceiling. Another flight of stairs led to the next floor.

Livios digested the sights even as he cast the squirming body down at the approaching *Kabu*. More screams greeted the heavy body, which flattened the leading pursuers. *Where'd all they come from?* he wondered as he slammed the door and wheedled closed its sticky latch. *Kabu* immediately struck the barrier, which bowed at top and bottom. Livios stuck his knife into a moccasin and swiped an armful of assegai from the closest rack before running up the next stairwell. The latched door snapped off its hinges before he reached the top and he was assaulted by a fresh wave of clamor. If anything the *Kabu* sounded even angrier than before.

A body filled the space before Livios and he opened the girl's stomach without thinking. She shrieked and slumped onto him but he grabbed her curly hair and cast her down the stairs, where she soon flopped to a stop. Livios reached the top, leaned the spears against a wall and turned to meet the *Kabu*, who were packed so tightly as to be a single entity of bristling weapons, white eyes and gnashing teeth.

Livios hefted a spear and threw it at the closest man, a dozen feet away. The *Kabu* took the point in his breast and staggered but others scrambled over him. Livios grabbed another spear and, loosing his war scream, charged down the steps. The assegai plunged into a razor woman's stomach, exited her back and skewered the man behind her. The amazon howled in his ear as he pushed the pike to one side, turned her and wedged the weapon between the wall and a step. He slipped on something wet then scuttled back upstairs where he locked the door.

"Roooaaarrr!" rang Livios' ear as a lion launched itself at him. He had barely lifted the razor in response before the beast was upon him. But a chain brought the cat up short, jerking it flat from mid leap.

Panting, Livios stared over the irate beast into the heart of the room. *Must be Danawayo's lair,* he thought. Lush wall coverings, a huge mound of pillows and tall silver candelabrum decorated the place. A dozen nubile young girls were huddled together on the pillows; they begged for their lives. He ran to the next flight of stairs.

Forgot my spears! he thought after a few steps and turned in time to see the door bending off its hinges. The *Kabu* saw him and continued the chase.

"Where will you now go?" a man yelled from below.

The steps emptied directly onto the flat roof, which was barren but for tall mounds of rocks and some casks. Stars shone in a clear sky. A short glimpse of the dark plain showed many campfires but little else. *This is it!* he thought and turned to face the *Kabu*. "Come up!" he shouted, a blade in each hand.

The *Kabu* needed no encouragement. They emerged from the lit flight with the satisfied howling of predators that had run their prey to earth.

The first man to emerge got kicked in the face so hard his neck snapped. The next warrior took Livios' razor across the scalp. Another threw an assegai, which grazed Livios' shoulder, and a fourth grabbed his ankle. Livios severed the grappling arm above the wrist but snapped the razor in the process. He threw the hilt and backed into the darkness, knife before him.

The *Kabu* were all smiles as they leaped onto the roof. "Just wound him!" a headdressed nobleman ordered as he came into view. "He must be taken alive!"

Three braves fanned out and rushed Livios. He sidestepped left to a long pile of rocks and met one of them head on. The first *Kabu* was big and very fast but the sword hung clumsily in his hand. *Like a recruit*, Livios thought and threw the knife at the soldier's face. The *Kabu* flinched and Livios grabbed his sword and simply twisted it from his hand. He sliced the *Kabu's* thigh to the bone then backpedaled into a better position to meet more of the breastplated swordsmen; there were now six of them. The other *Kabu* hung back as though content to cheer on these champions, who approached confidently. The man in the headdress was screaming orders so quickly they sounded like gibberish.

Livios didn't doubt these *Kabu* had been fine spearmen, but decided that whoever had trained them with blades should lose his head. They came on in a ragged formation with the apparent intention of pinning him against the rocks by sheer weight. Even so, they were going about it wrong. The man on the extreme left was too far back and the two in the center were too close to each other. *One's right handed, one a lefty*, Livios noted. *Might even wound each other.* He considered fleeing but discarded the notion. *I'll show them a real swordsman!* He instinctively divvied up the field into segments: far left, left, center, right and far right.

"Take him now!" Headdress screamed.

The *Kabu* rushed and Livios leaped at the man on the right. Two men in the center did indeed collide, jumbling their line for a considerable time—perhaps two heartbeats. Livios dispatched his first victim with a stab through the eye and leaned out of the way of the downward swipe from the man who had closed from the far right. Livios ground his heel onto this man's naked foot, pulled the sword from the dead *Kabu's* head, and thrust backwards under his own arm into the living man's abdomen. He charged both men in the center, still trying to untangle themselves, bowled them over with his left shoulder and skewered through the throat the man who had tried to swing around behind them. The latest corpse dropped to the bricks wearing a stunned *How'd he know I was going to do that?* look.

Livios ran over the body and invaded the far left section, back-stabbing the confused swordsman he found there. The *Kabu* screamed as a shiny blade screeched from his armored navel.

Livios proceeded to the roof's edge, thinking, *Is this the correct side?*

"Kill him!" officers cried, beside themselves with wrath.

Livios felt as though his feet were dragging. Surely someone would catch him from behind! It seemed an endless time before he reached the edge. He took one final step and dove from the roof into empty night; unseen assegai hissed past his head. The sensation of sluggish motion stuck with him as he tumbled through the air. At the end of his body's slow rotation he found himself looking up at the silhouettes of those *Kabu* leaning over the edge.

The black men began to jump after him.

Just when Livios was sure he would never land he slapped the water back first. The pain was sharp but not as jarring as striking the shallow river's muddy floor. Falling bodies splashed all around him as he came up for a desperate breath. He quickly submerged again and swam downstream.

COHAR

Arms wide, Phaetonis *Ikar* simmered in the center of the command tent while an armorer measured him for a replacement suit. First *Elhar* Tzetzos stood at attention before him with the eyes of a dog anticipating a whipping; gone was the cocksure attitude he had so recently inflicted upon his peers. Phaetonis hadn't eaten since his return, so anxious was he to get refitted. He intended to attack the enemy at first light.

"Aren't you done yet?" he griped at the armorer.

"That'll do it, lord. It'll take a bit to make the adjustments."

"Get to it." Phaetonis dropped into a chair and glared at Tzetzos from pitted eyes. "Guard?"

A legionary looked into the tent. "Yes, *ikar?*"

"Food and drink. And summon the other *elhari.*"

"They're here, sir," the sentry replied and turned to unseen comrades. "Bring the food!"

Tzetzos stood rigidly erect while Phaetonis devoured a bucket of boiled eggs, his favorite meal. He finished with a belch and asked the *elhar:* "Why'd it take so long to rescue me? They nearly killed me a hundred times."

"We didn't want to be hasty, sir," Tzetzos replied. "We—"

"Drop the 'we'. You were in charge and should've acted in charge. If you couldn't handle the Legion it was your problem alone."

Tzetzos remained silent.

"Right?" Phaetonis demanded.

"Yes, sir."

"Continue."

Tzetzos looked supremely uncomfortable. "I didn't want to risk getting you killed, sir. There was much to weigh and I had no precedents."

"Precedents? You need instructions for every problem, you idiot?" Phaetonis sneered. "Do you know what they did to me while you lazed up here?"

"No, sir," Tzetzos said sheepishly.

"And I won't tell you, either!" Phaetonis brooded for a long while. "Are the men ready?"

"We are, sir!" Tzetzos replied emphatically. "Lead us."

"Very well. Get the others."

The *elhari* were soon seated at Phaetonis' table. The *ikar* cut short their hearty greetings with an impatient, "Yes, yes, good to be back." His eyes regained some of their usual gleam. "Now let's talk of killing."

"Yes, sir!" the officers agreed.

Phaetonis produced a sketch map and laid out his battle plan. "I thought of little else while I was being tortured," he admitted. "Though it didn't seem too likely I'd get a chance at revenge." He slowly elucidated ambitious designs. True, the *Kabu* might expect an attack, but he had gathered invaluable intelligence during his captivity—where their best troops were stationed, what generals held Danawayo's favor and so forth. "They've never even drilled as a single unit," he revealed. The Legion, with its rock solid discipline, armor and superior communications, not to mention the benefit of the high ground, would have many advantages.

"They still outnumber us by thirty times," Polyphemos pointed out.

Phaetonis' temper flared. "What do you want to do, run? After what just one of my men did to them? Anyway, the lesser kings are unhappy with Danawayo," he went on. "The *Baswai* in particular want to run things and will use my escape to discredit him. I've no doubt they're bludgeoning him with it right now. That boy Kerebos has sorely damaged Danawayo's prestige."

"Nor can the *Chaconni* be happy about it," Lasctakos put in.

"Didn't see them too often."

"If Danawayo's not inviting them inside, they might not be on good terms," Tzetzos suggested.

"Doubt that," Phaetonis muttered. "The Old Kingdom likes him well enough to equip and train his elite troops. He's been one of their agents for years, it seems, and they've showered him with gold. Enough to forge alliances with some *Tantorri*, at any rate." He chuckled. "Did you see their swordsmen?"

"*Swordsmen?*" Lasctakos replied.

"Yes, Danawayo's 'black' Black Legion, as he called them. Modeled after us, if you can believe it."

"They use our formations?" Polyphemos sniffed.

"That's what I heard. They even have an "*ikar*". Handpicked by the king himself, or so he said." Phaetonis laughed. "I think he was trying to impress me."

263

"It takes more than muscles to make legionaries," Lasctakos said. "Who trained them, the *Chaconni?*"

"Apparently. I rather ruined his mood when I pointed out that we routinely maul the Old Kingdom's best divisions. He dropped a charcoal on my trotters for that remark." Phaetonis' mood swung again and he waved off further comment. "Let's get back to this map." After giving precise instructions he sent the *elhari* to bed, with, "Be ready before dawn."

"Yes, sir," they replied.

"Lasctakos," Phaetonis said as they rose.

"Sir?"

"Let me know if your boy makes it back. I'd like to thank him personally."

"Yes, sir. Shall he go into battle as a *cohar?*"

"What are you talking about?"

"He asked for Melas' position when he approached us with the plan for your rescue. Tzetzos agreed."

Phaetonis looked at Tzetzos. "It wasn't even your plan?"

"No."

"Get out."

*   *   *

Lasctakos rested on the corner of a cot, sharpening his sword. True, the armorers could put the edge on for him, but he liked doing it himself. The chore had become something of a sacrament to him over the years. Few things relaxed him like the sound of stone on steel. He suddenly dropped the whetstone and flexed his tingling right hand. He quietly cursed and massaged the palm. These attacks had grown more frequent in recent months. *You're training too hard,* he told himself. *What's that clamor?*

"Sir!" Azimos *Sestar* called from outside.

"Enter."

"It's Kerebos! He's back!"

Lasctakos' smile coincided with strength returning to his hand. "Very good news."

"Everybody's waking," Azimos said and ran back outside.

Lasctakos wiped clean and sheathed his blade then followed the *sestar*. Azimos had been right, the whole camp was cheering. Lasctakos sought his peers.

"Your pup has a charmed life," Polyphemos said.

It took Livios a good while to make his way through the crowd. Every man in the Legion, it seemed, wanted to slap his back or offer *kraal.* His smile grew strained as he wormed through the reeking throng; he had rarely been so tired. The assembly finally thinned as officers ordered men back to their posts. Eventually he found himself before Lasctakos and the other *elhari*—except Tzetzos.

Livios was warmed by the pride in Lasctakos' eyes and pulled a solemn salute. "Mission accomplished, sir," he rasped.

"I knew it would be," Lasctakos replied. "But I think we owe the salute, son. Gentlemen?" The *elhari* saluted in concert. "Congratulations, *cohar*!" Lasctakos finished heartily. "Your great deed shall outlive us all."

Livios' contentment faded with the sobering realization that he was now master of forty-two souls. "Thank you."

"Report to the *ikar*," Lasctakos said. "He wants to personally express his gratitude. Then rest, for we attack at dawn."

"My armor, sir?"

"It waits in your tent."

"Thank you, *elhar*."

Livios slowly plodded uphill to the command tent where some First *Elhar* men accosted him. The topknotted legionaries crowded around, shouting, "Ker-e-bos! Ker-e-bos!"

"Let go," he grumbled as they lifted him.

"Put him down," Pythen *Sestar* said as he arrived. He faced Livios for a short while then suddenly bowed. "Kerebos, we can't thank you enough."

Livios was surprised and embarrassed. "He's my *ikar*, too."

Pythen straightened. "You really must join the First."

"Thanks, but I'm happy with Lasctakos. Excuse me."

Pythen pulled a dagger and grabbed Livios' arm. "Can I have some of your blood?" he asked with frightful earnest.

"What?"

"For luck," Pythen replied as though the answer was obvious.

Livios bared his arm and Pythen pricked him a few inches below the elbow. The bodyguard wet, then sheathed, his blade. "Thank you, brother."

The other bodyguards wanted some, too. Livios grudgingly accommodated them. "You're lunatics," he said as he rolled down his sleeve. They thanked him for the compliment.

"Come," Pythen said. "I'll announce you."

Livios followed.

The *ikar* was donning armor when Livios entered. "Ah, there you are," he said. "Guessed that's what the racket was. You can sit."

The armorers finished with Phaetonis and left. The *ikar* buckled his sword belt. "I suppose you know I'm glad you cut me out of there?"

"I'm proud to serve, sir."

"Really? I'd be considerably happier if you didn't do it to get promoted."

It had never occurred to Livios that he might have to answer to this particular. "I would've done it anyway, *ikar*. But why not get Melas' job? Saves me the trouble of killing him come Winnowing."

Phaetonis turned toward a small mirror and placed a new helmet on his head. "You don't like Melas?"

"No. He never forgave me for getting promoted."

"Or for killing what's-his-name? Enyo?"

"Yes, sir. They were friends."

Phaetonis cursed and threw the helmet. "Someone get Aspendos back in here! This bucket's too tight!"

Phaetonis looked at Livios, who noted furrows in the *ikar*'s short hair. *Wonder how he liked having to grow it after the promotion?* he thought. First *Elhar* men were notoriously attached to their topknots. Some even killed themselves when baldness stripped their knot.

"What if Melas calls your name on Winnowing Day?" Phaetonis asked.

"Then I'll leave him dead in the grass."

Phaetonis gave a nasty chuckle. "I believe it. I'm confirming your promotion but it won't go into effect until after the battle. I can't have you making beginner's mistakes in such a crucial fight. Lasctakos will have to wear two helmets."

Livios was relieved. "I understand, sir."

"When we get home Lasctakos will tutor you. Dismissed."

The abrupt dismissal surprised Livios. He rose to his feet and saluted, thinking, *Suppose that's what passes for an ikar's gratitude.* "One more thing, sir."

"Yes?"

"I killed Danawayo. Cut his throat right in the throne room."

Phaetonis stared. "*What?*"

"You heard correctly, sir."

"I'd say that changes things. How'd you escape without him as a bargaining chip? I was sure that's how you'd manage it."

"I ran up to the roof and jumped into the river."

Phaetonis squinted. "This is true?"

"Yes."

Phaetonis looked thoughtful. "I would've paid anything, *anything*, to have seen that bastard bleed," he said quietly. "I thank you, Kerebos. You've done me a great service. Do the *elhari* know?"

"No, sir. Figured you should be first."

Phaetonis stepped close and grasped Livios' shoulder in an almost friendly gesture. "You were right. Summon them for me."

Livios found Pythen just outside, wearing an expression of adoration. Had he been listening? "He wants the *elhari*."

"I'll see to it, sir," Pythen replied, saluting.

Yes, he was listening, Livios decided. "Good luck tomorrow."

"Thank you, sir. Let me know if you need anything, anything at all. The First will never forget what you've done."

Livios turned to hide his disgust. *Last night he wants to kill me, now he's kissing my ass*, he thought. *Liked him better yesterday*. He had a brief glimpse as to how an *ikar* must feel, with sycophants' perpetual boot-licking. *Before they call you out on Winnowing Day, anyway. No wonder Phaetonis is the way he is.* The insight depressed him and the feeling intensified as he stumbled downhill toward a line of tents. He was disappointed by the change in Pythen and wondered how a blooded veteran could so easily shelve his dignity. *And I never even liked him. What if my friends start acting like that?*

Livios ducked inside his tent before anyone saw him. His armor rested on a T-rack, bathed in the soft red glow of a hanging lantern. He ran a dirty finger over the oiled breastplate, which seemed larger than he remembered. A note hung from his swordbelt. It read: *I am very proud of you. You'll get the new crest after the battle.* Lasctakos' thoughtfulness only temporarily halted the inexorable approach of a deep melancholy. *I should call Pythen down here and kick him*, he thought, though he knew the bodyguard had little to do with the malaise.

Livios lowered himself gingerly onto the cot. He had ridden hard to rejoin the Legion and had gone forthwith on the taxing rescue mission; he needed rest. An endless, slow moment was spent staring at his callused, crusted palms. *That can't be blood*, he thought. *Not after the swim.* The image of killing Danawayo's innocent young concubine splashed across his mind, causing him to twitch. *But she surprised me*, he consoled himself. *I would've just thrown her aside if she gave me more time.*

Like you did Vara? his conscience needled. *You had plenty of time to think about that one.*

"She should've stopped talking," he countered. "I warned her."

Yes, it's all her fault. She should've just let your men rape her, too.

Livios' heart sank.

Your father shouldn't have grabbed you, either, the voice pressed. *The stupid old man. Got what he deserved.*

Livios snorted as though from a kick to the gut. "No! Dad wasn't stupid!"

Then why'd he love you?

Livios closed his eyes tight. How had he ended like this, a murderer and master of murderers? *Kin slayer, woman slayer and slaver*, he tallied

267

his crimes. *And creatures like Pythen worship me for it. How can I get out?* He leaned onto his knees and moaned.

And leave Kassandra to your friends? the voice asked. *That's a smart idea.*

Livios slapped his knees in impotent frustration. "Shut up!"

Someone laughed. "Hey, you look like hell."

Livios looked up cautiously to find Luecos smiling at him. The *Boru's* blonde hair was long and he wore *Tantorri* garb. "I was sent out again as soon as I got back," he explained. "Had to position the riders. How you been?"

Livios smiled weakly. "Not well. I'm sitting here talking to myself. But I'm damn happy to see you alive."

Luecos doodled on the oily breastplate. "I'm too mean to die. Running with the horsemen was more fun than dangerous, anyway. Didn't want to come back." He gazed at Livios. "You look about a hundred years old. Want some good *kraal?*"

"We have to be up early."

Luecos pulled the drug purse from his belt. "Go ahead, it'll help you sleep."

Livios took a small portion and chewed. Relaxing heat spread throughout his cheek. "Thanks."

"What were you blubbering about, anyway, *cohar?* Cohar! Talk about moving up fast."

"You heard?"

"Of course I did! It's all anyone's gabbing about, the next chapter in the blossoming Kerebos legend. Freya's milk, you'd think it was Lex Desia they were talking about! You're the luckiest cutthroat on Pangaea, I swear, getting out of the castle alive. Must've been born with a horseshoe up your ass."

Livios laughed and it felt good, even if he was a bit delirious. "Yes, must have."

Luecos looked stern. "I wouldn't have let you pull that stunt if I'd been here. At least not alone."

"Someone had to do it."

"Don't expect me to start saluting you, now."

Livios laughed again. "You do and I'll break your teeth." He stood and gave Luecos a quick, grateful embrace. "Thanks, Krynn."

"For what?"

"For being your nasty self."

"Well don't get weepy on me. Come, let's find some shears and we'll trade haircuts."

"Later." Livios pushed him toward the tent flap. "Let me sleep."

Luecos stopped near the opening and snapped a salute. "Yes, sir!" he cried and then stepped outside.

Livios went back to the cot and fell instantly asleep.

For about an hour.

Luecos shook him awake, saying, "Have to get up. Lasctakos wants us." He was armored, shaved and his hair freshly shorn. Smelled as though he had managed a bath, too.

Livios was pulled into a sitting position. "Feels like I just dropped off," he complained.

"You did. Hurry up!" Luecos wriggled a gambeson over Livios' head and began working the laces.

"I can get it." Livios was soon following Luecos from the tent. The armor felt constrictive after being so long without it. They approached Lasctakos' dwelling and were admitted by the guard. The *elhar* was pacing before an apparently unused cot, his officers at his feet.

Livios was too tired to pay Melas much attention as he sat beside him. "Sorry, sir, I was sleeping," he apologized to Lasctakos.

"Let us begin," Lasctakos replied. "Since Kerebos has killed Danawayo the *ikar*—quiet, quiet! Yes, he's dead." The tent shook with shouts of surprise and approval.

"Good work!" Azimos told Livios and others agreed.

Lasctakos smiled them to silence. "Yes, it is big news. Because of it, Phaetonis feels we should attack before the *Kabu* straighten their chain of command. Hostilities will commence within the hour. Yes, Odyssios?"

"In the dark, sir?"

"Unless the sun decides to rise early. Now be silent." Lasctakos laid out the battle plan. The Legion would assault the center and right of the *Kabu* camps, ignoring the *Baswai* tribes near the river. "To allow them time to desert," he explained. "If the *Baswai* do run, we shall cut through to their 'legion' in the rear by the *Chaconni* horsemen." He went on to give a brief description of Danawayo's swordsmen then said: "These vaunted fighters are the heart of the enemy, though they've served but two functions until now—to protect the castle and to monitor the Royal Guards. Once we rout them all resistance should crumble. Yes, Kerebos?"

Excitement had made Livios much less tired. Back in armor, he felt virtually invulnerable. "Sorry to interrupt, sir. Looks like those phony legionaries hold the only bridge over the river. I'll bet they're supposed to keep the Guards in, too."

Lasctakos nodded. "I agree. The *Chaconni* are no more used to fighting in the dark than are we, and their alliance with the *Kabu* will be tenuous following Danawayo's death. It would be no surprise if they withdraw over that bridge once the 'legion' is engaged. They'll want to reassess their situation in the morning light, I think."

Lasctakos briefly touched upon the diversionary tactics Phaetonis had planned. A small party of saboteurs would infiltrate the castle while *Tantorri* archers harried the *Baswai* formations. "Some runners will be left to guard the hostages, however," he explained. "In case the horsemen suffer a change of heart. Questions?"

"How are we going to communicate, sir?" Melas asked. "Sounds like we'll be plenty short of runners."

"We'll employ runners but there will be *no strategic changes*. The *ikar* doesn't want anyone getting creative in the dark. If fortune dictates, we will retake the hill to consider our next move. Other questions?"

There were none.

"Good luck, gentlemen," Lasctakos said gravely. "Our future demands we eliminate this southern threat. We must crush the *Kabu* or fight a succession of rearguard actions the entire long road home. Only decisive success will leave us strong enough to stave off, and ultimately pressure, the Old Kingdom. See to your units. Dismissed."

A God's-eye view of the field moments before the battle would have revealed a relatively small group of legionaries quietly massing in the heights above a sprawling conglomerate of enemy forces. Phaetonis had divided the enemy host into six sectors, A through F. A, B and C made up the forward *Kabu* concentrations. A and B each numbered some eight thousand men from tribes most closely allied to Danawayo while C boasted twelve thousand warriors from the *Baswai* confederation and held the cramped position between B and the river. Sectors D and E were nestled just behind A, consisting of the ersatz "legion" and the neatly lined tents of the *Chaconni* VIIIth and Xth cavalry divisions. Sector F was the castle, remote and backed against the river.

Phaetonis had arranged his *elhari* in a straight line. The First, on the extreme right and which he would personally command, would join Lasctakos' Second against sector A. Menestheos' Third would hit the lightly manned area between A and B, splitting the *Kabu* forces. Anios *Elhar*'s Fourth and Naphios' Fifth were tasked with B sector while Polyphemos' Sixth would lightly engage B but leave itself in a position to slow a *Baswai* charge from C.

The *ikar* didn't think the *Baswai* would attack, at least not immediately. He anticipated duplicity, especially when they saw their traditional adversaries in A and B getting mauled. To further sway the *Baswai*, he had ordered two hundred *Tantorri* to fire upon C from across the river. With their numerous campfires, the *Baswai* would make good targets.

If all went as planned, the First through Fifth would rout A and B and thrash the *Kabu* "legion". The Sixth would tarry to cover the rear against regrouping enemies and to discourage the *Baswai* from joining the fight. To further baffle the *Kabu* and to rob them of refuge, Phaetonis had dispatched a band of runners to assail the castle. These men would rope onto the roof with the objective of torching the fortress. The roof was not chosen arbitrarily. During Phaetonis' captivity the Old Kingdom had delivered numerous barrels of potent *Chaconni* liquor to Danawayo, which were cached atop the castle. The high-grade spirits should flame up nicely.

The *landesknectos* let their fires burn low to shield their muster. They were ordered into formation about halfway through the night and stealthily joined ranks. Not even their captives marked the gathering.

Livios stood quietly beside his unit, which was arranged in rows, with Luecos' and Melas' *sestari* on either side. Every man held spear and shield with spare pila slung over his back. *Can't believe how awake I am,* he thought, palms itching. *Must be the broth.* He glanced at his men and found them looking back at him. *Didn't get to fill them in on where I'd been or to talk about the promotion. Must be killing Talos to keep quiet!* Talos suddenly didn't look so young or harmless; his freckled face was resolute. *Even he'd give those Kabu swordsmen fits.* Livios smiled at the notion and Talos' pasty face split with a grin. *This might be our last fight but we're going to take an awful lot of them with us.* He gazed back down the hill. *Are they really so unprepared? Got my sword and my metal skin and am the youngest cohar of all time. Kassandra will be impressed.* He chuckled softly. *Hurry, Phaetonis, let's get started!*

A runner ran up and said, "Sixty count, sir." Livios nodded and the man moved down the line. It seemed a much longer tally before they advanced. *Here goes!* he thought with his first step. He hardly felt his feet beneath him.

The legionaries moved silently and were only occasionally betrayed by the soft crunch of dirt clogs underfoot. *Chaconni* horses neighed in the distance. Livios restlessly scanned the dark slope and the crowded *Kabu* camps, tranquil in the campfire light. *Have they no guard?* he wondered.

When the legionaries were a hundred paces from the enemy, *Kabu* sentries leaped from the ground and dashed toward their encampment, shouting as they went. Livios' jaw clenched and his grip on the spear tightened. The *Kabu* armies stirred even as their scouts reached camp.

Just then screams rose from Sector C. Phaetonis had ordered the *Tantorri* to shoot at the first sound of activity and the horsemen were really feathering the *Baswai*. The cries from the stricken multiplied by the moment.

"At them, men!" Phaetonis shouted. The legionaries responded with a rousing battle cry and broke into a run.

271

Livios slowed to let his men catch up and merged back into the line. Before him the vast *Kabu* host shook off sleep like some great, rising beast. Enemy voices filled the air. *They didn't expect our tiny force to attack and haven't planned a proper defense!* he realized. *Or did it go out the window when I killed Danawayo?*

Sectors A and B were now fully active. Livios clearly made out the cowskin shields as the *Kabu* scrambled into position. Spear tips glimmered in the night. A commotion on the left caught his eye. *Is B splintering off to support C?* he wondered. *Yes! They think we're already hitting the Baswai!* The rest of B and all of A solidified into two long, curving shield walls that bristled with spears. Even in the scarce light it was obvious that the Legion was many times outnumbered. Livios' spirits sank at the enormity of the task ahead. *Going to be like rolling a tree uphill.* It would be a long night.

The *Kabu* shouted at the incoming legionaries and clashed their shields and assegai together, which sounded like the slamming of thousands of doors. Livios wondered if they had formed up quicker than Phaetonis had expected. He glanced right and saw Luecos' unit in perfect step with his. *Good old Krynn!* he thought. *Knew he'd be ready! Hope my elevation doesn't ruin things between us.*

There were some loud shouts from the massed *Kabu* and assegai pelted the legionaries like a hailstorm. Something sliced Livios' leg, a spear caromed off his helmet and another bounced from his breastplate. He did not slow.

"Answer them!" Phaetonis roared.

Livios was twenty paces from the teeming horde when he slowed and threw the pilum. He lost sight of the projectile but a different pilum pierced together a bunch of overlapping shields directly before him. The *Kabu* tried to free their shields but quickly dropped them in disgust. Angry warriors poured from the compromised wall like water through a burst dam.

Livios reached overhead and pulled another pilum. Heart racing, he threw the spear directly into a man's belly and was rewarded with the distinct snap of a spine. The *Kabu* shrieked and went down; his countrymen swept over him. A thousand spearmen raced towards Second *Elhar*. Livios shifted nervously on his feet. *Give the order, Lasctakos!* he thought.

"Front line, swords!" Lasctakos commanded. "Pila from the rear! Don't break, men!"

The last remark stiffened Livios' resolve, somehow, though he had no intention of breaking. Swords rang from their sheaths and he took position between Talos and one of Luecos' men. He felt a sudden pang of loneliness as the bare-breasted *Kabu* covered the last few feet. *Naked,* was all he thought. A spear snapped on his shield and he stabbed the offending *Kabu* in the chest. The smaller man tried heroically to trap the blade as he died. Livios yanked free the sword and had a fleeting glimpse of its wet blade as he stabbed over his falling opponent into another's gleaming teeth. He twisted the sword inside his victim's mouth, felt crunching, and ducked a spear he hadn't seen. Crouching against his greatshield while ineffective blows skid off his back, he sliced legs as a comrade covered him with a pilum. *Sounds like the men are using short strokes in this jam*, he thought as he stood. *Good*.

The swords of the forward Tridents kept the *Kabu* at bay while the second line speared the enemy. A legionary's pilum was not an ideal thrusting weapon, its shaft was designed to bend upon impact, but the *landesknectos* got off a few lunges before having to throw them. For his part, Livios felt reassured by the sharp points that kept darting past his ears.

The terrible swords and skillfully handled pila of the Legion took an awful toll on the *Kabu*. The ground grew thick with dead and wounded, so much so that the legionaries gave ground to keep dying enemies from grabbing their feet. The rear line of legionaries ran short of missiles, which they had snatched from the men in front of them, and drew their swords. Talos suddenly grunted and crashed onto his back, an assegai through his throat. Clios filled the breach before the *Kabu* could race over the gurgling legionary.

"Keep tight and cover!" Livios ordered as he fended off numerous blows. He felt the comforting warmth of Clios' leg as the unit constricted for maximum protection. A succession of *Kabu* howled as his blade struck; his gauntlet was soon dripping enemy blood. He saw quite clearly now, though the night had grown no brighter. Cut. Deflect. Stab. Crouch. Stab. His arm burned from exertion. The air grew fouler than a latrine's as death loosed men's bowels.

"Shift!" Lasctakos cried from behind. "We have the line, so throw deep!"

The first row disengaged and slipped behind the second but Livios stayed up front. Those recently graduated to the rear yanked pila from their forward comrades' slings and arched death into the *Kabu* ranks. The enemy assault slackened. Livios found himself with more room to maneuver and opened up his stance. He chopped through an assegai shaft and slammed his blade deep into a man's forehead.

"Press them!" Lasctakos yelled.

The *elhar* advanced a few steps and the *Kabu* surrendered ground. That they had room to retreat spoke to the effectiveness of the thrown pila. Livios found himself with considerable space and contemplated switching his sword to his left hand. He killed another man and it took a long moment for an enemy to fill the hole. *They can't already be running short?* he thought exultantly. A *Kabu* rushed in from the side and grabbed his arm; he dropped the shield, snatched his dagger and buried it between the man's ribs. By the time three other *Kabu* leaped forward Livios had cast aside the body. He met them with a blade in either hand, waving the weapons before him.

"I killed Danawayo!" he bragged.

The trio slowed to appraise the situation and Livios changed blades from hand to hand. *That feels better,* he thought and charged. He smacked the foremost man's spear aside, slammed him chest to chest, then stabbed at the other two with dagger and sword. As luck had it, he caught both *Kabu* in the solar plexus then swiped the head off the man he had thrown with the chest blow. Livios backed into ranks as the stabbed men crumpled over their decapitated mate.

"I forgot how good you were, sir," Clios gasped as Livios positioned himself.

"Got lucky."

"I saw that," Lasctakos growled in Livios' ear. "Any more bravado and you might just stay a *sestar.* Hear me?"

"Yes, sir!"

"Now retire. You've been too long up front. I'll cover you."

Livios dropped back and took water. Lasctakos merged into the line and effortlessly handled a spot while commanding the *elhar. What balance he has,* Livios thought as he savored another swig. *Wish this were broth. I'm getting winded.* After a brief spell he returned to the line. "It's time for the shift, sir."

Lasctakos disarmed a man then sliced him twice across the stomach. "I've just warmed up," he laughed. "SHIFT!"

The unit obeyed with smooth precision. Livios let Lasctakos pass and was confronted by a fresh mound of dark corpses smartly piled like firewood. He wondered if Lasctakos had so designed it, but concluded such skill was impossible.

A shrieking *Kabu* leaped at Livios, who flattened his face with the greatshield before killing three more men with an equal number of strokes. Still the *Kabu* came on. He got involved in a furious exchange with a big spearman, but eventually caught the man with a backhand slice across the eyes. The shrieking *Kabu* fell forward while two others rushed to fill his space. Livios stabbed low and killed the first but someone else dispatched the second. *Why've they gotten so reckless all of a sudden?* he wondered in alarm. *The fight should be draining out of them.* The unit fought valiantly to hold ground as blood mud formed beneath their feet. Blades rang and sang.

Livios' breath was now coming in gasps and his shield seemed thrice its normal weight. His sword arm felt hot. A rock struck his helmet and his sight dimmed. Terror gripped him as he flailed blindly, ears ringing.

"Watch out!" Clios responded to the wild strokes.

Livios calmed but continued to lance out with his blade. His sight returned in increments, to his great relief, but brought along a debilitating headache. Another *Kabu* died at his hands but he was finding it increasingly difficult to handle the endless string of adversaries. *Have they been reinforced?* he thought and opened a man's guts. *What a stink!* The Second shifted again and the giant swordsmen kept at their bloody work. The armored line held.

The *Kabu* died by the hundreds, but still they came. The source of their resolve eventually became clear. The First, facing a thinner line and fueled by Phaetonis' fury, had folded the *Kabu* flank back into itself. The enemy was actually retreating in the Second's direction! Lasctakos' group stood firm as an anvil, however, which placed the First in excellent position to play hammer. First *Elhar* savaged the turned flank, laying low rows of the crowded *Kabu*. The right corner of Sector A grew so compacted the tribesmen could hardly defend themselves.

It was Lasctakos who first gauged the *Kabu*'s peril and he took bold action to magnify the problem. "Second *Elhar*!" he cried above the din. "Fall back thirty paces and integrate!"

Livios echoed the command before realizing what it meant.

Integrate? he thought. *Going to one line?*

That was Lasctakos' plan. He discerned that Phaetonis' turning movement might rout Sector A, but only if the Legion acted quickly. By pulling back he would create the space needed to merge his lines and therefore bring more swords to bear against a faltering enemy. The unit retreated the necessary distance up the hill, high enough for Livios to see the entire frenzied battlefield, and completed the fusion just in time to meet the advancing enemy. There was panic in the *Kabu* voices now, as though they sensed fate had turned against them.

Lasctakos elbowed into the line. "Charge!"

The Second went to work with renewed fury. The *Kabu* were literally hacked to pieces as the legionaries advanced down the slope. Blood rained over the field. A severed, dripping arm flopped onto Livios' shield and hung there.

"Faster!" Lasctakos demanded, and his men leaned into their work. Heavily armored and moving downhill, they plowed right over the enemy.

Livios was moving too fast to be sure the men he hit stayed down. A dozen times he slipped on slick casualties. "Here comes Phaetonis!" he cried.

It was true. First *Elhar* had cut through the enemy and was now in view. The *Kabu* of Sector A had had enough and scattered in all directions. Weapons were cast aside as the majority of the force fled toward the castle.

Livios thought it a glorious sight and watched with grim satisfaction. Only moments before he felt spent and now he saw a vastly superior force fleeing in terror. The men of the First and Second hailed each other as Lasctakos ran to Phaetonis.

"Hey!" A smiling Luecos said as he approached Livios.

"Hello. Your head's bleeding."

"It's not mine." Luecos tossed his *kraal* purse. "Eat some. Battle's not over yet."

Livios peered towards Sectors B and C. The Legion was still heavily engaged but he couldn't tell how things were going. "I guess not." Tall flames suddenly rose in the east and groans lifted from the *Kabu*.

Luecos turned. "What the hell?" A rapidly spreading fire lit Danawayo's castle. Phaetonis' plan had worked. "Well that's pretty. Now we've some light to work with."

Lasctakos ran over. "How many casualties?"

"One of Kerebos'," Luecos replied. "Going after B now, sir?"

"No, to neutralize their swordsmen. Forward in Tridents, the *ikar* has the lead. Move!"

*   *   *

The runner Tissaphernos led six lightly armed men from camp just before the Legion attacked. The small detail swam the river to emerge on the other side as the *Tantorri* began to feather Sector C.

"I like the sound of that, T," a runner said as he rewound his grapnel rope. "Are there sharks here?"

"Not so loud," Tissaphernos commanded. His was a voice used to being obeyed. "Let's give it a minute. Orders are to wait until our comrades are busy." Twice the age of the average recruit, he was no stranger to hazardous missions. In fact, he so relished danger that he had deserted the *Chaconni* army because his unit had been regulated to garrison duty. Though thin of hair and craggy of face he had survived *landesknecta* training that would have killed his former comrades. "All right, let's go."

The runners moved out in single file and detoured the *Tantorri* to avoid being shot by accident. *Or maybe on purpose*, Tissaphernos thought. *I don't trust them. Sounds like the fighting's really heating up!*

The battle was in full swing by the time they approached the castle. Tissaphernos did not speculate on the fight. "Okay, one more swim," he said and slid back into the river. The others followed. They emerged

276

from the water and scrambled up to the castle wall. The din from the field had grown much louder.

Tissaphernos leaned against the clammy bricks and caught his breath. "Where's your rope, Nemesos?" he shouted to be heard.

"Lost it in the water. Five will do, right?"

"Idiot." Tissaphernos stepped back a few steps and began swinging his grapnel. The others followed his lead. *Now I see the use of all those rope drills*, he thought. "Toss 'em!"

Only three of the hooks caught hold on the roof. "Good enough. Up we go!" Tissaphernos said. He put a dagger in his teeth and led the way. Scaling the wall proved remarkably easy after rope drills. He reached the top and pulled himself over before grabbing the blade. *Good, no one up here*, he thought. *There are the barrels just like he said.*

"Move," a teammate growled.

Tissaphernos rolled over into a crouching position then helped up his comrade. The rest of the legionaries scratched onto the roof. "Let's get to work. Epidamnos, watch the stairs."

The runners spread out. Many of the barrels were empty and others held just water but there was still more than enough liquor to make the trip worthwhile. Tissaphernos rolled his barrel over to the sunken stairwell and started pouring the contents down the steps. The liquid splashed more noisily than he anticipated. The smell recalled that of his old barracks.

The job was soon finished.

Tissaphernos tossed the empty cask. "Good. Nemesos, work the flint, the rest of you scat. Wait at the bottom."

Nemesos picked up a barrel lid and hastened to a point far from the ropes. He kneeled, reached into his belt and produced a vial of tinder and a well-worn flint.

Tissaphernos walked to the edge and looked over the battlefield. *That's some swarm of Kabu*, he thought while rubbing a sore elbow. He paid closer attention to Sector C and saw that the *Tantorri* shooters were giving the *Baswai* hell. Even as he watched, some *Kabu* retreated for the protective darkness; the trickle became a flood. *Don't worry, archers, you'll have plenty of shooting light before long.* He couldn't easily identify the more distant legionaries but it appeared they were doing well. The *Kabu* defense was particularly confused and disjointed in Sector A. *Maybe Phaetonis isn't crazy after all?*

"Got it, T!" Nemesos shouted.

Tissaphernos turned to see his comrade's burning lid. "Throw it down the steps!"

Nemesos did as ordered and they bolted for the ropes. Their shadows leaped before them as flames roared into the air.

Phaetonis laughed heartily as Sector A crumpled. "Let them go!" he cried. "They'll get theirs soon enough." He felt euphoric, as though liberated from the disgrace of having been captured. He would have liked to watch his troops butcher the fallen *Kabu* but there was work to do. "I need a runner!"

The man arrived almost immediately, having been on the nearby slope. "Yes, *ikar*?"

"Get Lasctakos over here. And get me some water."

"Yes, sir!"

Phaetonis stuck his shield into the dirt, pulled off a gauntlet and wiped his bloody face.

Lasctakos arrived with runners in tow. "I thought you might need them, sir," he said.

"Good! How are your casualties?"

"Light."

Phaetonis pointed north across the littered plain. "Our mates haven't done as well as us. Looks like we're tackling Danawayo's 'legion' alone."

Sector B had given Fourth, Fifth and Sixth *Elhari* trouble but Phaetonis' success allowed Third *Elhar* Menestheos to threaten B's hitherto unexposed flank. The Third was ravaging the enemy rear but B proved well led and fought with resilience and skill.

"My strategy counted on B's dispersal," Phaetonis said. "I don't like the idea of leaving a committed unit responsible for my flank."

"We should be fine, sir. The Third will cover us."

Phaetonis grabbed a runner. "Tell Menestheos to hold no matter what, because I'm pressing on. Go! Lasctakos, form into Tridents and stay on my ass. Hit them hard. We have to scatter them quickly."

"Yes, *ikar*."

Phaetonis watched Lasctakos go, thinking, *A good man. Maybe too good.* "Tzetzos?"

"Here, sir," Tzetzos said from behind him.

"Rope them into formation."

Phaetonis tried in vain to see Sector C. Would the sun never rise? He turned to the runners. "What passes with the *Baswai*?"

"Some have run, *ikar*," a runner reported. "The horse masters are doing their job."

Tzetzos returned. "Ready, sir."

"And here comes the Second. Let's move!"

Lasctakos asked Luecos and Livios: "How many casualties?"

"One of Kerebos'," Luecos replied. "Going after B now, sir?"

"No, to neutralize their swordsmen. Forward in Tridents, the *ikar* has the lead. Move!"

Luecos smacked Livios' shoulder. "Good luck!"

"You, too!" Livios turned toward his men, who were clambering into formation. "Tridents need three men, Clios," he said hurriedly as he joined them. "I'll take Talos' spot."

Clios' cheek was visibly swollen and discolored; he had been stabbed in the face. "You won't lead, sir?" he replied as though around a mouthful of food.

"I'm a better lefty." Livios stepped behind Clios, Argos on his right. "Keep your ears open for which way to cut. Advance!"

They caught up with and took their place in the *elhar*. Phaetonis' unit led at a distance of fifty paces. The legionaries rumbled over the hard earth toward Sector D. Livios could see little but the jostling backs of Phaetonis' men and regretted not leading the Trident.

"Up!" Clios shouted as he jumped. Livios and Argos leaped high enough to miss a *Kabu* corpse. "Up!" They bound again, this time over a smoldering campfire.

Livios now heard the challenge from the *Kabu* swordsmen and wondered about the sturdiness of their breastplates. "Clios, hit them low!"

Phaetonis' Tridents shifted from triangular to linear formation and Livios caught a glimpse of the *Kabu* before the *landesknectos* struck their center. There was a tremendous crashing sound followed by screams and shouts. A few bodies actually flew into the air.

Lasctakos shouted: "Left!"

"Lance it!" Clios said and Livios moved directly behind him; Argos brought up the rear of the linear "lance".

Again Livios lamented his position. *I can't see a thing*, he thought. *Might as well be blind.* The noise of battle intensified by the moment. There was a clanging of swords.

"Here goes!" Clios cried.

Livios held his blade close and covered up with his greatshield.

Clios howled and rolled into the shins of three huge *Kabu*, who spilled forward.

Livios scrambled over the fallen men and dug in his heels. He and Argos whirled in tandem as Clios bound to his feet. They attacked the fractured enemy line. Livios shaved off the crown of a prostrate *Kabu*'s skull then ran left and pommel-spiked another in the back. Argos dispatched two men as Clios wrestled with a third.

The First and Second had breached and neutralized a narrow span of the enemy line, but the rest of Danawayo's 'legion' was quickly converging upon them. The *Kabu* were absolutely rabid to avenge their slaughtered mates.

Phaetonis ordered the *landesknectos* into a circle and screamed for Lasctakos.

"Yes, sir?"

"I saw the *Chaconni* forming up and the only way to keep them off our flanks is to not have any!" Phaetonis said breathlessly as he gestured toward Sector E with his sword.

"So much for the Guards retreating!" Lasctakos replied.

"Stay out of the line and keep a reserve to plug gaps. Here they come!"

The officers split for opposite sides of the circle. The *Kabu* chanted as they came.

"Every sixth man fall out for support!" Lasctakos bellowed. "This is it, gentlemen! Break their backs!"

Livios braced for the assault with Clios and Argos beside him.

"For hell's sake," Clios grumbled. "Do we always have to be outnumbered?"

Livios growled and braced for impact. The *Kabu* burst upon the legionaries and slammed shields. Blades flailed overhead, metal smacked metal. The circle shrank beneath the enemy's weight; the combatants were too tightly packed for effective swordplay.

Livios hammered away with his blade but hit shields, mostly. And still he was being pushed back. He screamed with frustration as he gave away inches. Never had he heard of *landesknectos* being muscled in this fashion, despite the odds, and the novelty terrified him. In the depths of his mind was the thought of running. *If we fall back much farther we'll bump ass with the First!* he thought frantically. He slid his sword into his belt, freed his dagger from its scabbard and began slicing *Kabu* sword arms. Blades glanced from his helmet, shoulder and shield as he leaned into his work. The stench of sweat and death stole his breath. Still the legionaries gave ground. *By God, that's enough!* he thought and with an incoherent yell threw aside his shield and ran smack into a *Kabu*. There was a brief tussle before he got his dagger under the tribesman's oval-shaped shield; the *Kabu* yowled as the dagger pierced his knee. Another *Kabu* filled the breech. Livios lay on the man's shield and stabbed down into his nose. The *Kabu* thrashed wildly but was too crowded by countrymen to fall. Other *Kabu* swung at Livios but the short blows didn't penetrate, nor could they effectively stab low due to their shields, and even when a sword did strike the legionary it didn't penetrate his armor.

Livios sliced exposed legs, groins and abdomens with increasing success. Arms grappled and pummeled him but their numbers were still a disadvantage. A large hand shot out from the scrum and grabbed his sweaty throat but he twisted from the grip.

Lasctakos was running back and forth behind his men. "Daggers! Use your daggers!"

The remainder of the *elhar* was shortly in on the action. *Kabu* casualties mounted but they were able to more effectively use their swords as the ranks thinned. The *landesknectos* were experienced enough to do well daggers versus swords but the *Kabu* began to make some kills of their own. Clios had his arm chopped off and floundered back from the action.

Lasctakos started to commit the reserves. "Back to swords!" he ordered.

Livios freed his sword without missing a beat but many of his comrades weren't so prepared. When the initial order for daggers came they had thrown their long blades back into the shrinking "safe zone".

Lasctakos committed the rest of his reserve and joined the fight. He called to men by name, his voice loud and soothing.

"Pielos, fill that gap!" he said. "Coming up on your left, Laertos!" "Kerebos, get back into line!"

Livios had held firm as the circle shrank and was now exposed but it didn't bother him. He had cleared a nice space for himself and was swinging away and the *Kabu* didn't like it; try as they might they couldn't get inside on him. Arms and heads were lopped off with increasing regularity. The dead and wounded covered the ground. A *Kabu* shot screaming from the darkness, blade overhead. Livios swung with both hands, swept the man's legs then struck downward with a quick windmill motion. The *Kabu* coughed blood as the sword breached his armor and lungs.

"Kerebos, fall back!" Lasctakos repeated.

Livios turned and leaped over some bodies then dashed to the line. He noted that the sky had grown lighter and marveled that he had been fighting that long. The battle continued but the *Kabu* were rapidly becoming outnumbered. Some *Chaconni* did ride up but withdrew after assessing the situation. The legionaries laughed at the cavalry.

Phaetonis stomped around the circle, cackling like a fiend. "Why these aren't swordsmen," he said. "Looks to me like they're about to run!" He faced the faltering enemy and asked in their language: "Will you tuck tail?"

Livios ducked a sword swipe, slashed his *Kabu* across both legs then opened the man's throat with a return stroke. The *Kabu*'s jugular spouted blood as he crumpled to earth. For once Livios was out of opponents. "Press forward, sir?" he asked Lasctakos.

"No, hold the circle."

The *Kabu* finally had enough and began to disengage. They ran in

281

small groups at first but the piecemeal retreat shortly became a general rout.

"Let them go," Phaetonis said then conferred briefly with Lasctakos.

"The *Chaconni* have pulled out and it doesn't look like they're coming back."

"You guessed correctly, sir. That castle is making a charming blaze, too."

Phaetonis glanced at the keep, where men and women were streaming from the gate. "So no one will be retreating there. Get the men into formation but have the runners get our wounded back to camp. We'll have to cannibalize units; patch them together as best you can."

Lasctakos nodded toward Sector B. "Over there, sir?"

"Right. Hurry."

Phaetonis maintained two *elhari* despite having suffered thirty percent casualties. "To the Third, men!" he shouted and led them forward at double time.

The Third through Sixth had contained B and those *Baswai* not scattered by arrows, but the line had grown static. Some of the *Kabu* had fled at the sight of their retreating swordsmen but most fought on.

A huffing runner caught up with Phaetonis. "Sir, Menestheos *Elhar* is dead!"

"Who took over?"

"Don't know, sir, it's all confused!"

Phaetonis scowled. "Get back to camp. Lasctakos, take over the Third!"

"Yes, sir!" Lasctakos peeled off from the formation.

"Let them hear you!" Phaetonis cried.

Livios tried to voice a war cry but nothing happened; his throat was drier than an old boot. Luckily, his comrades managed a respectable clamor—at least enough to catch the *Kabu's* attention.

The *Kabu* weren't prepared for more legionaries, apparently, and began to break before Phaetonis arrived. "No prisoners!" the *ikar* thundered as his unit crashed upon the enemy.

Sector B collapsed all at once and the *Kabu* raced for the river in the early morning light. Corpses, assegai and shields littered the field and those *Kabu* unable to retreat were massacred to a man. Lasctakos had to give the most stringent orders to keep the Third from pursuing the foe all the way to the water. The unit was most distressed by the loss of their *elhar*.

Phaetonis summoned runners and his commands were very swiftly forthcoming. The Sixth, which had suffered fifty-percent casualties, was ordered to round up the stricken before returning to camp. Two *elhari* were tasked with killing the wounded *Kabu*, none but kings and generals would be made prisoner, while another was sent to destroy the bridge the *Chaconni* had used to escape. The Second was directed to see if anything could be salvaged from the castle. Phaetonis parked his bodyguard in the middle of the carnage and he reviewed casualty reports; he made some battlefield promotions.

There was little exultation among the legionaries, so great was their fatigue and losses; it had been centuries since they had lost a quarter of their strength in a single engagement. They doggedly set to the clean up, which promised to take longer than the battle. Fortunately none of the enemy units returned to attack, though horses were seen on the horizon, and the legionaries completed their work in peace. The wooden bridge proved sturdier than expected and the Second was ultimately redeployed to assist in its destruction. The sun was almost overhead when the structure finally crashed into the water.

The *ikar* at last ordered his men back to camp. Fourteen thousand *Kabu* had fallen to sword and arrow, though fully half of these had been killed as they lay wounded on the ground. Four hundred and twenty-five legionaries were casualties, almost two hundred of them killed outright.

Livios staggered up the hill toward camp, his entire body numb. He bled from a dozen superficial wounds and his nose oozed a constant stream of mucous that he didn't bother to wipe. The slope looked as daunting as a mountain to his bleary eyes. Stoop shouldered legionaries slogged silently beside him.

Luecos caught up with him and grunted: "*Kraal?*"

"No."

They descended into the dry moat and clawed their way out with effort. Livios would have sworn that his tent was retreating from him, as it was growing no closer. He concentrated on each painful step. Either blood or sweat had pooled in his boots. "Luecos?" he croaked.

"Yeah?"

"Set a guard, then bed them down. See I'm not disturbed."

"All right, *cohar*."

AFTER

Livios woke with a gasp. It took a short time to get his bearings; he was lying on his cot, still in armor. He pawed clumsily at gluey eyes and creaked into a sitting position. A washed-out, empty feeling filled his body. Every muscle ached and his skin itched beneath stinking armor; his throat was parched. He fumbled with his canteen, which proved empty. Dismayed, he stared at the sunlit tent wall. A shadow passed.

"Who's there?" he rasped.

The tent flap opened and one of Luecos' men ducked inside. "Good morning, *cohar*. Sleep well?"

If you like burning alive, Livios thought. "Give me your canteen."

"Yes, sir."

Livios emptied the container's warm contents and felt slightly nauseous. "Help me up," he said at last.

"You really ought to get out of that plate," the legionary said.

Livios walked for the opening, his feet dragging. The sun burned in a cloudless sky. *Kabu* corpses carpeted the battlefield and had started to decompose, by the smell. "Uh," he moaned and stopped a few feet from the tent. Legionaries were busy in the trenches and the freshly churned earth of a mass grave rested at the bottom of the hill.

White haired Pielos *Sestar* approached and saluted. The veteran looked none the worse for the recent hostilities. "How you doing, *cohar*?"

"Could use some food." Livios paused. *Cohar? That'll take getting used to.* He recalled his days as a recruit. *Wonder how Boros would feel about that?*

Pielos' smiled knowingly. "We were starting worrying about you."

"How long was I out?"

"Two days."

Livios could scarcely believe it. "A long time to burn," he muttered.

"Sir?"

"Where's the food?"

"Oh, sorry." Pielos waved down the line of tents. "Luecos has stewed something down there. Looks like he retched it out. Want me to fetch?"

"I'll do it. Where do we stand?"

Pielos pointed at the still smoking castle. "Lasctakos sent men to see if anything's left. *Chaconni* scouts are still around but they're keeping a distance. Don't think we'll have any trouble out of them."

"The *Tantorri?*"

"Spent their arrows, so most were sent home. The rest are scouting us a path out of this hole and laying tribute demands on the locals."

Livios watched a runner dart for the castle and felt brief nostalgia for the simple job. *Now officers call me 'sir'*, he thought, uncomfortably. "How many men did we lose?" he asked softly.

"A hundred seventy three in the action, fifty since. Another *cohar's* worth will be joining them before long."

"How many from the Second?"

"Thirty."

"Talos and Clios?"

"Them, too."

Livios shook his head. It amazed him how much the news hurt.

"I'm going for some of Luecos' slop."

"I'd eat something first," Pielos called after him.

The sun made Livios blink. His head was beginning to feel better but his back throbbed and his shoulder hurt particularly. Men saluted as he crossed the dusty trail but the greetings grew swiftly irksome; responding was an inconvenience.

Luecos and four others were sprawled around a small black cauldron. The whistling *sestar* was sharpening his dagger when he spied Livios. "Stand up, boys, here's our new *cohar!*"

"At ease," Livios told them. "Glad to see you all made it. Anything left in that pot?"

"Sure, pull up a chair," Luecos replied. "We're taking a break from digging."

Livios sank to the ground, feeling each spinal vertebrae crack in turn. A legionary handed him a bowl of steaming gunk. "Isn't that dagger sharp enough?" he asked Luecos, still furiously at work.

"One of them dusky bastards took a bite off my edge," Luecos replied. His blue eyes sparkled. "Funny, but no matter how many men I tickle with this thing, I never get a laugh."

Livios picked a chunk of something from the bowl and blew on it before placing it in his mouth.

"Not bad for horsemeat, huh?" Luecos asked.

The meat tasted like boiled leather. "It's bad for anything," Livios choked.

"Thanks."

"Sir?" a legionary asked.

"Yes?"

Oloros, a hard-faced ten-year veteran, managed to look shy. "Could you teach me to throw knives?"

Livios was surprised by the question. "Not sure I can teach anyone, it just sort of happens, but I'll try when we get home."

Luecos chuckled to himself.

Pythen emerged from the *ikar's* tent and told Lasctakos: "He'll see you now, sir."

Lasctakos entered and saw Phaetonis concentrating on a scroll. "Reporting as ordered, sir."

"Sit."

Lasctakos found a small, backless chair and watched Phaetonis work. *How long since he slept?* he mulled, admiring Phaetonis' stamina. The *ikar* had far exceeded his expectations as both a leader and strategist, despite a tendency towards rashness. *Has shown more talent than he did as an elhar.*

"How much gold did you find?" Phaetonis asked without looking up.

"Only two small bags, sir. We did uncover a considerable amount of gems, however. Cut stones, probably of *Chaconni* origin."

"Worth?"

"Perhaps a hundred thousand King's standard."

"That takes some sting out of our losses," Pielos said. If you haven't guessed, we're not going on the Tribute Trail this year."

Lasctakos had suspected as much. "Everyone will have to pay double next year."

"Or more. You fought an exceptional battle. Meant to tell you before now, but I've been busy."

"I knew you'd see us through, sir," Lasctakos said.

Phaetonis put down his stylus and rubbed his eyes. "I brought along some barrels of wine in case we had something to celebrate. I want you to dole it out. Do it by unit, not man. Those that lost the most deserve more, anyway."

Lasctakos was impressed. *This from he who forbade wine?* "I'll see to it, sir."

Phaetonis studied his subordinate. "So how would you have handled the battle differently?"

"Well, sir—"

"Truly."

Lasctakos hesitated. "I would have committed archers to taking out the *Chaconni* horses, but that seems a quibble considering the Guards ran. And, if I may say, you were too much in the fore of the fighting."

"I considered that. At least I've thought about it since."

What has gotten into him? Lasctakos wondered. *So mild today. Has he already been drinking?* "We can't afford your loss, sir."

Phaetonis smiled. "Want me around for the Winnowing?"

Lasctakos smiled back. He could take Phaetonis with any weapon, as they both knew. "I am not anxious for a change."

"Really?"

"We see eye level about the direction of the Legion."

Phaetonis considered this. "Pleased to hear it. How do you fancy a haircut?"

"Excuse me?"

"I'm giving you the First."

Lasctakos liked the idea. *First Elhar!* he thought. *Gives me reign of the Scriptus and makes me his successor.* "Tzetzos certainly deserves it, sir."

"He's turned out to be pretty useless sub-*ikar*. I'll kick him over to your old unit. He should think about taking a step down so Kerebos doesn't have to kill him."

"You won't suspend the Winnowing?" Lasctakos asked.

Phaetonis appeared troubled. "I just don't know. Would the men stand for it? They're killers, not stable boys. Tribute's one thing but you know how they starve for the elevation sacraments. Keeps 'em in line all year long."

Lasctakos sat mute. He'd assumed the *ikar* would skip the annual trial. *The Brand lets him, due to our losses,* he thought. *And the pretext would keep anyone from challenging him.*

"That's it for now," Phaetonis said. "Keep your promotion quiet until I tell Tzetzos."

"Certainly, sir."

"And send in the *Tantor* chief. He's been doing some recruiting for us. All the tribes we're passing are being told to deliver their fighters who fit the bill. No harm in taking a look at them." Phaetonis suddenly let slip a torrent of curses directed at the *Chaconni* king, Pontis. "That pup has greatly injured me with his meddling. Even if I elevate all our runners we're going to be thin, not to mention short of scouts."

"We should recruit as soon as we get back."

"Of course we will. Dismissed."

Lasctakos saluted and left. He had much to chew over as he navigated the hill. Despite some minor criticisms, he quite approved of

Phaetonis' leadership. True, the war might yet kill them all, but that was hardly the *ikar's* fault; his predecessor's stupidity had forced the actions. *We've still to get through this and the less infighting the better,* he thought. *Besides, he's not hurting my objective.* A bitter taste filled his mouth as he remembered his ancient disgrace and slowly worked his stinging fingers. *But can I afford to follow him for a year or two?*

*   *   *

Next morning the Legion prepared to move out, but not before wrapping up loose ends. First, many *Kabu* corpses were tossed into the river to poison the water for tribes further south. Next, prisoners were liquidated. These men, captured kings and nobles, had not generated the desired interest from their subjects. No one had inquired after them, so they were bound and cast into the river.

Much more important was the necessity to ready the wounded for the journey and to attend fallen comrades. The hospital wagons were primed and dead men's kits bundled for the journey. *Landesknectos* gathered before the mass grave where Phaetonis, in his priestly capacity, said some appropriate words as enemy corpses rotted in the sun behind him. The *ikar* wore "Desia's miter" for the occasion; the tall purple headdress lent a regal air to the proceedings.

"When Lex Desia broke with Korenthis he did so to create the finest army in the world," he began. "He accomplished his goal. We are his proof. But even victorious armies suffer and death finds even the stoutest warrior. The war of life goes on and we march to meet it while our brothers sleep here. Honor them in thought and with deeds of blood, for you shall never see them again. Honor them as others shall one day honor you."

Tzetzos and a man bearing the Scriptus broke formation and approached the *ikar*. Tzetzos pulled a parchment from his belt, unfolded it and faced the Legion. "The following men have died in this, their first action, and have been buried separately." He read a short list of names. "The man formerly known as Cecalos, 6146, is being stricken from the Legion's records for cowardice. His body shall remain among the enemy dead. Bring forth his sword." A legionary approached with a weapon and a hammer. Tzetzos took the items and struck the sword until it snapped. He and the Scriptus bearer returned to ranks.

The Legion hit the trail soon afterwards and the going was slow due to the overcrowded convalescence wagons. The legionaries marched throughout the day and stopped only to inspect potential recruits, which the *Tantorri* had gathered. Over forty suitable *Kabu* were collected in this fashion.

How many will survive training? Livios thought as he slogged on. *Five?*

The Legion moved until dark and pitched camp in one of their previous sites. The next nine days of the journey were similar except that the wagons sped up as more wounded died. The *landesknectos* finally reached the black castle on the evening of the tenth day.

Livios never thought he'd be so happy to see the place and hoped Kassandra was all right. He found himself more eager to see her than any time during the campaign and wondered if he could simply march through the gate to the barn. Orders from Lasctakos quashed the thought.

A runner told Livios: "Lasctakos wants after-action reports before you turn in, delivered personally."

"All right," Livios snapped. The desire to find Kassandra became overwhelming. As he marched through the gate he thought, *I get more orders as an officer than I did as a recruit.*

Livios waited for his subordinates' reports before finishing his own. Most of the accounts made agonizing reading but Luecos' was surprisingly well-written—legible and succinct. Had the *Boru* some kind of formal education? Livios' own summary wasn't completed until long after dark. He carried it through the sleeping spoke to Lasctakos' room and knocked on the door.

"Come in, Kerebos," Lasctakos said.

Livios entered. "How'd you know it was me?"

Lasctakos was sitting cross-legged on the floor, a multitude of parchments about him. "By your walk." He looked up and smiled. "Besides, I already received the other *cohari*."

Livios handed over his scrolls.

"Four?" Lasctakos said. "I need facts not literature."

Livios stood in peeved silence. Had not Lasctakos wanted his best effort?

"Have a seat, son, I want to talk to you."

Will I never see Kassandra? Livios wondered as he eased onto the wooden floor.

"I think you know how pleased I am with your service," Lasctakos said. "I'm constantly amazed by your aptitude and expect greater things still."

"Thank you, sir," Livios replied softly.

"For these reasons and others it pains me to leave you to another's care, but I have no choice."

Livios was startled. "Leave me? What do you mean?"

Lasctakos' expression was enigmatic. "I've been ordered to First *Elhar*."

289

"Then I'm going, too!"

Lasctakos raised a hand. "Easy, son, let us consider that. Don't you some day want an *elhar* of your own?"

"No!" Livios retorted.

Lasctakos frowned. "No? Why not?"

Livios clenched and opened his fists, thinking, *How can he go to the First? Look at how pathetic I'm acting. Some officer!* "I'm sorry, sir, I'm very tired."

Lasctakos was openly disappointed. "I thought we'd settled your objections to our life."

Livios shrugged.

"Do you seriously believe you were born to be anything but a legionary? If so, you've not thought enough. There is no getting out, in any case. And what of your lady friend?"

Livios sighed deeply. "Sometimes everything seems fine but other times..." His gaze narrowed. "Tzetzos takes over the Second?"

"There's no helping it, son. Phaetonis will let me continue your instruction, however. You'll still report to me once a week."

Livios hardly listened. Why would Lasctakos transfer? "I guess I'll make the best of it," he mumbled.

"Yes, you will. You must. There are magnificent things in your future. Now go see that woman."

Lasctakos was an old hand with summaries and swiftly completed his own report. He reached Phaetonis' floor in time to see Tzetzos storming down the hall and surmised that the *ikar* had broken the bad news. He rapped on the door.

"Come in," Phaetonis said. He was seated at his desk and looked most put out. "You missed the drama," he muttered.

Lasctakos stood before the *ikar*. "How'd he take it?"

"Bad. Cut off his topknot and handed it to me." Phaetonis picked the raven hair off his lap and waved it as evidence. "We were recruits together, you know."

"Yes, sir." Lasctakos laid the report on the desk. "Perhaps you should rest?"

Phaetonis stared at nothing. "I've done a powerful lot of thinking about the Old Kingdom and how we're going to handle them when they come. The bridge." He yawned. "It can wait. I'm going to get some sleep. You're in charge till I wake."

Kassandra sat on the corner of her bed, feeling very small. *They've been home all day,* she thought. *Where is he?* She tried to suppress her fears; years of abuse had skilled her in that. The lumpy mattress seemed suddenly itchy so she rose and walked to the window. But all she could see was the candle's reflection in the glass.

Kassandra abruptly turned from the window and began to pace. She soon plopped back onto the bed and unbuttoned her dress so she could breath. She hated staying in the tiny room but didn't dare leave for fear of missing Livios. It was moments before she realized she was wringing her hands. Time dragged on. *Admit it, he's not coming back*, she thought. Rage, fear and grief swelled within her breast. *Just like a man!* She angrily swept a tear from her face. *He's dead.*

"You awake in there?" Mother asked from the other side of the door.

"Yes."

"Get yourself together, a *cohar* is coming up!"

Kassandra's glimmer of hope died stillborn. *But where's my sestar?* she wanted to scream. It surprised her that Livios' commander would deliver the bad news, but she didn't dwell on the thought; legionaries frequently did strange things. "I don't want to see him," she replied in a quavering voice, but Mother had already gone. She pictured Lasctakos in her mind. There was something disconcerting about the insouciance with which the handsome officer had treated her.

Footsteps in the creaky hall preceded a gentle rap on the door.

Kassandra shut her eyes. "What?" No answer. "What?"

The latch moved, the door swung open and Livios stepped inside.

Kassandra burst into tears.

Livios hurried forward and tried to take her hands. "Don't cry," he said softly. "Please, don't."

Kassandra slapped him. "You scared me to death!" she shouted. "I thought you were gone!" She struck him again then succumbed to his embrace. "Thought you were gone," she repeated and nuzzled his breast-plate.

Kassandra stowed her tears and wiped her face; she gazed up at Livios. He looked years older than when he left. A lot of flesh had fallen from his tanned face, leaving it gaunt and predatory. But there was still that flicker of kindness in his dark eyes, eyes that grew warmer even as she stared into them. "Where'd my young boy go?" she whispered sadly.

Livios seemed hurt; he dragged her small white hand to his heart. "In here."

Kassandra suddenly leaned forward and kissed him; they both tasted her tears. "Sorry I hit you."

"You did?"

Kassandra was no longer upset, merely worn out. "How'd you make *cohar* so fast? I thought for sure it was that Lasctakos bringing evil news."

291

Livios shook his head. "He's an *elhar*. And he wouldn't bother, anyway. I didn't mean to alarm you with the grand entrance, I just wanted to impress you."

Kassandra was already calculating the applications of Livios' promotion. She *was* happy to have him back but was no less glad that he could now better shield her.

Livios released her and stood. "I have to go."

"When will you be back?"

"A few days. Your pool of visitors will be shrinking, though. I'll be putting out new reminders just in case."

"But I don't want any of them touching me!"

"I'll do what I can!" he shot back. "If I do too much I might get demoted or even removed." He looked pained. "Do you think I like having to put up with this?"

Kassandra hugged herself as she shook her head.

He touched her cheek. "I'm a *cohar* now, though, so not many outrank me. I have to go."

"Livios?" she called before he stepped into the hall. He turned. "Thank you," she said.

He half smiled and was gone.

*   *   *

King Pontis of Korenthis disliked the War Room he had inherited from his father. The chamber's gilded walls and plush carpets seemed incompatible with military planning which, for Pontis, helped explain why his sire had suffered so many defeats. *My reign's going to be different,* he thought as he studied his olive visage in a mirror. *We're the richest state in the world and must regain our primacy, Black Legion or no.*

Pontis would wait no longer. He exited the room, closed the door and proceeded down the marble hall, a stout but upright figure in an outdated Scarlet Guard's uniform. Chandeliers hung from the white ceiling; watchmen stood at regular intervals. He felt their eyes, in fact he sensed the gaze of the nation. It had been six months since he secured the crown and the realm was anxious for signs of a foreign policy. Would he be cautiously unlucky, as was the king before him? *They won't have to wait much longer to find out,* he thought. The Council knew of the bribes to the *Kabu*, his father's policy, but only a few intimates knew his ambitions to destroy the *landesknectos*. Then again, only his closest associates would have believed him capable of such audacity; he was widely derided as a copy of his unimaginative and dispassionate forebearer. A battlefield victory would be just the thing to quiet his detractors. *Those legionaries have clipped our interests for too long. I'll see an end of it, so help me God.*

Pontis remembered something as he entered his favorite sitting room. "Tell the count I'm in here," he ordered the guard.

"Yes, my liege."

Pontis entered the "blue room" and found his favorite divan. He slid off his riding boots and relaxed; the cerulean marble walls always eased his mind.

The dashing Count-Colonel Fidelis Pyrros entered and sat opposite the king. His chiseled face was troubled and, at the moment, looked little like the busts that graced his estates. "My apologies, sire. I needed confirmation about the *landesknecta* dead. We pulled two hundred seventeen from the grave."

Pyrros and Pontis were related, as were many of Korenthis' patricians, but were friends nevertheless. They had also served together in the Scarlet Guards; Pyrros had been the superior officer.

Pontis smelled bad news. "Continue," he said flatly.

"All Danawayo's sub-chiefs are dead, and what's left of the tribe won't help us. Worse, we were unable to recover any of the money."

Pontis gave an "I knew it" snort. "So Phaetonis gets my gold. That's grand. And your two divisions didn't lift a finger?"

Pyrros looked grave. "Again my regrets, sire. They're anxious to redeem themselves, I assure you."

"They'll soon get their chance. Have the commanders executed."

Pyrros stared. "Are you sure? They're of the Kloz clan, if you remember."

Pontis was not at all sure but he was angered by the units' inaction and at the loss of money. "They ignored direct orders and abandoned our allies," he said. "Put them down. I think the rest of the army will get the message."

Pyrros looked at his hands. "Yes, sire." A short while passed. "So you still want the black castle?"

"More than ever. We must hit them while they're weak."

ADMINISTRATION

The black castle witnessed a flurry of activity during the next month. Endless streams of runners scoured the vicinity, when not drilling with their new units, while *Tantorri* horsemen probed deeply the Old Kingdom. The tribesmen's daring and Danawayo's jewels bought Phaetonis reliable, if not encouraging, information. It was learned that King Pontis had recently announced plans to "eliminate, once and for all, the godless *landesknecta* cancer"; he had dredged up numerous legionary atrocities and pointed to their "recent, crippling losses" as reasons for their removal. But the *Tantorri* also heard that the general public's enthusiasm for war, particularly in the urban east, was lukewarm. The Black Legion's reputation of invincibility was too firmly entrenched for anyone to really expect its defeat. Commoners were far more concerned about Pontis' tax collectors than an enemy who only troubled the western provinces. Korenthis' nobles, except for some enthusiastic impoverished houses, were taking a wait-and-see approach to the affair. Time enough to sing the crown's praises in victory, or to damn it in defeat.

Of the twenty-two divisions in the *Chaconni* army (fourteen infantry, two engineering and six cavalry) fourteen were being readied for action. Ten infantry divisions would move out, though most of the cavalry would be deployed to deter the *Tantorri* and *Boru*; Pontis had no intention of mishandling another "*Tantorri* invasion". Both divisions of engineers were slated for the attack. It was an impressive force of over twenty six thousand professional soldiers and it would hit the *landesknectos* when they were at their weakest point in memory.

Livios labored over an "armor preparedness" brief in his room which, he imagined, still reeked of Melas. He wondered if Melas wanted to challenge him come Winnowing Day. *I hope so*, he thought, though the officer had been acceptably tractable since his demotion. Livios realized he was being unreasonable. *If you can't handle men hating you, you're in the wrong business*, he told himself. "Don't I know it," he said with a sigh.

294

Tzetzos, however, was taking hard the public humiliation of losing First *Elhar*. He showed no inclination to get to know his new subordinates and was particularly hostile to the *cohari*. Also, he frequently reeked of forbidden wine. Livios considered it a blessing that his presence was never demanded and tried not to dwell on the fact that Tzetzos' indifference was damaging the unit. *Just do your best to stay ready*, he thought. *The ikar will sort things out.*

Or would Phaetonis go easy on his longtime friend?

Livios resumed his task. He hated administrative work and *cohari* had plenty of it, he had discovered. Fitness and readiness reports, tactical plans, disciplinary recommendations, cross-training suggestions, drills, parade, weapon inspections; the list was endless. It was demoralizing. He missed mixing with the men, particularly Luecos, and found it increasingly difficult to maintain concentration, or his physical prowess. It was to the point that he would have welcomed a tough forced march, or even one of Boros' torture sessions. *Small wonder subordinates sometimes take out better swordsmen on Winnowing*, he thought. And the lack of sweat work left him too much time to mull how unbearable life had become; there was hardly any time for Kassandra.

Livios could bear no more of the brief and leaped up from his desk. He seized his helmet by the crest and stomped out into the empty spoke, which was depressingly empty. Lined beds stretched past an equal number of T-racks. At that moment a man strode into the long hall. His walk revealed him as one uncomfortable in armor, a new legionary.

"Come here," Livios commanded, for no reason except that he was bored and lonely.

The man ran over, saluted and stood at attention.

"Who gave you leave to skip drills?" Livios asked.

The young legionary was obviously *Boru*. His skin was deathly pale and his eyebrows so blond as to be invisible. "My *sestar*, sir. Luecos."

Can hardly understand him, Livios thought, studying the speaker's hollow face. *He might be even younger than me*. "What's in your hand?"

"Cloth wrap, sir. Came to wash and bind a wound."

"Let me see it."

The legionary hoisted his kilt and revealed an ugly, deep gash above his bony knee. Blood covered the lower leg and plated boot.

Livios felt bad about grilling the man and hoped he wasn't becoming the sort of martinet that had made him so miserable when he was a recruit. "Did it hit the tendon?"

"No, *cohar*."

"Where's your boss?"

"In the yard, sir."

"Your name?"

"Triskeles, sir."

Livios slapped Triskeles' shoulder. "Didn't mean to hold you up. See to your patchwork. And eat a double meal tonight."

"Yes, sir!"

Livios headed toward the exit. *We'll have to put some meat on that one,* he thought.

It was a bright, early summer day. The grass was yet green, but where drills had bruised it flat. Livios saw Luecos and made for him.

Luecos was really chewing out his men, one in particular. "I'm more dangerous with a sausage in hand than you are with that pilum, Tissaphernos," he bawled. "Hit 'em with some sincerity!"

Tissaphernos' weathered face was blandly stoic but he repeated the movement and with more success.

"Keep at it," Luecos told them and turned to Livios. "Good day, sir. Come out for some honest work?"

"I wish. How are things?"

Luecos nodded at Tissaphernos. "My old recruit there is having some trouble with spears. Too many years in Pontis' army, it seems."

"Let's go watch the *ikar*."

"Right. Keep it going, Oloros."

"Yes, *sestar*!"

The two officers walked to the black wall and climbed the spiral stone stairs. They reached the top and gazed over the floodplain, where hundreds of shovel-wielding legionaries were completing a trench that stretched to the river. The *ikar* himself directed the labor from a mound of rolled sod; the grass would eventually camouflage a completed tunnel.

"Phaetonis has been possessed lately," Luecos noted and laid his tattooed arms on the parapet. "Saw him digging yesterday."

"He's become more involved since his capture by Danawayo," Livios agreed. "Can't say I blame him."

Phaetonis had revealed his engineering plan shortly after the Legion's return but hadn't proceeded until gathering favorable intelligence. His plan assumed a tunnel from castle to river, which would facilitate the destruction of the bridge at an opportune moment. It would not be an easy chore. The water table rose as they approached the river, which made the last hundred yards very muddy indeed.

"How long will the chain be?" Luecos wondered aloud.

"A furlong, I'd guess. We'll need that because of the water." Livios wondered if sharks could fit in the tunnel.

"Glad I'm not one of them ditch dogs," Luecos said.

"I'm not. Haven't had a good sleep in weeks."

Luecos looked fretful. "Being the old man's tough, huh?"

"I don't care for it much, Krynn," was the soft reply.

Voices rose from the yard behind them.

Luecos turned and pointed. "Isn't that Tzetzos?"

It was. Two legionaries were dragging the bare-chested *elhar* from the spoke; Lasctakos brought up the rear.

"Is he beaten or drunk?" Luecos asked.

Livios had a sinking feeling. "Don't know. Maybe both."

Livios entered the First's spoke. Most of the men were asleep but some were attending weapons by candlelight. He approached Lasctakos' door and knocked.

"Come in."

Livios entered and saluted. "Reporting as ordered."

Lasctakos was sitting on a crate, sharpening his sword. "Make yourself comfortable."

Livios grabbed a chair and whirled it around. "I still can't get used to that topknot, sir."

Lasctakos smiled and stroked his shaved head. "It feels particularly queer under a helmet. How's your unit?"

"No problems. We're one of the few back to full strength, but are short of runners."

"How short?"

"I have two."

Lasctakos whistled. He put down the sword and flexed his hand. "How are *you*, son?"

Livios shrugged and glanced away.

"Are you able to see that woman on a regular basis?" the *elhar* asked.

"Not really."

"That concerns me. Perhaps I have some good news for you, though."

"What news, sir?"

"I've been studying a lot of Scriptus law," Lasctakos began. "Fascinating information, really. I came across one of Desia's pronouncements which you'd find interesting."

Livios leaned forward. "In what way?"

Lasctakos stared. "It would allow you to exit the Legion without recrimination."

"What!"

"Sit and allow me to finish. The doctrine is from his Primus Pilus revelations—the laws that deal with succession."

Livios could hardly contain himself.

Lasctakos continued. "In essence, Desia stated that a man, upon achieving the rank of First *Elhar*, might reduce his rank or leave the Legion altogether."

"Leave!"

"Correct. More importantly, he may do so with honor. His name is not stricken from the Great Book."

Livios' mind raced. "But is it on the Scriptus, sir? Would Phaetonis let me?"

"No, not on the brand, it's commentary, but it is definitely canonical. The action has been twice executed. A kind of safety valve, I believe." He grinned. "You're not yet First *Elhar*, son, so I doubt it will be Phaetonis' decision."

Livios was dreaming and missed some words.

"…but it has to be on the Winnowing. So give the Legion your best and your hopes shall be realized," Lasctakos concluded.

Livios grinned. He would do almost anything in order to defect and take Kassandra. "Yes, sir!"

Lasctakos leaned back. "I appreciate your enthusiasm, especially since I need a favor from you."

Livios' smile grew strained. "Sir?"

"Phaetonis is quite unhappy with Tzetzos' drinking and plans to make an example of him. He offered me the honor of the disciplinary action and I have a fine idea. I want *you* to administer the punishment."

Livios asked mechanically: "In what manner?"

"Standard execution for an insubordinate officer. You've never seen it done?"

"I've heard about it," Livios said quietly.

"Barely a challenge for your sword."

"Phaetonis didn't want you to do it, sir?"

"He leaves me to my own devices. I think your involvement would send the proper message, anyway, you being an ascending star. You look troubled."

Livios was stonefaced.

"What's wrong?"

"Well, I'm not sure."

Lasctakos stared hard. "Then let me even your path. You'll do this because I want you to and because it's in your best interest. Yours isn't the only imperfect life, you know."

Livios felt chagrined. "Yes, sir."

"You must learn to think ahead," Lasctakos said with disappointment. "Do you take me for a simpleton?"

Livios was astonished by the question. "Not at all, sir."

Lasctakos furiously squeezed his palm. His anger ebbed slowly. "You need to trust me, son," he finally said.

"But I do, sir!" Livios assured him.

"With Tzetzos out of the way, I'll own both *elhari* and will be in a position to elevate a man of my choosing." Lasctakos read Livios' expression. "I've already cleared my plans with the *ikar*."

Livios' head was spinning. "Sir, I'm honored by your trust in me, but I'm not ready. Not by a long way."

"I agree, which is why your promotion will be delayed. I'll continue your instruction in the meantime and will teach you to think strategically. Anyway, I see no purpose in elevating you before the Winnowing. No need to entice your subordinates."

Livios was pleased by that last part; the Second's *cohari* were all gifted swordsmen. He thought of how Lasctakos had nurtured him along and was swept by gratitude and affection. "I can't thank you enough for all you've done for me," he said sincerely. "You must know that I'd never challenge you for First *Elhar*, whether it meant getting out or not."

Lasctakos smiled. "I admire your loyalty, son, but never let another stand in the way of your dreams."

Something in the remark snagged Livios' curiosity. "What are yours, sir?"

Lasctakos' stared blankly as he kneaded his hand. "To put my birth town to the sword. Though it looks ever more likely that I'll have to delegate the deed."

"What's wrong with your arm, sir?"

Lasctakos stirred from his fog. "Eh? Oh, nothing. I jammed it during drill. It loses feeling from time to time." He picked up his sword. "Now leave me, but keep our conversation secret. Be prepared to slice Tzetzos tomorrow."

Livios disliked Tzetzos but had no desire to kill him. Except that it brought him closer to leaving the Legion. Where would he take Kassandra? The world suddenly seemed so wide. "You can count on me, sir."

As he left, Livios tried to recall when last he saw Lasctakos drill.

Kassandra was drawing water when she saw Livios headed in her direction. She marveled that he endured armor in such heat. Livios' eyes danced, though his face was somber. *He's not fooling me, though I'm sure he thinks he is*, she thought. *I see right through him*.

"Hello, *cohar*," Kassandra said as he arrived. "I was starting to think you forgot about me." She talked lightly but there was more than a little admonishment in her voice, which frightened her.

"Not likely. Let's go inside."

"Mother said—"

"I'll handle her."

She reached for the buckets.

"Leave them," he said.

Kassandra wondered if she had misread him. *Something bad has happened?* she thought. *He's so stern.*

They entered the musty building and saw three legionaries on the couches. Mother was nowhere to be seen. "Out!" Livios told the men. They looked disappointed but gathered their gear and departed. Livios shut the door behind them and turned to Kassandra. "I've great things to tell you."

Kassandra stopped holding her breath.

Livios smiled impishly. "Scared you, huh?"

"Yes. What things?"

Livios looked around then leaned close. "I'm going to get us out of here. Lasctakos is helping me."

"Out of where?"

"Here. The Legion."

"When?" Kassandra replied, grabbing him. "When?"

He took her hands. "A year or two, I think."

"A year or two!"

Livios dropped her hands. "I thought you'd be grateful."

Kassandra's expression moved from shock to sorrow. She leaned against his breastplate. "I'm sorry. I can wait."

The comment irked Livios. "I don't think it's ideal either, but it must be this way. Don't you understand?"

"Yes," she replied in a resigned voice.

Livios' heart softened as he laid his chin on her head. He gave a brief description of the Primus Pilus code and how it would benefit them. "So I can leave with the thanks of the Legion, instead of as a hunted man. That's the way it has to be. I owe Lasctakos that much."

"I don't trust him."

Livios grunted. "Who do you trust?"

"You."

Livios laughed unexpectedly and squeezed her. "You'd better! I'd expect nothing less from my wife."

Kassandra slowly backed away. "What?"

"My wife. Why else would I take you?"

Kassandra's eyes filled with tears; she touched her breast. "You'd marry me?" she asked in disbelief.

Livios was grieved by her self-loathing and felt a swell in his throat. "Of course."

Her tears flowed. "Why would you do that? You've never even touched me."

300

Livios popped the gold *cohar's* ring from his sword's tang bolt. He stepped forward, grabbed her hand and slid the ingot over her thumb. It was too big for the digit. "That's how serious I am."

Kassandra covered her mouth to mute the sobs but soon stopped trying. She squeezed the ring with her other hand. "They'll take it from me."

"Like hell they will." Livios touched her face. "What's this crying? I thought you were an ice maiden?"

"I guess you thawed me." Kassandra smiled through her tears. "I'll be the best wife I can," she vowed. "I'll give you strong sons."

The words pleased Livios, until he thought of Daedilos. "I know you will."

Kassandra felt the rapid onslaught of a curious, desperate pang, which took a moment to identify. "Come upstairs," she invited.

Livios pushed hair from her eye. "I can't. And I wouldn't if I could. We'll wait and do it right."

They embraced briefly and kissed before he turned to go. Kassandra clutched tightly her ring as she watched him leave. *Two years isn't so long*, she thought.

*   *   *

Livios slid from bed and girt himself. A growing uneasiness, fear really, had made sleep impossible. It was as though he was marching inexorably toward some peril he could neither see nor escape. He had even prayed for the first time in many months, but relief and rest had eluded him. *Bet it was an even harder night for Tzetzos*, he thought as he strapped on his swordbelt.

Someone knocked on the door.

"Yeah?"

"Word came from Lasctakos," Luecos yawned. "I'm getting 'em up."

"Right. See you out there."

A short time later the Legion was assembled in the yard. Two thick vertical poles supported a horizontal third in the clearing before the formations. Clouds had rolled in overnight and the sky was foreboding. *Dark for dark business*, Livios thought dolefully as he waited before his unit. He imagined the difficult duty ahead and closed his eyes.

Phaetonis and Lasctakos stood before First *Elhar*. The *ikar* talked while Lasctakos nodded.

Luecos whispered to Livios: "What's the holdup?"

Livios shook his head once.

The slaves arrived and occupied the space Phaetonis had left for them. Nothing indicated the *ikar*'s displeasure so much as the fact that he would allow outsiders to witness Tzetzos' humiliation. *Oh, no!* Livios thought; Kassandra was in the front of the crowd. She shot him a bewildered look. *Don't watch!* he wanted to shout.

Phaetonis nodded and a runner made for the First spoke. Four legionaries soon hauled out Tzetzos, who was stripped to his breeches and covered in bruises. His wrists and ankles were chained to the vertical posts, leaving him spread eagle. A noose was tightened around his neck and thrown over the horizontal post. Tzetzos turned a defiant glare at Livios and bared teeth through swollen lips.

Light drizzle started. There was no sound but the gentle pats of rain on armor.

Lasctakos stepped forward and opened a scroll. He read. "The man formerly known as Tzetzos, 1112, has been found guilty of gross insubordination during a state of war. The just doom is death by sword. His name shall be stricken and his remains gifted to the sharks."

Tzetzos cackled at the words. Lasctakos told the guards: "Lift him."

The legionaries hoisted Tzetzos into the air then staked the rope to the ground. Tzetzos struggled as he hung suspended in space. His breaths came in slobbery gasps and his swarthy face darkened even further. Livios was repulsed by the sight but refused to show weakness. He avoided looking at Kassandra.

Tzetzos struggled with his bonds. "Phae-ton-is!" he choked.

Legionaries laughed at the sight. Luecos whispered, "Wiggling like a starfish in a frying pan."

Even at this stage of his career, Livios was surprised that men could enjoy the spectacle.

"Carry out the sentence," Lasctakos said firmly.

Livios approached Tzetzos, who was staring forward, eyes bulging from his purple face. Time passed. Livios couldn't find the will to begin. *God have mercy on me*, he thought, but the hopelessness of the prayer robbed its strength.

"Kerebos!" Lasctakos called.

Livios' sword rang from its sheath. Snarling, he severed Tzetzos left leg with a downward strike then sliced off the right with an upswing. Tzetzos had barely begun to howl when Livios pivoted and chopped him in half just above the pelvis, causing a veritable eruption of blood and innards. Livios followed the stroke, hacked through the left elbow, did a half spin and took off the other arm in the same place. What was left of the rapidly draining body swung gently from the line. The grass was dark with blood. Tzetzos' eyes and mouth worked ever slower until they stopped altogether.

Livios stared at the dismembered corpse, disgusted and awed by his swordsmanship. He barely recalled the strokes he had made.

"Finish it," Lasctakos said.

Yes, I'll do that, Livios thought. *Like this!* He drew and threw his dagger, which sank into one of Tzetzos' eyes, then sheared the neck in two with a hissing backhand slash. It seemed that the torso fell slower than a feather; he kicked it before it hit the ground, reclaimed and hurled the dagger, and pierced the heart even as the remains flopped to earth.

Livios wiped his sword on his glove and sheathed it before turning a fierce gaze on his comrades, who stood in slack-jawed amazement. Even Lasctakos seemed astounded. "Thank you, Kerebos," he said. "Return to ranks."

Livios ground his teeth and struggled to corral his emotions. Again he felt that mixture of exultation and dread that accompanied one of his terrifying feats, but this time it was worse. And better. Put to it, he would have oathed that something larger than himself had directed his movements. The language wouldn't have occurred to him, but the feeling was the closest thing to a spiritual experience he had ever known. "Yes, sir," he replied and returned to his unit. Tremors ravaged his body.

"Hot damn, man!" Luecos intoned, smacking Livios' back. "Sprained my eyes, seeing that!"

They kept formation as slaves gathered up the pieces. Phaetonis eventually gave the word and Lasctakos cried: "Fall out!"

Legionaries instantly crowded Livios. Some offered praise but most seemed content to merely stand nearby. Even senior commanders walked over to congratulate Livios on the impressive display, which Lasctakos would later dub an "epiphany".

Livios cared nothing for the adulation. He looked for Kassandra, but she was gone.

Livios sat in his room later that evening. The tears had long since dried, but they hadn't really bothered him. Nor was he concerned over the almost embarrassing approbation from his comrades. He could even get over Kassandra having seen him at work. After all, he had had no choice in the matter.

Alone in the dark, he finally determined what ailed him and was forced to embrace a repellent fact: he had enjoyed enormously Tzetzos' execution.

So much for God's mercy, he mused.

ATTRITION

Midsummer.

The air was heavy and the mood grim in the *ikar*'s war room. "Be seated," he told the *elhari*. "Just got word from my spy in Korenthis and it's not good. Pontis won't attack until after Winnowing."

"To bleed us," Polyphemos said.

"Yes."

Naphios asked: "Do we know who will run their campaign, sir?"

"A General Diakonos of the Guards. Most of his staff will be Guards, too. I didn't recognize the name. Do any of you?"

"Yes," Lasctakos said. "He's a scion of a dispossessed royal house. How peculiar that Pontis placed a cavalryman in charge of a siege."

"It is," Phaetonis agreed. "Maybe we can exploit that. My source believes this Diakonos was picked as an apology for the execution of two of his divisional commanders."

"Those sods with the *Kabu?*" Polyphemos asked. "The ones who wouldn't fight?"

"None other. Lasctakos, any word from our *Tantorri?*"

"Yes, sir. It was in the brief."

Phaetonis scowled. "I didn't get to it. Enlighten me."

"*Chaconni* cavalry is making things difficult for our allies. Twenty units have been seriously degraded and eleven have failed to report. We must assume that information shall grow more irregular."

"Then squeeze their chiefs a bit and get some more men in the saddle."

Lasctakos smiled. "Nothing left to squeeze; they already have boys of ten riding. Unless, of course, you released some hostages."

"Forget it." Phaetonis looked at Anios. "How's the wall?"

"We've completed the modifications and have rigged the tunnel. A couple moved stones and it will collapse. We'll be covered if the *Chaconni* think to come that way."

Phaetonis had grown visibly annoyed. "Fine. Get back to work."

304

The *elhari* rose and made hastily for the door. "Stay a moment, Lasctakos."

Lasctakos returned. "Sir?"

"About this idea of you running both units. I've been thinking that I don't like it. I've never gone into battle missing an *elhar* and can't believe you talked me into it."

"Are you going to reverse your decision, sir?"

"Maybe."

"Sir, if Kerebos is elevated, it may encourage the *cohari* to challenge him," Lasctakos said quickly. "Any such engagement will cost us a needed officer."

Phaetonis waved off the comment. "Who'd risk fighting him after that execution?"

"Rodios, for one."

"Then he'll get killed."

"My point exactly. Or perhaps he might win, which would put a brand new *elhar* in place the day before the battle."

Phaetonis rubbed his forehead. "Maybe I should just put it all off till next year."

Lasctakos ignored the bait.

"Well?" Phaetonis growled.

"Sir?"

"Don't give me that! What do you think?"

Lasctakos smiled. "I'd proceed with the ceremony, especially since you've already promised not to cancel it."

"We're in a fight for our lives here, Lasctakos. Getting dead is bad for morale, too, you know."

Lasctakos held his tongue.

"Speak, damn it!" Phaetonis roared. "If I want my ass kissed I'll get the rest of those fools back in here!"

Lasctakos proceeded with caution. "Let me talk to my peers, sir. We can discreetly pressure the men to initiate challenges only if there is a real grievance, not just because they itch to wear a different crest. We could imply it's their duty without denying the right. No one need suspect the direction comes from you."

Phaetonis sat in silence.

"Let me hold the First and Second," Lasctakos continued. "None of the officers will challenge me or thwart me about the challenges."

Phaetonis looked unsure. "You can make all this work?"

"Well enough, sir; I can be quite persuasive. Spirits will remain high and we won't lose many men. If it were peacetime I might have some problems but things being as they are..." Lasctakos trailed off.

Phaetonis folded his arms. "All right. Do it."

305

Livios was supervising drills when a guard approached.

"There's a *Riiz* at the gate asking for you, sir," the man said. "Asking by name."

"Who?"

"A fellow named Baso."

Livios chuckled. He had often wondered about Baso, especially with the casualties the *Riiz* had suffered. *My time up north seems so long ago,* he thought. "I'll be right out."

"Yes, *cohar.*"

Livios delegated his duties to Melas and headed for the gate. He walked from the castle and saw the *Riiz* a short distance away. *Don't remember that horse,* he thought. Baso dismounted and Livios was shocked by how short the *Riiz* was; he loomed much larger in memory.

Baso extended a leathery hand. "I heard of your promotion."

Livios shook heartily. "I'm very glad to see you alive."

Baso hesitated. "And I, you. Many of my people have died, though."

"Yes, I've heard."

Baso's black eyes were piercing. "We need your help. You must speak to your *ikar.*"

"About what?"

"Enemies have attacked our homes while we've been here. Phaetonis must let us defend our women and children. And our herds."

Livios sympathized, but knew what the *ikar* would say. "I understand, but there's nothing to be done. We're already short of scouts."

Baso was unmoved. "Will you ask him?"

"It won't matter."

"We aren't cowards, and aren't avoiding the fight," Baso said bitterly. "Half my kin have died doing your bidding. If Phaetonis lets our families perish, why should we stay?"

Livios regretted his previous responses. Baso was a devoted family man who had every right for concern. "I'll talk to my superiors."

Baso stared. "Truly?"

"Of course. You've earned my support."

Baso bowed his head. "Thank you. I didn't think you would."

"No?"

"Forgive me, but you've changed."

Livios was bruised by the remark, but had no argument. Would Kassandra say the same when next he saw her? He looked at the horse. "Where's the other one?"

"The Guards are using *Aharoni* mercenaries. They're good shots."
Baso showed the ghost of a smile. "Not so good as you."

Livios wished to ride off with the *Riiz*. Only Kassandra restrained
him. "Where will you go now?"

Baso's face darkened. "Back to my people to await Phaetonis' permission."

"And if it doesn't come?"

"There are four hundreds left in my town of Mistaaka, and four old
cripples to guard them."

Livios nodded broodingly.

Baso whistled and the horse trotted over. He mounted lithely.
"Come with me."

Livios lifted a hand and wiggled his digits. "Can't. Still have those
raccoon fingers."

"I hope it proves worth it, *cohar*."

"Me, too. Give the men my best."

"I will." Baso kicked the horse and galloped across the plain.

Livios didn't feel like going back inside. He wandered over to the
tunnel, where returned sod had all but eliminated signs of construction.
Can hardly see the scars, he thought.

"Absolutely not," Lasctakos told Livios. "The *ikar* wouldn't hear of
it."

"Sir, the *Riiz* have been brave and loyal allies."

"What good are allies who desert before our greatest battle?"
Lasctakos asked. "In any case, Phaetonis would be violently opposed,
and I stress 'violently'."

"But, sir!"

"Enough, Kerebos. Perhaps you should concern yourself more with
the men your friends' absence place in peril, not to mention the danger
to that paramour of yours." Lasctakos' expression softened. "It was all I
could do to convince Phaetonis to not demand more riders. I advise you
to seek contentment in the current state of affairs."

Livios saw the futility of further argument. "Yes, sir."

"Get back to work."

Livios went into the spoke, where men prepared for bed. He could
not bear the thought of returning to the reports piling up on his desk.
He wanted to visit the barn. *I've put her off for too long*, he admitted to
himself.

When Livios entered the barn, Mother was bent over the register.
"Hello," he said.

Mother lifted her enormous head. "Hello, Blackie," she replied in
her soothing voice. "Or should it be Blackie *Cohar*?"

"Whatever. She's alone?"

Mother looked embarrassed. "Yes. I wanted to speak to you about that, actually. The other girls are complaining that Kassandra's not carrying her load."

Livios cared nothing for the "other girls'" protests. How dare they try to muscle his wife! "I'd tell them not to complain too loud, Mother."

"Oh, it's not that bad," Mother backpedaled. "They're just cranky and winded, that's all. Don't your troops get tired?"

Livios seethed; it was bad enough he still had to share Kassandra with senior officers. He leaned on the counter. "I could make them feel a damn site more cranky. If not now, then one day."

Mother leaned away. "No need to get rankled. I'll put them straight. We could use a few more girls, though, that's all. I'm trying hard to shield Livia, you know."

Livios' temper rose higher. "That little thing? You're not thinking of using her?"

"I've my job to do, *cohar*, same as you. If things don't straighten themselves out I'll be answering to Phaetonis. He doesn't like waiting in line any more than the rest of you."

Mother's face had remained friendly but Livios smelled the threat. Schemes raced through his mind. "How much does one of your girls cost?"

Mother cocked her head to one side. "Depends on the girl."

"Livia."

"She's fresh, Blackie. At least fifty crowns in a city, maybe a hundred out here."

That much! Livios thought. All he owned was his kit and a few trinkets. He guessed Mother was inflating the figure, but knew it would be wise to let her profit. "I'll pay your hundred," he said, though it would be difficult to get the money. *Luecos will have it,* he decided. "Keep her scrubbing floors."

"You want to buy her?"

"I do."

"The hundred won't cover feeding and clothing her, you know. If I'm going to have to take care of her."

"Feed her what?" Livios snarled. "She looks like a skeleton and probably eats less. And she's wearing rags. You're lucky I won't charge you for all the work she'll be doing."

Mother chuckled. "One hundred it is, *cohar*. You're a shrewd bargainer."

Livios stood down. "You were starting to give me a headache, woman. I'm not much good at this sort of thing."

308

"You did all right."

"I'll get your crowns when I can scrape them together. See you later," he concluded and walked past.

Mother watched him march down the hall. *A hundred in gold for that little bag of bones, plus I keep her as a maid!* she thought. She knew the *ikar* would frown upon the business deal, but saw no reason he need learn about it. *Certainly not from me.* The best part of the transaction, though, was that Livia would again be hers, and for free. *Once Blackie finds some way to get himself killed,* she reflected with a touch of sadness. *They always do.*

Livios knocked as he entered Kassandra's room. She stirred and woke.

"Didn't mean to rouse you," he said and sat on the bed.

Kassandra yawned as she sat. Her blue eyes were mere slits, her hair disheveled. "I've been so tired lately. How is everything?"

Livios interpreted the question as *Where have you been and why haven't you sent word?* "I'm sorry you had to watch the execution," he said.

Kassandra looked away. "I closed my eyes."

"Oh?"

"Yes, but the rest of the girls have talked about it."

Livios felt ashamed. To make himself feel better he related how he had purchased Livia. "I know that my father would've liked it," he said. "It's only one good deed, though. I know he was watching when I carved up Tzetzos."

Kassandra moved close and snuggled against him. "You were under orders."

"Yes, I was."

"I'm sure you couldn't like such a thing, either." A moment passed. Kassandra looked up. "Did you?"

Livios stared blankly ahead. "No," he lied softly.

"Then release it," she concluded and again lay against his arm. "One day we'll be gone from here."

"You please me," Livios replied, though was taken aback by her attitude. Almost he wished that she had condemned the violence. "I didn't think you'd understand."

"My brother was accused of murder by another house and had to fight trials by combat. I was very young, but I remember how the towns-people honored him after the holmgangs. Eventually, the challenges stopped."

Livios pondered the words. "You sound like Lasctakos."

Kassandra gasped. "No I don't!"

Livios faced her. "You were right when you said we'd leave here. We will. Nothing will stop that, I swear. I don't care how many men I have to kill."

Kassandra hugged him to hide her worried face.

*   *   *

The Legion gathered strength throughout the summer. Grains and livestock flowed through the black gates until the barns and cellars were filled to bursting. Iron and coal were requisitioned from the *Stalenzka* and medicines purchased from as far away as the *Hsia* kingdoms. Money and threats were spent lavishly to procure necessities, and so quickly that the loot was collected before Diakonos could cordon the territory.

Phaetonis prepared for the worst and vowed to be ready, "even if the siege lasts ten years". Extra wells were dug and rain barrels placed around the compound in case *Chaconni* engineers diverted the stream that fed the keep. A very great store of lumber was piled near the southern wall across from spoke four.

Recruiting slowed but never quite stopped. One hundred volunteers were gathered but most died in training. Phaetonis ignored pleas to soften instruction in order to maximize the number of graduates. His decision proved popular; the vast majority of legionaries would rather go into battle under complement than trust their skins to half-baked replacements, saying that it would be better to lose the war than disgrace the uniform. The effect of the semantic wrangling was that training was made even more brutal. Only nine men survived the branding and two of these were Judged when revealed as *Chaconni* spies. Information was extracted from the men before they were handed over to the executioners. The most important revelation being that many *Tantorri* had quit the theatre of operations, leaving behind only enough strength to maintain the illusion of activity. Phaetonis didn't believe the confessions until he personally interrogated some *Riiz*. The truth proved disheartening. Nearly all of the Legion's mounted "allies" had gone over to Diakonos in exchange for autonomy. Evil as the news was, it would have been much more damaging had the Legion been in the field as opposed to awaiting a siege. Phaetonis would deal with the betrayals at a later time and few doubted he would make a particularly gruesome example of the *Riiz*, if given the chance.

Winnowing Day proved anticlimactic, to Phaetonis' vast relief, with a mere eleven challenges issued. The conflicts resulted in only three promotions, none from the First or Second. As the sun sank behind him, a jubilant Phaetonis gave a speech lauding the Legion's solidarity in the face of imminent attack.

Livios listened with half an ear, concentrating instead on the fact that no one had contested his leadership. He hoped his subordinates abstained because they believed him a good commander, though he suspected it was because of his prowess. *But that's good enough,* he thought.

"Let us now look to the task ahead," Phaetonis went on. "The challenge is great, but I have confidence in each of you. After we clear this obstacle we can look forward to a new dawn, one where none dare challenge our power or question our just retribution. Be vigilant because the enemy is very near."

*   *   *

General Diakonos and his staff reined their mounts to a halt; they gazed over the sloping plain toward Cemetery River and beyond. It was a beautiful autumn day and the black castle sat peacefully on a sea of green beneath the pale sun. Diakonos removed his gilded helmet and hung it on the saddle. He scratched the scalp beneath his black hair. The staff, an even mixture of career officers and well-connected nobles, knew better than to interrupt the general's thoughts.

Diakonos eyed the narrow bridge. It would take time to get his men over the trestle but, fortunately, there was no chance of an ambush; it was a naked mile from the river to the walls. *Dumb of them to leave the bridge standing,* he thought. *Are they that anxious to knock heads with me? They don't even have archers to keep me off the gate.* Diakonos' contempt for the *landesknectos* was well known, but it was the disdain of one who had never fought them. Perhaps the legionaries possessed supreme heavy infantry but there was more to war than cracking shields. Rotating lines were outdated, anyway. How would Phaetonis' little band handle the flexibility of highly trained divisions, as opposed to a bunch of unskilled, naked savages? *They're lucky Korenthis has had its head in the sand all this time.* He imagined toppling the antique, hexagonal wall and allowed himself to fondle royal ambitions. *It was unwise of Pontis to have given me this army.*

"Pyrros?" Diakonos called.

"Yes, general?"

"Scour their perimeter with some horse while Third, Fourth and Eighth Infantry secures the approach. Clearidas, have your engineers poison that creek upstream. Maybe we can kill some of the scoundrels before turning off the flow."

"Yes, sir."

Diakonos recollected his last meeting with Pontis. The king had wanted the siege in place by midsummer, but Diakonos had ignored the suggestion. Better to wait until after the Winnowing. *Pontis!* he thought

311

in disgust. *An even poorer king than he is a general.*

Phaetonis got word of the *Chaconni* arrival and promptly scaled the wall to see the enemy with his own eyes. What looked to be a couple divisions had already crossed the river and many more were massing on the far plain. Phaetonis paid special attention to the siege equipment; dozens of wheeled catapults, ballistae and trebuchets were lined to cross the bridge once the enemy had secured a foothold.

"Ain't never seen so many standards, *ikar*," a legionary said. "You think the king's there?"

I wish, Phaetonis thought.

"A lot of bodies we'll have to get rid of," another man added.

Two *elhari* arrived. "Quite a show of force," Lasctakos said. "How unfortunate Diakonos can't squeeze them all onto our side."

"Yes," Phaetonis agreed. "What do you think he'll deploy?"

"Certainly the engineers and equipment. Half of the infantry, perhaps."

"Sounds about right. Lucky for us it's still early. We'll be able to trap a good portion of them. Get below and make sure the men are prepared."

"Yes, sir."

Lasctakos took to the enclosed, spiral stairs at a brisk clip. He emerged into the yard where some of the units were already forming. The legionaries looked calm and confident, though some of the recruits were obviously excited. To his surprise, Lasctakos found himself equally anxious, perhaps because this might be the last battle he would enjoy adequate control of his limbs. Some days he could hardly feel his extremities. He approached Rodios' *cohar* and accepted the man's salute before smiling at the unit.

"Ready, gentlemen?"

"Yes, sir!" they roared.

Lasctakos walked to Livios' *cohar*, which was precisely lined and stood ready in the sun.

"Hello, sir," Livios said. "Fine day for a fight."

"Be prepared to assist the *ikar* if I become a casualty, son."

Livios' face indicated how remote he thought the possibility. "Yes, sir."

"I see you ordered extra spears. A good thought."

"Thank you, sir."

"Luecos, come here."

Luecos looked baffled as he arrived front and center. "Yes, *elhar?*"

"Could you spare some *kraal*? I find myself in the mood." Lasctakos disliked the drug but it increased blood flow to his hands.

312

Luecos smirked as he reached for his stash. "I was racking my brains to figure what I did wrong," he said as he handed over the purse.

Lasctakos took a large pinch and stuffed it under his upper lip. He pulled the drawstring and returned the cache. "Thank you."

Livios took the bag before Luecos could. "I got it, sir," he said and appropriated some *kraal*.

Luecos stared at his friend. "That was a healthy handful, sir."

Livios laughed. "Add it to the crowns I owe you."

Lasctakos dismissed Luecos with a glance. "This is the most important engagement of our lives," he told Livios. "Keep a firm hand on your unit. Stay alert."

"Yes, sir."

Diakonos watched his forces deploy from the north side of the river; they proceeded deliberately to maintain maneuvering room. It took the better part of the afternoon for nine divisions to cross the bridge. *And a right silly little catwalk it is,* he thought, eyeing the span. *Think they'd widen it, if those stories about the sharks were true.*

But the more Diakonos studied the defenses, the more he appreciated how carefully Lex Desia had chosen the spot. The broad river was a fine obstacle and the grassy span leading to the castle was too small to comfortably host an army. The waterway's angling path narrowed the approach to the castle, too, which would bottleneck an attacking force. The dry moats were dauntingly deep and the gate was cleverly placed so the brightest sun was always at the defenders' backs. There was no timber for fuel close by, either. *Desia was no fool,* Diakonos silently admitted. *No matter what they teach at the Academy. Not that it'll make much difference.* It seemed impossible that any fifteen hundred men could long stave off his divisions; time would see them storm the wall. He would make every effort to take the fort without destroying it. *My coat of arms will look excellent over the gate. What would Pontis think about that?*

A cloaked cavalryman rode up and saluted. "Sir, General Clearidas' compliments! He's poisoned their tributary but it will take time before they taste the effects. He also began the counter trench and has our heavy equipment in place. May he start ranging the weapons?"

Diakonos knew how a long haul might knock siege equipment out of calibration. "Proceed, but no general assault until I give word."

The messenger saluted and rode away.

Diakonos considered putting the attack off until morning. His men had covered eighteen miles today and he wouldn't mind digging in, just to be safe. *Hell, Phaetonis might even parley when he sees the straits he's in,* he thought.

313

Phaetonis had stayed on the crowded wall all day and now the sun was sinking. It deeply injured him to see the *Chacconi* on his land and the sight grew more unbearable with every moment. He would never get over the spectacle, no matter how temporary, and wondered if Diakonos really believed he would remain unmolested. *First my capture, now this,* he thought drearily, imagining the scorn of his predecessors. *Only blood will erase the stain on honor.*

"By Desia it sticks in the craw," a legionary complained to a comrade.

Must've read my mind, Phaetonis thought and decided right then to personally lead the offensive. "What's your name?" he asked the speaker.

"Sicyon, *ikar.*"

"Well, Sicyon, I hate it too but I promise this: we'll one day have Diakonos' head. Until then keep quiet."

"Yes, sir," Sicyon replied. He fretted with his belt before fumbling for his canteen.

A legionary raced up to Phaetonis. "Sir, Lasctakos reports that men have fallen seriously ill! They can hardly breathe!"

Phaetonis leaped forward and slapped the canteen from Sicyon's hand, shouting, "Don't drink anything!" He immediately took off in search of Lasctakos. Lasctakos was in the hospital, where six legionaries were suffering through various stages of asphyxiation. One man, frothing at the mouth, convulsed and kicked while four others held him in bed.

Phaetonis cursed. "They must've poisoned the creek! I should've thought of that."

Eight more legionaries were carried into the hospital and dumped onto beds. Men vomited and soiled themselves as they choked and wheezed. The floor grew sticky with reeking fluids.

A soldier grabbed Lasctakos' arm, crying, "What do we do, sir? What do we do?"

"Compose yourself, for one thing," Lasctakos replied icily. "And find that dratted surgeon." He turned to Phaetonis. "Arsenic?"

"Possibly. There's nothing we can do for these men. Put them out of their misery. I'm going outside to spread the word about the creek."

"What if it was a well?"

"The slaves will be testing them for us, so we'll soon find out. Finish up here and move on the bridge!" Phaetonis yelled over his shoulder as he headed out the door. No sooner had he departed than more casualties were hauled into the room.

Lasctakos summoned the able-bodied and said, "Draw swords, gentlemen. It is the last mercy we can gift our brothers." There were no complaints. The killing was swiftly done. Lasctakos wiped sweat from his face. "Tissaphernos?"

"Yes, *elhar?*"

"Tell Kerebos to take the bridge."

"Yes, sir!"

Livios and his unit were waiting in the yard. He saw Tissaphernos and asked: "It's time?"

"Yes, *cohar*. Lasctakos wants us to do it."

"Very well." Livios faced his men. "Leave helmets and swords here. Melas, strike those torches!" Melas and his men ignited and began distributing brands while the others shed unneeded kit. The weapons were laid in precise groups.

Livios took a torch from Melas, shouting, "Keep it to a whisper down below! Let's go!"

Smoke from *Chaconni* cooking fires was wafting into the keep before they reached the wide hole in the ground, a stone's throw east of the gate. Livios was first to descend the crude earthen steps into the damp coolness of the passageway. Luecos came next.

The path was barely large enough to accomodate Livios; his torch lent the tight quarters a hellish glow. Crouching, he loped down the tunnel. The soft thudding of feet and the rush of air filled his ears. He was surprised how little he could see before him and regularly bumped his head on the uneven roof. Jagged stones took bites from his scalp. Blood leaked into his eyes. The going got rougher as the ground grew muddy. A man slipped and fell, causing a pile up. There was some muted profanity but things were quickly set in order.

Running at a stoop is difficult under ideal circumstances but Livios was shocked to find just how taxing it could be; his back burned and sweat streamed off him, despite the clammy air. They had been running a long time, it seemed. Surely the river was close? But the gloomy path went on, growing ever wetter until the unit was splashing through ankle-deep water.

This is ridiculous! Livios thought. *Are we going in a circle? Damn it, what kind of*—he suddenly sprawled into a deep pool. It took a moment to claw out of the cold, slimy bilge.

Luecos dropped to a knee and pulled a four-inch thick chain into sight. "Yep, here it is. You tripped over it." He turned to those behind him. "It's underfoot. Stick those torches into the wall and grab some."

Livios threw the extinguished torch back over his shoulder and glared at Luecos.

"What?" the *Boru* asked.

Livios struggled from the water and grasped the chain. "Nothing. Let's pull."

"Huh?" Luecos said to someone behind him. To Livios: "We're out of chain. Half the men don't have anything to grip."

"Damn it," Livios said. "Come on, back we go." They waded into the black water and shuffled forward until it tickled their chins. The distant torchlight did little to illuminate the walls around them. "Did that do it?"

Luecos turned and asked, "We ready?"

They were.

"Pull!" Livios ordered.

The chain held at first, but soon began to slide. Livios thought he felt each time a link cleared the distant mud wall. The chain suddenly slackened and everyone spilled backwards. Livios emerged from the water, sputtering, "Keep pulling to make sure!" The water began to rise rapidly. "Out!" he bellowed. "Luecos, get them out!"

"What's wrong? Is it getting deeper?"

Livios flailed for higher ground. "Hurry, or we're all dead!"

There was some noisy confusion but no one seemed to comprehend the situation. Livios yelled instructions but no one heard him. *Why aren't they listening?* he thought frantically, terrified he might drown underground. "GET MOVING YOU FOOLS!" he screamed.

The legionaries sloshed up the slant towards the castle, dropping many of the torches in the chaos. A hundred paces later they were laboring through two feet of water. Everyone believed themselves mere moments from drowning.

Livios pushed Luecos' back as he ran, thinking, *For God's sake, are they moving backwards?*

Did that bridge just shake? Diakonos wondered. *No, I'm just tired,* he decided after a while. The bridge shimmied again. "Did you see that?" he queried those staff members still present—Memnon, Theris and Philip.

"No, sir." "See what, sir?" "Yes, you just rubbed your eyes."

Diakonos pointed in agitation, insisting, "That bridge moved!" He looked at his men, who did their best to remain circumspect. "All right," he said at last. "I'm seeing things."

Mreeeaauunchh! The structure's support pylons slowly tilted and dumped the walkway into the river. Diakonos watched the last stones plop into the sluggish water and turned to his underlings. "I suppose you missed that, too?"

"We saw that one, sir."

Diakonos muttered under his breath. "I thought that arch looked dainty." He glanced at the darkening sky. "Philip, cross over and ask Clearidas if he has the means to rebuild the bridge."

Philip, an effete political appointee in burnished armor, asked:

"How should I do that, sir?"

"By swimming."

Philip cleared his throat. "But general, there are supposed to be sharks in there."

Diakonos smiled. "I wouldn't worry about it. I haven't seen any."

"They were probably scared off by the ruckus our army made," young Theris offered.

Diakonos nodded at the water. "Get going. It's almost dark."

Philip straightened in the saddle and eased his horse down the slope. He rode to the river's muddy edge before showing Diakonos a long face.

"Hurry!" the general snapped.

Philip spurred the mount into the inky water. The animal bucked in the shallows but things smoothed out as it reached deep water; the glassy surface rippled in the horse's wake.

Diakonos and the others watched in silence until Philip was half-way across. "See, nothing to worry about," Diakonos said.

Memnon pointed out a triangular shape that was moving swiftly toward Philip. "What's that?"

Theris said: "There are two more. Look, there's a bunch of them!"

It was true. Over a dozen fins of varying sizes were slicing towards the oblivious Philip, who continually smacked the horse's rump.

"Faster!" Theris cried. "Philip, behind you!"

Philip finally saw the sharks and began to shriek, sounding for all the world like a hysterical woman. The first predator struck the horse so hard Philip flew into the air. The screaming steed was dragged under in a pool of foam while Philip splashed wildly toward shore. A very large, mottled shark swam in and bit off his arm just before two smaller brutes locked onto his torso; Philip's cries were cut short as he was ripped in half and carried in opposite directions. A leg floated downstream.

Diakonos could hardly believe the sharks' dimensions. Their size and ferocity surpassed all rumor. He unwittingly slid backwards in the saddle. Troops on the opposite plain, hundreds of yards inland, were just now investigating the commotion. "Theris, summon the signal corpsmen. We must alert Clearidas."

There was a low rumble like distant thunder and the men looked about for the source. More rumbles lifted into the twilight from the riverside, where sharks were emerging onto the muddy flats. The animals moved with ease despite short, stubby legs.

They're even bigger than I first thought! Diakonos realized in alarm. *How'd Intelligence fail to plan for this?* "Theris, get the signalers!"

More sharks were beaching themselves. Night was coming and they wanted to scavenge the plain for the bodies and offal that legionaries invariably dumped there. Those of Clearidas' men who had come to investigate Philip's screams voiced some of their own and darted back to camp.

The throaty bawl of curved cornu trumpets soon filled the air, calling men to arms. *Chaconni* soldiers dropped entrenching tools and grabbed weapons or rose from bedrolls. Officers spilled from walled tents. More sharks made their way into the vicinity, drawn by blood in the water; roars filled the air as they moved inland.

The commander of Third Division quickly assessed the situation and ordered archers to the perimeter. Volleys were fired as the first hulking masses came into range, but did little more than enrage the beasts. These bowmen were regular army, not *Aharoni* mercenaries equipped with the dreaded, recurved desert bow, and their missiles scarcely penetrated the thick-skinned, muscular animals. A full-grown shark could take hundreds of such hits without being put out of action and many did. Ballistae were recalled from the forward positions but it would take time to reposition the machines.

Clearidas ordered Eighth Division's sturdily armored pikemen to engage the sharks while he redeployed heavy weapons. The armored spearmen launched a disciplined attack and halted some beasts not far from Clearidas' command tent, where a mighty battle ensued. Men died by the scores but the brave soldiers put their spears and halberds to skillful use; the sharks' roars were deafening. Spilled blood summoned yet more sharks to the scene.

Phaetonis swore like a madman because it was too dark for him to see the fight. "Oh, our friends are giving them trouble!" he told his officers as he peered over the wall. "Just listen to that fuss! Why can't there be some moon tonight?" Roars, shouts and the sounds of crunching armor filled the night.

"Should we attack while they're in disarray, sir?" Nicios *Elhar* asked.

Phaetonis wrung his hands. "No. Let big teeth do the work."

"Those 'legionary sharks' deserve a promotion," Polyphemos joked.

Phaetonis laughed. "Maybe you're right."

The conflict raged through the night with varying levels of intensity. The *Chaconni* ballistae were eventually brought into play and proved effective. The tide of battle slowly turned against the sharks. The soldiers developed a method of separating and surrounding their toothy assailants. Rings of determined pikemen took out smaller sharks while larger ones were kept at bay until heavy weapons could bring them down. There was no quit in the sharks, however, and they fought with a frenzy that depleted entire regiments. Only dawn scared off the remaining animals, though few made it all the way back to the water. Sixty-three sharks lay dead or mortally wounded on the field.

Clearidas wasted no time preparing for a *landesknecta* assault; it seemed inconceivable that Phaetonis wouldn't take advantage of his weakened state. He did a good job of reordering his lines, despite having sustained thousands of casualties. The Eighth had suffered particularly, which was significant because they were his only heavy infantry.

Inside the keep, Phaetonis gave final instructions to his officers. A portion of Sixth *Elhar* would remain to man the walls while the rest of the Legion struck the enemy. Those chosen to stay behind were sour on the prospect but dared not complain.

Phaetonis took his place at the head of First *Elhar*, fully intending to play an active role in battle. He licked thin lips at the prospect of blood-shed, thinking, *Those Chaconni are in trouble.* Yes the enemy still greatly outnumbered him, but they had just suffered severe, demoralizing losses at the hands of a most unexpected foe. *And that after marching and digging all day,* he reasoned. *Besides, these King's men don't know a point from a pommel.*

Phaetonis gazed at the columns behind him; the motionless, black-clad legionaries stood in shadow. He drew his sword, turned to the gate-keepers and nodded. The bolts were pulled and the gates dragged open. Light from the rising sun spread over the Legion. Phaetonis lowered his eye slits. "Follow me!" he shouted and led First *Elhar* through the gate and over the moat. Their booted feet thundered over the wooden bridge.

Squinting, Livios waited for the order to move out. His heart pounded as though it were his first action, fueled by the feeling that something momentous was about to happen. After all, when was the last time the Legion had fought for its very land? He liked the idea; it lent legitimacy to the violence. Pilum and shield in hand, he looked over the column, six men abreast.

"To victory!" Lasctakos cried and chased after the *ikar*.

"Victory!" the Second echoed and stormed through the gate.

Livios was out front and had a good view of the field. The First had crossed the bridge and was forming into lines before the enemy trenches. Hissing arrows arched from the *Chaconni* interior and rattled off the legionaries' greatshields. Phaetonis' loud voice exhorted the men to hold fast. Company after company of *Chaconni* pikemen lined the opposite side of the gulch as mounted officers shouted orders behind them. Thousands of soldiers were massing in the rear.

Livios and his comrades noisily crossed the moat. One man stum-bled and pitched into the pit but the unit moved on. Lasctakos sprinted across the grass to halt behind the First, where he whirled toward his men and directed them to Phaetonis' right flank. "That way, gentlemen!" he shouted while motioning with his sword.

Livios attached himself to the left end of the front line as the Third hit the bridge. There was a brief empty space between himself and Phaetonis' group; Luecos stood to his right. Arrows struck their greatshields and ricocheted overhead but the ineffective shooting tapered off. "We might have trouble with those bowmen later," he told Luecos.

The *Boru* laughed. "Nah, they can't shoot when they're running! Damn, can you smell all that fish, though? Now *that's* a problem."

Livios had tried to forget the sharks, which smelled worse than dead men.

Lasctakos joined them. "The *ikar* will crash their line once all units are in place," he said. "Use the trenches to cover your flank until the enemy has broken."

"Yes, sir!" Livios said.

"Nice of them to dig those gullies for us, eh sir?" Luecos asked.

Lasctakos' stared frostily then turned back to Livios. "And beware their archers once the rout starts. They'll have greater success if our formations get sloppy."

"I'll sit on the men, sir," Livios promised. Merely hearing Lasctakos boosted his enthusiasm.

"I know you will." Lasctakos smiled and dropped behind the second line, crying, "Melas!"

"I don't think he cares for your humor," Livios told Luecos.

"You may be right. See that look he gave me? It hurt my feelings."

The legionaries were speedily in place. Four *elhari* formed a skirmish line with the Fifth, and elements of the Sixth, in reserve close behind. The enemy appeared content to cede the initiative.

What cowards, Phaetonis thought. *Here they have a smaller force with its back to a moat and they won't even push! They're bloated and rotten, like a dead ox with a belly full of maggots. And I'm just the man to kick them open.* He called a runner and gave instructions; the man fell back to deliver the command.

Without warning, Fifth *Elhar* burst into action. Hundreds of pila soared over the First and riddled the *Chaconni* center. Men voiced their pain and surprise even as a second volley was loosed. First *Elhar* threw their spears, pulled their swords and leaped into the trench. The enemy center had softened under the assault but rallied in time to strike the vulnerable First. Second, Third and Fourth *Elhari* dispatched a concentrated rain of pila that bought Phaetonis' unit time to scratch onto level ground. *Landesknecta* swords went to work with terrifying efficiency. First came the sound of spears being chopped in half, followed by the

320

screams of stricken *Chaconni*. The superbly armored and shielded legionaries simply waded into the pikemen.

Breaking enemy lines had been the Legion's specialty from time immemorial and, because of the sharks, Clearidas couldn't counter with heavy infantry of his own. Phaetonis' giants improved their position while more *elhari* arrived in support. Some legionaries were wounded as they navigated the dusty trench but not enough to stem the offensive; they fanned out and soon held a significant portion of the enemy camp. Fifth *Elhar* crossed unopposed.

A brief, bloody exchange left hundreds of *Chaconni* dead. Clearidas sent bowmen on a flanking maneuver but Phaetonis ordered Fifth *Elhar* east to head them off. The *ikar* took advantage of a brief stalemate and dispatched runners.

Livios was holding a position in the crowded line when he received orders; he kept hacking while a runner shouted in his ear.

"The Fifth will continue to occupy the archers, while Two and Three kick the enemy!" the messenger said. "You fellows keep step but Lasctakos is leading a *cohar* to flank them bowmen! You got it, sir?"

Livios was irritated. *It's so obvious*, he thought. *Can't he see I'm busy?* "Right!"

The runner moved on to the next *cohar*, identifying the officer by his helmet crest.

Livios was confronted by a seemingly endless supply of *Chaconni*. Spear points screeched on his shield and darted at his head but none found that exposed inch between aegis and helmet. He sliced weapons, arms and heads and impaled men with his shield's boss spike. Six times he swatted aside a lance, feinted with his sword and buried the spike into an enemy's chest and each time the victim looked shocked. *Don't these idiots learn?* he wondered and faded back into line. Blaring horns shook the field and the pikemen withdrew, regrouped and charged. The new formation so bristled with spears that Livios was reminded of a porcupine.

Clearidas' men fared even worse the second time around. Phaetonis had used the lull to swap lines and maximize his killing zone. The pikemen died bravely, contesting every foot, but they were perpetually driven back. The legionaries picked up steam as the *Chaconni* ranks thinned and eventually reached the first row of siege equipment. A brigade of *Chaconni* swordsmen arrived to stabilize the line but Clearidas' forces were now wedged into the narrowest part of the plain. The stabilization gave the Fifth time to reposition and their falling spears again struck the *Chaconni*. It was then that Lasctakos' group returned from a fruitless pursuit of the archers.

The Legion was preparing to split the enemy when the unthinkable happened. A *Chaconni* slid from beneath a catapult and backstabbed Phaetonis, who had dropped back to view the field. The howling *ikar* killed his assailant before clawing at the spear in his back. Phaetonis cursed and fell to his knees even as Lasctakos arrived to help. A collective, drawn out wail lifted from the First and a few men began to disengage.

But Lasctakos had arrived. "Get back in ranks!" he thundered with such fury that the retreat stopped cold. "You! You!" he identified two officers. "Keep them busy!" He knelt beside Phaetonis and took gentle hold of the spear. "How bad is it?"

The *ikar* had gone white. He scratched feebly at his breastplate, as though at an itch he couldn't reach. "I'm through," he said, looking both sad and angry.

"I relieve you."

"Kill 'em, Lasc," Phaetonis slurred with quivering lips.

"With pleasure."

Phaetonis blinked a few times then crashed onto his face. Lasctakos twisted the spear from the dead *ikar*'s back and cast it aside. He turned to the castle walls and waved his arms for attention; he motioned toward the catapults before turning back to the fray.

One of the First's officers approached. The man looked spooked. "Is he dead?"

"Yes. I've assumed command. Come, let us avenge him."

Together, they ran to the front, which had stalled with news of Phaetonis' fall. Lasctakos darted to and fro behind the line, spurring men with praise and invective.

"Is this how you honor Phaetonis, by fighting like women?" he demanded. "Dress that line, Pythen, or give back that topknot! Come, now, who will slay a *Chaconne* for Phaetonis? Yes, Theseos, that's how we kill a man! Good work! Your *ikar* has fallen: what will you do about it?"

Lasctakos had soon transformed their grief to rage. He waited until legionaries from the castle began turning the siege weapons before shouting, "Now push them all the way to the river!"

Livios heard his comrades' groans and glanced to see Lasctakos running toward the *ikar*. A spasm of terror passed through him when he saw the spear in Phaetonis' back. It was all he could do to hide behind his shield. The sensation in his breast defied description.

"Oh, hell," Luecos muttered beneath the clamor.

Livios mastered himself with effort. "Hold together men!" he ordered. "Lasctakos will get us through!"

Other officers picked up the cry. "Hold the line!"

322

The legionaries of the Second fought on doggedly, albeit without their former fire, until the First began to advance. There was scant warning of a renewed offensive, aside from shouts of "Phaetonis", before the First tore into the *Chaconni*. The other *elhari* redoubled their efforts to keep pace.

At this point, most of Clearidas' pikemen had fallen and the legionaries came face to face with swordsmen. The *Chaconni* were game but clearly outmatched by the enraged *landesknectos* and were further hampered by conflicting orders and bad leadership.

Cries of "Phaetonis!" had spread through the Legion, whose advance was again gaining momentum.

Livios found himself with more room as the units spread out and grinned at the prospect of unencumbered swordplay. He advanced fearlessly into a knot of four *Chaconni*, resplendent in their chain mail and scarlet jupons.

"Take him!" a *Chaconne* said and leaped forward.

Livios crushed the man's face with his shield and stabbed another in the stomach. The second victim screamed and doubled over as Livios withdrew the blade and ducked right towards another closing soldier. Livios smacked his foe's sword to the ground and slammed his shoulder into the man's chest so hard that bones crunched. Livios sensed the remaining man closing on his left and raised his shield as another legionary ran the man through. Livios turned back to the fight; the *Chaconni* dead had really piled up and he'd have to climb over corpses to get at his next prey.

There were still thousands of able-bodied *Chaconni* in the vicinity but the fight was going out of them. It was understandable, perhaps. Nothing had gone their way since crossing the river. First the bridge had collapsed, then came the all-night battle with the sharks and now the legionaries were slaying them with maddening ease. The *Chaconni* were tired, hungry and discouraged and started a measured retreat despite the demands of their officers.

Legionaries began discharging the captured catapults and large stones flew deep into the enemy camp. Livios couldn't see the rocks land but doubted they struck anything important.

Having their own terror weapons turned against them proved the last straw for Clearidas' men, however. The shouts of battle changed to those of panic as whole units quit the fight. The legionaries redoubled their efforts and the entire *Chaconni* host began to break. That was when Clearidas arrived. The white-bearded general, sword high, made an impressive sight on his gray war-horse. His voice was deep and powerful and had an immediate effect upon his men.

Two legionaries discharged a ballista at Clearidas and came close enough to spook his horse. Clearidas was thrown. Nothing could stop the *Chaconni* stampede after that. Men threw their weapons and ran screaming for the distant river. Lasctakos gave stern orders for the Legion to proceed as a unit. The *landesknectos* stomped forward at a deliberate pace while the enemy scattered like mice. The ground was littered with the staring dead and the moaning wounded.

Livios kept pace with his men, thinking, *Where are those King's men running?* He wondered if enough sharks had been killed to make swimming viable. The legionaries dispatched wounded as they passed them but maintained their double-time march. They filed through a wagon complex before crossing a vast field kitchen; the fires had long since expired.

Livios sized up the wagons, food and abandoned kit. *What a mountain of loot for the ikar!* he thought as the mental image of Phaetonis melted into one of Lasctakos. *Lasctakos will give me the First, surely. He's already said as much. Oh, Kassandra!* That being First *Elhar* would make him sub-*ikar* scarcely crossed his mind. All he cared about was reaching the Winnowing and stepping down. *I'm getting married sooner than I thought.* Waves of gratitude broke over him and he looked forward to thanking Lasctakos. *He's been like a father.*

There was minimal enemy contact as the legionaries crossed the plain. Indeed, the *Chaconni* reached the river far in advance of the Legion. Clearidas' mob was shouting to Diakonos' divisions, which had gathered on the other side, but no one was ready to risk the water.

A runner tapped Livios' shoulder. "Sir, Lasctakos is meeting with the *elhari* and wants you there."

Livios saw that Lasctakos and some others had fallen behind. "Right. Luecos, keep at it!"

"Will do."

Livios joined the senior officers. None appeared injured, though Polyphemos had a scratch over his empty socket.

"Kerebos, good," Lasctakos said. "You take the Second."

"Yes, sir." Livios' immediate reaction was disappointment but he calmed himself. *Of course he wouldn't hand me the First during a battle,* he decided.

"Fine work so far, gentlemen, but peril remains," Lasctakos said. "We haven't found Clearidas and must assume he lives. Look for the *Chaconni* to turn at bay."

"Let's slow down and regroup," Polyphemos said.

"The five of us are regrouping right now. I want to speed things, actually. It will keep them in a panic."

"Let's go back to a rotation, at least," Polyphemos countered.

Lasctakos' eyes smoldered. "This isn't a council, *elhar*. Phaetonis is dead, not captured, which means *I* assume control. If that hurts we can discuss it on Winnowing day. If you make it that far."

Polyphemos nodded.

Lasctakos scanned their faces. "Strike hard and fast before their leaders rise to the challenge. Take no prisoners, unless Clearidas turns up. Understood?"

"Yes, sir!"

Livios noted they had yet to use Lasctakos' new title. *Habits die hard*, he thought. "Is that the rest of the Sixth coming from the castle, *ikar?*"

Lasctakos smiled. "Just in case. Time to finish, gentlemen."

The officers ran back to their respective units, a hundred paces from the river. Livios fell in beside Luecos. "I've got the *elhar*. We're keeping one line and taking no slaves. Pass it on."

Lasctakos gave the order and the Legion broke into a run. The *landesknectos* hastened over the plain. The *Chaconni* were packed onto the shore and yelling in confusion. Some mounted officers tried to rally the disorganized horde, but to no avail.

They're not going to fight back, Livios decided. *Not one in ten has a weapon.* "Let them hear you!" he shouted and his men responded with battle cries. The rest of the Legion followed suit.

If the *Chaconni* were panicked before, they were now in an absolute frenzy. Many turned toward the legionaries with raised arms while others sprang into the river; a minority took off down the shore in an attempt to slip from the closing noose. A few soldiers organized a defense and managed a sloppy line; swordsmen and pikemen, caped officers and barechested engineers stood shoulder to shoulder.

The legionaries covered the last steps to the *Chaconni*. Greatshields slammed the enemy line, throwing men off their feet. The *landesknectos* hacked with maniacal bloodlust. Limbs and heads flew through the air. Stumps squirted blood. The sounds of clashing weapons trailed off as the remaining *Chaconni* fighters turned and attempted to cut through their countrymen to the river.

The legionaries closed and mercilessly hewed the shrieking soldiers, heaping corpses onto the ground until the bodies slowed their advance.

Livios dropped his shield and waded into the sea of fallen as the remainder of Clearidas' army began diving into the river. Only the strongest swimmers made it to the depths, weighed down as they were by mail, belts, helmets and boots. Those who reached deep water suffered the wrath of the sharks. Cries of agony filled the air as the vengeful fish mauled the soldiers.

"Cover!" legionaries roared.

Livios dropped before he knew it and covered himself with a body. He wondered why the alarm had been voiced until arrows started appearing in the cadavers around him. He felt the impacts of missiles on the body above him and grunted as a barb skewered his calf. The volleys continued for a short while. *Why is Diakonos shooting his own men?* he thought before reminding himself that most of the *Chaconni* were in the water. He could still hear their screams and wondered how many would reach the other side.

Azimos *Sestar* labored over the dead and knelt beside Livios. "Brought your shield, sir. They stopped shooting for now."

Livios cast off the corpse. "Thanks. Guess I deserve some lashes for dropping my cover, huh?"

Azimos grinned. "Start stripping the bodies, sir?"

Livios looked around. There were still some sharks visible, but not many. A surprising number of *Chaconni* had survived the swim and were being attended by Diakonos' men. *The sharks must've suffered a lot of casualties*, he thought. Bowmen lined the far shore but there were no arrows notched, which made sense; they wouldn't again catch the Legion off guard. "We'll wait for Lasctakos' orders." His heart skipped a beat. *Are those some of my Riiz on the other side?*

"Want me to dress your wound, sir?"

Livios remembered his leg. He would have to cut off the boot to prevent further muscle damage. "No, just break it off." He yelped as Azimos snapped the shaft then said through clenched teeth, "Thanks."

Azimos helped Livios to his feet and they toiled back to open ground. Legionaries milled about while waiting for orders. "I'm going to take a seat here," Livios said and eased to the ground. "Summon my *cohari*."

"Yes, sir."

Livios was a bloody mess and stank from the corpses' foul fluids. The injured calf ached and swelled. Again he looked across the river where the *Chaconni* were forming up and preparing to depart. He pondered how Diakonos would break the humiliating news to his liege. *They haven't suffered such a beating in years*, he thought. *The general might just lose his head.* His thoughts wandered and he considered just how lethal archers would be in the hands of a good commander. Would Korenthis retain a large number of *Aharoni* mercenaries? *Hope not. Too bad we don't have any.*

Azimos ran up, his fair face flushed. "Sir, come quickly!"

Livios was tired and testy. "What?"

"Luecos was hit!"

Livios was on his feet. He saw a circle of men in the distance and knew he'd find his friend there. "What's he doing with the Fourth?" he

326

asked Azimos.

"Stripping the dead of gold."

Livios reached the gathering and tossed someone out of the way. He fell beside Luecos, who lay gasping on his back, an arrow in his neck. Bright blood seeped from the wound and spread over the ground. The skin was discolored, as though bruised. Luecos' purse lay open beside him; gold rings had spilled onto the mud.

Livios dizzily sized up the wound. "Damn you, Krynn, what have you done to yourself?" he asked in a shaky voice. "Get back!" he snapped at the others. "Give him some air!"

Luecos' eyelids fluttered and he reached for Livios, who squeezed the hand and slid closer. Luecos tried to smile but coughed and blood sprayed the air. "S-s-sorry," he choked. "I-I'm s-sorry." He convulsed and spat red again, then lay still. He died with his eyes open.

Livios sank onto his haunches, still grasping Luecos' hand.

*   *   *

The next few days were spent clearing the battlefield. Rarely had the Legion achieved such a victory and most everyone was in high spirits. Having lost forty men, the *landesknectos* had witnessed the elimination of five *Chaconni* divisions including irreplaceable engineers, while securing fantastically expensive siege equipment.

Clearidas and another general were captured along with the paymaster's wagon, foodstuffs, the baggage train and many thousands of quality weapons. Some consideration was given to pursuing Diakonos, but the lack of a bridge made the mission impractical. Anyway, Lasctakos wanted to refit and replenish before going on the offensive.

Word reached the Legion that Diakonos' forces had retreated to his hometown of Thebis, where he declared himself king. Apparently he thought little of returning to Korenthis for execution. Lasctakos was pleased by Diakonos' decision, not least because a civil war left Korenthis no time for revenge.

Livios was summoned to Lasctakos' quarters a week after the battle and was admitted without comment. The *ikar* was eating. A plate of fowl, a flagon of wine and *kraal* leaves sat on the table.

"Hello," Lasctakos said without looking up. "Wine?"

Livios hadn't imbibed since Lasctakos rescinded Phaetonis' injunction. "Okay, sir."

The *ikar* poured. "It saddened me to bury Luecos without honor, but he should've been with his unit, not searching for trophies."

Livios swallowed. The pain of his friend's death was still near the surface. "I know."

"In many ways he turned out better than I expected."

"Yes, sir," Livios replied quietly.

Lasctakos crossed his silverware over the plate of bones and wiped his hands. "Interrogations confirm that the *Riiz* served, and may still serve, Diakonos. I will punish them. *Severely*."

Livios was surprisingly unaffected by the proposition. The arrow that killed Luecos had borne *Tantorri* markings. "You want me to handle it?"

"Of course. My best man for my biggest task. Blot them from Pangaea. We must send the proper message. Take all the men you need."

Livios ignored niggling thoughts of Baso. "Yes, sir." A moment passed. "When did you start carrying *kraal*, sir?"

"Have the *cohari* groused over your elevation?"

"Not a peep, sir. They know better."

"Excellent." Lasctakos held Livios' gaze. "You have grown very, very much."

Livios merely nodded.

"Do you still plan to step down next year, son?" Lasctakos asked.

Livios sat a little straighter. "I do, *ikar*. I wanted to ask about that."

Lasctakos chuckled. "Why I've yet to give you the First?"

"Yes, sir."

"It would be impolitic to bump you again so quickly. It would cause resentment. I think next spring should do."

Livios wanted the First *now*, so nothing could derail his plans, but he knew the *ikar* had larger concerns. "Thank you, sir."

"I want your battle plan before you retire tonight. As I said, take all the men you require."

Livios stood and saluted. "Yes, sir." As he left the room he marveled that he could so casually discuss annihilating the *Riiz*. The indifference bothered him. *They did kill Krynn, though*, he rationalized.

Five nights later Livios sat down to write an after-action report. It read:

By order of Lasctakos Ikar, the Riiz town of Mistaaka was destroyed on the 7th day of Daphna by Second Elhar, Kerebos Elhar commanding.

The enemy had warning of our arrival but, having lost most of their horses, could not vacate the town. Mounted archers harassed our southeastern approach and inflicted three casualties, one killed. Mistaaka was taken and its women violated in plain view until the mounted assailants surrendered. The noncombatants were then executed before the bowmen. The archers, including members of the tribal council, were crucified before being burned alive.

The heads of the women and children were impaled along the road leading north from town. Total dead: 41 men, 226 women, 90 children.

Mistaaka was looted and gems and gold taken (value = 2000?). All buildings were burned and razed. Livestock was killed and the surrounding fields salted.

Legionary Aristedes (2246) was buried with full honors and his sword recycled. One casualty was admitted to the hospital.

Livios reread the document and found it lifeless. There was nothing in the report that spoke to his feelings, though they stood out clearest in his memory. *Where should I write that I cried after killing Baso?* he wondered. *Or how I wanted to gouge out my eyes for what they saw?* He admitted to himself that the end couldn't possibly justify his means, even for Kassandra. The desire to run far away was overwhelming. *I'm dying inside, one piece at a time.*

He blew out the lamp and sat long in the dark.

GLOAMING

The Legion spent the autumn rebuilding the bridge and, of course, recruiting. The construction went well. There were far fewer sharks than before the battle and a steady dumping of *Chaconni* corpses kept these occupied. Stones were reclaimed from the river's floor and fashioned into arches without losing any men to sharks. The bridge, complete with easily demolished "tumble spans", was in service before the start of rainy season.

Recruiting went even more smoothly. The effortless drubbing of Pangaea's largest army lifted the Legion's prestige to unbelievable heights. Men swarmed the traditional recruiting spots and a force of zealots even presented themselves at the castle. It was with some reluctance that Lasctakos destroyed this last group, but allowing uninvited visitors onto his territory would have sent the wrong message.

Surprisingly, and to Lasctakos' enduring satisfaction, hundreds of *Chaconni* deserters sought entry into the Legion. These recruits cited Diakonos' incompetence and *landesknecta* valor as reasons for their defection. Nor were they bad soldiers. Many arrived wearing medals and a few officers even produced their service records! It was an historical zenith for the enrollment process; the pickings had never been so good. Only the very finest candidates were selected and an unheard of twenty percent survived training, which created a glut of runners.

That winter the Legion began to reassert itself. Gone was the garrison mentality that had characterized the latter stages of Phaetonis' command. Emissaries and *Elhari* marched constantly forth and returned with treaties or heads. Loyal allies were rewarded, questionable ones punished. A mountain of captured arms was given the backward yet reliable *Razkuli*, who used them to attack *Kabu* and *Chaconni* trade routes. The fractious *Kabu* suffered particularly from these raids and lost entire tribes. The *Stalenzka*, a clan of metal smiths from the continent's interior, were relocated onto *Riiz* land where Lasctakos could keep an eye on them.

It was an impetuous time for the Legion, which increasingly intruded into Pangaea's affairs. Lasctakos masterfully played his enemies and bound distant nations into a growing coalition against the *Chaconni*. He received diplomats and ministers in the great hall and seemed poised for unprecedented power. But he always had time for his men. Youthful but tested, wise and terrible, his supreme confidence promised an age to rival Lex Desia's. The men believed him and, more importantly, believed *in* him. Geraestos had reveled in pettiness and Phaetonis bulled opposition, but Lasctakos' orders felt inherently right, as though issued for universal benefit. There were no executions under him; there was no need. Men were united in spirit and bound fast by his charisma. Legionaries welcomed drills as building blocks to the golden future and there was no grumbling when their tough but beloved leader placed First *Elhar* into seventeen-year-old Livios' hands. To the rank and file, Livios was a god whose towering exploits bordered upon legend. Who better to own the Scriptus? To officers, "Lasctakos' golden boy" was a clever, gifted, brutal force of nature to be admired and feared. That Livios would one day be *ikar* was apparent, that he would deserve it seemed equally certain.

Livios slipped from First spoke and crossed the muddy yard. The night was crisp and the air fresh. *Tired,* he thought as he zeroed in on the barn. He had worked hard since getting First *Elhar* and it was catching up with him. Not that the unit was difficult; he had never seen a sharper group. The problem was that Lasctakos kept saddling him with administrative duties. *Either he's forgotten about me leaving or is squeezing the last drop of work out of me,* he thought, consoling himself that toil would make the time fly. *But Winnowing Day will be here soon enough.*

Where should he and Kassandra go after he stepped down? Farming he knew, but he had no land, and he couldn't return home. *Home.* Sorrow filled him whenever he thought of the cabin.

Livios was content to blame his troubles on fatigue because he didn't want to examine too closely those things that really bothered him, like Mistaaka. *Be strong,* he counseled himself. *It'll get better.* He entered the barn and crossed the crowded lounge. "Mother," he greeted as he skirted the big woman and headed down the hall. Talking to the old madame had ceased being fun; she always brought up Luecos.

"Hello, Blackie!" she called after him.

Livios pondered Luecos' last moments as he trod down the hall, wondering, *What had he been sorry about?* He climbed to the second floor and almost bumped into Livia. The skinny girl was lugging a huge slatted bucket. Dirty water sloshed onto the floor.

"Hello," he said and moved aside.

"Hello, Mr. Kerebos," she responded without slowing.

331

Livios wondered if she knew he owned her. He hoped not. *Maybe she should come with us?* he mused. He slapped open Kassandra's door.

"You frightened me!" she said and set her book down.

Livios unhitched his sword belt and tossed it onto the bed. "I'm a scary man." He sat and rubbed his eyes, which ached from writing by lamplight. "Any visitors today? There's a real crowd downstairs."

"No. They must think you're scary, too."

"They'd better." Lasctakos had never broached the topic of privatizing Kassandra, which Livios counted as approval. It was inconceivable that the *ikar* was ignorant of the arrangement.

Kassandra moved closer. *He's having another bad day,* she thought. "Livios?"

"Yes?" he replied, distracted.

"I'm *so* happy you stopped them." She took and kissed his hand. "You have all of me."

Livios nodded absently. "They'll never touch you again."

Kassandra had hoped for a warmer response. *He's been so withdrawn,* she thought, searching his eyes for traces of the youth who used to sleep on her floor. She felt a blooming guilt.

"What?" he asked.

Kassandra touched his stubbly face. Was she the only one who saw his pain? *Probably,* she thought. *I'm certainly the only one who cares.* She decided that she had no right to judge the changes in him, especially since she had profited by them. *But I'd wrestle every pig in the Legion, one after the other, to get back even half of what he's lost.*

"What?" he repeated.

She sighed. "Oh, Livios, don't you love me anymore?"

He looked puzzled. "Of course I do. Why would you say that?"

She touched his mouth but he shook her off. "Why do you think I've eaten every crap detail that they've asked?"

Kassandra couldn't answer. *He's right,* she thought. *Whatever's happened, we'll just have to live with it.*

Livios looked rueful. "I'm sorry. I know I've been...different. But I do love you. You have to believe that. You're all I have."

Kassandra could no longer hold the tears.

"Last night I had this dream," Livios began tonelessly. "It wasn't about burning, like usual. I was gone from here, from the Legion, and was back home. When I opened the door, though, the cabin was crammed with everyone I've killed. They were all looking at me."

Kassandra shuddered. "It's just a dream."

Livios guffawed. "Of course it was. That shack's too damned small to hold all my victims."

332

Kassandra wanted badly to make him feel better. "Come here," she beckoned.

He gave a haunted stare. "Why? Can't you see the slime all over me?"

"Please."

Livios allowed her to drag him flat. She pulled his head onto her stomach and fingered little circles on his temple until he lay still. "When I was little mother used to talk about the land of Frey, where the gods kept all things lost on earth," she said in a small voice. "I thought Frey was where I'd find my dolls and such, but now I know she meant loved ones and the feelings we've lost."

Livios was long quiet. "I wish it was true."

"It is. Mother wouldn't lie."

*   *   *

Livios was summoned by the *ikar* at the end of the week. He walked unannounced into the audience chamber and caught the seated Lasctakos in the act of biting his own hand. Lasctakos immediately desisted and shot an angry glare, demanding, "Why didn't you knock?"

"I'm sorry, sir. You told me I didn't have to."

"Well, start!" Lasctakos fumed a moment before saying, "Belay that."

Livios happily changed the subject. "Something wrong with your arm, sir?"

"Training accident. How are your men?"

"They appreciated the wine you sent."

"Phaetonis was hoarding the stuff. I was referring to their overall readiness, though. No issues?"

"None, sir. They're razors. I'm real happy with them and they seem the same about me. That's what they say, anyway."

"They wouldn't lie. Show me your topknot."

Livios removed his helmet and wiped moisture from his scalp. "You were right about it feeling slippery."

"It fits you. How does your grisette like it? Your woman, that is."

"She doesn't."

"Are you aware that you're the youngest First *Elhar* in history?

"Yes, sir. Read it in the logs. I admit that I like having access to the Desia's volumes," Livios said with a sheepish smile. "Good reading."

"I thought you would. Have you reached his discourses on Uniformity?"

"I have."

"And?"

Livios shrugged. "Body and mind are one. I don't see that it matters."

Lasctakos leaned onto the desk. "Of course it matters, son. Causality and Determination are *all* that matters." He saw Livios' bewilderment. "Keep reading. A leader needs a philosophy."

"Yes, sir."

"Now to business. I found mistakes in your logistics report. Water and food are the most important element of any army. Pay closer attention."

Livios had merely copied Lasctakos' winter allotment for the First and hadn't taken warmer weather into account. *It's not like I'll really need to know these things,* he thought.

Lasctakos shook his head. "I expect better from you. Suppose tomorrow required you to assume supreme command."

"You're *ikar*, sir."

"Don't spar with me. I said 'suppose'. Are you ready?"

Livios tried to not sound flippant. "I could do it, sir."

"Would you be at your best?"

Livios didn't answer.

"And *that* is what concerned me," Lasctakos said. "We can absorb sloth from a few *sestari*, but not in the *ikar* himself. Am I making myself clear?"

"Yes, sir."

"Very well. Even if you can't see fit to believe, you must trust me. I think the future will teach you that these trifles matter. When have I erred regarding your career?"

Livios had frequently pondered that. *He's been right about everything,* he thought. *How things would play out, what it'd take for me to survive, where I'd end.* "I believe you, sir. I promise to always do my best."

"Excellent." Lasctakos rolled a scroll across the desk. "Now take this supply summary and find the errors. Assume summer conditions and a northern campaign."

Livios grimaced.

"Make it perfect, son, or you'll find that you're not too special for rope drills."

Livios took the parchment. "Yes, sir."

"What were you about to say?"

How's he always do that? Livios wondered. "You really want to know?"

"Of course." Lasctakos sat back and folded his hands.

"It's like this, sir. I don't understand why you're grilling me with these things. Shouldn't you concentrate on the fellows who'll be here after I'm gone?"

"Perhaps, but I still have hopes that you'll remain with the Legion."

Livios cocked his head. "Sir, you're not going to try to keep me from leaving?"

"I might have a card up my sleeve."

Livios didn't like the answer. "Sir?"

"Son, I wouldn't have you here at any rank unless you chose to stay. You know how I feel about conscripts."

Livios nodded, satisfied. "I do."

Livios returned to his quarters and delved into the test, finding it far more complex than he'd anticipated. In addition to the six *elhari*, the *ikar* had to plan for runners, hostages, livestock and emergency communal supplies. There was a commotion in the spoke and the sounds of men scuttling to their feet.

"Carry on, gentlemen," Lasctakos said then entered Livios' room.

Livios stood. "I'm not done, sir."

"I know." Lasctakos picked up the mathematical calculations. "Not bad. You need a separate water supply for medical purposes."

"I forgot that."

"You might have remembered. I'm going for a stroll. Care to come?"

Livios wondered if he was in trouble. He quickly tidied his desk and grabbed his helmet. "Let's go out my private entrance, sir."

"Yes, no need to disturb the men."

They walked into the muggy night and made for the wall. They found a spot over the gate, where Lasctakos dismissed the guards. Livios was keenly interested about what was on the *ikar*'s mind.

Lasctakos looked over the plain. "I like to come here. I find it relaxing."

"Yes, sir."

"How do you salve your mind?"

"I've been reading Magos' books." A moment passed. "I enjoy seeing Kassandra, too."

Lasctakos nodded. "How will you feel once out of armor?"

"A little naked, sir." *Very naked!* Livios thought. The prospect troubled him greatly.

Lasctakos pulled *kraal* from his belt and tucked it into his mouth. "I would suppose so."

His mentor's growing habit disturbed Livios. It wasn't that he disapproved of the drug on principal, but Lasctakos had always possessed admirable control. The narcotic would change that. "Sir, what about all the *kraal*?" he asked, trying to sound uncritical.

"Are you disappointed in me, son?"

Livios' silence spoke loudly.

Lasctakos laughed hollowly. "I'm dying by inches, Kerebos. The leaves help mask the fact."

Livios waited for some indication of a joke. "What?"

Lasctakos looked at his hands, which trembled ever so slightly. "I'm dying in parts. Last year it was only a tingling in my fingertips, but now I barely feel them. It has spread to my arms and legs and I weaken by the season. Some days I can hardly hold my sword. If I have to fight come Winnowing Day, I'll surely lose."

Feelings of desperation shook Livios, not unlike those he felt after losing Daedilos. "But this is terrible! What can we do about it, sir? Let's summon physicians!"

"Nothing to be done, I fear, but the *kraal* helps."

Livios fought a choking panic. "Sir, too much of that trash will kill you."

"I know. The *Aharoni* priests call it 'the doctrine of double effect'."

They stared at each other. At last Livios said: "This is why you're working me so hard."

Lasctakos nodded thoughtfully. "It must be you."

Livios wanted to weep. How could Lasctakos, of all people, be so sick? The *ikar*'s illness made him want to flee the Legion that much quicker, so he wouldn't see his hero's end. "Sir, I can't take over," he said miserably. "I'm getting married and I don't want it, anyway."

Lasctakos reached for more *kraal*. "I understand. Keep this conversation to yourself, will you?"

Livios didn't sleep that night or even try. He paced the hot room, sat at his desk or sprawled on the floor but couldn't get comfortable. Would Lasctakos enter at any moment to reveal the whole story as a ploy to get him stay? *I wish*, he thought, but knew better. Thinking back over the year he picked out telltale signs of Lasctakos' illness. *How terrible it must be for him—to lose his skills. But he never fails his duty. The Legion's always foremost in his mind. All I've ever worried about was myself.* The last realization struck hard.

Livios couldn't remember placing the unit's welfare above his and was reviled by his selfishness. *Lasctakos is a true leader and even frets over who'll care for his men when he's gone*, he thought. *He's nurtured me from my days as a recruit. Can't I give him an extra year to ease his going?* It was a hard question, not just for himself but also for Kassandra. *But I owe him that much. I wouldn't be where I am without him, and Kassandra would still be on her back. I won't abandon him when he needs me.* The decision brought peace.

The spoke came alive as *sestari* chased men from bed. *Morning already?* Livios thought. He looked and saw pale light in the window shutters. *I'll tell Kassandra after mess. She won't like it, but there's no other way.*

Livios ate lightly and didn't join in table talk. He had lots on his mind, particularly how to break the news to Kassandra. The others were still eating when he rose from the table and deposited his plates into the wash barrel. He returned briefly to his room before exiting the barracks, walking slowly to give himself extra time. The more he considered his decision, the more he grasped how tough it would be for Kassandra to understand. She would certainly hate the prospect of another year under Mother's roof.

Livios looked up as he approached the barn and saw a runner groping Kassandra no more than fifty feet away! The bald assailant held the petite blonde against the well, one hand on her throat, one up her skirt. Water buckets lay on the ground. The leering recruit said: "Come now, girly, don't struggle!"

Livios broke into a run; the runner turned to catch a fist full in the teeth. Livios rode the man to the ground and punched until his nose hung by a flap of skin. Blood bubbled from the runner's mouth and snout as Livios choked him with both hands.

"You stupid bastard!" he screamed shrilly. "Not even officers touch her! *But you?* I'll twist the head right off your shoulders!"

Kassandra frantically pulled Livios' arm, saying, "Others are coming!"

Livios grew even angrier as he realized that the runner had ruined his plans. How could he keep Kassandra here another year after this? Fury lent him an ogre's strength and he yanked the limp recruit into the air and slammed his head against the stone well. He felt a swell of intense satisfaction. Laughing, he smashed his quarry's face against the rocks until gray brains oozed from a broken skull. Someone seized him from behind and he whirled, snatched the man and pitched him bodily over the well.

Chest heaving, Livios gazed over the gathering crowd. *Sixth Elhar,* he realized. "Who grabbed me?"

"Polyphemos, sir," a legionary replied.

Livios gazed at Polyphemos, who lay in a heap. "See to him." He took Kassandra by the arm. "You all right?" Terrified, she nodded. "Get inside while I clean this up." He watched her into the building before approaching Polyphemos, who was being attended by four men. The injured *elhar* lay flat on his back and blinked stupidly with his one eye, a dark bruise on his forehead. "How is he?"

"Broken arm and a concussion, maybe," a legionary said.

Livios recalled throwing Polyphemos through the air, marveling that he seemed so light. "Get him to the Hospital."

337

"The *ikar!*" an officer bellowed. "Attention!"

There was the report of snapping heels then Lasctakos was among them. He wound through the ramrod straight legionaries and stopped beside the well. His amber eyes burned as he looked from the corpse to Polyphemos to Livios. "What happened?"

Only now did Livios fully comprehend the gravity of the situation. Far worse than killing a man, he had embarrassed his benefactor. "My fault, sir," he replied feebly. "I attacked the runner because he was molesting a woman. Polyphemos got in the way."

"This was over a *woman?*" Lasctakos sneered.

Livios couldn't look the *ikar* in the face. "Yes, sir."

"You are confined to quarters until further notice," Lasctakos ground out. "Get out of my sight."

Dazed, Livios saluted. "Yes, sir."

Livios spent a bitter, regretful day in his chamber. Had he clawed his way up the ranks only to hang because of a momentary lapse of discipline? *That damned runner!* he thought. *Wish I could kill him again.* He was summoned after the Legion had eaten. Two bodyguards, First *Elhar* men, halted him at the *ikar's* door.

Pythen looked terribly uncomfortable as he said: "Sir, I'm sorry, but I need to—"

"Right." Livios unhitched his swordbelt. "Here's the dagger, too."

Pythen looked relieved. "Thank you, sir." He rapped on the door. "He's here, *ikar.*"

"Bring him."

The sentries trailed Livios into the room. Pythen laid the confiscated weapons onto the *ikar's* desk beside a mound of *kraal.* The guards took flanking positions behind Lasctakos.

"No gentlemen, that won't be necessary," he tiredly told them. "Wait outside." He motioned for Livios to sit. "You've put me in a most painful position, Kerebos *Elhar.*"

"I know, sir," Livios replied guiltily. The contrition was no act; he hated to have placed undue stress upon his ailing leader. "I'd do anything to take it back."

"I know, but you understand that I can't simply ignore such behavior, especially *your* behavior? That's the price for being *ikar's* pet and thus we are both ensnared."

"Yes, sir." *He's going to have to execute me!*

Lasctakos thoughtfully rubbed his chin. "On the other hand, I play no small part in your guilt. I should never have allowed that charade with the woman. I wasn't thinking clearly."

Livios saw a ray of light. *He's not talking like he's about to kill me*, he thought. *Should I say something?*

"Still, justice must be served."

"Yes, sir."

"I could circumvent the penalty for killing an unassigned recruit but," Lasctakos laid a hand upon a stack of books, "Desia was very specific about assaulting officers. If we were on battle footing I would have no choice but to Judge you for injuring Polyphemos to the point that he can't perform. Fortunately, action is not imminent."

"So nothing happens, sir?"

"Not exactly. You must taste the whip."

Livios cringed. He bore ugly scars from his previous flogging, which had hurt worse than anything he had ever felt.

"And more," Lasctakos continued. "You are First *Elhar* and are supposed to set an example."

Livios pulled a brave face. At least he wouldn't be demoted; he need only survive the summer to leave with Kassandra. "Yes, sir, I understand."

Lasctakos smiled wanly. "A good deal better than being Judged, though, right?"

"Yes, sir."

Lasctakos nodded at Livios' blades. "Take them. I have work for you."

Livios scooped up the weapons. "Anything, sir."

"Take a *sestar* to visit our friends the *Stalenzka*. Their headmen have been instructed to provide children as hostages."

"Only a *sestar?*"

"As evidence of my disappointment, because *I am* displeased with you. I would send you alone, but for security. You'll eat your lashes in the morning and will depart as soon as the doctor paints them. Dismissed."

Livios and seven others marched in single file over the grassy plain. They had been moving for the better part of the day and his strength was ebbing. His back oozed and itched from the whipping he'd received that morning; blood had soaked his loincloth.

"*Sestar*, come here," he called from his position in the rear.

Pythen fell back. "How are you, sir?"

"Bleeding. You're going to have to change my dressing when we stop."

"Sir."

"That forward runner's made a number of mistakes today. Make sure he waits on top of the hills instead of going over them. We need to keep him in sight."

"I'll straighten him, sir. If I may?"

"Yes?"

"There's an old campsite no more than four thousand paces ahead. We wouldn't have to do any digging and you could rest up."

"I know. That's where we'll stop."

Pythen returned to point. Livios found it increasingly difficult to keep up with his men. A constant flow of sweat stung his lacerations and he felt weak in the knees. *Lasctakos could've held the flogging until I got back*, he thought miserably.

The unit reached the campsite and Livios immediately lay on his stomach. Pythen set the men to work repairing the old trenches before kneeling beside Livios.

"Want me to look at your wounds, sir?"

Livios lay shivering. He felt faint and nauseous. "Take off my plate."

Pythen unstrapped and removed the breastplate. The smell of fresh blood so filled the air they could taste it. "Sorry, sir, but you'll have to sit so I can slither off your chain." Pythen slid off the mailshirt but had difficulty with the underlying gambeson, which stuck to the wounds. Livios groaned as the padded shirt was peeled free.

"I'll have it washed, sir."

Livios grunted.

Pythen thoroughly cleaned the wounds, which caused Livios great discomfort. "That lash did a real job on you, opened up the scars. Now get some rest, sir, and I'll wake you for grub."

Livios fell into a restless slumber. The camp sounds mixed with his dreams of fire, father and Kassandra. It was dark when Pythen shook him awake. The *sestar*'s face showed concern. "Heat some dinner for you, sir?"

Livios nodded and rolled onto his side. The pain in his wounds had subsided to a dull ache and his temperature seemed normal.

"I tried to rouse you earlier but you were dead," Pythen said, then called one of the men. "Gylippos, fix the *elhar*'s meal."

Livios reached around and felt the taut bandages. The blood had crusted. "A good dressing."

"I've had practice, sir. How do you feel."

"Better. The hot shakes are gone."

Gylippos soon brought over a bowl of stewed grains. Livios spooned into the meal, which had the consistency of mud. He finished the bland dinner and rolled back onto his stomach. "The guard set?"

"Yes, sir."

Livios woke to the sounds of the stirring camp. He felt rested and struggled to his feet unassisted. Pythen and another man were shaving their scalps over a bucket of water. The *sestar* hurried over, saying, "How are you, sir?"

"Fine. Give me a moment." Livios staggered to the latrine and relieved himself. He stopped at the campfire on the way back and got a tin of broth. It was a thick, potent brew that brought Luecos to mind.

"I wouldn't drink that, sir," Pythen called. "It thins the blood."

Livios looked into the cup, weighing the drink's benefits. He took a small sip and poured the rest back into the pot. "Where's my gambeson?"

"On your bedroll, sir. It's not quite dry."

They were presently back on the trail. It was overcast, which made marching easier. Livios held up well for a time but his shirt was completely soaked by the first halt. The world was spinning as Pythen replaced the bandages.

"Sir, why don't we stop here for the day," he suggested. "We could set out bright and early tomorrow."

The idea tempted Livios but the longer they tarried the greater the chance of misadventure. "Thanks, but that won't do. We can't waste a day because of my scratches."

"Yes, sir. We might slow down, though. Double time won't get us there and back to the campsite before dark."

"It will if I don't slow us down. Help me get that iron back on."

They reached the huge *Stalenzka* village later than Livios had hoped. Despite his best efforts he hadn't kept pace nor had he complained when Pythen dropped to quick time. He felt shaky, feverish and irritable. The remains of town Mistaaka lay on the horizon.

"Industrious folk," Pythen said as they halted a spear's throw from the ocean of tents.

Hundreds of grim civilians labored at tasks ranging from log splitting to smelting. Potbellied, wheeled furnaces belched filth into the air.

The metal smiths were well on their way to finishing their first permanent structures, low brick buildings with tin roofs and many chimneys. Outlines of roads had been carved into the earth. A delegation of grimy, barechested men approached Livios. They were short, sallow people, the *Stalenzka*, but built like blacksmiths.

"Welcome, legionary," a toothless *Stalenzka* said in passable *Chaconni*. "I've sent for Prince Tharba."

"Who are you?" Livios asked.

"Po."

"Well, Po, I was told there were twenty thousands in your tribe. I count tents for only a tithe of that."

"The main body stayed behind to dismantle our workshops."

Not the way it was presented to Lasctakos, Livios thought. The groups silently faced each other. A squat, gray bearded man rode up and dismounted. He wore a leather jerkin and gloves; his brown face was deeply creased from years of toil and looked as though it would crack if he smiled. *This must be the prince. Not one to shirk labor, it seems.*

Tharba walked to within a few paces of Livios and bowed. "You honor us, *elhar*," he said though his tone didn't agree. "The children are being gathered."

Livios nodded.

Tharba's dark eyes took measure of the legionary. "Refreshment?"

"No, just the hostages. And be quick." *Must clog his craw to be bossed by a handful of men*, Livios thought. *But he knows what'd happen if he disobeyed.* Another *Stalenzka* arrived with a train of unkempt girls in tow. Tharba gestured as though presenting a priceless treasure.

Livios eyed the scrawny children. "Where are the males?" It was known that the *Stalenzka* considered useless anyone without a strong hammer arm.

"Our boys remained with the main host to help," Tharba said. "But look at these young pearls, the finest of our people."

Livios drew his dagger, stepped forward and slammed it up under Tharba's chin so that he saw the blade edge in the man's eye. The prince crashed to the ground as the girls shrieked. Livios pointed the shiny blade at Po, who gaped in amazement. "Twenty noble's sons, right now! Any further delay and I'll return with the entire Legion and slay the lot of you! And get these yapping tarts out of my sight before I shove them in pieces back where they were birthed from!"

The girls were herded off as Po disappeared into forest of tents. Pythen gazed at Livios, who said: "Draw swords." He turned to the steppe and waved, setting his runners in motion. "If there's a fight, none of us are to be taken alive. Got that, men?"

"Yes, sir!"

Stalenzka began to arrive by the score, ringing the legionaries. Women wailed over their fallen leader and men stared at Livios with murderous glances. A large number of armed nobles arrived and ordered their people to fall back.

They want a fight? Livios wondered. *No way out of it if they do. Best to press on.* "Who's doing the talking?"

A serious looking young man in mail and helmet stepped forward. He raised empty hands. "Me. Twalla."

Livios nodded at Tharba. "He your father?"

"No. His sons are being restrained."

Good, they're keeping the hot heads back, Livios thought. *They're not going to fight.* "Po tell you what happened?"

Twalla nodded.

"Are you playing the same game?" Livios asked.

"No," Twalla said firmly. "You'll have your hostages. Give us a moment to draw straws."

Livios looked over the tents. "I don't see fighters back there, do I? Do you know what the *ikar* would do if you resisted?"

"We're craftsmen, lord, not warriors. Tharba chose poorly and paid."

A thought struck Livios. "You're not one of his kin, are you?"

"No."

"Does your clan take over with him out of the way?"

Twalla stared blankly. "Our sept will now be heard," he admitted.

"Fine. Don't betray the *ikar*, or you'll all end up like Tharba." The fresh batch of hostages arrived. Livios eyed the scared boys. "Be quiet and obedient and one day you'll see your families again. Pythen, rope them and set the pace."

The *Boru* stepped forward. "Yes, sir. All right you little rats, out front!"

As he turned his back on the *Stalenzka*, Livios couldn't help but wonder why anyone would hand their family to the Legion. Where he previously might have felt pity, he felt only scorn. *Not even to the Legion, but to eight of us,* he corrected himself. *Hell, I'd stand alone against the world before surrendering Kassandra.* Thoughts of the girl chased away the bleak feelings. He hoped she hadn't heard about him being flogged, as she'd surely fret. But at least she cared enough to worry. *Wish I'd seen her before leaving. Lots of things I should've said.*

Livios was relieved to see the black castle the following evening; he was dizzy and at the end of his endurance. If the unit hadn't slowed for the young prisoners, he never would've managed the journey. His fever had returned and his wounds had gone all day untended; he was out of bandages. Flies buzzed around him and he could feel them under his armor.

Pythen led the procession through the front gate and called the men to muster outside of their spoke. The dazed, whimpering children dropped to earth as Livios consulted with Pythen.

"Cage the captives and feed the men," Livios ordered. "I'm going to the hospital. Get word to the *ikar* for me."

Pythen saluted. "Yes, sir."

Livios staggered to the infirmary, where the old surgeon looked surprised to see him. "I'm glad you made it back so quickly, *elhar*. I didn't think you'd get in under your own power. They were the nastiest whip stripes I've seen."

343

Livios flopped onto the nearest bed. "The stitches pulled."

"Thought they might. You've a lot of scar tissue, especially for your age." The surgeon deftly removed the armor. "Yes, they're bad. The whipmaster really must have something against you."

"He couldn't go easy on an *elhar*," Livios grumbled. "And I got twice the number as was usual for the infraction."

"Why so?"

"Because the *ikar* expects more out of me, I guess."

The surgeon prodded the swollen flesh. "Smell that rot? I'll have to do some cutting. Unless you want me to cauterize."

"Cut me."

The surgeon ordered a slave to fetch his 'slicing kit'. "Just as well," he told Livios. "It'll let me remove some of that scarred matter."

Livios would have left the hospital the following morning but Lasctakos ordered him to remain until freed by the surgeon. The wizened physician proved impervious to Livios' nagging; it was days before he signed the release.

Livios gazed blearily around the room. "Where's my kit?"

"One of your officers claimed it," the surgeon said. "He said it'll be in your quarters."

As he tottered from the infirmary Livios realized that the forced convalescence had probably prevented him from a speedy relapse. His legs felt like rubber. *But that's to be expected after lying idle for so long,* he thought. He wanted to go directly to the barn but duty called; he ducked into the spoke and suited up, then lumbered into the crowded yard. The First stopped drilling at his approach and broke into spontaneous, sincere, applause.

Livios smiled as he stood before the cheering unit. "Who told you to stop working, you sluggards?" he admonished good-naturedly.

"How you been, sir?" a legionary called.

Livios' smile broadened as the men had unwittingly gravitated into formation. "I lost a pound of meat but am fine, Patroclos. I'm looking forward to cracking shields with you men."

The legionaries howled their approval.

"Let me speak with the *cohari*," Livios said.

The officers arrived as training resumed. Livios asked and answered general questions while trying to get a feel for how things had been in his absence. There had been no problems. "Cyros?"

The First *Cohar* had a hooked nose and a chin cleft so deep it hampered shaving. "Sir?"

"Pythen performed excellently. He reads terrain well."

"Thank you, sir. I'll pass on the compliment."

"Who cleaned my armor?"

"I saw to it, sir," Cyros answered.

"Good thinking. All right gentlemen, carry on." As he walked off Livios sighed, thinking, *Did I really just say 'gentlemen'? They'll think I'm parroting Lasctakos.*

Mother's expression was grim. "She's gone, Blackie."

Livios stopped in his tracks. "Gone where? What do you mean?"

"The *ikar* sent for her after you went away. She never came back."

"What in hell do you mean?"

Mother looked scared. "That's all I know."

Livios had a hard time digesting the comments. What would Lasctakos want with Kassandra? Fear, anger and shock peeled him in different directions. It felt as though a cold rock rested in his stomach. "Woman," he said gently, "I'm going to ask again. Where is she?"

"God help me, *elhar*, I told you the truth!"

"You better have or even God won't be able to put you back together." Livios turned to the legionary sprawled on a divan. "Don't let her leave."

"Yes, sir."

A sense of unreality weighed Livios as he strode from the building. He racked his brains to come to grips with Mother's report even as he denied the possibility. Could Lasctakos have sold Kassandra or, infinitely more terrible, taken her for himself? He was in a dreamlike trance by the time the guards stopped him outside the *ikar*'s closed door.

"Sorry, sir," a sentry said. "He wants us to announce all visitors from now on."

"Then do it." As Livios waited he wondered what he'd do if Lasctakos had sold Kassandra. *Why'd I leave her here?* he asked himself, as though he had a choice. He couldn't even begin to contemplate a course of action if Lasctakos had claimed Kassandra as his own.

The guard returned. "He'll see you, sir."

Lasctakos was sitting on the desk. A stern mask had replaced his customary benevolent expression. "Sit," he ordered.

Livios collapsed into a chair, all hope gone.

"Yes, the girl is gone," Lasctakos said in a businesslike tone. "I couldn't cover my top officer's antics with a mere whipping but had to remove the source of trouble."

It took a moment for Livios to find his voice. "But you promised to keep her here, sir."

Lasctakos shook his head emphatically. "I did nothing of the sort. I promised you could one day leave, if you so chose, and that you might take her with you. To that I hold."

345

"But how will I be able to buy her back? Where is she?"

"There will be no purchase, because I didn't sell her. I freed her."

Livios' jaw dropped. "Freed her?"

"Why should I sell her? How would that serve my purposes? I needed to draw an irritant from my command while putting my best man back on path. The manumission accomplished both."

Livios' grim mood was dissipating rapidly; why, Lasctakos had done him a service! *She'll have no more trouble with the other legionaries*, he thought. "Where'd she go, sir?"

Lasctakos gave a small, knowing smile. "I suppose she awaits you in Nilfheim by now."

Livios didn't know where Nilfheim was but would certainly find out. There were charts of the *Boru* lands in Magos' library. He was swept with relief. *At least she's out of this place, and I will be soon enough*, he thought. *Now I need only focus on getting through the summer.* "Why didn't you warn me, sir?"

"To what end? You wouldn't have gone on the mission, which would have further eschewed matters. You sitting here only confirms the mess I would have had."

"I suppose so." Livios mentally tallied the days until Winnowing.

"How's the back?"

Livios had forgotten the injury. "I haven't thought about it since talking to Mother."

"I've no doubt."

The meeting ended and Livios departed in good spirits, feeling tremendously grateful. By all rights the *ikar* should have sold Kassandra or forced her back into circulation at the barn. Livios wondered if there'd be any carping over the resolution. *No one knows I'm leaving, so they'll think I've been punished,* he decided. *Maybe I should act down for a few days?*

The situation wasn't perfect, but Livios had confidence in his ability to locate Kassandra. Anyway, she was smart and would leave him a clean path. He pictured her lovely face and thought: *It's going to be a long summer.*

*   *   *

Livios remained active throughout the summer. He led an abortive campaign into the south then spent the rest of the season on administrative duties. Thoughts of Kassandra, soothing at first, grew to haunt him until he was swamped by an endless series of horrible possibilities; worrying over why she hadn't sent word, or if she had fallen for another man were typical examples. And when he persuaded himself that he was being irrational, or otherwise succeeded in casting out one of the demons, a fresh fear came to mind. The situation grew so unbearable that he tried to not think of her at all, which was impossible. He suffered this state until halfway through the summer, when he found comfort of sorts by visiting Kassandra's old room. Spending time in the drab cube brought him some peace.

As summer drew to a close Livios learned that Cyros *Cohar* planned to challenge him on Winnowing Day. The news shocked him at first, since he had treated his officers so well, and he almost pulled Cyros aside for an earful. But further introspection brought him to the conclusion that his mildness might have caused Cyros' dissatisfaction. "Too nice and they think you're weak, too cruel and they want your blood," had been Luecos' mantra. *I started letting up when I decided I was leaving,* Livios thought. *My mistake, but Cyros will have to pay for it. How to do this without leaving the ikar even more shorthanded?*

Next day.

Livios waited until his men were into their drills before wandering out into the yard. The unit had a standing order to not stop training to salute him so he had to halt the proceedings. The First quickly fell into formation.

Their blood's up, he thought, noting the fire in their eyes. *Working with whetted blades today. Yes, that'd do it.* He didn't mind the men practicing with honed weapons every so often. It kept them sharp.

"I need your help, men," Livios began. "I'm getting fat sitting all day, working on reports. Who wants to help me lose some sweat?" He stared straight at Cyros. "What do you say, First *Cohar*?"

Cyros shot a nasty glance at a peer before saying, "Surely, sir. Need to warm up?"

"That won't be necessary?"

Livios feigned distress as he looked over the unit. "Didn't mean to disturb things. You men want to watch?" The roar of affirmation was deafening. "Come out front, Cyros. No need to form a circle. This won't last long."

Cyros stalked warily forward. He was a fine swordsman but his eyes betrayed concern. "With or without shields, sir?"

"Keep yours. I'll go without." Livios pulled his sword. "Begin!"

They circled each other at ten feet. Cyros was right-handed so Livios stayed to his left. Cyros tried to change direction and Livios pounced so suddenly the *cohar* beat a clumsy retreat. Livios chuckled; he was much faster than Cyros had expected. *That shield doesn't feel so friendly anymore, does it?* he thought.

The First watched with bated breath. Livios had frequently joined in drills but never demonstrated in single combat. Men from Second *Elhar* ambled over to watch.

Livios liked the audience, the thrill in his chest and a hilt in his hand. He eased over the sparse grass so smoothly and silently he might have been naked. Cyros looked a bundle of nerves, as though he might explode at the slightest touch.

Three different paths to get at him, Livios decided. *And he wanted to fight me for real?* "Relax, Cyros," he goaded. "It's only an exhibition."

Cyros' dark eyes narrowed. "Don't worry about me, sir."

Livios switched his sword from hand to hand. "You remind me of the woman that married a mule."

Cyros didn't respond.

"She bit off more than she could chew."

Livios closed quickly and Cyros responded with a desperate downward stroke. The blade blurred past Livios' nose and he assisted it to the ground with his own then trapped it with his foot. He grabbed Cyros' greatshield and twisted it so savagely that the *cohar* was obliged to release it. Livios slid his sword arm under Cyros', kneed him in the groin, and slapped him across the face hard enough to make the crowd wince. Livios walked off with both swords while Cyros stumbled about.

The legionaries hooted over Cyros being disarmed and there were catcalls from the officers. Cyros pulled his dagger and recovered the shield. Livios faced him at ten paces while balancing a pommel on either palm. "Sorry I struck you so hard," he said. "It'll bruise. Ready to yield?"

"No I'm not!"

Livios ran straight at the *cohar*, one sword high, one low. Cyros struck fiercely with the boss spike and barely missed; Livios brought the high sword down onto Cyros' dagger then swept the *cohar*'s legs with the flat of the lower sword. Cyros crashed loudly onto his back and Livios leaped in, stabbed the meaty part of Cyros' hand and sauntered away with the dagger. Cursing, Cyros pulled off his gauntlet to assess the damage.

The spectators went wild, especially those who had never seen Livios in action. Chants of "Kerebos!" lifted over the yard. *Half the Legion has joined us*, Livios thought smugly.

Cyros removed his sword belt and held it as a whip; the buckle gleamed in the sun. He looked very irate. "Let's finish this. Sir."

"What, I have to take your boots, too?"

"Come on!" Cyros cried, swinging the belt.

Livios sheathed his sword then threw the dagger with such force that it was but a blur—until it chirped into Cyros' shield. The *cohar* stared at the knife with a blank expression. Livios walked over and gave back Cyros' sword, saying, "Thanks for the exercise. Get the men back to work."

Cyros could only nod.

KEREBOS

Livios woke early on Winnowing Day and polished his kit. It seemed incredible that the day would be his last in armor; he didn't quite believe it. More incomprehensible, but far more exciting, was the pending reunion with Kassandra. He hoped the meeting would be all that he had dreamed and imagined in detail what he'd say when he saw her.

Livios dressed. Holding the helmet at last, he roughed its crest, which was white and tipped red. He regretted having disappointed Lasctakos by not achieving an *ikar*'s plumage but his life was for Kassandra. He longed to raise a family; Daedilos surely would have liked that. *At least Lasctakos hasn't pressed the matter,* he thought and buckled his helmet strap. *Another thing to bless him for.* A sack of cloth soon housed his possessions and he set the bundle onto his bed. A brief search through the room revealed he'd forgotten nothing. He walked to the desk, pulled a parchment from the drawer and scrawled, *Good fortune, Cyros. Give them hell. Kerebos.* He girt himself and took a final look in the mirror, thinking, *Goodbye, First Elhar.*

The spoke had woken by the time Livios left his room. The men moved with more purpose than usual and there was an indescribable charge to the air. It was definitely a big day.

A *sestar* hurried over. "Morning, sir. Ready for mess?"

Livios grunted in reply as he headed for the door; he had grown to detest small talk. Outside, it was shaping up to be a fine morning. Dew glistened on the grass and a faint mist lingered in the air. It would be one of those clear, mild days between fall and summer that he had treasured as a boy. He marched to the barn and found a willowy girl drawing water from the well.

"Thalia, right?" he asked the raven-haired slave.

"Yes, lord."

"Where's Mother?"

"Sleeping, lord. She don't wake before breakfast."

"Get her."

Thalia made off at a brisk pace. Livios sat on the well and casually searched for traces of the runner he had killed; he found teeth marks in the stone.

The house's door creaked open and a disheveled Mother emerged. A tight robe and a lack of makeup left her more hideous than usual. Her attempt to smile was unsuccessful. "Morning, Blackie. What's the fuss?" Even her voice was ugly this early.

Livios stood. "The girl, Livia. Have her ready to travel."

Mother's eyebrow lifted. "Livia?"

"Don't concern yourself."

Mother scratched her hairy chin. "All right, *elhar*."

Livios turned on his heel and headed back to the spoke. Smoke was issuing from the kitchen chimneys; the morning meal would be ready shortly. *Too nervous to eat*, he thought, but smiled. *Kassandra!*

Lasctakos marched onto the plain and the Legion snapped to attention; runners watched from the castle wall. He stopped before the First and said: "Bring the Scriptus forward."

Livios lifted the bulky brand and placed it beside the *ikar*, whose eyes were bloodshot and face damp. *Kraal*, Livios thought. *Lots of it.*

"The Winnowing has arrived, gentlemen," Lasctakos pronounced. "Every man who desires shall be heard. 'Then only shall brothers take arms against each other and in success, shall take their brother's place'" he quoted Desia. He nodded at Magos, who approached with the Winnowing tome. Lasctakos softly bade Livios to take over.

He can't even look at me, Livios thought sadly. *I suppose it's too much to ask for him to be happy about me leaving.* "Yes, sir. Sixth *Elhar* Polyphemos?" he called.

"Here!"

"Who of your men will challenge their *sestari*?"

And so it began. There were some challenges within the Sixth. Livios wondered how Polyphemos' unit had gotten so unbalanced. It was an *elhar*'s task to limit the carnage by correctly juggling his men, and in this Polyphemos had undeniably failed. That half of the combats resulted in elevations proved he had lost his eye for talent. A surer proof of his ineptitude surfaced when Polyphemos himself was challenged and killed.

He didn't put up much of a tussle, Livios thought. "Do you think that arm was still bothering him?" he asked Lasctakos, who shrugged.

Livios went through the motions of facilitating the action but his heart wasn't in it. Nobody he cared about was fighting, so he spent time trying to mend the fence with Lasctakos, but the *ikar* refused conversation and wavered between silence and one-word answers. Livios grew increasingly demoralized by Lasctakos' behavior and had dropped behind the spectators by the time Third *Elhar* finished. *Will he ignore me all day?* he wondered.

Livios was interested in the Second's purges, though, and recovered enough to watch attentively. There weren't many contests but he didn't doubt that he could have prevented most of these. Rodios, who had taken over the Second, could've done a better job of arranging the men. None of the challengers earned elevation but old Pielos *Sestar* was sent to the hospital with what appeared a mortal wound. It was with some trepidation that he called the Legion into formation and returned to Lasctakos' side. Looking at the First he thought, *Now we'll see what kind of leader I've been.*

Lasctakos broke his silence. "Are you positive you won't remain?"

Livios looked at the *ikar*, who seemed his old self, right down to the smile; it distressed him to kill the mood. "I'm sorry, sir."

Lasctakos nodded thoughtfully. "I wanted to hear it a last time." He cleared his throat. "Come, let's conclude the day's work."

None of Livios' men would challenge their commanders, which wasn't very surprising. He couldn't help but stare at Cyros when reporting, "The First is content, *ikar!*"

"Return to formation," Lasctakos ordered.

Livios faced the *ikar*, snapped a salute and fell back into ranks. Magos started closing the Winnowing book but Lasctakos stopped him with a glance. Lasctakos said, "Our new Sixth *Elhar*, Chalcos, is not eligible to challenge." He looked at Naphios *Elhar*. "What about you? Do I kill you today?"

"No, sir!" Naphios shouted without hesitation.

"Anios?"

"No, sir!"

"Nicios?"

"Not today, sir."

Lasctakos turned a cold gaze upon the young Second *Elhar*, whose ambition was common knowledge. "Ready to die, Rodios?"

The *ikar*'s acting skills impressed Livios, who thought, *If they only knew how sick he is!* Startlingly, he realized that he didn't know the proper words to resign, if there were any. Would that forfeit his chance?

Rodios thought a moment. "No, sir."

Lasctakos turned a gentle smile upon Livios. "I don't suppose First *Elhar* Kerebos wants the Legion?"

Livios swallowed. "No, sir." *How could he even suggest I'd fight him?* he thought. Lasctakos kept looking at Livios, who finally blurted, "Permission to address the *ikar!*"

"Step forward and be heard."

There were many puzzled faces when Livios broke ranks. He fumbled with his scabbard but managed to slide it from his belt; he presented the sword with both hands. "Sir," he said thickly. "As First *Elhar*, I request to be released by the Legion."

A spontaneous outburst shook the rows of soldiers. Some voices held anger but those of Livios' men held shock and grief. A number of legionaries loudly disputed the legality of the action.

Lasctakos lifted a hand to quiet the army and the grumbling slowly subsided. He looked at Livios. "That is your right, First *Elhar*. Are you resolved in this?"

Livios was daunted by the *ikar*'s hollow gaze and felt suddenly unsure. Could he go through with this plan and destroy Lasctakos' dreams? Maybe he could bring Kassandra back for a time? *Be strong! Be strong! It's almost over!* he told himself. "I am."

A murmur passed through the crowd. Lasctakos held out his hand authoritatively. "Your sword." Livios tried to hand it over but the *ikar* merely gripped the sheath and barked, "Fight me!"

Livios was stunned. "No, sir!"

Lasctakos tore off the scabbard and tossed it to the ground.

"You must!"

"I can't!" Livios shot back. "Kassandra."

Lasctakos laughed. "Stupid boy. That's not reason enough."

"No?" Livios retorted. *Why is he doing this?*

Lasctakos sneered. "Do you think some farmer's son gets his way of me? When I said I released your wench, I meant that I freed her of the burden of an earthly existence. I killed her."

The words struck Livios like a hammer. He slowly doubled over and hot stomach acid filled his mouth. Stumbling forward, he reached blindly with his free hand but Lasctakos moved out of the way. "Whyyyyy?" he wailed.

"Because I don't care about you," Lasctakos replied indignantly. "But there's no need to be cross; you can still leave. You might even be able to dig up your woman, though I don't suspect she'll make much of a wife anymore."

Livios covered his eyes with his fists and stamped the ground in an orgy of anguish. He screamed incoherently and frothed and wept. He wanted Kassandra and Lasctakos—*Lasctakos*, not the imposter before him—for comfort. "No! No! No!"

"Shatters the heart, doesn't it?"

Livios felt his guts had been ripped out. Seeing red, he turned a face of such fury upon Lasctakos that the *ikar* stopped smiling. Leaping, he buried his sword into Lasctakos' chest so the hilt rang on the breastplate.

Lasctakos grabbed him and they fell onto the ground, the blade snapping beneath them.

Lasctakos' handsome face was filled with pride. "Thank you," he gurgled.

Only now did Livios realize what he had done. He grabbed Lasctakos' shoulders and shook him. "Why! *Why!*" he cried, sobbing uncontrollably.

But Lasctakos was dead.

Livios was senseless with rage and grief. He clawed Lasctakos' face and smacked his own onto the *ikar*'s breast. At length he crawled up the corpse and, whimpering, wrapped an arm around the neck.

That night a silent Kerebos *Ikar* stood alone above the castle gate. Long he stared north as tears streamed down his face.

Epilogue

Grand Master Dokein stirred in troubled sleep before waking to a dark room. He stared at the arched ceiling until his rapid breathing returned to normal. At length he wiped his sweaty brow with an equally damp hand. *Lord, what a nightmare,* he thought, swallowing on a dry throat. *The Black Legion!* But he knew it had been no dream. *They never are when they feel like this.*

Dokein had hoped he'd heard the last of the Legion when he ransomed children a few years before but had suspected that wouldn't be the case; he had feared the *ikar* would some day visit *Kwan Aharon. But it didn't feel so soon. And who is Kerebos?* he wondered, mystified. He tried in vain to relax but eventually admitted there was no more sleep to be had this night. He rose from the low bed, walked barefoot across the cold brick floor, and sat at his desk. After lighting a lamp, he pulled the scriptures close and prayed for guidance. Then, for no apparent reason, he pushed the heavy tome aside and withdrew a much smaller book from the desk; he opened it to Nestu 11:17 and read:

God will once again show his compassion and patience by choosing the most wicked of serpents as Pangaea's last prophet. Mark it well, the very guard of hell shall be beaten into a drawbridge over which the faithful will march into the kingdom.

Dawn was far off, which gave Dokein plenty of time to contemplate the passage.

A week later Dokein was again at his desk when he learned that Lasctakos Ikar had been killed in single combat.

"His successor's name?" he quietly asked the messenger.

"Kerebos, Grand Master. Nobody's heard of him."

Dokein felt a tingling in his spine. "Thank you. You may go."

As was usual when his "dreams" proved true, Dokein thanked God for entrusting him with vision but lamented that the premonition came without instruction.

That evening as he labored in his garden Dokein was joined by his trusted lieutenant, Ehu. Ehu, shy a hand from his days in the Korenthis' coliseum, had come to give the Grand Master a full accounting of the day's affairs. Dokein rarely learned anything from these nightly meetings but he enjoyed the old priest's company.

"Still have that cough?" Dokein asked.

"Yes, Grand Master."

"Then I won't ask you to help me with the compost. Did you manage to straighten out Torra's mess in the market?"

"I did," Ehu replied with a smile and sat on Dokein's rarely used chair. "It was a lot less expensive than I thought it'd be."

Dokein put aside his shovel. "Well, that's good. Wine?"

"Please."

"You know where it is. Save me some this time."

Ehu fished a jug from an empty barrel and took a long pull. "By the way, I ended up finding homes for the last of the children. All but one, that is."

Dokein nodded. "God be praised. I didn't think it would take this long. Which one's still in our care?"

"Antiphon. Little dark fella."

Dokein smiled. He liked the skinny, thoughtful child. "No matter if we can't find a family for him. Something tells me he'd make a fine acolyte."

APPENDICES

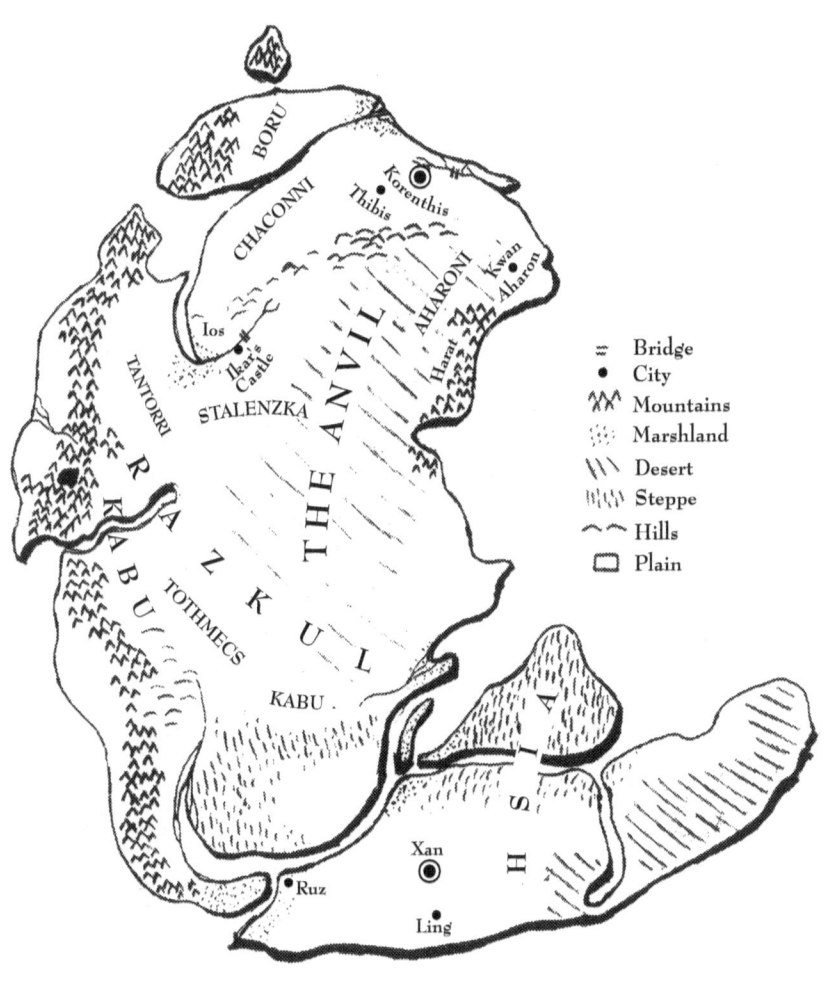

BORU

CHACONNI

Korenthis

Thibis

AHARONI

Kwan
Aharon

Ios

Ikar's
Castle

TANTORRI

STALENZKA

Harat

THE ANVIL

R A Z K U L

K A B U

TOTHMECS

KABU

H S A

Xan

Ruz

Ling

	Bridge
●	City
ʌʌʌ	Mountains
░░	Marshland
\\\	Desert
░\\\	Steppe
~~	Hills
▢	Plain

Pangaea

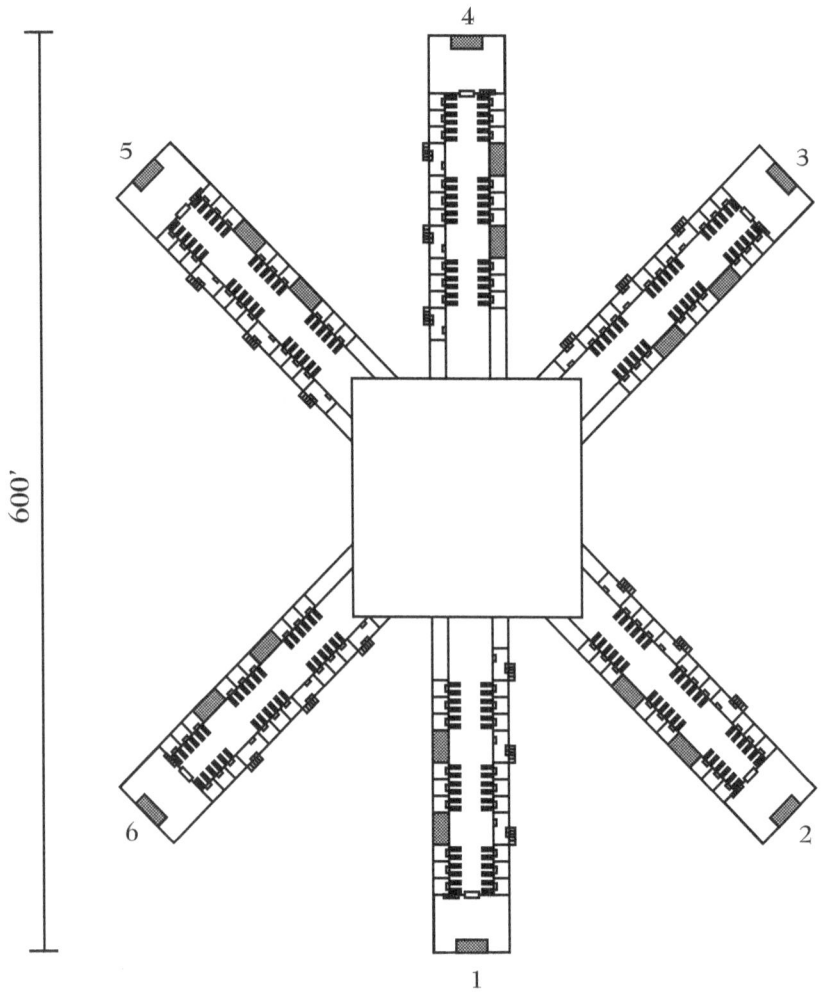

600'

The Black Castle

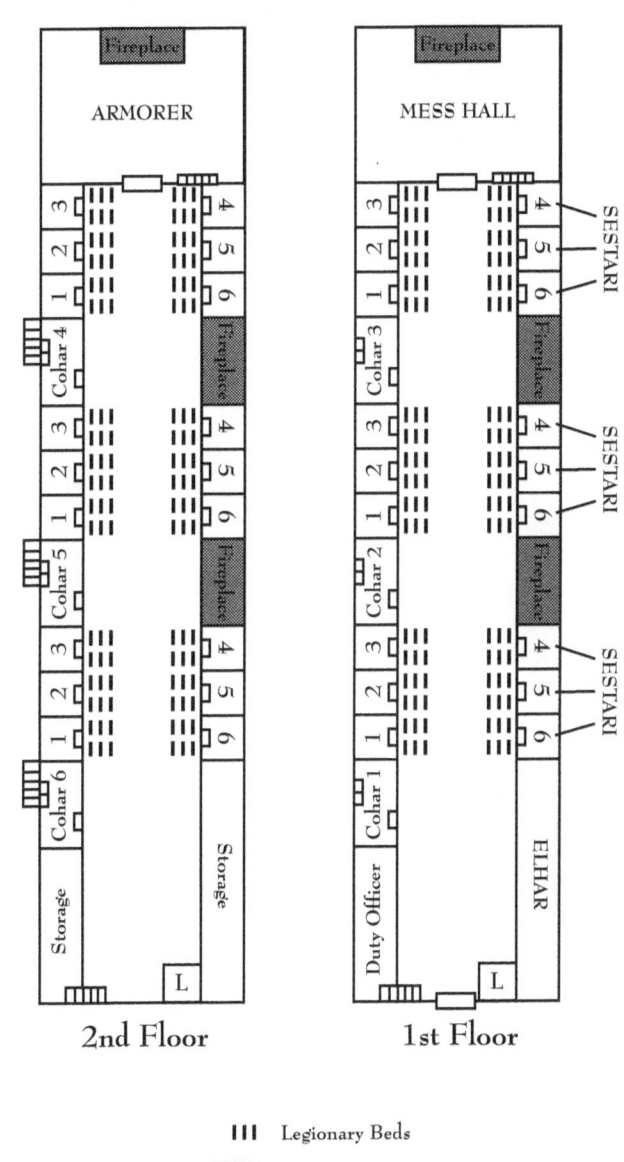

2nd Floor

1st Floor

|||	Legionary Beds
⊞⊞	Steps
▭	Door
L	Latrine

The Black Castle: Detail of a Spoke

361

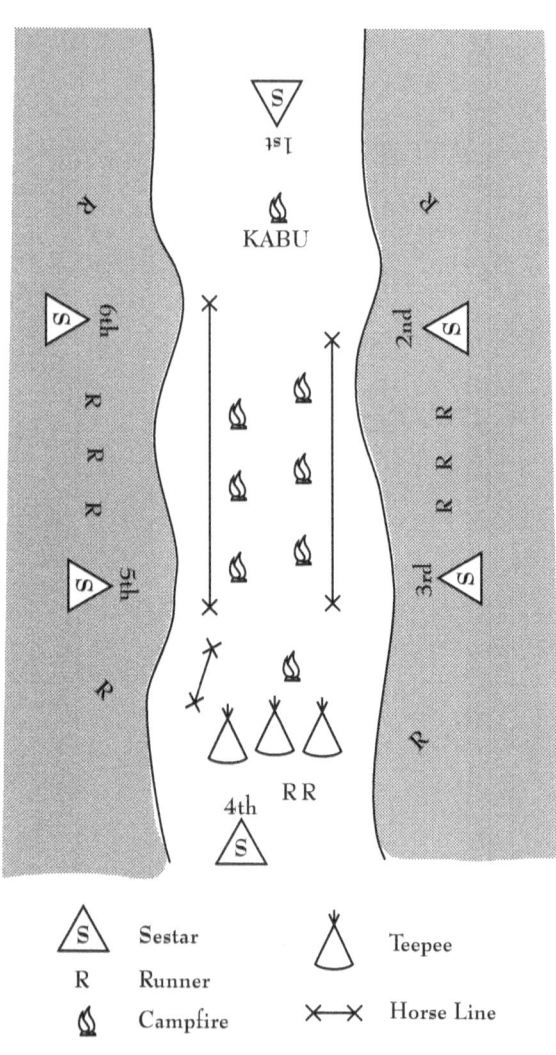

△S Sestar	△ Teepee
R Runner	
🔥 Campfire	✕—✕ Horse Line

The Riverbed Battle

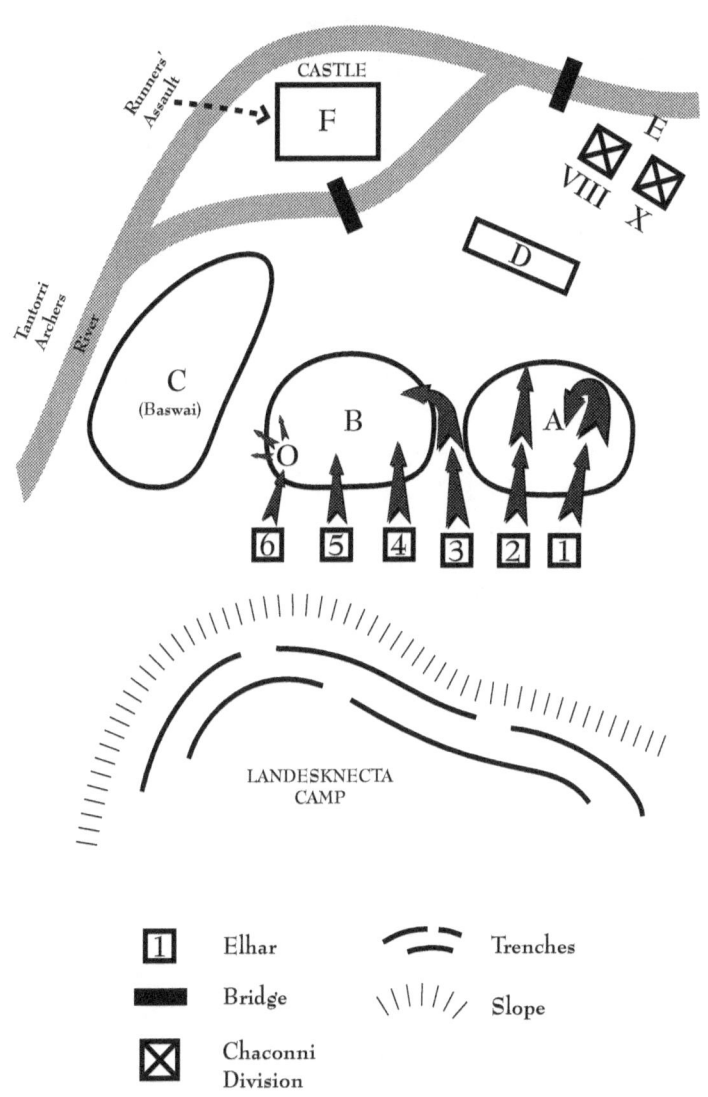

The Kabu Battle

The Alphabets of Pangaea

	Aharoni	Chaconni	Boru
A			
B			
C			
D			
E			
F			
G			
H			
I			
J			
K			
L			
M			
N			
O			
P			
Q			
R			
S			
T			
U			
V			
W			
X			
Y			
Z			

364

Glossary

Aharoni "people of Aharon" A mostly nomadic, desert dwelling folk. Their cultural and historical hub is Kwan Aharon.

ala/alaes A Chaconni designation for a column of cavalry. Size varies, depending on adjacent infantry.

Boru A fierce, warlike race from the inhospitable northwestern region of Pangaea. The last people to cling to feudalism.

Cemetary River Brackish river that separates the Chaconni and Legion's territory. Populated by large, man-eating sharks.

Chaconni The most populous and industrious of Pangaea's people. Once fully half the globe paid homage to their crown.

chiampuglia "battle name" The nom de guerre given a landesknecta recruit after his "branding" and before final assimilation into a unit.

cohar A junior officer among the landeskectos, equivalent to a Chaconni lieutenant.

Ducal Wars A period of internecine warfare and internal strife for the Chaconne. Many noble families were permanently dispossessed (or killed) before a democratic protectorate was established in what became the "Second Republic".

elhar A senior landeskecta officer who reports directly to the ikar, equivalent to a Chaconni colonel.

Heretos Ikaros	Kraal in its most potent form. This claylike drug is manufactured for the ikar alone.
Hsia	A numerous folk from the south of Pangaea, easily distinguishable by their narrow eyes and copper skin tone.
Imperial Rangers	A collection of small, mounted squadrons charged with keeping the extensive Chaconni highway system free of thieves, while collecting tolls and regulating trade.
Ios	Western province of the Chaconni kingdom and the capital city of that province.
irbarzi	A dangerous wolf-like creature of the steppe. This bony, striped animal is capable of great speed, its legs being over three feet long.
ikar	The supreme commander of the landesknectos. The ikar holds life and death decisions over his men and, in theory, is their spiritual leader.
Judges	The Legion's cadre of executioners. Practicing execution by cannibalism (on live transgressors) they were equal parts internal terror mechanism and exemplary practitioners of Desian Uniformity.
Kabu	Negro tribesmen from Pangaea's south-central plains who are perpetually at war with the Razkul.
King's Guards	"Scarlet Guards" "Royal Guards" This elite division recruits exclusively from the Royal Marines and remains under the direct command of the crown. They serve as bodyguard, maritime soldiers, cavalrymen and, in rare cases, shock troops. Only a fullblooded Chaconne could hope to rise in their ranks.
Kobold	Northern Boru island populated by seamen who prey primarily upon Chaconni shipping.
Korenthis	The Chaconni capital. By all accounts a majestic and beautiful place. Notable for its many public works, including baths, sewer systems and running water.

kraal	A strong, leafy narcotic favored by the landesknectos and culled for them by their subjects, the Tantorri.
landesknecta	A common legionary.
Pangaea	The world. A single continent surrounded by rough oceans.
Power Guard	A landesknecta unit charged with a specific task of short duration. Consists of two cohari.
razai	A squad of archers.
Razkuli	A collection of uncivilized plains dwellers. One of the few groups on Pangaea to openly practice cannibalism and human sacrifice. What laws they possess are dictated by their chief tribe, the Tothmecs.
Royal Marines	A branch of the Chaconni military with a reputation of effectiveness and élan. One of the first units to discontinue usage of the tactical legion in favor of interchangable divisions.
sestar	The most junior commander in the Black Legion, equivalent to a Chaconni sergeant. Commands six legionaries and is responsible for the development and assimilation of recruits. A sestar maintains power of corporal punishment over his charges.
Second Republic	A transitional period for the Chaconni people wherein the Senate and popular elections were revived. Ended with the restoration of the Grasmilios line.
Stalenzka	Relatives of the Chaconni. This tribe is noted for its skill as artisans and in the working of all metals. Its peerless armor sells at fantastic prices.
Tantorri	"the horsemasters" This folk once ranged far and wide through the interior of Pangaea but for decades had lived under shadow of the ikar's "protection". They are charged with maintaining the legion's lands and supplying slaves. Tantorri horses are greatly desired by all and turn great profit in all corners of the world.

367

Thibis   The ancient capitol of the Chaconne. Once nearly
                    destroyed by counterrevolutionaries, it is the perma-
                    nent seat of the powerful Vasilex clan.

Tothmecs   "the enlightened ones" This class of Razkul is gener-
                    ally feared and despised as both bloodthirsty and cruel.
                    There is reason to believe their philosophy influenced
                    Desia during his first years as ikar.